Australian Selection

PENGUIN BOOKS

DOWN BY THE DOCKSIDE

Criena Rohan is the pseudonym of Deirdre
Cash. Born in 1925, she grew up in the
inner-suburbs of Melbourne, and in South
Australia. Her mother, Valerie Cash, was a
professional singer, and her father Leo a minor
poet. After a Catholic education, she studied
singing at the Albert Street Conservatorium for
a year. Later she worked as a singer in night
clubs and taught ballroom dancing. She had two
novels published – *The Delinquents* (1962) and
Down by the Dockside (1963).

Criena Rohan died of cancer in 1963, at the age
of thirty-six.

*Penguin Australian Selection contains lively and
enjoyable books which have been lost for too long. Some
have been out-of-print, others never published. All
have been chosen because of their intrinsic interest
now, their readability and the pleasure of discovery.*

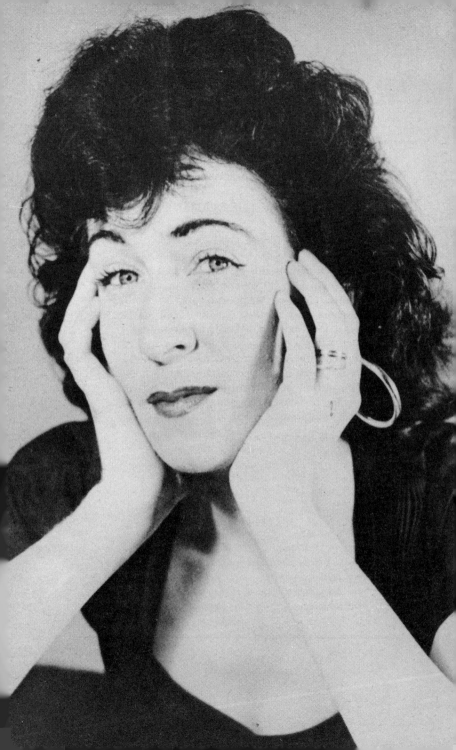

CRIENA ROHAN

DOWN BY THE DOCKSIDE

With a foreword by Barrett Reid

PENGUIN BOOKS

Penguin Books Australia Ltd,
487 Maroondah Highway, P.O. Box 257
Ringwood, Victoria, 3134, Australia
Penguin Books Ltd,
Harmondsworth, Middlesex, England
Penguin Books,
40 West 23rd Street, New York, N.Y. 10010, U.S.A.
Penguin Books Canada Ltd,
2801 John Street, Markham, Ontario, Canada
Penguin Books (N.Z.) Ltd,
182-190 Wairau Road, Auckland 10, New Zealand

First published by Victor Gollancz Ltd, London, 1963
Published by Penguin Books Australia, 1984
Reprinted 1985
Copyright © The estate of Criena Rohan, 1963

Offset from the Victor Gollancz edition, 1963
Made and printed in Australia by
The Dominion Press-Hedges & Bell

CIP

Rohan, Criena, 1925–1963.
Down by the dockside.

First published: London: Gollancz, 1963.
ISBN 0 14 007506 2.

I. Title.

A823'.3

FOREWORD

CRIENA ROHAN (1925-1962):
A NOVELIST ELUDING HISTORY

Barrett Reid

Criena Rohan's two novels, *The Delinquents* (1962) and *Down By The Dockside* (1963) have slipped out of history's net. Yet for a brief time twenty years ago they had a moment of fame, here and in England, and their author with her beauty, high-spirits and wit, became a celebrity for a day or two. Then, like lively fish diving deeply into an unchronicled ocean, the two books swam out of sight.

Or at least out of the sight of the literary surveyor. For example neither work is mentioned in *The Oxford History of Australian Literature* (1981) edited by Leonie Kramer. And although *Modern Australian Prose 1901-1975* (1980) edited by A. Grove Day examines individually the work of fifty-four Australian authors, Criena Rohan is not one of them. An earlier work *The Literature of Australia* (1976) edited by Geoffrey Dutton gives two and a half lines to *The Delinquents*, describing it as "a forceful and accomplished story of adolescent experience in the Australia of the 1950s", but does not mention the larger and more ambitious novel published one year after it. But, as I was to discover, the two books developed a life of their own outside, as one might say, of "literature".

For many years I was in charge of the development of public libraries in Victoria. One day an English publisher came to see me. He specialized in reprints aimed at the library market and he wanted to develop an Australian list. He asked what out-of-print Australian books were still in demand in our public libraries. An interesting question and interesting that he was one of the few publishers I knew ever to ask it. I promised to ask around.

When I did I was intrigued to find how often mention was made of two books by an author unknown to me, Criena Rohan. The two books had developed a word of mouth reputation particularly amongst teenagers and young adults. One librarian pointed out that quite often those who asked for these two books were not regular users of the library; indeed often they seemed to be people who did not read much at all but who were very determined to find these particular novels. The demand seemed to come, she said, "off the street".

Who was this author? What were her books like? What were the reasons for their unusual impact? Yet, why were they out of print?

Finding the answers to these questions took rather longer than I had expected. Yet to answer them is, I think, essential in understanding *Down By The Dockside* and in preparing a claim for its place in modern Australian literature. The quest went further and was more devious than I would have thought, and was much more interesting. The story of Criena Rohan, just like her books, took on a life and glamour of its own.

Both *Down By The Dockside* and the earlier book, *The Delinquents*, convey much of the quality of autobiography, of first-hand accounts of people and events directly experienced by the writer and still warm, if not hot, in recollection. The skills this writer employs are close to the skills of the raconteur. And Criena Rohan like a raconteur appears to draw her stories from embellishments on the events of her own life. In using the age-old gifts of the raconteur, the attention-getting opening remarks, deadpan humour, pathos, colour, solidarity with "common humanity", the throwaway ending, is the novelist embroidering the facts and, like many a Celtic story-teller before her, drawing a long bow?

The questions I ask above occur very early to most who read Rohan. To them, questions about the novel and questions about the author herself are closely related. We want to know how "true" her account is. The author and the narrator are not clearly separated. The personality of the author seems to have as much presence as her main characters. We appear to need, perhaps more with these two books than with some other kinds of fiction, to test their factual accuracy. We feel that if certain central episodes in the novel are not "real" then the whole thing falls down. What we are asking, of course, is a question about art.

Early in my search I was fortunate to meet Mary Campbell. We had met to discuss the poems of an unpublished poet, Leo Cash, who had died in 1974, not long before this meeting. I discovered that Criena Rohan was the pseudonym of Leo's daughter Deirdre Cash. Mary Campbell and her husband were close friends of Leo Cash and his family. Mary Campbell has a vivid store of memories of Leo's remarkable daughter and of her books. What began as a conversation about the father's poems continued, and continues, to be a conversation about the daughter.

I first met Leo Cash at a meeting of writers at a television studio. The studio had planned a programme satirizing the week's news. Leo was regarded as a likely contributor.

A slight, good-looking man, about sixty then, he had an enormous knowledge of literature underpinned with some knowledge of Greek and Latin, hallmarks of a sound Catholic education. It was clear immediately on meeting him that books, and talk about books, took first place in his life. His enormous charm was of the kind most impressive to strangers. For those who came closer to him, especially those with the duller virtues, there was often disillusion. One such said bitterly that "the only good thing about Leo was his poetry". It is the kind of tough remark that Leo himself or his daughter could have made. But it should be balanced by the knowledge that he was capable of life-long friendships, his relationship with the Campbells being one example.

He came from a family of Irish intellectuals a good many of whom, after coming to Australia, went into the law. (The currently famous young tennis player, Pat Cash, is the son of Leo's lawyer nephew.) Leo worked in some general managerial capacity in the family button factory in the inner-Melbourne suburb of Richmond. This is the factory described in *Down By The Dockside* but transferred in the book to Port Melbourne.

Few of Leo Cash's poems were published. Yet there is no doubt that he saw himself primarily as a poet and was seen as such by his family and friends. It was, too often, a romantic justification for his life. I find it sad, now, to look over some of his earlier poetry. Very little in these verses survive their period or circumstances. The wit and flashing phrase-making of his conversation are echoed hollowly, if at all.

He sought to express both his wit and his Marxism in writing for the theatre. Leo was associated with the left-wing New Theatre which, for a time, was a very lively part of Melbourne life.

I have diverged to look at the work of the father because it is, I think, the ground, or one of the grounds, from which the daughter's writing grew. It would not be reckless to assume that if literary talent can be inherited, then Criena Rohan got hers from her father. We do know that her love of books, her devouring need of them, grew out of the same qualities in Leo. And like him, she was shy of publishing under her own name.

Daughter, like father, was the product of an Irish–Catholic culture, but of an especial part of it, that part in revolt against the church. It was a culture that saw authority, of church or state, as the natural enemy, as the pruning shears cutting back the natural free growth of human qualities. It was a culture of both oral and written traditions, a culture of argument, be it Jesuit or Marxist, and a culture which saw the poor as having particular virtues denied to the bourgeoisie and the money–maker. Both Leo Cash and Criena Rohan came out of a Celtic tradition which, in its main branch, produced such writers as James Joyce, Sean O'Casey and Brendan Behan. I would be very surprised if Rohan did not read O'Casey. Different from each other as these writers are, and as all three are from Rohan, it is yet possible to find them all celebrating the same things. We can note, also, that in the works of all four, popular songs keep breaking in to provide a pathetic or humorous grace note. It was said of Criena Rohan, as it could be said of these other three writers, that she had the Irish gift of felicitous melancholy. And her sense of humour, so alive that eyes light up remembering it decades later, was purely Celtic.

Yet, while the cultural connection between father and daughter is clear, Leo was in the main a father in absentia. He had separated from his wife when their two children, Deirdre and her younger brother, were small. Their mother, Valerie Cash, is said to have been a beautiful woman in her early years and a singer of talent. She was more interested in a possible career as a singer in operetta than in domestic life and her attitude to her children was, if not cold, careless. One of the less successful characters in *Down By The Dockside*, because she is hard to believe in, is Lisha's mother, the department store buyer who is always somewhere else and who strains the reader's credulity with her lack of any maternal concern for her daughter. But, in essentials, this character is drawn from life. The writer draws badly here because she evades the enormous emotional charge of the mother–daughter relationship.

Valerie Cash had an opportunity to tour South Africa as a professional singer and took it. Clearly neither she nor Leo had much talent as parents. The children stayed with various people at various times, mainly members of the family. Deirdre was at one time in the care of Leo's sisters and they appear, cruelly distorted and unjustly maligned, as the aunts in *Down By The Dockside*. Her early childhood was spent with a grandmother on a farm in South Australia and it is this grandmother who provided the basis for that memorable portrait in *Down By The Dockside*. Only some essential characteristics are common to the real and the fictional grandmother, and this is a good example of the novelist's art in selecting only those aspects which fitted the story she wanted to tell. The real life grandmother was well–off, not poor. She was a marvellous teller of tales and passed on to her granddaughter a fund of Celtic folk–wisdom. These characteristics are used to colour the fictional portrait.

In later childhood Deirdre came back to Victoria. She attended the Convent of Mercy at Mornington as a boarder. She was particularly fortunate there in finding a teacher, Sister Dymphna, who encouraged her love of books and who gave her confidence in her writing ability. In his anthology *The Imagined City; Melbourne in the mind of its writers* John Arnold writes that at this time as a school girl Deirdre "got in touch with Alan Marshall to whom she sent her stories and sketches for criticism. He remembers her enormous zest for life and her conflicting mixture of Irish romanticism, Catholic mysticism and an intermittent rebelliousness." Mary Campbell believes that while Deirdre was glad of the help of an established writer like Alan Marshall (he had had great success with *I Can Jump Puddles* in 1955) so as to learn how to go about the business of being published she was, in fact, not influenced by Marshall and indeed was not particularly interested in Australian writing. However there is surely some sharing of taste or attitude implied in her choice of Marshall and not some other well–known author as advisor.

After matriculating Deirdre spent some time with her mother now back in Australia and living in West Melbourne. As far as we know, at no time in her childhood did Deirdre live in the Port Melbourne so memorably evoked in her novel. There is a Station Street in Port Melbourne but the street of that name in her novel is much more likely to have been drawn from the Station Street in Richmond which was the address of the family button factory. And many of the street scenes described were scenes she would have experienced in West Melbourne.

At this time Deirdre's mother offered to pay for her full–time training as a singer and she spent a year at the Albert Street Conservatorium. She was a beautiful girl greedy for excitement and she had a singing voice which people still remember. She was emerging into wartime Melbourne, a Melbourne crowded with soldiers and sailors from many countries, and she was enjoying it. It was a time of not much money but of endless parties. She often sang at these parties – ballads, songs of the left, songs of Ireland, the blues. People still remember the party clamour suddenly stopping, the stillness and the heartache as she sang.

While still very young she had an affair with a student at Melbourne University. They married, much to the disapproval of the boy's parents. His father, a doctor of medicine, considered the whole thing a disaster – and so it proved. There is little trace of this marriage in either of her books. Deirdre had a son, Michael, from this marriage. Later, on her second marriage to the seaman Otto Olsen, she had a daughter, Leonie. Predictably she was to prove as lacking what the established values of her time called "maternal instincts", as did her own mother. But of course it must be remembered that she was very ill for much of her later adult years.

We catch glimpses of her at this time, glimpses of someone trying to define herself on her own terms and not in the terms of a daughter, wife, mother or girl friend. She fought, often tigerishly and in desperation, for an emotional integrity defined by her own actions, her own decisions. Friend and contemporary, June Factor, wrote in an obituary notice in the literary magazine *Overland*:

She grew up a turbulent woman, emotionally very close to the heroine of her last book. Like Lisha she worked in night-clubs, taught ballroom dancing, and married a sailor. Like Lisha, she too alternated between a strong allegiance to her religion and an equally powerful defiance of all social restrictions, including those of the Church.

There is no doubt that Deirdre Cash as a woman and Criena Rohan as a writer were products of their time and that, to a degree, they were prisoners of their time. It is moving to observe this vivid, passionate woman – on the one hand, she observes the old values, and subjects herself entirely to a man. On the other hand, she strives to become her essential self – a highly independent person as free as any man to make for herself the crucial decisions about her life.

"What are you getting so hot under the collar for?" Charlie was genuinely delighted now. "I'd never leave you. I might go away but . . . "

"But I'd always come back to you", I finished off rudely. "I'm sick of hearing that, Charlie. In the first place it sounds like a B–class film, in the second it's so damn condescending, and in the third place it's a bore."

Charlie put down Napoleon and looked at me. "You're very independent all of a sudden," he said. "A man ought to shoot through for six months just to show who's boss."

"You shoot through any time you like."

It was after her first marriage and before meeting her great love, the coastal seaman Otto Olsen, that Deirdre worked as a singer. She sang and danced in night-clubs in Melbourne and with dance bands in Melbourne and Brisbane. She also became casual friends, as did many in that milieu, with well-known criminals of the time. The Charlie Barton episodes in Part III of *Down By The Dockside* are based on experiences of that time though, in the main, they were not first-hand but based on stories told to the author by her friends. Part of the reason for knowing criminals was simply consanguinity: they lived in the same streets. But the criminals were also "agin the government", disturbers of a status quo of a dreariness hard for young people today to imagine. It was much more usual in the bohemia of the 1940s and 1950s, in the smaller more rigidly stratified cities of those years and in a world where established powers were often censorious, narrow-minded and hypercritical, for the "free" spirits to form alliances and these included underworld figures, if only superficially. "They're a dead respectable lot are the criminals" a disappointed Lisha concludes.

The criminal boss Normie Morrison, described so amusingly in the novel, was based on the real-life criminal boss Norman Bradshaw. Readers might well find Normie's house at Portsea, and his social pretensions, a little hard to believe, but for a while it was true: Bradshaw did have a Portsea house and did entertain some of the local set, gamblers mostly, who today would be surprised, not to say embarrassed, that they had been observed by a sharp-eyed novelist.

While the novel is drawn, and gains immensely, from the novelist's own life, a life of unusual range and variety at that time for one so young, it is also clear that autobiography has been changed quite consciously into fiction. Deirdre Cash is not Lisha Flynn, not quite, and Lisha's world, her circumstances and her friends, differ in important ways from that of the novelist. Art has compressed, elided, heightened and refocused much of it, not only in the interests of telling a good story, but of illuminating the inner life of a young city woman of her time.

That this difference was important to the author herself we know from contemporary newspaper interviews. In discussing her first novel *The Delinquents* she said the story "was not drawn from her own experience or anyone else's experience. I have never been in trouble with the police. I don't drink. I do enjoy a good 'bad' joke." While allowing for the novelist's self-protective colouration, this has the ring of truth. She was doing something more than telling her own story.

To conclude her personal story: after marrying her seaman she moved to various ports to be with him. Her health deteriorated and she lost a lot of weight. Tuberculosis was suspected but in fact, and after a period of mis-diagnosis, it was to prove to be cancer. She spent four months in hospital in Perth and it was then that she wrote *The Delinquents*. "I preferred doing that to this occupational therapy business..." She went to London briefly. As her illness developed she again had spells in hospital and *Down By The Dockside* was written in convalescent periods by a patient rapidly losing strength and, indeed, mortally ill. She wrote the final pages wearing an oxygen mask. She was not to live to see *Dockside* published. Such, however, was the extraordinary force of the woman that, on the evidence of friends such as the writer Adrian Rawlins, she had completed a third novel – *House with the Yellow Door* – before she died at the age of thirty-six. Sadly this manuscript which she said was by far her best work, seems to have disappeared.

She had forfeited some of the sympathy of many of her family. But amusingly, her family critics did not include her father, the detached Leo. It is true that he said he was very annoyed by one thing in the book but it was not a question of morality, religion or family loyalty. For Leo it was a much more serious matter: a misquotation from Tennyson, one of his favourite poets.

She sent the manuscript of *The Delinquents* to several Australian publishers, without success. She then sent it to a literary agent in London and eventually it was published by Victor Gollancz who was also to publish her second novel *Down By The Dockside* in 1963. It is interesting that she chose to publish in London and perhaps some measure of her alienation from local writing, though too much should not be made of this. "Australian publishers," she said at the time "won't touch a book unless it builds up Australians as great heroes..."

The Delinquents was given considerable attention when it was published in 1962. Kenneth Alsop in the London *Daily Mail* called it a "back-street *Tristan and Isolde*." He praised not only her "rare freshness of eye and warmth of heart, but an even rarer understanding of young proles desperately trying to inject a meaningless and drab existence with excitement and purpose." The *Times Literary Supplement* critic found the heroine of the book, Lola, a triumph – "generous, defiant and basically very touching."

A prominent Australian writer of the time, Kylie Tennant, was one of the first to recognize Rohan's talent. Kylie Tennant came to prominence twenty years before Rohan with novels such as *Foveaux* (1939) and *The Battlers* (1941), which interestingly were both published by Gollancz, who was to be Rohan's publisher. Tennant can be seen as the precursor of a number of women novelists whose preoccupations were with urban life and its social injustices, especially those faced by women: Ruth Park (*The Harp in the South* 1948, *Poor Man's Orange* 1949), Dymphna Cusack (*Come In Spinner* 1951) and Dorothy Hewett (*Bobbin Up* 1959). Park and Cusack have both been criticized for sentimentality and a too facile realism, faults which reviewers such as John McLaren also found in Rohan. Hewett's *Bobbin Up* has been said by one commentator to be "incompletely realized. With her as with other writers of that generation, and of that persuasion in matters both political and literary, the impulse to create is secondary to the commitment to social protest." Certainly Hewett's novel is an expression of the author's wish to change things as they are, specifically in this case factory conditions.

Though her commitment is less clear-cut than Hewett's there is little doubt that Rohan also saw the novel as a vehicle for social change. Certainly Rohan is one of those "of that persuasion in matters political and literary" who see the novel as a form in which to express outrage at the bastardies of mankind and the social conditions that create them. All honour to her for this. To devalue her creativity or Hewett's because it serves as social protest is to devalue a tributory, however minor, of a great tradition: the tradition of Zola, Dickens, Gorky, Dreiser and Solzhenitsyn.

These women writers can be seen as part of a social realist literature in Australia which also included such writers as Alan Marshall, Judah Waten, John Morrison and Frank Hardy. Interestingly all of these writers, like Criena Rohan, wrote books in the 1950-60 period which described working class life in inner-Melbourne suburbs.

While there is no direct evidence, except for the contact with Alan Marshall, that Rohan saw herself as connected with these other writers, it is clear that she had much in common with them.

Much work has yet to be done on her literary origins. We know that she read most of Maxim Gorky available in English (the pre-Stalin editions). We know, too, that she read John Steinbeck. His *Of Mice and Men* (1937) and *The Grapes of Wrath* (1939) were highly popular in Australia during the war years, partly due to being brought in by American soldiers. In particular, I think that the writer of *Down By The Dockside* has much in common with the writer of *Cannery Row* (1945).

But perhaps of all writers it may be that Charles Dickens was the one who provided the young writer with her most enduring model. It was Dickens surely who provided the licence, as it were, for her bold narrative style, her highly–coloured simplified character drawing, and her use of fiction as a demonstration of where emotional loyalties lay. Her most memorable characters, Grandma, Mrs Phillips the St Kilda landlady and Uncle Shaun, are all Dickensian. There is a sense in which Criena Rohan is a valid inheritor of the tradition of the novel as part of popular culture, of fiction as entertainment and uplift for the mainstream, a tradition whose force and strength derives in large part from Dickens.

So when Rohan and novelists like her are called sentimental and adjudged to be using the novel for social protest, it is as well to note that these are criticisms commonly made, and with equal validity, of Dickens himself.

All readers, of course, bring to the novel their own preoccupations, their own notions of what the novel ought to be doing. Whether one accepts Rohan as a novelist of importance to her time and place depends to a degree on one's notions of what fiction should be.

At one extreme there are those like that prince of novelists, Nabokov, who believe that literary masterpieces are "wonderful toys" and that good readers do not "read books for the infantile purpose of identifying oneself with the characters, and not for the adolescent purpose of learning to live . . . " He asks that books be read "for the sake of their form, their visions, their art."

On the other hand there are those who believe that the novel has a valid purpose in conveying information, in educating, in teaching us how to live. For these critics the craft of fiction can take on a lot of cargo: history, biography, politics, philosophy, indeed any matter on which the author is deeply informed or, preferably, obsessed. And surely it is not impossibly pluralist to turn from the excitement and interest, say, of Nabokov's *Pale Fire* and find comparable interest and excitement, albeit of a very different kind, in Solzhenitsyn's *The First Circle*. All that is needed is breadth, relativist and not monolithic values, and the ability to find important virtues in the very different things which each book sets out to achieve.

It is misguided to expect the fictional ironies of, say, a Martin Boyd in Criena Rohan, or to look for Rohan's sympathy with low-life or her power of direct assault on our emotions in Martin Boyd. This is not to say that Rohan can be compared with Boyd, one of Australia's greatest novelists, but to compare the skill and originality of her two books with Boyd's first two books is not so far-fetched. Certainly her first novel *The Delinquents* is much more successful as a work of art than his first novel *The Montforts*. The fact is her writing skills, like his, would have developed. But I imagine she would have always drawn clearly, and without irony, on her autobiographical and everyday sources. After all, it was Nabokov himself who wrote: "There is a lot to be said for mingling now and then with the crowd, and he must be a pretty foolish and shortsighted author who renounces the treasures of observation, humour and pity which may be professionally obtained through closer contact with his fellow men."

This, I think, brings us to an explanation of the disappearance of Rohan's two novels from current accounts of Australian literature, as was noted at the beginning of this *Introduction*. It is a matter of the swings and roundabouts of critical fashion. Just as forty-six years ago, F. R. Leavis excluded Dickens from his "great tradition" of the English novel, so today in Australia, and perhaps as a consequence of the influence of Leavis on the study of fiction, the social realists and *their* tradition are undervalued or, in some cases, ignored. When the time comes for assumptions to be made about the function of the novel, other than those allowed by the current critical orthodoxy, we will find Rohan's achievement reassessed. In the meantime her books get passed from hand to hand and the "common reader" lucky enough to come upon them, and unaware of the rules of the games critics play, goes on just enjoying them!

There is another reason for the two novels falling from critical view which is not to do with current literary standards but with circumstance. For books to be kept alive it is best if the author is visible and if a publisher has an interest in a continuing output. All authors to some degree create their market as they go along. The combination of an overseas publisher and an author who has died or has stopped writing does not keep a local reputation alive.

It is a pleasure to return to this book twenty years after it was first published. We experience vividly the character of Lisha developing over the years, with the quickness of one who has learnt from "the faces in the street". A good example comes early in the narrative when Andy takes her to the hotel in Williamstown.

"Of course old Jim's pub was a Jack's Ashore. Not even his best friends would have tried to deny it."

Andy dragged on his trousers and his shoes (a scouse never goes bare-footed to open a door. This is not personal vanity but a wise defence precaution. Indeed I have known particularly cautious souls who always took an empty bottle in one hand as well.)"

But other aspects of Lisha are uncovered. She can be tender:

I remember it was a misty morning, misty and still, as though autumn were trying to prolong its time. A soft vapour lay along the top of the Yarra and I knew that later in the day the sunlight would not break through the clouds, it would just filter down in a golden web, wrapping itself around the buildings, throwing a sheen over the trees and putting beauty into the faces of the people that went up and down the streets.

And she learns to be realistic despite the Celtic mists of her romanticism:

I had seen this street bloom with the money that came with war, and now, if we were to have the poverty that came with peace, I would face the fight here where I was already a veteran in poverty and struggle.

Another pleasure is Rohan's ear for the spoken word, her gift of absolute pitch. Much of the dialogue in Australian novels of Rohan's contemporaries reads woodenly today. But the speech of Rohan's characters was authentic then and is authentic now. Here is Andrew Michael Kelly surprised in his seduction of the young Lisha:

xvi

He saw the gentlemen in the grey felt hats and said, "O.K., you didn't waste much time did you. Right y'are, just give me time to get the tweeds on, well."

And here is Mrs Phillips:

My landlady raised her tea–cup to the photo on the mantelpiece. "Here's to you," she said to Phillips, "the greatest cad on the astral plane."

The book of course has many flaws. I believe Rohan lacked critical support. She also lacked time and a good editor. If she had had more time, if she had written in less isolation, and if, above all, she had developed under the eye of a good editor she would undoubtedly have cut some of the sentimentality and those passages where she seems to be writing not a serious novel but for the women's magazines of the day. Many of the worst passages occur in the middle of the story between Andy's death and the arrival of Joe. They could have easily been cut and the book would have been better for being shorter.

Indeed one can appreciate the arguments of those who claim that *The Delinquents* is the better book, being less diffuse, more concentrated in its purpose and with much less flab in the prose. On the other hand *Down By The Dockside* has incomparably richer characters and covers much more, and fascinating, territory.

Neither book sacrifices its realism to its message and to that degree they are more successful than much of the fiction in the social realist tradition to which they belong. They do not instruct, they celebrate.

What attracts us to Criena Rohan's work is the colour and humour of her world and the vitality of her style. What was an everyday and not very attractive world to those of us who were her contemporaries, the world of wartime Melbourne takes on compelling glamour for people who are Lisha's age today. Lisha – Eilishe Cahaleen Deirdre Flynn – may seem at first consideration to have little in common with a twenty year old of today but her courage, her street wisdom and sheer cheek, her gutsy grasp of the essential merits in a man or woman, escape her time and make her a character with which a new generation can easily identify.

Acknowledgements

I am indebted to my friend Mary Campbell of Garden City, Victoria, for much of the information about Criena Rohan and her family. Librarians of the La Trobe Library, State Library of Victoria, were unfailingly helpful especially the Deputy Librarian, John Arnold. He has a particular interest in Criena Rohan, and enabled me to see copies of Leo Cash's poems. Thanks also to Adrian Rawlins and Vane Lindesay for their recollections.

Barrett Reid

PART I

GRANDMOTHER

WHEN I WAS a child I would lie in bed of a morning and watch the wall opposite my window. It was the wall of the Perfection Paper Bag factory and it was separated from my window by only a narrow path that ran beside our house. I would watch it with the cold, slow Melbourne rain running down its grimy face. I would watch it grow and take clearer shape in the first light of the winter morning. It would grow bigger and bigger. It would swell before my eyes. I would feel that I was choking before it, that it would come tumbling down on top of me and I would be buried—buried for ever. I would jump out of bed and run into the back yard; from here I could look down the back lane and get a glimpse of Prince's Pier and the ships lying at anchor. The sight of the ships could always comfort me, and my courage would rise again and I would tell myself that there was nothing to fear, just to wait till I was older. I would win a scholarship and go on to college, and even if I did not win a scholarship, something would turn up. My father would come home with a fortune, or times would get better, or Uncle Shaun would raise the wind, somehow. Something would happen, for sure. I could scarcely wait to have a go at life. Standing there in the yard I would hear the streets coming to life, the hurrying feet, the snatches of conversation, the heart-lifting sound of ships' whistles and, over and above all else, the wailing and roaring of the factory sirens, clamouring like the voice of some huge monster that held the whole district in bondage. I would listen awhile and then I would throw back my head and take a deep breath that drew into me some mysterious strength that seemed to float in the very air all around me. Inside myself I would say to the factory sirens:

"You won't get me. You'll never get me."

I lived with my grandmother. She had been born and reared in Dublin. Her father had been a ship's captain, and so also had her husband. She had borne two sons and six daughters and her husband had died when the youngest child was six weeks old. The shipping company gave her a clock. She then set out to raise a family single-handed. The eldest boy had died of what we always called in our family chest trouble. We were not a clan given to euphemism or evading issues but the dread word tuberculosis (or consumption, as everyone seemed to call it round our way) stuck in our throats. The second boy had been on a ship that was torpedoed in the first world war. The daughters were married and scattered far and wide. When I knew my grandmother, she was an old woman, her face deeply lined, her hair snow-white, but her eyes were still bright green like emeralds and thirty years in the slums had done nothing to destroy her gaiety and her courage. She gave me all the warmth, love and hope that I needed. I felt she was my whole family. It is true that there was my brother and I was very fond of him, but Grandmother could not keep the both of us, so he lived with my Aunt Lucy, who was married to a country police constable and had three boys of her own. She was a big, easy-going and very pretty woman, and she said she never noticed one boy more or less. Aunt Rose lived with Grandmother and me but I never liked Aunt Rose. She was a tall, gaunt, good-looking woman whose husband had left her. He probably discovered that he could no longer go on living with a woman who so deeply resented the whole male half of the human race. Or perhaps he could not stand her violently bad temper. Always she seemed to be consumed with dark and secret rage that would suddenly break out into the most terrible fury. She had such a crazy hatred of my father that some of it extended to me.

"She's the spit out of his mouth," she would scream. "She'll never be any good, coming from a swine like that."

My grandmother, wanting to comfort me, would say, "He has his good points, and he's very entertaining. He's not so bad considering he's a scouse."

"What's a scouse, Grandma?"

"A Liverpool Irishman, darling, the scum of a noble and intelligent race."

When she said things like that she had a special smile that took one side of her mouth higher than the other and made her look indescribably young and cheeky.

8

My father was Owen Flynn, the descendant of a long line of Liverpool packet rats. I am very proud of those ancestors of mine. Recruited from the slums of Dublin and Cork, they were the only men tough enough and mad enough to sail the famous mail packets to America with the wild old skippers who kept the mail away from the steamers longer than any man thought they could, by the simple method of heading straight into the raging Atlantic gale with about twice as much sail as any ship should carry. And up amongst the masts and spars were the skinny half-fed scouses with Hold Fast tattooed on their fingers, and let us hope it was a great help to them, for it is told of some of these Atlantic crossings that the men were never out of the rigging. My Uncle Shaun used to sing to me about them :

"There was Jack Lynch from Ballynahinch,
 Mick Murphy and some more
And I tell you well they suffered like hell
 on the way to Baltimore."

My Uncle Shaun was my grandfather's brother, the last of the great chanty men. He had sailed out of Bristol fifty years before when he was a boy of fifteen, and he had sung his way round all the oceans of the world. His stories, his songs, my grandmother's dreams for me, they filled my childhood.

"When I'm grown up," I told Swede Ryan, "it won't take me long to get out of this dump, I can tell you. I'm going to have two diamond rings and a fur coat twice as big and furry as Mrs Woodley's."

Mrs Woodley was the wife of the pub-keeper at the corner. I was sitting in the fig tree that filled almost all our back yard when I made this boast. Swede looked up at me. He was a quiet little boy with a heavy white face under a shock of wavy black hair.

"I wouldn't want to look like old Ma Woodley," he said. "She's an old bastard."

"Why?" I asked. In actual fact I agreed with Swede but I liked to hear him amplify his statements. I liked everybody to amplify their statements. I liked probing around in people's minds.

"I'll tell you why," said Swede. "She keeps my old man down in that pub of hers filling him up with beer, and then he comes home and beats the hell out of my old woman. He's a real bastard, my old man."

Here again I was heartily in agreement with Swede, but I made a *pro forma* protest about his language. Swede was indignant. He pointed out, with truth, that, by local standards, his language was mild in the extreme.

He was a great favourite with the nuns, being a very polite and quietly spoken little boy, and a talented server on the altar. Not only was his Latin word-perfect, but his hands were so deft and his every movement so soft and well co-ordinated that any other boy serving with him always seemed a clod-hopping lout. Take, for example, Charlie Barton. Charlie was a dear little boy with snowy curls and, as far as anyone could make out, two left feet. It was his ambition to be a priest. (He had an extremely religious mother.) But every time he went on the altar he stuttered so desperately and stumbled around so consumed with nerves that to see him move the Book to the Gospel side was to witness a sort of ecclesiastical obstacle race.

We three always walked to school together. Sometimes Philomena Foley joined us, but she was a little older and had terrible scorn for little boys, so usually she came along later with her friend Chrissie Brady. Swede and Charlie and I would set out together along the rain-washed streets. Even in Melbourne, there is many a sunny school morning, but when I think back there is always the same set of pictures in my mind. Swede's bare feet skirting around the puddles in the pavement, and Charlie, with a book in his hand, asking us the catechism questions for the day—three questions every day. Charlie always knew the answers, and usually Swede knew them, and sometimes I did. I would go skipping over the pools and jumping the gutters. My feet felt so light, and my long legs so springy, it was agony for me to sit or stand still. I would answer Charlie carelessly as I danced around.

"What does 'Amen' mean?"

"Amen means 'So be it'."

"Who is God?"

"God is the Creator of Heaven and Earth and the Supreme ..."

"Lord of All," prompted Swede as he went along with his own books under one arm and mine under the other. Past the warehouses with the men outside looking for jobs, past the factory with the women outside looking for jobs, past the hotel with the dead-beats outside waiting for the doors to open so that they could get a threepenny dark for breakfast, past the State School where the children played, looking very small and defenceless in the shadow of the match factory, past the little park on the corner with its trodden grass, its smoke-stained trees and its notice that said football and cricket were not to be played there on Sunday. We lived in an area where front gardens were the exception and back yards were so small that we could almost be said to have had indoor lavatories—most of them were about two strides from the kitchen door. So when we didn't play in the park we played in the streets, but it is comforting to think that the Sabbatarians did not neglect us.

There was also to be no playing on the swings or the horizontal bars on the way to school, by order of Sister Mary Angela, but every morning I would run across the grass to the swings and demand that the boys push till I was flying right out as far as the swing would take me—weightless and free.

"I'm flying. I'm flying," I would cry.

"Come on, you'll be late," Charlie would protest, but Swede would stay behind with me.

"You go on Charlie, if you're a squib," he would say. "I'll stay with Lisha."

So Charlie would stay because he had been called Charles Jarman Barton after Charlie Jarman, a long dead hero of the Seamen's Union, and he didn't like to be called a squib. Then we would all be late.

"Lisha Flynn, it's all your fault."

We were happy. At least Charlie and I were happy. Charlie would be a priest, and I would marry a rich man, but Swede did not say what he would do. The only indication he ever gave that he planned for the future at all was that sometimes he would ask me, "When I make a lot of money will you be my girl?"

I always answered, "My Grandma says there's plenty of time before I begin to worry about things like that."

Swede was so loyal and devoted that I had not the heart to tell him that his chalky face and heavy, secretive eyes repelled me. In the meantime he was welcome to do my arithmetic homework, and maintain against all comers that I was far prettier than Philomena Foley, the beauty of the school.

One day when I was about eight my grandmother sent me across to Mrs Clancy with a pair of little boy's shoes which someone had given Aunt Rose when she was working somewhere in Toorak. Mrs Clancy lived in one of the dreadful little bug-ridden sustenance houses at the corner, and had three children under the age of five—Lonnie who needed his tonsils out, Mary Teresa who needed attention to her adenoids, and Patrick Joseph who was not thriving on the powdered milk supplied by the relief authorities.

Ted Clancy was a big handsome lad of about twenty-four who worked on the wharves when he could. He had gone up the country about two weeks before on relief work, and Lila stayed behind in the three damp rooms and coped with the three ailing children.

When I arrived all three children were taking their afternoon sleep at the same time. It was the first time I had ever been into that house and not heard the sound of children in tears. Now everything was still and peaceful, and Lila sat alone in the kitchen, her elbows on the table, her face cupped in her hands. She was staring into space, and she looked as though she had been crying. She rose to take the shoes, and then suddenly, as she smiled her thanks at me, her face went the colour of chalk and she arched her back with both hands pressed down on the table.

"Stay awhile, Lisha," she said, "and mind the kids. I'm just going down the back."

I waited awhile, and then called out to ask if I could go to the park to play.

"Wait awhile, Lisha. I might want you to do something for me. Don't go away for a while, like a good girl."

She seemed to be sobbing.

So I stayed a little longer. Then Patrick Joseph woke up and commenced to grizzle, so I put on the kettle for some water to heat his bottle. I had fed him and was trying to change his napkin before his mother walked back into the kitchen. Her face was grey and beaded with little drops of sweat, and she had bitten through her bottom lip till it bled. Suddenly she rushed outside to the gully trap and vomited violently. Then she came in and took Patrick Joseph in her arms and cried hopelessly. She said, "Go down to Mrs Frazer's shop and ask her will she give me a bottle of Solyptol on tick. If she says no, tell her for Christ's sake."

I brought back the disinfectant and put it down beside the sobbing woman. I was afraid and embarrassed before such hopeless grief, so without another word I went away, and Lila Clancy cried out, rocking her baby backwards and forwards in her arms.

I told Aunt Rose and Grandma about it at tea-time that night. They exchanged glances.

"She said she'd do it," said Aunt Rose. "What a thing to do, and she calls herself a Catholic."

"It's easy to sleep on another man's wound," said Grandma. "How would you like to have three children already, and all of them sickly, and your husband out of a job?"

"Serve her right for being a fool. I've no sympathy for her. You have to be tough in this world, and you have to be smart. If she hadn't let Ted Clancy get her into trouble with the first one, she wouldn't be in the mess she's in now."

My grandmother turned and signalled me out of the room.

"Not in front of the child," she said.

Soon after this, Charlie Barton's father dropped dead. He had been a good man, and a good father. He never drank, he never raised a hand to his children, and if there was work to be had on the docks Paddy Barton could get it. His family had always been the luckiest in the street. They had what seemed to us a big garden in front of their house, and Mrs Barton could afford new curtains for the front window every spring. It was even said that she was putting a little money away to send Charlie on to the Christian Brothers when he had finished primary school. The Barton children always had weatherproof shoes and hand-knitted jumpers, and they were always promptly on their feet each Friday afternoon when the question came : "Stand up all those who have paid their school money this week." Then suddenly one morning, on 7 North Wharf, their father reeled beneath his load, and fell. They carried his body home to his wife, and Charlie and Terry and Brian were called home from school.

My grandmother helped Mrs Barton prepare her husband for burial, and in the evening I went down with Swede Ryan to join the people thronging into the small house to honour the dead man, and to try to comfort his widow. Everybody in the street was there : the doctor, the priest, the secretary of the Waterside Workers' Federation, men from his gang on the wharf, relations from all over Melbourne, Leo Grady the local communist. Blessed candles, white roses from the presbytery garden, the small red lamp beneath the picture of the Sacred Heart, the soft murmur of voices as the priest led the rosary, the sound of someone crying quietly in the kitchen, Mrs Woodley entering with a huge bunch of lilies and chrysanthemums, the two younger Barton boys, exhausted with crying, being carted off to bed by some kindly neighbour, Charlie refusing to be parted from his father and sitting by the bed all the evening—and amidst it all, the dead man lying wrapped in the brown Franciscan shroud with a rosary wound around his hands.

His hair had been neatly brushed back and lay, wavy and black, against the pillow, and his fair Irish skin, freckled across the short wide nose, looked clear and fresh. But his hands were covered with callouses, and where the sleeves of the shroud turned back from the wrists, the veins of his arms shone out, blue and twisted—the arms of a man who had carried loads far beyond his strength.

One of his workmates came up to the bed and covered the clasped hands with his own huge fist. He was limping, this man, for he had been in an unemployed demonstration the previous week and he had been beaten black and blue in a baton charge.

"Poor old Paddy," he said, "he was such a good little chap. He was too little to be a wharfie, and he never poled and he never bellyached, and many a time he paid my Union money when I didn't have it. He was a damn good little bloke. Well, he's worked his last shift."

The winter of the next year was bad—very bad. Aunt Rose was out of work. Swede Ryan's father was in jail again. Mrs Woodley had had her face slapped by a frantic woman who was tired of seeing her husband's sustenance pay go over the Harp of Erin bar. Little Harold Rowlands, youngest of twelve, had

14

died of rheumatic fever, and Lila Clancy was expecting yet another baby within the month.

Then I developed tonsillitis and was home from school for weeks. I became so delirious that I had the doctor and, believe me, even at the best of times doctors were not considered a necessity in Stawell Street until all else had failed. He pocketed our last 10s. 6d. and advised my grandmother to keep me in bed till the temperature had gone down, and paint my throat with glycerine and tannin.

"And get those tonsils out as soon as possible," he said.

So I stayed in bed day after day and watched the grey sky, and listened to the worried discussions between the two women in the kitchen.

"How much have you got, Rose?"

"About two bob—one and nine to be exact."

"Well if I get some gravy beef and carrots and potatoes, I can make a stew, and I'll give her the broth off it."

"Better get a couple of oranges too, and she can have the juice."

"Yes, that should do her good. She's very sick, Rose."

"I hope to God she's not going to be delicate."

'Delicate' meant tuberculosis in the female.

Grandmother said, "For the love of God, Rose, don't even talk about it."

"Well you have to face facts."

"I'm facing about as many facts as I can cope with at the moment, Rose."

I don't know how we would have survived had it not been for Uncle Shaun. He swept into Stawell Street like a breath of warm tropical air on a day when things were at their grimmest —my throat was so swollen that I could swallow nothing but hot tea, and there was sevenpence halfpenny in the house. Aunt Rose had torn the lining out of her bag in a frantic search for what, down in one corner, felt like a sixpenny piece, but what turned out to be a St Christopher medal. The electric light had been cut off the day before and the gas was to go at any tick of the clock. Everything pawnable had been pawned—including most of the blankets. I was the only one in the house who still had a full quota on my bed. Next door on the left hand side both the gas and electricity were just happy memories, and next

15

door on the right hand side Carl Andersen had taken his box trolley to the market and brought it home piled high with stolen cabbages. For this splendid effort he was sent to a reformatory.

Yes, things were bad in Stawell Street when Uncle Shaun arrived. True, he had not much money and very little prospect of a job, but he had the boundless resourcefulness of one who has been stony-broke in every port of the Seven Seas. Greatest advantage of all, he had an extremely gentlemanly bearing, and a faultless English accent which he had practised and perfected for his world famous imitations of shipping company representatives.

The first thing he did was to go out and buy a huge meal for us all. The lovely smell of frying steak and onions circulated through the candlelit house, and there was Uncle Shaun in the midst of all the cooking and preparations, running between the kitchen and my bedroom, lighting the fire, telling us bits of news about the relatives in Ireland and Liverpool and the States, singing snatches of songs, and refusing to be daunted by any tale of woe. He told Grandmother that, in view of the poverty and fertility of the Rowlands family, the death of baby Harold was 'the action of a gentleman, my dear, the action of a gentleman'. He piled more wood into the grate till the fire roared up in a great extravagant, heart-warming flame that beautified the room, shut out the approaching night, and threw a ruddy background around his figure till the great curling dragons tattooed on his arms shone like etchings on bronze.

Next day he went out and had the light put on again, and dealt very expertly with a policeman who came to the door with a distress warrant for Aunt Rose.

"Does a Mrs Morton live here?" asked the policeman.

"She does not," said Uncle Shaun, "I wish she did and I'd have plenty to say to her."

He leaned, confidentially, towards the policeman : "She did live here, constable, and left owing me six weeks' rent, and that's all I can tell you about Mrs Morton."

"She seems to have owed money everywhere," said the policeman, "this is a distress warrant I have here."

"You don't say." Uncle Shaun bent over it and examined it with interest, not at all like a man who has seen in his day more distress blueys than the whole Victorian Police Force would serve in a twelve-month.

"Well, constable, I can't help you. She's left no forwarding address, for very good reason"—I wish I could describe to you the scorn in Uncle Shaun's voice for people who left no forwarding address, for very good reason—"and there's people calling here all day and every day trying to collect from her. It's very annoying to my wife and myself."

The policeman was sure it must be, and left in a spate of apologies :

"Sorry to trouble you."

"Not at all, constable. You must do your duty."

"This is a job no policeman likes."

"Well so long as the neighbours don't think there's trouble in the house. Lived here, man and boy, sixty years, and never a bit of trouble with the police as anyone could tell who you cared to ask."

The copper beat a retreat in the face of all this oldest inhabitant brand of volubility, and Uncle Shaun went out and joined the local branch of the Returned Servicemen's League.

With his usual happy fortune in such matters he joined at a time when local politics were running high, and official positions were being resigned from at the rate of about three each Thursday night meeting. Into this turmoil strode Uncle Shaun playing the part of the pourer-of-oil-on-troubled-waters, the white-haired and dignified old gent who had travelled so extensively, obviously been so well educated, and had such thrilling experiences in the Boer War. In fact Uncle Shaun had been profoundly pro-Boer at the time when he was fighting them. In our family, right up until the time of Dr Malan we saw the Boers as brave and clever fighters who had put up a terrific struggle to keep their beloved farm lands from the grasp of Imperialistic Britain. "Of course, by the same token," said Uncle Shaun, "it is only fair to remember that as well as being brave and tough, they are also arrogant, narrow-minded, ignorant and suspicious, and they treat the natives vilely, and I'm no longer worried as I once was about the brave old Boer farmer and the land he stole from the native people. But in those days anyone who fronted up to the might of England received my support, my moral support at least, and I was the first Flynn ever to don the British uniform, and so with one thing and another I felt a disgrace to the clan when the band played 'Goodbye Dolly Grey' and off I marched."

"Why did you go, then?" I asked.

Uncle Shaun grinned. "It wouldn't interest you, me little love," he said.

On the contrary I thought it would possibly interest me very much indeed, so I asked my grandmother, "Why did Uncle Shaun go to the Boer War?"

Grandmother looked sideways at me from out the wonderful green eyes and I saw the corners of her mouth lift. "Something to do with a widow who kept a boarding-house at Southampton," she said. "I never did hear the full strength of the affair."

Then she remembered to whom she was talking, she pulled down the corners of her mouth and finished off much more primly, "It was nothing to your Uncle's credit, I can tell you that, and it's probably better forgotten. The whole business was nothing to his credit, if it comes to that—going off to shoot people who had never done him any harm."

Be that as it may, this graceless epoch in Uncle Shaun's career came in very handy in our hour of need for without it he could not have joined the R.S.L., and once joined, so well did he soothe ruffled feelings, heal chairmen's wounds, and suggest ways and means of augmenting branch finances, that in no time at all he found himself organising secretary of the Benevolent Fund, and very benevolent we found it.

"Just a little bundle of groceries for a distressed family," he would say, dumping a sugar bag filled with tea, flour, potatoes and such like on the kitchen table. Then there would be much celebration, and those other distressed families, the Andersens, the Clancys, the Ryans, the McShanes and numerous others, would swarm in to help divide the spoils, and none would go away empty-handed. And all would bless the name of Shaun Flynn, and pray that long might he stay out of jail to continue with his good work in alleviating the lot of the poor bloody working man.

Nor did his rough and ready socialism stop short at food. There were huge piles of clothes brought in to the R.S.L. for distribution to various charities. Uncle Shaun appointed himself chief sorter—shoes in one pile, underwear in another, and so on. In my capacity of assistant sorter I scored a very nice little black velvet dress, a bit rubbed around the cuffs and seat, but still warm, and capable of looking very dashing under my heavy coat. "I saw a picture the other day of Marlene Dietrich's little girl wearing black velvet," said Uncle Shaun. "You look twice as good." Our greatest problem was shoes for Auntie Rose. Just to be different from the rest of the family, who had short, thick Irish bog-trotting platters, Aunt Rose had the longest and thinnest feet I have ever seen. If a pair of shoes long enough was raked out of the big hessian bag from the R.S.L. they were so much too wide that, to use the phrase of the day, you wouldn't wear them in a dole queue. If they were narrow enough, they were about as long as her big toe. At last there arrived a pair of goloshes that more or less fitted, and in these she spent the rest of the winter. One of my most vivid recollections is of the early morning, and Aunt Rose, about to set out on the round of employment agencies, registry offices and factories, looking out the kitchen door and praying for rain. "It's pouring, you can wear your goloshes," became one of the best pieces of news you could tell Aunt Rose.

Uncle Shaun was also glad to see the rain, for he had gone into the window-cleaning business with Ted Clancy and after the rain business boomed. Each morning they would set out with their buckets and mops and walk up to the more prosperous suburbs. Uncle Shaun, being a born chanty man in every way, had it all so arranged that Ted did most of the hard labour, and he did all the valuable spieling so important in the matter of cups of tea, cast-off clothing, and so on. In this line Uncle Shaun was an artist. In the kitchens of those who still had some money he held forth on his adventures in Valparaiso and such far-off places, varying his tone to his audience, sometimes the simple sailor, sometimes the hard-bitten adventurer, sometimes the philosopher.

"What did you do today?" we would ask him at tea-time.

"Today," he would say, "I fought an octopus, single-handed, beneath the blue waters of the Caribbean."

Or else: "Today I lay three months becalmed in the Doldrums. Half the crew down with typhus and the skipper gone mad."

Or: "Today I was wrecked on the desolate Island of Dead Man's Elbow."

"And where is the Island of Dead Man's Elbow?" asked my grandmother.

"Your guess is as good as mine," said Uncle Shaun.

Late in July, I helped the two younger Andersen boys run down the Harrops' pet rabbit. Captain Cook had escaped from his hutch two days before and had been sighted browsing in a vacant allotment. I was a good sprinter and my services were called upon. Either two days' freedom had gone to his head or instinct warned him that the hungry gleam in the eyes of the Andersen boys was something to be avoided, for he refused to be cajoled with lettuce leaves or carrot tops. We chased him round the allotment and over a dozen rubbish heaps, and through countless back yards, before we finally ran him to earth; whereupon Johnny Andersen wrung his neck and carted him back to the Andersen kitchen. There, in company with two onions and three potatoes, he staved off starvation for the five little Andersens for another day, and I went back to Mrs Harrop to tell her sorrowfully that all our efforts to recapture Captain Cook had been unsuccessful.

The result of all this tearing through wet grass was that my throat swelled up afresh. I went back to bed for another week. Grandmother told me that it was God's punishment on me for stravaiging the streets with the Andersens, but Uncle Shaun backed me up. He said that Harrop was a highly successful bookie's urger and in clover compared to the rest of us, and one rabbit in the poor man's pot was worth half a dozen in the rich man's hutch.

I was very sick this time, but somehow it did not seem so bad, for when there was no window-cleaning to be had, and no odd jobs available, Uncle Shaun would sit on the end of my bed and tell me stories of revolutions in Mexico, temple dancers in Bali, earthquakes in New Zealand, or cattle punching in the Argentine—and soon the drabness around me was gone, lost in the warmth and colour of his story-telling.

The orchid-hung jungles of the South Americas and the lacquered temples of Burma were jumbled together against the fading background of the factory wall outside my window, and when I went off to sleep the wall was not there at all. In its place were the glittering peaks of the Andes, the palaces of India, the orange trees of Spain, and through my dreaming came the sound of tropical seas breaking around palm-fringed islands.

The songs that Uncle Shaun sang as he sat there with his white hair shining in the firelight! Beautiful songs like :

> Oh Shenandoah, I'm bound to leave you,
> Away, you rolling river.

Gay songs like :

> As I strolled down the Broadway one evening in July,
> A full rigged Yankee clipper at once did catch my eye.
> And away there, Johnny,
> My dear honey
> And all you New York girls, can't you dance the polka?

And my favourite of all, the inexpressibly sad :

> I dreamed a dream the other night,
> Lowlands, Lowlands away my John,
> I dreamed a dream the other night,
> Of the Lowlands away.

The wattle came out in August, and Uncle Shaun kept fidgeting around the house and going down to the docks to look at the ships, and then within a week he was gone, leaving a new pair of shoes for me and a month's rent on the mantelpiece, and a letter to say that we could go down to Burns Philp and draw half his pay twice a month.

Aunt Rose got a job working in a hotel up the country. It only meant her keep, but at least it was a job.

It was an early September day of surprisingly warm sunshine when I went along to the public hospital with Lila Clancy. Lila's latest baby was not at all well, and the social worker who went the rounds of the Port Melbourne sustenance houses advised her to take him to hospital. I went along to keep Lila company, and she undertook to fix up about having my tonsils out, at the same time.

"You'll be alright, alannah, when they come out," said my grandmother, "and thank God we've all come through this winter."

She was fixing my scarf around my neck, and as she spoke she turned her face up to the sun, and in the morning light I could see that she was very tired, and that there were tears in her eyes.

I was very quiet as I walked along beside Lila, and the baby was quiet too—lying in his mother's arms, wrapped in a worn-out shawl, one small finger in his mouth. At the hospital we stood for about an hour and a half waiting until there was room for us on the long wooden benches in front of the small glassed-in office where you got your card. On the card you stated the nature of your illness, whether you were working, whether your husband (or wife, as the case might be) was working, how much you earned, dependants if any, and how much you felt you could pay.

The mighty one who conducted this probe was a large, well-fed and heavily-pimpled youth wearing the blazer of a very expensive and well-known public school. I should think his father must have been one of the biggest honoraries in the hospital. This being the day before Psychology For The Worker, he employed the old-time method of disciplining the proletariat —that is to say, he offset his near idiocy by an imposing show of physical omnipotence.

"Sit down and wait your turn," he roared every five minutes, in a voice of such pathological brutality as I had never heard before in my life. As he shouted he would wave his arms and poke people in the ribs.

And we sat and waited our turn, as instructed—men with poisoned hands, boys with broken arms, women with T.B., a child heavy-eyed with diphtheria, clutching his mother's hand, a factory girl pressing her hand against her appendix, Leo Williams who went to school with me, a huge abscess on the back of his neck. We waited, and when our turn came most of us answered humbly and quietly because we were afraid. We were very afraid. But I promised myself that when my turn came to walk into that little den beside Lila I would give myself the fun of reeling off my difficult Irish name very fast, and very Irish. "Eilishe Cahaleen Deirdre Flynn, said with a good thick brogue," I thought. "Let the bastard make what he can of that."

A woman passing us on the way into the next room to wait

for the doctor showed us her card, whereon her husband had been described as a meatle worker. This novel way of spelling metal made us all laugh, but our friend in the office looked up and decided he was not amused. He came out like a charge of the New Guard. He bellowed his slogan till the roof re-echoed. He gave poor Lila, who was still standing, such a shove in the back that the baby was jolted in her arms and gave a thin solitary little wail.

"And you," he shouted at the girl with appendicitis, "stop putting on an act."

An attractive woman with masses of dyed, black hair, and very shiny high-heeled shoes of patent leather, decided that she had had enough. She stood up with her arms folded and motioned the girl up into her position.

"You can have my place, love," she said.

"No swapping places," yelled he of the school blazer. "If you give up your place you go to the end of the queue."

"That suits me all right," said the woman. And as she sauntered down the waiting line she remarked to all of us in general, "The rotten pig."

"Don't you go making a scene," shouted the flower of higher education. "You can't go making a disturbance here or out you'll go."

A door on the left flew open and a woman wearing a matron's veil looked us over with a bleak grey gaze which she flattered herself could quell a riot. After pausing to let us recognise the mien of true authority, she spoke :

"Come, come now, people ! If this noise goes on you will all have to go home. There are a few genuine cases present who are really in need, so please don't waste our time. You are not paying for this, you know."

We all looked guilty. 'You are not paying for this, you know' was calculated to be the ultimate insult, and it was, for in those days we clung to the precepts that had destroyed us. We helped dig our own graves because we believed that it was the greatest of all crimes to be out of pocket. Better to rob your fellow man, better to murder your unborn children, better to sell your body on the street, than to admit that you could not pay. We sat crushed, accused of the final indecency.

Time went on. Lila and I at last got a seat beside a very fat woman seamed all over the legs with varicose veins. We ate the lunch of bread and butter and bananas we had brought with us and Lila asked timidly if she could have the baby's bottle heated. A red-headed trainee nurse snatched it out of her hand and whisked it away. When it came back it was boiling and we had to wait till it cooled. Lila was worried about this, but the baby neither whimpered nor stirred, but just lay with his little hands clasped together and his eyes growing larger every moment. He sobbed a bit, in a half-hearted fashion, while his napkin was being changed, but soon gave it up and relapsed into his wide-eyed stare at the ceiling, and when we offered him his bottle he turned his head wearily away. The woman with the varicose veins looked at him with a practised eye. "What's wrong with him?" she asked.

"He just won't take his food at all," said Lila. "He doesn't weigh any more now than when he was born."

"Don't worry about that, love," comforted the other. "I've had seven, and my fourth, young Shirley, was just the same way. Have you tried Nestlé's milk and barley water?"

"I've tried everything," said Lila.

"Well they'll fix him up with something here. They're wonderful here. All the same I'd try to get up to the head of the queue with him. It's no good for him hanging around here in the cold. I wonder if he is cold. Feel his little feet."

Lila let the other woman feel his feet. She just sat with the child lying in her lap and her eyes gazing straight ahead. Had we been permitted the luxury of nervous breakdowns Lila would have had one months ago. As it was, she was bereft of hope, energy, the will to live, and the capacity to help herself. She was not yet twenty-five, and completely finished.

The baby's feet were cold so we wrapped them in my woollen gloves and wrapped him again in the shawl. Then I nursed him while Lila prepared to walk up and ask could she be attended to straight away. She had not taken two hesitating steps before he of the office was out like a whirlwind.

"Sit down and wait your turn," he roared. "You people with children should take them to the Children's Hospital. Just too bone-lazy to go the extra distance. Sit down there and wait."

Lila began to cry and the woman with the varicose veins gave us her place and went down to the end of the line. I suggested

24

that the next time a nurse went through we should ask her to take Jimmy straight into the hospital. I was frightened by the lightness of the bundle in my arms. But the only person who seemed to go in and out was the red-headed trainee, who glared at us and said she was too busy before we had time even to open our mouths.

Then the girl with the appendicitis began to vomit violently and fell to the floor, where she lay writhing and moaning. She was helped in to the doctor, and about a quarter of an hour later went past us on a trolley on her way to the operating theatre. Her appendix had refused to sit down and wait its turn. It had burst.

Suddenly Lila took her child out of my arms and started walking straight towards the door. She ignored the roar of 'Sit down' and walked straight on. All the women rose and thronged around her. Something new had come into the atmosphere of meek and hopeless misery. As yet Lila had said nothing. The youth in the office swallowed hard, pulled at his tie, and made one last stand in the name of inborn privilege.

"What's going on?" he blustered. "Sit down the lot of you or all get out. I . . ."

And now the door on the left opened and the doctor came out.

"What is it?" he asked.

"She's got to sit down and wait her turn like everybody else," yelled the youth. "She's got to . . ."

"It doesn't matter now," said Lila. "My little boy is dead."

She spoke very quietly and rocked her baby in her arms in a soothing sort of way. Then she held him up against her shoulder and put her face down against his face, and patted his little back as though to bring up wind.

"Yes," she whispered. "He is dead."

Suddenly the stony silence was broken by the woman with the dyed hair and the lovely legs, who came charging down from her position at the back of the queue. She hurled herself upon the youth in the public school blazer and tore at his face.

"You rotten bastard! You lousy swine! You're not fit to be in a drum, let alone a hospital. You're not fit to be alive, you stinking rotten . . ."

Her voice, hysterical with hatred, went on and rose in a spate

25

of filth and obscenity, the terrible language a prostitute uses to reassure herself that she is inured to the horror of her life—the protective colouring of the street-walker. She was still screaming and doing her best to kick the youth in the blazer to death when they dragged her away to the city watch-house.

"Come along out of this, love," said the woman with varicose veins, touching Lila gently on the shoulder. "Come along. I'll get you home."

As we went down the hospital steps she asked, "Where do you live?"

"I don't know," said Lila.

"We live in Stawell Street, Port Melbourne," I said.

I remember it surprised me that my voice still sounded the same—that after all that had happened I was still the same person.

"Well I'll get you into a taxi," said the woman. "Come on, love."

She led Lila down into the street.

"What about your varicose veins?" asked Lila.

I was horrified at myself, but this pitiful effort to keep a grip on things struck me as terribly funny. I wanted to laugh. I wanted to stand there in the street beside the dead child and laugh my head off.

"Oh bugger my varicose veins," said the woman. "I've had them since my first was born. I can put up with them a while longer."

So Jimmy Clancy was taken back to his home, and we laid him out on his parents' bed, and I folded back the shawl and looked at his little wasted body, the tiny hands still clasped together, and the little stone-cold feet wrapped in the gloves that now would never warm them. Lila dressed him in the silk dress he had worn at his baptism only a month before, and handed me back my gloves, but I put them down on the pillow just beside his face.

"He can have them," I said.

And I knelt down with my head on the edge of the bed and cried bitterly.

Because my grandmother considered that Jimmy's death was a bad omen, I went to have my tonsils removed at another

26

public hospital where tonsils, adenoids and post-nasal growths (as a big printed notice so gruesomely put it) were attended to on the first Monday of every month; which day was called Bloody Monday.

Along with a swarm of other children and their mothers, Grandmother and I were shown into a huge hall filled with wooden trestles about the size of single beds. Here we children were undressed to our underclothes and shoes, and swathed in the shapeless white smock which the hospital provided. Then we waited.

Across the passage was an identical hall where the children were carried after the operation. They lay on the same sort of trestles, and bled and were sick while their mothers hovered over them and waited for them to come out of the anaesthetic. Some of the children cried and clung to their mothers when the nurse came to take them into the operating theatre, but I was filled with such a rage of rebellion against the fear and pain and unhappiness all around that I resolved that if I did any crying or flinching it would only be in front of my own—those whom I knew, and who knew me.

So I sat and held my grandmother's hand and glared at the nurses as they hurried back and forwards.

"Gee, what beautiful eyes you have," said one of the nurses, intercepting one of these glares. "You must be Irish to have eyes like that. Let's look at your card."

Grandmother held out my card, and I saw that her hand was trembling.

The nurse read my name. "Well, come along with me, Irish Eyes," she said.

Grandmother's face had gone white. She had never had anaesthetic in her life. She kissed me lightly on one cheek and smiled at me. "Run along there, darling," she said. "When you wake up they'll be gone."

And in good time I did wake up, and when I had recovered enough to walk I went home in a taxi. There were hardier types who took the tram but I did it in style with my legs wobbling and a big chunk of blood-stained towelling held up to my mouth. I had the usual few days in bed, living on soup, ice-cream and mashed potatoes, and I read *Les Misérables* and *Kidnapped*. It was not so bad, all things considered. I have always been of the opinion that the only way to spend the Melbourne winter (and most of the spring) is to hibernate, with a plentiful supply of good books beside the bed in readiness for moments of wakefulness.

Only one thing worried me. On the morning that we went to the hospital, Grandmother said to me just before we left home, "Lisha, when I fill in your card I'm going to say that you are an orphan and I am your legal guardian. Now you know that nothing has happened to your parents so don't be frightened when I say it. We had a letter from your mother only last week, as you well remember, and Owen Flynn will never died young, but it doesn't do to tell these people all your business."

I said, "All right, Gran," but I thought it very puzzling indeed and, of course, I must go discussing it with my little friends.

"Why do you think Gran said it?" I asked Phyl Foley.

Phyl said she didn't know, but Chrissie Brady tossed her plaits back over her shoulders and said that when I was older I would be told. "You wouldn't understand," she said, "you're too young."

This riled me.

"What has age to do with it, Chrissie?" I asked. "I'm two years younger than you are and I'm in the same grade at school so I should think I would understand anything that you knew, so what are you making such a big secret about?"

So there you are. I would go meeting trouble head on. I asked for what I got.

"Well," said Chrissie, "if you must know, you're a deserted child, and if the Welfare knew they'd take you away from your grandmother."

I was as near to fainting as I have ever been in my life. I felt as if the sky were crashing down about my head. 'Deserted child', 'on the welfare', 'neglected child', all these were the most dreadful insults.

"Chrissie, you're awful," said Phyl.

That gave me time to get back my breath.

"You don't know what you're talking about," I said. "Anyway, even if it were true, what good would it do to say I'm an orphan?"

"Makes a lot of difference. If you're an orphan your grandmother is really your guardian, but the way it is the Welfare could take you any time, because your mother and father don't want you and you're just living on your grandmother's charity."

CHARITY!!!

Chrissie had spoken the unspeakable word—the dirtiest word in the slums. Had I been smart I would, there and then, have burst into tears and Chrissie would have been voted, by one and all, to be the greatest bitch to ever walk down Stawell Street. But just at that moment I did not want to weep (that came later), my one desire was to throw myself upon Chrissie and gouge her eyes out. I kept my voice even and downfaced her.

"That's all you know. My mother and father send money every week for me."

"First I knew about it. What I heard was they'd cleared out and left you."

"Who told you that lie?"

"My mother, and my mother doesn't tell lies. Anyrate everybody says so."

I looked down the street to where Mrs Brady was standing by her gate talking to her friend Mrs Lascala, and, without a word more to Chrissie, I turned and ran, straight to the Bradys' gate.

"Did you tell Chris that my mother and father had deserted me and my grandmother kept me on charity?" I demanded.

"What!"

Mrs Brady was astonished. She was not used to being bailed up by white-faced, breathless, enraged little girls.

I said it again. It had not choked me to say it once. Obviously, I could repeat it without dropping down dead. It's wonderful what we can get used to.

"Well of all the cheek," said Mrs Brady. She turned to Mrs Lascala. "Did you ever hear anything like it?" she asked. "Isn't she a little madam? Her grandmother has filled her so full of big ideas that there's no doing anything with her."

Mrs Lascala smiled nervously. She liked my grandmother, but the Bradys were a big family and very good customers at the Lascala fruit shop. At that moment, she wished most heartily that she did not speak the English. Mrs Brady turned to me.

"You run along home now, this instant," she said, "and tell your grandmother to learn you a few manners."

Suddenly I realised, as I looked up at that mean, unkind face, that Mrs Brady was enjoying herself. I had always been taught to keep my head up and not make a show of myself. I had already shown too much hurt and distress. I picked up my school-bag and walked away home, and the hardest thing of all to bear was that I heard someone running up behind me, and then Phyl was beside me, tugging at my arm, trying to make me turn and look at her, saying, "Don't take any notice, Lisha. I don't believe what Chrissie says. She's cruel. I don't want to be friends with her any more. I've been going off her for a long while. She's only jealous. Mum says Mrs Brady talks about everybody. Don't worry about them. Don't take any notice."

Well, of course, this was the word of sympathy that always makes the recipient burst out into those enormous sobs that seem to tear the chest apart. I don't know how I got inside my front door without breaking down. Phyl said, "See you tomorrow", and I could only nod my head.

Grandmother was busy baking in the kitchen and called out to ask if I wanted an apple turnover. I managed to answer, "No, thank you", then I methodically put my pillow over my head and had a long, relieving cry. Grandmother came in after a while and wanted to know what was wrong. I dried my eyes and said it was just something that had happened at school and it was all over now, and I thought I'd have an apple turnover after all.

But the next evening Grandmother looked at me across the tea-table and said, "I hear you had a run in with Mrs Brady yesterday."

"Yes."

"That was wrong of you, Lisha. It never does any good to go giving people the chance to say you're cheeky. Do you think I like it when Mrs Brady is able to say that you're not well brought up? You let your grandmother down when you behave badly."

My grandmother's voice was so gentle and sorrowful that I almost began to cry again. I knew that, somehow, she must have been told about what had happened, and that she was talking about manners and good behaviour only because she felt she should; that really she was intensely sorry and grieved for me. She reached over and patted my hand.

"Lisha," she said, "you should never worry about what people say. Usually people who say the sort of things that Mrs Brady said are so mean and small-hearted that they just cannot understand how the average person thinks and feels. They are to be pitied because they miss so much, just because they cannot love enough. You have never been anything except a joy to me. I would be an old lonely woman with nothing to do except look to the grave, if I didn't have you. When you are grown up you will understand what a great thing it is, and how it gives you your own life over again, to have a young one that you love growing up in the house. Come on, eat your dinner."

I looked around the table and I realised that Grandmother had spent a good deal of money preparing the meal I liked best. There were lamb chops and tiny new potatoes in their jackets, and French salad and a long crusty loaf of bread.

"Confusion to the Bradys," said my grandmother.

She lifted her tea-cup, as though in a toast, and gave that crooked smile of hers that could only be called a grin. I burst out laughing. She had a great gift of making people happy, had my Gran.

The Christmas before the war started I was thirteen and I took my first job. I was finished with primary school and I had just managed to get a Diocesan Scholarship. This meant that if I could raise the money for uniforms, books and fares, I could go to an expensive college in the eastern suburbs. My grandmother wept for joy when I won that scholarship. We had been buying the *Age* for a week and looking for the exam results and telling each other that we were not anxious about it, really, but it would be nice all the same, mind you. We weren't greatly hoping, there were my maths to be reckoned with when all was said and done, and it was no use getting all worked up in advance, and if I did not get one this year, why, I could try again next year. For sure it was no disgrace to go for a scholarship and not win. Not everyone could win, so we were not going to be disappointed if it came to nothing, and so on. Sensible, that's what we were going to be. So there was the pair of us on the Thursday morning, step-dancing round the kitchen, laughing, crying, singing and pausing every so often to hug each other and take another look at the blessed *Age* where my name appeared in characters clear. The next Sunday it appeared also in the *Advocate* and the *Tribune* and my grandmother was a proud woman that day—buying a copy of each in the church porch and telling her friends, "It seems that her ladyship is famous in a small way."

In a small way, forsooth. Grandmother was absolutely certain that every parish rang with my glory and that, if she lived long enough, she would certainly have the happiness of seeing me receive the Nobel Prize.

Sister Mary Angela and Sister Mary Paul paid us a special visit of congratulation and Sister Mary Angela said she had lost count of the Diocesan winners she had taught but, this she knew, never had she had a child before who was as good as I was at History, English and Geography.

"I'll admit when it came to her maths I was praying to St Jude," she said. "Good old St Jude, Hope of the Hopeless."

Sister Mary Angela had been teaching for fifty years, and never once had she lost her zest and joy in her vocation. If ever a woman was born to train the young, it was she, and every scholarship winner who went out from her classes was a source of the purest happiness to her. I decided to go over to see Phyl Foley before I was embarrassed any further by hearing such flattering things about myself.

Next day came Aunt Nell, who was my grandmother's sister. She had also been left a young widow with a large family. It was a hot day and Aunt Nell's bunions were giving her hell, and none of her grandchildren had been the least clever at school, so when told about the scholarship she said she had already heard about it from her friend Mrs Bourke. As for Sister Angela's claim that I was her most brilliant pupil in English, Auntie Nell sniffed to demonstrate incredulity, and said it was a well-known fact that Sister Angela always said things like that about pupils who reflected any credit on her.

"She said practically the same thing to Mrs Brady about her Bernadette."

This was perfectly true. Sister Angela, in her excitement and delight, always decided that the child in question was a genius in her own particular line, but Grandmother was indignant.

"Rubbish," she said. "Are you saying that the holy nuns tell lies?"

Aunt Nell said there was not much point in arguing about it, because I would not be going on to college, anyway.

"Indeed," said my grandmother, "that's where you're wrong, Nell. She most certainly is going. She will have her chance."

"You're mad, Kate," said Auntie Nell. "You can't afford it. It'll kill you."

"Shaun always sends money when he's in work, and her mother sends what she can, and we heard from her father only last month. He's still in New Zealand. He sent five pounds."

"That will probably be his contribution for five years," said Aunt Nell, with more truth than charity.

My grandmother rose and put her tea-cup on the sink. She turned towards her sister and held out her hands.

"While I have these two hands to work with," she said, "the child *will* have her chance, even if I have to go out scrubbing."

Aunt Nell looked at her, and shook her head. "Cathrine McCormack," she said, "you are a fool." (It was fifty years since my grandmother had been Cathrine McCormack, but we always used clan names in moments of extreme earnestness.) "You spoilt your own and now you're determined to spoil this one."

"And what's wrong with my own, if I may ask?" said Grandmother, mighty civil and dangerous-sounding.

"Well where did all their education get them? Oh I remember well, you worked yourself to a shadow while your boys took scholarships and, God rest their souls, they're dead and gone now, and what good did it all do? And look at your girls. They had to have piano lessons and they had to have this and that, and the one you spent most on was her mother, and she's so fine a lady that she can't even be bothered with her own children."

"You know very well," said my grandmother, "that her mother has to spend money and dress well to keep the job she has. She does what she can and she sends what she can in presents and money. At any rate, even if she sent nothing, I'd thank God every day of my life that she got out of here, and Lisha will have her chance to get out too."

"Lisha will have her chance. Lisha will have her chance. That's all I've heard since I came here. Very well, go ahead."

"Thanks, Nell, I will."

33

"Ruin her. Turn her head. You've got her half ruined already, you and Shaun between you. All the Flynns were too big for their boots and she's no exception. Not but that she's not like the Wards, as well—getting around with her head in the air and the lungs melting in her chest."

"That's no way to talk in front of the child, Nell. Besides, she's been strong and sturdy since her tonsils came out."

Aunt Nell looked ashamed, because she was really a very kind-hearted woman, but bunions, combined with new shoes on a hot day, can turn a dove into a tiger, as I have often had opportunity to observe—so she stuck to her point.

"Why don't you put her to a trade?" she said.

"Never."

"A trade was good enough for my girls."

"Well it wasn't good enough for mine, and it's not good enough for Lisha."

Aunt Nell said that, perhaps, she was not good enough to visit such high and mighty folk.

Grandmother said Aunt Nell could please herself.

Aunt Nell said that, in that case, she'd be going.

Grandmother advised her to hurry back to West Melbourne and the good sensible people who could think of nothing better to do with their children than to put them to trades and trap them in factories for a few miserable shillings.

Aunt Nell said that her girls were good girls to her, and she might not be so ready with the grand talk but she hoped she was better than some she could mention that were for ever skiting about their fine family, and holding out their hand for the pension come every second Thursday.

This was delivered on the doorstep in good clear tones for the benefit of such of the neighbours as might be interested.

Grandmother, fine old veteran that she was, waited till Aunt Nell was half way up the street and then leaned over the garden gate to beg her not to be too haughty about the pension.

"I've seen the day when you were glad enough if I could give you the cast-offs that my own children were finished with. The pension, is it? I mind the time when you weren't too good for the St Vincent de Paul's."

Aunt Nell whirled round. "I'll tell you one thing I was always

34

too good for, Cathrine Eilishe McCormack. I was too good to marry into a pack of dirty thieving, traipsing tinkers."

"You were so, Nell. I'll agree with you there, Nell. True for you, Nell. Soupers and informers were always more to your taste, weren't they, Nell?"

And at that Aunt Nell answered never a word. She put her head down and hurried up the street. She seemed suddenly to have shrunk to about half her normal size.

Grandmother and I went in and brewed a cup of tea, and Grandmother said that it was the last we'd be seeing of Nell for a while, and what a relief it would be not to have to listen to her silly, pessimistic talk.

"Lisha, I've heard it for years : 'you have to come to terms with circumstances, you have to cut your coat according to your cloth'." Grandmother laughed gaily at the mere idea of doing anything so ridiculous and weak-kneed as coming to terms with circumstances.

Aunt Nell appeared about ten o'clock the next morning. She wore her old shoes with the bunion slits and was in a happier frame of mind. She sat down and said that if we had the kettle on she could do with a cup of tea. Grandmother served tea with a sort of bright, sharp courtesy—and flickers of affection showing in her eyes and at the corners of her mouth. Having had her tea and three scones, Aunt Nell produced a tape-measure and asked Grandmother if she had a pencil and paper.

"I told Florrie," she said, "and she's as pleased as punch, of course. She says that with all her own home for the Christmas holidays she won't have much time, but if you get the materials and send over the measurements, she'll try and get the uniforms made for you before the school term starts. She says she'll be able to get the blazer and at least one tunic done, and it takes no time at all to run up the blouses. Then she can take her time with the other tunic."

Florrie was Aunt Nell's eldest girl, and a wonderful dress-maker—that being the trade she had been put to on the first day that she could legally leave school.

Grandmother sat looking at Aunt Nell. Her face trembled and then she smiled. "Ah, Nell," she said, "you were always a good sister to me and your children have hearts of gold, the lot of them."

35

"Well it's a fine thing if you can't help your own," said Aunt Nell, "and it isn't every day that you get a scholarship winner in the family. We're all very proud of her."

That night when Grandmother and I were drinking our cocoa before going to bed, I said, "Is it true what you said, Grandmother, about Auntie Nell's husband having an informer in the family?"

I sensed a family scandal here, and it is always handy to know any family scandal. You may never need to use it but it is good to have it there.

"Well, you'll not hold it against her I know, Lisha, but it is a fact that her husband's grandfather was something in that line."

"Well, he's no relation to us."

"None at all, thank God."

"It's kind of Aunt Florrie to make my uniforms."

"Nellie's girls were always the kindest people in the whole clan," said Grandmother, "and Nell, herself, was always my favourite sister. Even when we were little girls back home we were closer to each other than to any of the other sisters. Eight of we girls, there were. Honora married very well, but she's dead and gone this many a year and so is Clare—God rest their souls. And Brighid is in the Dominican convent in Dublin, and Annie and Mary and Bibiana are all in America, all with a dozen or more grandchildren apiece. Bib had a lot of money left her by her first husband and she came over once for a trip. I never saw such clothes, nor heard such a Yankee accent. The others I haven't seen for fifty years. But Nell and I, we've been through it all together, all the hard times, and some good times too." Grandmother stirred her cocoa and smiled, and her smile went way past me, back to the days when she was young and handsome.

"It's more than thirty years ago and yet I can see it now, as though it were yesterday—Nell arranging to meet me in town the next day so that we could go to the theatre because some-one had given her two tickets to see Daisy Jerome. Nell was so excited that she couldn't stop laughing. It was a long time since we'd been anywhere and Nell was always a great one for knocking a bit of fun out of things. Those were the days when anyone who hoped to be taken for even half a lady had to wear a hat if she so much as stepped foot outside the door, and there was Nell in the most dreadful old wreck you've ever seen and it was the only one she possessed, and her gloves were splitting at every seam. She was the very picture of the poor little widow woman, and as she got on the old horse tram she called out to me so that all the world could hear, 'You'll have no difficulty seeing me in the crowd, Katey. I'll be wearing me high-buttoned boots, me feather boa and me hat with the Lancer plume.' "

Grandmother laughed, and then she looked up at me and came back to the present again.

"I'll go down to Byron's tomorrow morning," she said, "and see if I can get any carding to do. It will all help."

She rubbed her hands. I have seldom seen her in such high glee as she was at that moment, beset as she was with worry and work and expense.

"This all makes me feel young again," she said. "The old war-horse sniffs the battle from afar, as you might say, Lisha. And you can believe me, darling, this is one battle I'm going to enjoy."

The Byron Button Factory was the most extraordinary establishment. It had this unique gift of never going quite broke. Small, rackety and ill-equipped, it was run by the two Byron brothers, who combined engineering genius and lack of any sort of business method, in a manner which would have put the great Henry Ford himself in the hands of the Public Receiver. But Byron's Buttons survived. Every Friday evening, Robert, the elder Byron brother, remarked, as he paid his employees, "Come in on Monday. God knows if we'll get the doors open, but you can come in on the off-chance." And sure enough on Monday morning the doors opened and Byron's was saved for another week. It supplied Stawell Street with its one cottage industry—carding. This was simple enough and not at all strenuous. All you had to do was to sew buttons on sample cards which were usually about six inches wide and nine inches long. The pay was a halfpenny a card, but it was not such sweated labour as it sounds. It is surprising what a nice little sum a good carder could knock up in quite a short time, and it was pleasant to sit by the fire in winter, or under the fig tree in summer, your hands busy with the cards and your mind

37

thousands of miles away, lost in dreams and fantasy. I've done plenty of it, so I should know.

Now I had an idea. Byron's always put on a couple of extra girls over Christmas. I would go down and see if I could get a job.

"Just for the holidays, Gran," I said. "I'd love to be earning some money."

"I don't want you getting so tired that you're no good for study when the school year starts," said my grandmother.

But I begged and coaxed, and promised that if it made me too tired I'd leave, and finally Grandmother was persuaded, and the following Monday I went to work.

I worked from 8 a.m. to 5.30 p.m. with a half-hour for lunch and ten minutes for morning tea. I stood all day on a concrete floor that made my feet, legs and back ache till I wanted to cry, and with every breath I drew into my lungs the all-pervading casein dust. For this I was paid 12s. 6d. per week. I was in the picking, sorting and packing department. In company with three other girls—Dawn, Eily and Gladdie—I spread the buttons on the long racks, waited till they dried, and then sorted them into their types, sizes and colours. We developed a technique whereby you picked up the button and threw it into its colour compartment in the one movement. When you became a good sorter you became ambidextrous and your hands worked so quickly that they looked as though you were using a typewriter at top speed. And believe me we worked fast. We had Gwen Brown the forewoman standing right behind us to see that we did. We also had what Robert Byron was pleased to describe as 'a very healthy and wholesome fear of the sack'. I was not a very tall child at that time and picking from the higher racks made my shoulders and arms ache, but I picked buttons with a sort of dumb, stolid rage all the Christmas holidays.

It was a hot summer, and the elder Byron brother, who was very clever at all the little shifts and meannesses, decided that if the drying racks were moved under the windows the sun would dry the buttons, and thus electricity would be saved. So over to the windows the racks went, and it was just unfortunate for us that the windows faced west and got all the afternoon sun. The perspiration stuck our dresses to our backs and ran off us in streams. It even ran off our hands and fell in small drops on the cardboard that covered the racks. Gladdie fainted. The smell of the fat and good natured Dawn made me feel sick. Every time you put up your hand to push your hair back from your face you left wet streaks of dirt across your forehead.

Miss Brown took orders as they came in over the phone, put through calls for the Byron brothers, and, in between whiles, packed the buttons into gross and great-gross boxes. When packed they were neatly stacked away on shelves around the dispatch, and it was her boast that she could lay her hands on any colour or type of button within a minute of receiving an order. She was one of those terrible people with a superhuman capacity for work. Efficient and tireless, she liked to see everyone around her completely exhausted. She toiled away all day, one pencil in her hand, another behind her ear, and a cigarette in one corner of her mouth, while Eddie, the messenger boy, came whistling through to take out some of the smaller orders that did not warrant the personal attention of Eugene Byron, the younger brother, who ran the car.

Robert Byron raved daily about the output, and the expense, and the weekly wage cheque. And still we picked on, our eyes narrowed against the glare.

Toilet facilities were represented by two dilapidated lavatories —I never knew the time when both chains were working properly—and an ancient enamel sink with a grey towel beside it. It was a matter for wonder to me that Dawn would sometimes brave the wrath of Miss Brown and shut herself in this malodorous apartment to smoke a cigarette, for I avoided it as much as possible, which put me in well with Miss Brown, who would have been much happier in charge of three robots. She would say, "Dawn, do you think you're paid to sit there all the afternoon? Mr Robert has been asking for those blue type thirty-sixes."

"Sorry, Miss Brown," from Dawn. And then, out the side of her mouth as she rejoined me at the rack, "What does the old bitch think we bloody well are—fairies?"

Dawn, if you could cope with her smell of stale sweat with fresh sweat superimposed, was an interesting personality. She was almost sixteen, had left school for two years, and was going steady with a boy called Alan. She told me all about her mother's internal operations, her sister's illegitimate daughter, and her cousin who had married Mick Gleeson. The Gleesons had been the criminal royal family of our suburb for years, and Dawn was full of fascinating stories about them. Local legend had invested them with a Robin Hood quality. Bluey Gleeson— the elder and tougher of the two brothers—was 'a wonderful boy to his old mother'.

'No Gleeson has ever shelved a mate.'

'The police didn't give the Gleesons a fair go. . . .'

'The Gleesons wouldn't take a trey piece from those who needed it. . . .'

'You just leave the Gleesons alone, and they won't worry you. . . .'

'Many a family have had their wood bill paid by the Gleesons when times were bad. . . .'

How often did I hear these claims? All I know is that no Gleeson ever paid for our wood, or the wood of anyone personally known to me, and I have heard Bluey Gleeson and his dear old mother indulge in a slanging match in the middle of the street, in which the burden of Mrs Gleeson's remarks was that a worse son than James Patrick Aloysius Gleeson had never stepped foot in shoe-leather. Certainly they were both handsome men, and Mick had a sort of superficial good humour and sometimes handed ice-creams around amongst the younger children, exclaiming as he did so, "Gawd, I love kids."

He had also been seen to help old ladies across the road and he always patted dogs upon the head.

He made me sick.

But he and Bluey (and, to a lesser extent, their dear old mother) did provide us with colour and excitement of a sort, and we were prepared to glamourise them to show our gratitude. Certainly on the one occasion when I had witnessed a Gleeson going about his professional business I had abided by the injunction : Leave the Gleesons alone and they'll leave you alone.

There was I, with my head stuck around the corner of the lane which ran down beside the Harp of Erin, watching entranced while Mick went through the pockets of the local S.P., who always conducted his business in this lane on a Wednesday and Saturday. I had been just about to turn the corner looking for my old friend Johnny Dawson on this sunny Saturday morning, and I was lucky enough to see the knock-out punch. The bookie lay in a limp unsightly heap on the cobbles, and Mick worked with feverish speed but apparently little success. He had one huge hand in the S.P.'s back pocket when Bluey came rushing down the lane.

"For the love of God, Mick," he shouted. "You must be bloody well mad. There's three flatfeet outside the Harp, and they're coming in here any minute."

Mick wrenched his hand out of the tight pocket. "I've just got to get a tenner by lunch-time," he gasped, "I've got to get it."

He scrambled to his feet and he and his brother disappeared around one end of the lane just as the police came in at the other.

I had managed to learn what, in Stawell Street, were always called the facts of life by the time I was eleven. At about twelve I knew, in a hazy sort of way, that some women sold their bodies, and these women were called prostitutes, but it remained for Dawn to tell me that the Gleesons operated thirty brothels in Little Compton Street. Houses, Dawn called them. She said they stood, one next door to the other, all down one side of the street. The numbers involved were not so horrifying as one would imagine on first hearing the story of the Gleeson Empire, for it should be explained that each one of these houses was that dreariest, dullest, loneliest and ugliest institution in the whole history of harlotry—the one-woman drum. They were little damp, secret-looking three-roomed cottages, built in a terrace, no curtains in the windows, no flowers in the patch of front garden, no smell of cooking, no sound of singing, no sign of anything that could truly be called life—just the women; a woman on each verandah, her hair in curlers, her feet in felt slippers, a magazine, or some knitting, in her hand.

"You've got to give this in," said Dawn, "they're quiet and they're well run. Never any trouble. Blue Gleeson sees to that. My Dad was overseas in the war and then he was on the ships afterwards, and he says that what he's seen in Europe would make your hair curl. They're that brazen, especially the French and the Eyeties, or all those Dagoes if it comes to that. They've got their houses going full blast day and night, dancing,

41

drinking, fighting. He says him and a mate went to a place in Spain. It was before he was married, of course, and you know what men are."

I didn't know any such thing, but I nodded and looked very wise.

"Well off they go and there was this terrible brawl and his mate nearly got carved up. There was a bar there and all. Imagine a bar in a place like that. What I mean to say, you'll always have it. It always has been since the beginning of history. Mum says if it wasn't for those girls a decent woman couldn't walk down the street in safety. But you can keep it quiet. You don't have to rub people's noses in it."

One thing was sure, no frivolous Frenchman, no rorty Spaniard would be getting a drink or a dance or a fight, or anything that could possibly gladden the heart of man, in one of our brothels. We kept it quiet. We had Little Compton Street, where vice was reduced to its ugliest and dullest. I decided that I could forgive the vice and, to a certain extent, I could excuse the ugliness—but never, *never* was I going to be able to tolerate the dullness.

Dawn had a theory that, with only one woman operating per building, the law with regard to using premises for purposes of prostitution was, in some way that was not very clear to us, circumvented. I never found out if this were true, but I daresay it was. Pat, the wife of Bluey Gleeson, ran this side of the Gleeson enterprises, and I presume she knew her business. She'd had heaps of time to learn. She'd been in it since she was ten. Showing great aptitude for the work and a natural brilliance at handling money, she had risen from Condies girl to Madam in a very short space of time. From then on all had been plain sailing. She had married Blue Gleeson, who was fifteen years younger than she, when he was just a bright lad, ambitious of getting ahead in the underworld, and now she lived in what might almost be termed retirement. She rented the Little Compton Street houses for 17s. a week. She then let them out to the girls for £5 a week, and she took a certain percentage of protection money.

"None of the Gleesons would take a regular cut out of the earnings, like," explained Dawn. "They're not as bad as some I could mention, but those girls have got to have someone to see that no one stands over them or pikes on them. Someone's got to look after them, so it might as well be the Gleesons."

I agreed doubtfully. I was not at all sure that I did agree, but I was afraid of appearing soft.

Then something happened which made it clear to me that I was not tough enough yet. Not nearly tough enough yet.

One evening when I was working overtime I stood alone in the small lunch-room eating my tea, and gazing out the window into the lane at the back. It was the end of a lovely day—the noises in the streets were hushed and the sunset lay, red and gold and beautiful, on the huddle of roofs and chimneys that stretched away before me. I was humming softly to myself, a mournful old song that my grandmother had taught me . . .

"Oh beat the drum slowly and sound the fife lowly,
    Play the dead march as you take me away,
    And down on my coffin throw heaps of red roses,
    Throw the red roses to soften the clay."

I was perfectly happy in the peace of the evening and the sad old song, and then into the lane came a little girl in a pink fur fabric jacket. She was very smart with her hair dyed blonde and arranged in Shirley Temple curls. She also wore white buckskin Shirley Temple boots, and under the pink jacket she wore a *crêpe-de-Chine* dress. I knew her at once. She was known around the neighbourhood as Pat Gleeson's kid, for general opinion was that she was not Bluey Gleeson's kid, that she was either Pat's grand-daughter or else the child of one of the girls. She always had plenty of short frilly dresses with pants to match, and she was a leader amongst the little girls around our block.

Now she stopped in front of a back gate and called, and two little girls came out to join her. Then a couple more came out from a gate farther up, and another, with a doll in her hand, came down from the top of the lane.

"Let's go up the street," said the one with the doll.

"No!" little Bonnie Gleeson caught her by one arm. "You can have better fun here. We're going to play girls and customers. I'm going to be the girl."

She made a gesture so knowledgeable and obscene that I was frozen with horror, and then she skipped off and stood herself

43

in a half-open gateway. She was obviously completely happy in her environment.

"This is a doorway," she announced, and leaned against an imaginary door-post with her hands on her hips and her legs crossed in the traditional stance. She was about nine years old and her little friends were somewhere round the same age.

Then followed a faithful reproduction of a prostitute serving a customer. Apparently the Gleeson brothels did not cater for the carriage trade, for 5s. was the price which little Bonnie demanded, and which she was very firm about getting. One of the customers, to infuse a little variety into the proceedings, asked would it be possible to pay 3s. 6d. down and 1s. 6d. next pay day.

"I just haven't got it on me right now, love."

Bonnie was adamant. Five shillings was the price she said, and very cheap too with lousy pikers like the customer in question trying to do a girl out of her rightful earnings.

"Get home to your wife, you mingy old bugger."

The defaulting customer slunk up the lane followed by a barrage of insults all reflecting most pointedly upon the manhood of those who tried to get a woman on the cheap. If you could believe Bonnie Gleeson, generosity and virility were as one.

The customers who were in the funds were made to display an imaginary 5s. which Bonnie pocketed before they were allowed through the doorway. Going through the doorway was represented by the action of shutting a door, and Bonnie calling out, "The door's shut. There's a customer in with me."

The mime that followed was completely faithful and realistic, even including a little cleansing ceremony over in one corner with which Bonnie rounded off every performance. At that time I could hardly be expected to know what this final flourish was all about—which but made it the more gruesome.

I had been curious when the game began. I was only thirteen and there were a lot of things I wanted to know. Half way through I would gladly have run away and hidden somewhere, but I forced myself to stand and witness everything. I was enraged that life should force me to look upon its terrible cruelty, should show me what it could do to a little girl of only nine years.

44

"This is life," I kept telling myself. "It's not pretty, is it? Look what it can do to people."

So I stood where I was, to defy life and show it that I was not afraid. But afterwards I discovered that my paper packet of sandwiches was still untouched, and I threw it into the rubbish bin and then went into the lavatory and was very sick. Then I cried for a long time, leaning against the back of the door.

When I arrived home I found that Grandmother and Aunt Nell had gone into the city for Friday night shopping. They often did this. Sometimes I went with them. We loved wandering through the big city stores that glittered with light and bulged with Friday Night Specials. I knew that soon they would be arriving back, laden with packets of cinnamon scrolls, and pickled cucumbers, and curly rolls with poppy seed on top, and heaven knows what that they had picked up in Myers Basement. I wanted to go to bed but I decided to stay up. We always had a whacking big supper after Friday night shopping. I put on the kettle in readiness.

"Why should I go off to bed and bawl some more?" I asked of myself, or of fate, or of life. I did not know to whom or what I was talking, but I had already made up my mind that nothing was going to put me out of my stride. Whatever I saw, whatever happened, whatever I learned of misery and squalor and injustice, I would never again allow it to turn my stomach and set my legs shaking and fill my mind with a sort of black horror that was like a physical pain.

I got out milk and sugar and began to set the table.

"I'm all right," I told myself, "and life can do its worst. It can kill me if it likes, but as long as there's breath in my body I'll never again cry out for mercy."

Uncle Shaun and I were sitting on the jetty at Williamstown watching the gulls glide around the four tall masts of the *Killoran*. We had arrived at about eleven o'clock to see her come in under full sail. We had gone aboard and Uncle Shaun had gone up the mainmast to show me that he could still do it. The captain was an old friend of Uncle Shaun's and when he saw us he clapped one enormous paw upon his shoulder and, without one word of formal greeting, burst out with a bellow of :

"I zerved mein dime in de Blackvall Line,
   Do me vay ay ay 'oorah-o,
   In de Blackvall Line I zerved mein dime . . ."

He must surely have been heard down at Geelong. He beamed down at me and pumped Uncle Shaun's hand up and down.

"Goot to zee you," he said. "Goot to zee you. Best zinger that ever zailed the zea. 'Ow iss it mitt you?"

Uncle Shaun said it was great to meet the captain and everything was fine with him and I was his niece whom he always made a point of taking to see any sailing ships that might come into Port Phillip.

"Nod many now, bat lok," the skipper shook his head, sadly.

Then he cheered up and said we must come and have a drink with him before he went ashore to see the agent, so I had some coffee in the galley and Uncle Shaun had something stronger in the captain's cabin, and it turned out that the cook was also an old friend of Uncle Shaun's and they had to give one another the news of all their mutual friends, and then the captain said he really must go or the 'adgent' would think he was dead, and he went off roaring, "Komm down the Glub domorrow efening. Ve vill zing de goot olt zongs. Neffer 'ear dem now ad zea."

"What on earth nationality is he?" I asked.

"Zome zort of Zgandinavian," said Uncle Shaun.

Now we were sitting looking at the sea. Suddenly Uncle Shaun spoke:

"It was the summer of 1882 that I sailed out of Bristol on the four-masted barque *Claremont*, and it was a day just like this—very little wind. We had every stitch of canvas out, and the girls were all down on the dock. I remember my girl. She was a little thing with her hair tied up on the top of her head with a red ribbon. I told her I was eighteen, and there I was only fifteen, and setting out to see the world. The gulls were screaming all around and the sun felt warm on my face, and I was singing as they worked the capstan round. . . .

   'We're tired of women, we're tired of the land,
      Oh Rio,
   It's there where the river runs gold to the sand,
      And we're off to the Rio Grande.'

That's what we sang."

46

"You must have been fit to burst with happiness, Uncle Shaun."

"Believe me I was. I've had everything I wanted. I've sailed down south where the icebergs are as big as cathedrals, and in the tropics where the stars seem to glitter round your head. I've sailed in the Dutch Indies where the smell of the spices comes miles out to sea on the wind, and in the British Indies where old Spanish treasure lies, still waiting for those who know where to look for it. I've seen the Northern Lights more times than I can count, and I've seen the dragons off Dondra Head. I've won a hundred pounds in gold in Mexico and I've seen the gypsies dancing in Cadiz. I've been in sail and I've been in steam, and I've been in jail, and I've been in the money and I've been flat broke, and now I'm over seventy and I get dizzy when I'm half way up the mainmast, but it doesn't matter now. I saw all I wanted to see, and learned almost all I wanted to know. What do you want to do with your life, Lisha?"

"I want to get as far away from Stawell Street as ever I can," I said. "I want a fur coat and some diamond rings, and a house of my own, and I'll never have to worry about the rent because this house will belong to me and no one else, and I'll get lovely clothes, and when I go travelling I'll go first class, and I'll never be poor or hungry or shabby or cold again as long as I live."

"How will you get all this, Lisha?"

"I suppose I must marry someone who has it."

"Now what do you really want, Lisha? That blueprint you've drawn up for the future doesn't sound like you. Think hard, go right down deep inside yourself, and think what do you really and truly want. Forget that you've ever been cold and hungry and sick and humiliated—now what would you really be wanting?"

Then he added hastily, "Don't tell me if you would rather not. Sometimes these things are a secret."

"Well," I said, "if I were a man it would be so easy. I would just go off and see the world as you did. But I'm not a man so I think I would like to marry a sailor." I began to speak slowly because it was difficult to bring this dream out into the daylight. It belonged to a part of my mind and heart that I neither encouraged nor cultivated.

"He would be very young when we married, he would be just

47

going for his mate's ticket, but when we got enough money I would leave work and I would live in a little house down by the beach in just some small port so that I could watch for his ship to come in, and then, maybe, when I felt like a change he would get on another run and I would move to another port, and he would bring me home presents from all over the world, and I would write to him three times a week and send him photos of myself and the children. We would have four sons, Owen and Shaun, and Cashel and Terry, and I'd always be waiting for him when he came home. Then when he was a captain he would take me for a trip to England, and I'd go to Liverpool and see all my people there. And," I finished, "I'd like to be a very good dancer, and to play the guitar."

Uncle Shaun laughed at this anti-climactical ending to my dreaming, but he turned round and looked at me, and he said, "Well, if you wish for a thing hard enough, and work for it hard enough you will get it. I believe that; but you must be prepared to accept the limitations of your dream."

"I don't think I fully understand what you mean."

"Well it's like this. If you want to marry a sailor it's likely you'll get your wish, but there won't be too many fur coats or diamond rings for you, and you'll lie awake many a night and listen to the sea and think that it is crying aloud for his life, and you'll have to bring up those four boys of yours single-handed. Their father won't be beside you when they're ill or kicked out of school, or when they run away from home. And I've seen many a sailor who loved his wife with all his heart lose four months' pay at poker, or in a gambling house in Sacramento Street, or in a dozen other places, too many of them to remember now. You'll never be rich, Lisha, if your dream comes true. Life is like a pair of scales. Your wishes go in one side and you must be ready to throw something into the balance. Look at me, for instance. I've seen the world as very few people have seen it and I've been in the loveliest ships that ever were afloat, and if I had stayed at home I would have my own home, maybe, and my children around me, which is comforting when you're looking to the grave."

"Did you ever miss it, Uncle? Miss your own home, and want a wife and family and so on?"

"I was never much of a home body, Lisha. I didn't miss that, but many a time and often I missed my wife."

"Your wife!" I was astonished. This was the first word I had ever heard of Uncle Shaun's wife.

"It's all such a long time ago, Lisha. Long before even your parents were born. She was a little Burmese girl just a little older than you. Just about fifteen she was, when we met. She had tiny little hands and feet and a little smooth face with skin like bronze-coloured satin. She wore chains of gold all round her wrists and ankles, and a collar of jade and gold around her neck. I stayed with her about four months in Rangoon, and then I shipped aboard the *Paloma* bound for Macao, and for the first time in my life I missed someone. I missed her so much and she was so unhappy without me that I decided I'd take her home and get into the Home Trade. But she died that first winter. My own home port of Liverpool killed her. She got pneumonia when I was across in Ireland. She died with no one she knew around her, not even anyone who could speak her language, or anyone of her own religion. She died completely alone, because she was a sailor's wife. Lisha, I can tell you that now, after more than fifty years, it doesn't bear thinking of that I left her to die alone."

"You didn't know," I said, "that she would get pneumonia." My throat and eyes were aching because I wanted to cry.

"No, I didn't know," said Uncle Shaun, "but it has never made any difference. That's what she paid, you see. She wanted to marry me. She had her wish and she paid for it with her life. I wasn't worth so high a price. And for a long time afterwards I would cry for her in the night when no one could see and hear. I was pretty tough by the time I was nineteen—a lot tougher than I am now. I'd had fifteen years in Liverpool and four years at sea, and it was part of my religion that you must never cry, but I cried then, bitterly and often, very quietly because they packed us close in the fo'c'sle then. There was not much scope for howling your eyes out in private. I often think now, Lisha, that if it is true that we all meet again after we die, I hope that the next world is really like the old Irish used to say—Tir nan Og, the Land of the Ever Young. Because she won't be looking out for an old man with white hair. She'll be watching for a red-haired boy of nineteen, a boy wearing a

49

navy-blue jumper and canvas trousers, and a big thick ring of Mexican silver. Ah, Lisha dear, don't cry, no weeping on the dock. I've had a good life, and as for children, you've been like my family, all the children I ever wanted, you're all of them to me."

The next September brought the war and everybody said, "There'll be jobs for everyone now", and the unemployed men joined up and had some money to spend for the first time in years, and it did make a difference, but not such a great difference, at first, as everyone seemed to think it would. Aunt Rose came down from the country and moved in with us again. She got a job at the Fishermen's Bend Munitions and soon rose to the position of forewoman, and was worse tempered and more overbearing than ever. Fortunately we did not see a great deal of her. When she was not at work she spent most of her time out with her friends from the factory. They seemed to be a group of women about the same age as herself, who had all had unfortunate experiences in marriage and near-marriage and who hated all men as a consequence. They were all hard-working and efficient and more than capable of looking after themselves financially—so therefore why should they need a bloody man about the place, they asked. They were all terrific sports (to use an expression which they themselves used almost constantly) when it came to alcohol, and aggressively puritanical when it came to anything else. They were an unattractive crew. Aunt Rose often talked of taking a flat with Hilda or Doris or Kath or Pat, and how I prayed she would! But most of the time I had no thought for the war or Aunt Rose or anything else—I was lost and overwhelmed and completely preoccupied with the new, the great adventure that commenced for me that summer.

It was four days before Christmas and we sat on the steps of the old Perfection Factory enjoying the cool of the evening.

"So far," I said, "I have two bob saved for buying Christmas presents."

Everybody laughed. Phyl had said that her mother was buying her a new pair of bathers and a sun-suit, which had brought the conversation round to Christmas presents and what we expected to give or get.

"What I'd like to do," said Phyl, "would be to take a house down at Frankston or somewhere. Just to get out of this dump for a while."

"Houses at Frankston—listen to her," said Clarrie Harrop. "We'll just drive down in the Daimler. Or would you prefer the Bentley?"

"Just for a couple of weeks," Phyl went dreaming on. "I'd lie on the beach in my new bathers and get lovely and brown."

"What say we all put together next year," said Tom Mannix, "and take one of those beach houses for a week?"

Phyl and I looked at him in the sheerest amazement.

"We'd never be allowed," we said both together. We had never heard such a radical suggestion in all our lives.

Phyl decided she must stand on her dignity. "What do you think we are?" she asked. "You'd better invite Vi Hodges for trips like that."

Poor Vi Hodges was what we called a lair. I always felt a bit sorry for her myself, or perhaps it would be more correct to say that I always felt a certain sympathy with her. She had her hair dyed an astonishing shade of blonde which, in my secret heart, I thought looked extremely striking and which I had decided to imitate just as soon as I thought I could do so with safety.

"I like Vi," I said. "She used to teach me dancing when I was a little kid and just busting to be another Shirley Temple. She's never done anything to hurt you, Phyl."

"I'm just irritable this evening," said Phyl. "Vi's not so bad."

"Even the bad girls have their uses," said Clarrie, who was just seventeen.

We all roared laughing at him.

"You devilish old dog," said Tom. "What would you know about it? Your next time will be your first."

"What do you bet?"

"Me last remaining trey bit."

"Not worth worrying about."

"You're right there, sport." Tom took the threepence out of his pocket and looked at it sadly.

I smiled absent-mindedly. My mind was not on Clarrie or Tom. I was studying Johnny Dawson as he stood leaning against the door of the Perfection with his legs crossed and his hands in his pockets. I thought all this talk about Vi Hodges in bad taste when Johnny was around, for his family, the Dawsons, the Bakers, the Kiernans, the Dales (whatever you liked to call them), had been the talk of the street for a couple of generations. His grandparents, the Dales, had come out from Ireland at the same time as my grandmother, and they had proceeded to raise a family of one boy and five girls. Two of the girls died in childhood and the son married when he was over in England with the first A.I.F. Then the excitement started. Lily Dale married Jim Dawson. Bessie Dale went into the Convent. And Annie Dale had a baby and did not seem to know who was the father, which was the sort of thing that caused a bit of a stir in 1919. The baby was bundled off for adoption and eighteen months later Annie had another. She had four all told and her mother allowed her to keep her last son. After that she was perfectly happy. She had no more children. She had no time for men. She was busy at home with her baby. Then Bessie Dale left the Convent.

"I remember the day after she came out," I once heard Aunt Rose say, "she went into town in the morning, and there she was in the afternoon, standing at the gate with her hair marcelled and her face painted up like an advertisement. They were always mad, those Dales, full of religion and sex. They're the funniest combination I've ever met."

And while all this was going on Lily Dale was having her adventures. Jim Dawson just went out one day leaving Lily with her six months old son, Eugene, and £2 in the tin in the dressing-table drawer. He was never seen or heard of again. Lily made no attempt to get a separation or maintenance from him. She did not know how to go about it, in the first place, and in the second place she knew that she would never get back the money she would have to pay out to have him found and brought into court and so on. After a while she just moved into the position of *de facto* wife to a wharfie called Bluey Kiernan. She had a daughter to him, and no one was sure whether the child should be called Grace Kiernan or Dawson. "Kiernan is more polite," said my grandmother.

Then when the child was about a year old Bluey came home from the wharf complaining of a pain in the head, and the next day he was dead of meningitis. At his funeral, Lily cried and went on like a mad thing and tried to throw herself into the grave. She had to be watched for weeks afterwards lest she kill herself. Then she became extremely devout and was always up in the church burning candles for the repose of his soul. Six months later she had found someone else to look after her, for she was a strangely attractive woman with a thin fragile-looking body and untidy black curls. Her latest protector was Jack Baker. He was tall and handsome and very good to Lily. He never beat her as Dawson had done, nor did he gamble his wages, which had been Bluey Kiernan's failing. He was a shearer and he always brought his cheque straight home. He was a half-caste.

Now I sat and looked at his son, who stood with the last light of day glinting on his face. In that light his eyes looked big and luminous in the thinness of his face. He was so slim and brown, and his head was beautiful, plenty of back on it, and covered in soft black curls. Behind him the wall stretched away into the night and up above it the first stars came out in the sky.

Phyl suddenly became all dignified.

"You're childish," she told Clarrie and Tom. "Anyrate I'm sick of the sight of the same old street and the same old faces. I'm going home."

At that moment I became aware that Johnny was watching me while I watched him. He came across to my side of the steps and stood looking down at me. Then he smiled.

"Home's a dump, anyway," said Phyl. "I'm only going there because there's nowhere else in the world to go."

Johnny put out his hand and took me by the wrist.

"Don't go yet," he said.

"I'm all right, I can go by myself," said Phyl.

She flounced off.

"Coming into town with us?" asked Tom Mannix.

"I wouldn't be allowed," I said.

"How about you, Dawson?"

"I'm not keen," said Johnny.

Tim whistled and raised his eyebrows. Then he smiled and took Clarrie by the arm.

"Let's get out of here," he ordered. "Me, I'm smart. I can take a hint. I don't need a ton of bricks to fall on me."

Johnny was laughing, and so was I, though I was nearly choking with a mixture of embarrassment and pride. When

Tom reached the bottom of the steps he turned and raised his hand in something that looked vaguely like the Papal Blessing.

"Have a good time, my children," he said, sorrowfully, "because when the Swede comes out he's going to blow the both of you to hell." (Swede was doing his first stretch. Only Park Royal Reformatory this time, but, as all readers of the papers know, he went on to bigger and better things later on.)

"Isn't he silly?" I said. "I don't care about the Swede."

"Neither do I," said Johnny. "So will you come down the beach with me, Lisha?"

We went down and sat on the bluestone wall and watched the people come and go.

Port Melbourne on a hot December night, how I love you! The lights of the ships anchored at Prince's Pier, the broken down little jetty where the children play, the barking of the dogs that play with the children, the lovers lying on the sand, the shop straight across the road that sells such quantities of soft drinks, ice-cream and potato crisps. Dear old ugly romantic beach; I love every bit of you in a way I will never be able to love St Kilda, or even the surf-washed beauty of Bondi or Manly, or the desecrated strip of blue and gold that is Surfers' Paradise.

We talked about how we were going to get out into the world, and the wonders we would see and do, and when we began to feel cold we went over the road and bought some potato crisps and walked home. We walked with Johnny's arm around me, and it was the first time either of us had ever attempted anything of this sort—so it was an inexpert performance. We bumped each other's hips because I could not match my walk to Johnny's long stride, and though our shoulders jostled, we held our heads rigidly apart because we were much too shy to go along cheek to cheek, and we both ignored the embracing arm—carrying it off with what we hoped was the completely casual air. Having both arms free, I fed Johnny potato crisps as we went along. It is indicative of the rapport between us that he farewelled me at the back gate. I was not so besotted with love that I did not realise that to arrive at the front on the arm of Johnny Dawson, or indeed the arm of anyone at all, would cause a family crisis. And then he said, "Lisha, can I kiss you good night?"

And so well had I been trained by the nuns and my grandmother that I replied, "Well I'd rather you didn't."

But Johnny, like his Aunt Annie, was a persister. He wanted to know why not. This was a curly one. I knew that the correct answer was supposed to be, "Wait till you know me better." But that seemed a silly sort of thing to say to a boy whom I had known all my life, whose grandparents had come to Australia on the same ship as mine, and whose mother and aunts had gone to the same school as my mother and aunts. So I countered with another question :

"Why do you suddenly want to kiss me? You've known me all my life and you never wanted to kiss me before."

Johnny grinned. "How do you know?" he said. "Lisha, I've wanted to kiss you for about a year. Truthfully speaking, I've wanted to kiss you since I was about twelve, but the wanting's got real painful over about the last year."

"I sympathise," I said. "Nothing is so annoying as waiting," and I held up my cheek to be kissed.

Johnny took my face very gently between his hands and turned it round till my mouth was against his. Then he kissed me. It was the soft clumsy kiss of the young and innocent but it left me without even enough breath to say good night. I sat by myself in the darkness under the fig tree for a long time before I felt collected enough to go in and face Grandma and Aunt Rose.

For the rest of the summer I was so obsessed with my love for that skinny brown-faced boy that I thought of nothing else at all. I can say this in all honesty. I worked in Myers (Xmas Wrappings Section) during those holidays, and I found I could serve a customer with five yards of tinsel rope for the Christmas Tree, and give correct change, and pass on to the next customer, who wanted two dozen sprigs of holly, and do it all quite efficiently while I was thinking of Johnny Dawson's brown eyes and black curls and the long slender lines of his body.

"I can't see why you think he's so good-looking," said Phyl, who was amused and impatient with the whole affair. "He's a quarter-caste. How can he be good-looking? He's all skinny and scruffy-looking. His hands remind me of claws. Oh well, trust you to have to be different."

This last was said kindly but it made me feel both guilty and eccentric. Being different was not encouraged at all in Stawell Street, and, worst of all, it was never considered to be anything except the most appalling affectation. But if my conception of beauty was a little too exotic for Stawell Street there was nothing I could do about it. I thought Johnny Dawson was glorious from the curls on the top of his head right down to his small-boned feet.

"Honestly, Phyl," I defended myself, "I'm not bunging it on just to get notice. I like the way he looks. I can't help it."

"You don't want to help it," said Phyl. "You're just crazy about him. Well, good luck to you, kid. He was always a very nice boy and that's more than you can say for half the members of the Junior Wandering Hand Society that live round here. I loathe and detest men half the time, honest I do, Lisha."

Of course it did not last long. How could it in a street where everyone knew everybody else's business, and usually had nothing else in life to talk about? How could it last anyway? Anything so lovely and innocent and young must finish soon. So one Friday night when I was eating my tea, in came Aunt Rose with her breath smelling of brandy, and grabbed my hair with one hand and started hitting me around the head with the other.

"You dirty little slut," she kept gasping. "You rotten little strumpet. You're like your dirty swine of a father."

I twisted out of her grasp and turned to confront the hatred that distorted her face.

"What's wrong with you?" I tried to bluff. "You're drunk."

But I knew what was coming. I had known all along what must come, but I had not expected it so soon.

Grandmother came in from the back yard, where she had been gathering the first of the figs, at the moment when I was deciding that if Aunt Rose attempted to hit me again I would hit her back. I had been brought up with an exaggerated respect for my elders. Other families round about could have knock down and drag out brawls—but not us. We were not common. We were lace curtain Irish. Down on our luck, certainly, but lace curtain none the less. I was not supposed to be the sort of girl who thumped her aunt under the ear, but that is precisely what I would have done but for the entry of my grandmother.

"For the love of God, Rose," she said. "What is it?"

56

"Do you know what she's been doing, the crawling little go-the-road?" shrieked Aunt Rose. "Sneaking off with Lily Dale's bastard, that's what she's been doing."

"Stop that language, Rose," said Grandmother, "and keep your voice down. Do you want all the street to hear you? Now, Lisha, what's all this?"

Suddenly I could bear no more. I could not bring myself to offer apologies and explanations, even to my grandmother. Her "what's all this?" savoured too much of a cross examination. Without a word I turned and ran from the room. I was just aware that Aunt Rose made as though to follow me and Grandmother stopped her at the door.

I tore up the street, sobbing to myself as I went. I did not know where I was going. I had some dim idea that I would perhaps find Johnny and, sure enough, there he was on the Perfection steps, talking to Tom Mannix. As I passed he swung on to his bike and rode up the street ahead of me; he was waiting for me as I turned the corner.

"Trouble?" he asked.

I nodded and he put up his hand and gently touched the finger marks across my face.

"Don't cry here, Lisha," he said. "Listen, darling, I'll put the bike away and then we'll go down the beach."

I stood in the Dawson back yard, still sobbing and shaking, while he put his bike in the shed, and his father came out and invited me in for a cup of tea. I said, "No, thank you", and he stood a moment looking at me with his big worried brown eyes. Then he patted me gently on the shoulder and went away. Johnny and I went on down to the beach. We sat for a while on the sea wall, saying nothing, then I began to cry again and say, "I'm so sorry, Johnny. I'm very sorry."

Johnny turned and looked at me and put his hand on my arm. "It doesn't matter, Lisha," he said. "I don't blame your family. Everyone thinks the same around here. We've always been the ones who weren't good enough. Everyone in the street knows that Eugene is the only one in our family who's not a bastard, and I'm the greatest bastard of them all because my father's a half-caste."

"Don't talk like that."

"He is a half-caste. You just can't get away from that, and it's a great crime round here, we all know that."

"I don't like to talk about it," I said, "I don't want to hurt you, Johnny."

"It doesn't hurt me, Lisha. What hurts me is when people just won't talk about it as though it was something real dirty that you must never ever mention."

"I'm sorry."

"Don't be sorry, Lisha. I had no right to say that to you. I must be going mad to pick on you. You're just not used to thinking about it, but we've all had to live with it for years and years because we've never had enough money to get away from this lousy, stinking place. And do you know what, Lisha? I honestly don't care. What's the good of caring? They're never going to think I'm good enough. So I'll just have to get on as best I can on my own. I'm not just talking about your family. No one is ever going to think I'm good enough."

"You forget," I said, "I'm no great social success myself. Have you ever heard about my father from my Auntie Rose? Haven't you heard her screaming 'bad blood will out' and all the rest of it?"

"Yes, I have. I think what your Aunt Rose needs is a good man to give her a good thump in the jaw."

I laughed, but in my heart I knew that I would never be able to say of the people who had rejected me 'I don't care'. I knew that I wanted to join them. Somehow I would do it. I would be a great success or marry great wealth. Somehow I would make myself admired and sought after, and then let everyone who had looked down on me take care.

"One of these days, Johnny," I said, "I swear it, I'm going to make them all eat dirt."

After that night I made no attempt to lie to Grandmother and Aunt Rose. I simply told them nothing. Grandmother watched me anxiously for weeks, and Aunt Rose openly spied upon me. She had a great triumph the evening she put the hose on us. There we were in the back lane and Johnny was teaching me to smoke. I was coming on very well with the draw-back, and then suddenly we were spluttering and choking, and wet to the skin and helpless with laughter, while a furious Aunt Rose stood in

58

the gateway yelling, "Get inside, you little strumpet. My God, you're your father over again."

There were several little incidents of this nature, culminating in the evening that Aunt Rose chased me half way into town and gave me my last public box on the ears. I had set out to walk into town with Phyl. The two of us walked miles in those days—looking in shop windows, flirting with soldiers, talking about love and what we were going to do. Phyl listening, all admiration, while I spouted yards of poetry to her. Myself all ears while Phyl told me about work and her latest admirers, and on this fateful night I was comforting Phyl for the collapse of yet another romance (someone or another had turned out to be a brute—no respect etc.) with a large slice of Mr Swinburne, whom I found a great help in sublimating the vague and disturbing yearnings of adolescence.

> "From too much love of living,
> From hope and fear set free
> We thank with brief thanksgiving
> Whatever gods there be
> That no man lives for ever,
> That dead men rise up never
> That even the weariest river
> Winds somewhere safe to sea"

I declaimed as we turned the corner out of Stawell Street, and there was Johnny with Tony Mannix, Tom's youngest brother.

"Surprise, surprise," said Phyl sourly because, though flattered by Tony's devotion, she could not but admit that he was at least three inches shorter than she was and Phyl demanded six footers.

But there they were, announcing that they were just thinking of walking up Bay Street. What could we do?

Now it was just unfortunate that Gracie Dawson should be walking past our house with her soldier boy friend while Aunt Rose was talking at the gate to Mrs Anderson, and Aunt Rose did not like to see young and pretty girls, or girls of any sort for that matter, enjoying themselves in masculine company, so when the innocent Gracie said, "How are you, Mrs Morton?" Aunt Rose opened fire.

She said she was well and would be all the better if none

of the Dawsons, Kiernans, Bakers, Dales or whatever they called themselves ever spoke to her again.

"And tell your brother not to come hanging round our Lisha," she finished. "We've got other plans for her."

Afterwards Gracie was apologetic :

"Honestly, I wouldn't have said anything, but it was that string of surnames that did it. I was that furious I didn't know what I was saying."

What she did say was, "If you want to know where my brother is right at this very minute, Mrs Morton, he's walking up Bay Street with Lisha—she knows when she's lucky."

Then Aunt Rose gave chase. We had a good start but rage lent her wings. She tore along like a woman demented, and we were all so absorbed in our own company that we were not aware of her coming. The first I knew of it she had swept up behind us and suddenly I received the smack across the ear that made my head spin. Johnny and Tony disappeared up a side street like savages into a jungle. Even at such a terrible moment I had time to feel admiration for such superb streetcraft. Aunt Rose did not hit me again, but she ordered me home, and my loyal old friend Phyl came with me, her head up and her cheeks pink with embarrassment. She ignored Aunt Rose and so did I. We stalked along in silence pretending not to hear the half-crazed abuse that surged around our heads, but in my heart I was deciding that if Aunt Rose did not leave and go and take the flat she was always talking about, then I would ask if I could go.

Aunt Rose, however, saved me the trouble. The minute we got home she tore into her bedroom and dragged her suitcase from underneath the bed. Then she started packing. She would not stop, she said, in a house which my behaviour was turning into a brothel. Grandmother went in to her and said, "That's enough of that language, Rose."

"I'm not a kid. I'll say what I like."

"I'll ask you to remember that I'm your mother and this is my house, and I may be a doddering fool of an old woman but I'm still entitled to say what goes on under my own roof."

"That's all I wanted to know. If you prefer Owen Flynn's brat to your own daughter—"

"I don't have favourites, Rose; but if that's the way you feel you had better go."

So Aunt Rose went.

She came back frequently to see us—usually on a Sunday afternoon, and she and I managed to be civil to each other, and Grandmother was always very affectionate towards her. She was sharing a flat with a friend called Pat and they seemed to be having a wonderful time. Altogether it was a very happy arrangement and Grandmother and I were much more comfortable without her.

This was the first of the many changes that 1940 was to bring. The second change was that I suddenly found myself out of love with Johnny Dawson. There is something about a public ear-boxing that makes the victim wish to shun the company of all who were present to witness the humiliating business.

"I don't know what it is," I told Phyl, "I still like him just like I used to when we were at school, but I'm just not crazy about him any more."

"Well, that's the first one over," said Phyl, "and you're lucky you didn't end up hating him. It's just as well anyway. He could never have got you out of this dump."

Phyl, herself, was to move away within the next few weeks. Her father was in the Railways and he was shifted out to be stationmaster in one of the eastern suburbs. Phyl was wild with delight. "It's not Toorak but it's a start," she explained.

I went out and helped them move into the new house. It was a small cottage with a very old rose-bush in the front, not really very much different from the house they had left.

"But when you look out the window you don't see the bloody old Port," said Phyl.

"And you don't see the sea," I thought. "I don't think I'm ever going to be able to live happily away from the sea."

Just across the road from Phyl's house stood the home of my father's two sisters, Margaret and Theresa. They were both unmarried, and one worked in a stockbroker's office and the other in the Public Service. They lived alone in that narrow brick house filled with quiet and good china and cedar furniture. By all the rules of clan protocol I was obliged to go and visit them for a few minutes whenever I went out to see Phyl. Not that I minded this. They were friendly women with shelves

61

full of the most fascinating books, which they allowed me to borrow whenever I wished, and in their kindness they always gave me pocket money which it made my cheeks burn to take. But I was always so broke and shabby—so I took it.

Now I said to Phyl, "What do you think of my aunts?"

"They're nice old girls. Wonder why they never got married. They're both good-looking."

"Perhaps they didn't want to."

"More fool they. I tell you, kid, the only thing you can do is marry money. It's the only chance you've got if you haven't got money yourself. Otherwise you're stuck in a dump in some crummy old suburb for the rest of your days. Anyrate, that's what I want to do."

"Want to do what?"

"Want to fall in love with someone with a lot of money, of course—preferably an Air Force Officer."

"I want to be a dancer."

I think that was the first time I had ever spoken of it to anyone outside my own family and I thought, "I'm committed now. I have spoken of the dearest wish of my heart to someone who may not understand—not to Uncle Shaun or to Gran but just to a friend. Now I'll have to make good what I've said."

Phyl was not very impressed. She said, "When you've been around as much as I have, Lisha, you'll find that kids from real high-class suburbs are often lousy dancers. They seem to think it's a bit common to be able to dance extra well."

I knew this already. It was one of my mother's most tenaciously held theories. She first let us know of it when my grandmother sent her a photo of her only daughter dressed up in gauze and spangles—an angel in the Olive McSweeney School of Dancing Monster Christmas Pantomime. One way and another I had danced ever since I could walk. My first memory is of Uncle Shaun whistling "The Blackbird" and clapping his hands in time, while Grandmother (who'd been a noted stepper herself in her day) led me through the first simple steps of a reel.

"She's a born dancer, Katey," Uncle Shaun had said, "she has the love for it and she has the build for it and she has the feet."

He had taken my foot in his hand and stroked the high arch with his forefinger. "Look at it," he said, "she could walk on eggs without breaking them."

So every Saturday I went off to Miss McSweeney's National Dancing class, and as the years went by I wore out many a pair of buckled shoes and won many a medal. On one great occasion I even won a Cup. That was in the big Australia Day Competition when all the Irish and Scots used to get out and dance around their swords and twirl their kilts and flash their shoe-buckles and blow their pipes till they were near to bursting. The Scots were better pipers but we could dance rings round them and that's a fact. "Four hundred years of Presbyterianism has done their stepping no good," said Uncle Shaun.

It was soon after this that the Misses McSweeney (always known as the McSweeney girls, though even Sally, the youngest, must have been about my mother's age) approached my grandmother after Mass one Sunday morning and offered to take me into Sally's class without charging any fee.

"Think about it, Mrs Ward," said Olive, who was the eldest and most dignified of the McSweeney girls, "it's not a decision to take lightly, but I've talked it over with the girls and they both agree with me that the child has a future. Don't say anything now, but I'll be down to see you this afternoon, if I may, and you can give me your answer then. But that child, Mrs Ward," she laid one long gloved hand on Grandmother's arm and lowered her voice impressively, "that child has laurels waiting—with the right training of course, Mrs Ward. Now is the time to start the right training."

Miss Sally took Character, Ballet and Tap, as the sign in the window said, and I learned for a couple of terms with great enjoyment even if nothing else. We kept it a secret from my mother, intending to dazzle her with the report of my progress and the photo of myself, so glamourised, at the end of the year.

Mother's reaction was not as expected. By return mail we received a letter which left us all speechless with astonishment. Gran did not discuss it with me, of course. She simply told me that my mother did not want me to go on with the dancing lessons because she felt it would interfere with my school work. The letter was folded up and put away in the box on top of the wardrobe (the box that was made of all the different types of wood that grow in Ireland) and as soon as I was alone in the house I read it. I flattered myself that I loved my mother very much. Actually, I did not know her and I had for her a sort of fairy-tale worship born of the fact that she was beautiful and far away. I believed that she could not be wrong in anything, but I can tell you that letter tested my faith.

No daughter of hers, she said, would be turned into one of those unbearable, precocious dancing-school kids. She was nearly mad with worry, she said, wondering just how I was growing up. It was bad enough my living in such a suburb and going to the little parish school. My God! what wouldn't she give to see me at a decent college. Had Grandmother forgotten how people with a bit of background behaved? National dancing was permissible, though didn't Grandmother think that all this Irish business was a wee bit silly after all these years? After all, Grandmother could just face it, it was a British world and the best thing anybody could do was to make the most of it. If Grandmother could see the filthy rich people up in Kenya and Rhodesia who had acres of land and dozens of natives to do all the work she would just wonder how she had borne Australia so long and would strain every nerve and make every effort, as she herself was doing, to make a decent life for the child and see that she got in with the right people. The way she was going she would end up dancing on a tightrope in a bloody circus.

So that was that. There was no answer that could possibly be given. No polite answer at any rate. My studies of Character, Ballet and Tap came to an end, but I took to waylaying my little friends as they came home from classes on a Wednesday evening after school.

"What did you learn today?" I would ask. "Teach me some new steps."

Vi Hodges, who was a big girl and making a great name for herself at the South Street Competitions, was very kind to me. She taught me a great deal. Now, in this first year of the war, she was earning good money as a ballroom dance instructress and when I went down the street to the four-roomed cottage she shared with her parents and two younger brothers she would teach me anything I wanted to learn, standing there at one end of the kitchen changing the old 78 records and shouting instructions at me or at her brother, who was a good dancer himself and came in very handy as a partner, and she would say to me, "It's a crime not to let you learn properly. You can follow anyone like a duck and that's the first thing you need to be a championship winner."

There was a saying in our family that we always died in July —nothing else could kill us except the terrible Melbourne winter. And it was in the middle of the next July that Aunt Nell dropped dead of a stroke. She was buried in the family plot at Williamstown Cemetery on a day of bitter rain and the wind howling in from the sea. When we got home Grandmother said she thought she had caught a chill, and three days later she was in the Alfred Hospital and they told Aunt Rose she was dying of pneumonia. But she did not die of pneumonia, my brave old Gran. She fought through, and on the first day that I was allowed to see her again she lay there with her hair spread like snow across the pillows and she winked one of the emerald eyes.

"It would take more than a drop of chill to kill me, Lisha," she said.

But that was the last big fight of all her fighting life. Her heart was quite worn out and she died a month later in her own bedroom with the picture of the Sacred Heart above the bed and the photo of my grandfather (taken when he was twenty and a third mate) on the mantelpiece, and her own white honeycomb quilt over her, and in her hands the Rosary with the Cross of black bog oak that her grandmother had brought from Kerry to Dublin a very long time ago. It was a Sunday evening, the end of a fine mild day—the sort of day that sometimes comes towards the end of a Melbourne August to reassure people that spring will come and, though when it does come it will bring hail and influenza, still there will be some fine days and the earth will warm and if you can just live through till about November you'll be saved. Grandmother had been very well that day. It was the first Sunday that she had, been allowed up to go to Mass, and Leo Grady had driven her there without so much as a word out of him about 'the fear of hell and the bribe of heaven' and such like—which was kind of Leo, for he had been a very convinced rationalist for many years. Apparently Gran also thought it kind of him for as she stepped from the car she patted him on the cheek and said, "You're a good boy, Leo. You always were. When you get to

65

heaven I'll personally see to it that you don't have to associate with St Peter or St Patrick or any of the rest of that wrong-headed collection."

After Mass Aunt Rose came in and I helped her cook the dinner, and I made my first batch of scones. The scones on a Sunday were a family tradition that I was not going to see neglected. The actual baking was always referred to as 'knocking up the scones'. So I made my first effort in this direction. Very hard they were too—just like all the others I've made since.

When dinner was over and Aunt Rose had gone and Grandmother was having her rest, Vi came in and asked would I like to drive up to Ferntree Gully in the 1928 Riley which her boy friend had bought for £25. But, for some reason that I have never been able to explain, I wanted to stay with Gran. It was not that I had any premonition of what was to come. On that last beautiful afternoon there seemed nothing abroad in the air except happiness. When Gran woke up she said she would like to go out into the sunshine and have a look at the ships, so we walked along Station Pier, and half way back Grandmother said she was tired, and she sat down on a bollard and stayed awhile there—looking out to sea with the wind blowing her hair and the sun bringing a touch of brown back into her cheeks. Just to the port side of the Gellibrand Lighthouse a cargo boat made its way towards the Rip and the open sea. Closer inshore a Bass Strait schooner was making for its anchorage in the river. We watched it skim in before the south wind.

"When I first met your grandfather," said Grandmother, "he was on a little boat not much bigger than that; she was a little mainsail schooner called the *Nesta Bach* and she sailed out of Fishguard in Wales."

She turned from the sea and looked up at me. For a moment she studied me, her eyes holding my face, then she nodded and smiled. "Yes," she said, "you're the image of him, long-faced and black, the very picture of your grandfather, Hughie Ward. Small wonder I loved you better even than my own children."

She rose and took my arm, and when we got back home she said she would go straight to bed. "The old lady has to take it easy a while longer, Lisha."

I made her comfortable and went out to make a cup of tea.

66

I pulled back the damper of the stove and blew on the coals and it was beautiful in the kitchen with the fire blazing into life, and the kettle beginning to sing and the clock ticking on the top of the dresser, while outside the first shadows of evening sloped down the branches of the fig tree, and sitting on our back fence were three sea-gulls—come in amongst the houses to bring promise of bad weather. I sang to myself as I warmed the tea-pot and buttered the scones and practised my new dance steps. It was not easy to dance in a kitchen as small as ours. I turned and pivoted and did a run through that brought me up against the ice-chest and set the copper pans jingling on the wall.

"What in the world are you at?" called Grandmother.

"I'm practising how to do a run through on a threepenny bit."

My grandmother laughed.

It was not five minutes later that I went into her room with the tea things on a tray—and there she sat, dead, leaning back against the banked-up pillows. And because she had always done everything with style and distinction, she had closed her eyes—and so I may remember them always, beautiful, emerald, glittering with life.

Within a few days of Grandmother's burial the cables and then the letters began to arrive from my mother and father. The two children must be kept together, my father instructed. We were to go to his sisters, Margaret and Theresa. My brother came down from the country and did as he was told. I, who considered myself more bound to the Wards, refused to be beholden to the Flynns. I gave up my scholarship, moved in with the Clearys, who lived farther up the street, and got myself a job in a sweet-shop in town. I wore a floral overall with a huge pussy-cat bow at the neck. It was a most attractive uniform, and usually I felt fairly content with myself, but sometimes my erstwhile school friends came in to buy two shillings' worth of rocky road or half a pound of peanut brittle, and then I would feel like the poor but honest mill girl—obliged to give up higher education to earn her beggarly bread and so on. I would remember my voice, filled with hurt against the echo of the sea :

"One of these days, Johnny, I swear it, I'm going to make them all eat dirt."

So I would tell my friends, "This is only temporary. I'm going back to school when Mother and Father get home."

Mother and Father were both on their way and, to judge by their letters, we were all going to have the most glowing times when they did arrive.

"I'm so excited," wrote my mother, "what fun we're all going to have together."

"It will be wonderful to see you again," wrote Father. "You and I, my lady, have a great deal to talk about. There are so many things to which I wish to introduce you—symphonic music, the French poets, Mallarmé, Verlaine, Rimbaud and the rest—"

Father was a shocking intellectual snob. Mallarmé and Verlaine forsooth! I was struggling with good old Lamartine, let alone any of the more exotic boys.

"When I think," said Mother in her next letter, "that next Christmas I shall be sitting down to dinner with my own boy and girl, well I can hardly believe it."

She need not have bothered to put so great a strain upon her faith, for the reality was all a little different.

Mother arrived first. Father appeared some weeks later, and straightaway they had a violent fight about who was to have the children. I say 'fight' advisedly, because it did end in actual physical violence with my mother throwing anything she could lay hands to at my father, and my father warding her off and repeating over and over again, "Maeve, you must be insane", till finally he became tired of it all and gave her an open-hander under the ear that stopped her in full spate. This all took place at the home of Aunts Margaret and Tess, and I was irritated at the expression of uppity disapproval on their faces, though I was obliged to admit to myself that I had a fair understanding of how they must feel. Apart from that, I did not take much interest in the whole affair. It had already become so obvious that what they meant by "who will have the children?" was "who will have disposal of the children, who will say where they will stay or to what boarding-school they will go?"; for in one thing alone my parents were in accord—wherever the children were going to stay it was not going to be with either of them.

Not on your bloody life, as we used to say in those days. They had skilfully and successfully escaped from the boredom and responsibility of being householders and parents. They were not going to be trapped back into it. So after a while I saw very little of them. I visited my mother about once a week and she was very affectionate and occasionally bought me clothes. My father I saw perhaps once in six months.

And so it was that their coming made very little difference in my life, after all.

PART II

ANDY

IT WAS A sweltering evening in February when Phyl Foley and I went down to St Kilda to look the field over.

Phyl called for me and finished making up in my room. We dressed with care and a kind of suppressed excitement, for to-night we were going hunting. Our current Yankees had gone north, and very light-hearted they had been about it. At any rate they had taken us out half a dozen times and, as we were both virgins, it was doubtful if we could have held them much longer—and remained virgins, that is. At least I doubted it. Phyl always maintained that she could inspire respect in a big way. I envied her this gift. I did not seem to have it at all, and I had found that Jimmy Burns from Providence, Rhode Island, was becoming very restive.

So there we were with our hair piled high in the front and cascading down past our shoulders at the back, our uplift brassières thrusting our breasts forward like Ack-Ack guns (in this respect I was way ahead of the beautiful Phyl, which just goes to show that sometimes there is justice), rouge high on our cheek-bones and each wearing a huge Yankee graduation ring; off to St Kilda to walk arm in arm on the Esplanade. Phyl, be-cause she was 5ft. 8in., wore flat suède shoes which we con-sidered looked very American and sharp, but I wore my first pair of real true high-heeled courts. What I called real, true high heels meant about five inches high. They made my long brown legs look like stilts, and my mother said her feet ached every time she looked at them.

We pushed through the crowd at Flinders Street Station. It was packed as usual. Never will I forget those wonderful war-time nights. The crowds of servicemen, their girls, tight-skirted, bare-legged, long-haired; the brownout, the noise, the couples kissing in doorways.

71

> "I shall have lived a little while,
>   Before I die for ever,"

I said, and Phyl laughed and said, "You're a funny girl", but she gave me a sudden look of affection to show that she knew what I meant. We ignored all would-be pick-ups on the way to the St Kilda tram.

"I just feel like St Kilda tonight," said Phyl, and I let her take the initiative because she was two years older than I, and a beauty.

We sighted our quarry after about five minutes parading the Esplanade. They were standing outside the shooting gallery nearest the Scoota Boats—one a tall blond and the other shorter and barrel-chested, with hair that was reddish-brown in the half-light. Phyl looked at me as we strolled past them. There is no need for words in such a situation. I nodded.

"So long as I can have the refined-looking blond," said Phyl.

"The tough-looking red-head will do me," I agreed.

Phyl was red hot on refinement.

"Are they following us?" she asked.

I turned my head slightly and looked out the corner of my eyes. This ability to roll the eyes was a great asset on this sort of expedition.

"No," I reported.

"Walk slower," advised Phyl, "and pretend we're looking out to sea."

We did so, and they began to saunter towards us. The blond wore a white T-shirt with M.N. across the chest in big block letters.

"I thought you didn't like the M.N.," I said to Phyl.

"Maybe they're officers," said Phyl.

"All M.N. are officers when they're shooting a line."

"Don't be nasty"—Phyl came from a shore-side family. "Why don't they hurry up? I've just got my mind set on that blond now. Go slower."

"We can't drop down on all fours and crawl along the street."

"Take off your shoe," said Phyl.

So I put my hand on the sea wall and, stooping, slipped off one of the glamorous court shoes. Then I stood stock-still pretending to look for a nail or a pebble, and while I stood there the red-head came up and slipped one hand under my arm. I looked up into the square-cut face. I saw the broken nose, the brown eyes, the wide mouth and the hair that fell down across the forehead. I saw the strength of the over-muscled shoulders and the arm that held me. It was brown and powerful against the rolled-back white shirt-sleeve. I saw the hands, hard and spatulate with red hair growing on the backs, and I felt my mouth go dry and my legs begin to tremble. I slipped my foot back into my shoe.

"Thank you," I said, "are you always so helpful?"

"Only when I'm looking for someone to help."

He had a faint accent which I felt I should know.

"It's a grand evening," said the blond to Phyl.

Phyl, who was not much good at the preliminary sparring, merely smiled and said, "Yes."

It was a smile so charming and beautiful that I sighed within myself. "No wonder," I thought, "that I have had to develop a right good line."

I said to him now, "Do you come from the Highlands or Lowlands?"

"My folk are highland," he said.

"That's good," I assured him.

"That's my girl," said the red-head, "I can see you have the right ideas." He put his hands under my elbows and swung me up to sit on the wall. "Now make yourself comfortable while we get the introductions over. I'm Andy Kelly from Liverpool and my friend here is Lachy McLaughlin from Glasgow."

"Laughlin McLaughlin the Pride of the Clyde is my official title," said the blond.

Phyl and I both laughed. We thought they were charming.

"My name is Eilishe Flynn," I said, "and my friend is Philomena Foley."

"Flynn and Foley," said Andy, "both good old names. I approve of them. And where are you both to this evening?"

"Nowhere in particular," we said, both together, "just walking."

"Well we're just walking too," said Lachy, "so isn't it lucky for us we met you—so accidentally and all?"

Phyl gave him her famous haughty look. Then she relented and gave him her famous lovely smile, and we all walked on together. It was still too early to go anywhere and they asked us had we eaten and we said 'yes', so we went and sat in the park that is on past the Baths. Phyl and Lachy sat on a seat but Andy threw himself down on the grass, and he took me by the wrist and said, "Come down here to me."

"Why?"

"Why! Because, woman, I want to lie with my head in your lap."

"I don't want to sit on the grass."

" 'Oh I'll not sit on the grass', she said,
    'Or be a love of thine,' "

he sang, and he had one of those fragile and sweet Irish baritone voices that teachers turn into tenors, and thereby ruin.

"Why won't you sit on the grass with me, Lisha Flynn?"

"Because this dress is new."

"And it surely fits you something beautiful."

It did too. It was pale lilac, cut on princess lines, and it followed closely my waist and the narrowness of my hips before it swirled out wide to the hem.

"You have a lovely figure," he said.

It was so simple and direct a statement and so devoid of any sexual import that I made none of the usual coquettish backchat. Then he sat up and pulled off his shirt. He spread it on the grass.

"Now," he said, "I've given you the shirt off my back—sit down and be a comfort to me."

I sat down and he lay there with his head resting on my knees, and I pulled up a long blade of grass and tickled his face.

So we sat till it was completely dark and other young couples stumbled over us as they prowled round looking for a likely spot for a little love-making. Then I said, because both Phyl and I believed you should cost a man as much as possible, "Well we can't sit here all night. Let's go somewhere."

We decided on Palm Grove. Then before we moved off the refined-looking Lachy drew something from the coat he carried over his arm. It was a whisky bottle.

"You don't drink, maybe?" asked Andy.

"Of course I do."

I was insulted.

74

"How old are you?"

"Eighteen."

Phyl, loyal old friend, always backed me up in this lie.

"Old enough in wartime," he said. "Right you are, Laughlin my boy, give my girl a drink, well."

Phyl had tasted whisky before, but it was the first hard liquor I had ever drunk in my life and it made me gasp. In the darkness I saw Andy's mouth curl into a smile, so I took another mouthful before I wiped the mouth of the bottle and handed it back to Phyl.

"I just feel like drinking tonight," said Phyl.

"So do I," I said.

I felt wonderful. The high-heeled shoes had made my legs tired but now there was not an ache or a pain anywhere.

"We can buy lemon squash at Palm Grove," said Phyl, "and lemon with our whisky should be O.K."

"Can you not buy soda?" asked Lachy, anxiously.

"Of course you can."

"Then what are we waiting for?" said Lachy.

"Look out for that one of yours," Phyl warned me as we renewed our make-up in the powder room. "He looks very hard to handle, to me."

"I'm all right," I said. "I'm no sleep-walker."

I went on with that sort of nonsense all night, and I showed a surprising amount of knowledge about the Merchant Navy without bothering to add that I had more relatives at sea than ashore.

Then about ten o'clock Phyl said, "It's too hot in here. Let's get out."

Outside in the still night air it was beautiful, and we went into a coffee lounge in Fitzroy Street and drank coffee. Lachy put his arm along the back of Phyl's chair, and Andy and I sat very close together on a bench against the wall.

In the taxi going back to the city we finished the whisky. I pretended to drink. Something told me that I had no head for liquor and was never going to develop one. In this I was absolutely right. Suddenly Phyl had an inspiration.

"Let's get out at Princes Bridge," she said, "and go home to Hawthorn on the ferry."

Of course the ferry was full of lovers. It always is; even in peacetime. I was astounded to see in the half-light that Phyl and Lachy were holding hands. Phyl would scarcely ever hold hands with a man. They were the natural enemy and they had to be kept right in their place. "You have to be mean to them before they start getting mean to you," she would say, "and you have to make them take you to all the expensive places. That is," and here she would sigh gloomily, "you have to try to make them take you to all the expensive places."

And here she was on the old Hawthorn Ferry (I think it was sixpence a ride in those days) holding hands with a sailor. Of course I will admit that Lachy had the charm. Andy and I stood in the stern looking at the ripples in the wake of the boat.

"How many knots do you think she is doing?" I asked him.

He laughed and put his cheek down against mine.

"What a funny kid you are," he said. Then he said, very softly, with his face still against mine, "Where can we go? It's early yet. Do you live near the Duchess here?"

"Right opposite," I said cruelly.

"Damn it, well. Does she have to come and tuck you into bed?"

"No, my Auntie does that."

"Can we not walk awhile?"

"Yes, we can walk awhile."

I expected Phyl to disapprove. I was astonished when she turned round on the landing at the Hawthorn Tea Gardens and said, "Lachy and I are going to walk by the river awhile. See you later, Lisha."

She bestowed on us her rare sweet smile, and then they were crossing over the road from us with Lachy calling over his shoulder, "See you back on board, Kelly", and then they were lost in the shadows.

"That was easy," said Andy.

"Lachy must practise hypnotism," I said. "Phyl never goes walking by the river."

"Do you?"

"Sometimes."

He stood looking down at me as though he wanted to say something, and then, as though he had changed his mind, he

76

said, "Well at any rate come on now. Show me a good spot on this river bank."

Phyl and Lachy had gone off in the direction of Fairview Park. We took the river on the other side of the road and when we had gone a little way we stopped by an acacia tree. It smelled sweetly of resin and its branches dipped almost to the earth. Andy stooped and put his hand on the ground. "In under here," he said, "there's still a little soft grass left. This lovely tree has been keeping the sun away from it all day—just for us, Eilishe Flynn."

"Poor fellow," I thought, "I'm going to be very cruel. But I'll just sit a little while with him. No need to be too cruel. It can't hurt to sit a little while, and besides I don't want to leave him. But I will. I'll go home very soon."

He stayed crouched beneath the tree. With one arm he pushed back a branch so that it formed an archway around his head. Beneath the leaves his eyes looked up at me, limpid, watchful in the shadowed smudge that was his face. What light there was seemed condensed in those eyes, it glittered and ran together in tiny points like light on the surface of a pool. For the rest all was silence and stillness and waiting. Slowly I pushed the leaves a little farther out of the way, then I stooped and went in beside him in the long cool grass and the resin-scented darkness.

"Why didn't you tell me?" he asked.

He was sitting with his back to me, one arm resting on his updrawn knee, and with his right hand he kept pulling up grass and throwing it in the river.

"I didn't think," I said, "I just didn't think of anything."

He still kept his back turned to me and went on maddeningly tearing up grass. Then he said, "How old *are* you?"

"Sixteen."

"God Almighty. You said you were eighteen, and how was I to know you were a virgin?"

Suddenly I was angry. I was tired and cold and my body hurt me. And now when it was all too late in the day, I felt afraid. I said, "Well I'm not any more, so what are you worrying about?"

He laughed a little at this and turned and faced me. "You're right," he said, "it's not my worry. So why am I all about like this? I don't know myself."

"Don't worry about me," I said. "I can take care of myself."

"Don't talk like that. You've been going on like that all night."

"Yes I know. I asked for it."

He came over and lifted me up, saying, "Get up off the ground now, maybe it's damp, and don't go taking the blame. I wanted you."

"And I wanted you."

"Yes but I knew I wanted you, and I don't think you had any mortal idea what you wanted."

"I just thought I'd like to lead you on."

"My poor little Judy."

He lifted me up and sat me in a cross branch of the tree, and he stood there with his arms around me and his face against my breast; talking to me, trying to comfort me.

"Listen," he began, "do you know how to look after yourself?"

"How do you mean 'look after yourself'?"

"You know what I mean. I don't want to Jonah you, but suppose you have a baby?"

"I don't know. Do I know how to get rid of it you mean?"

"Yes."

"Well I think you drink Lysol or something, don't you?"

"Hell! You're only a baby yourself. Look here, well. You'll most likely be all right. It doesn't so often happen to first trippers. But if you do find out that you're not all right, don't go taking Lysol or anything like that. And don't go running off to any old woman who offers to fix you up for a couple of quid."

"There's a woman at work who always fixes herself up with a steel knitting-needle," I suggested helpfully.

"For God's sake, Lisha," he took me by the shoulders and shook me, "you have to listen to me. Do you think I want to kill you on top of everything else? You've no idea of how to look after yourself. Everything like that is deadly dangerous. We're sailing tomorrow morning so I can't stick around, but I should be back by May."

"Where are you going?"

"I'm not supposed to tell you, but it's the States. But while I'm gone look after yourself. I've only twenty pounds left. I'll give it to you. I don't know what a good doctor charges in

78

Australia. In England it would be enough. If you should need it, use it. Phyl or someone should know the name of a doctor who does that sort of thing."

He pulled the money out of his wallet and put it in my hand.

"You won't come back," I said.

"Listen, honey, I want to come back very much."

"Just because you feel you should."

"I like you a lot. Better than any other girl I ever met."

"You don't have to say that sort of thing."

He sighed impatiently and took off his watch and handed it to me.

"I've used that watch for a marker more times than I can count," he said, "and I've always come back to collect it. Now do you believe I'll come back to you?"

"What's a marker?" (How strange to think that I should ever have asked that question.)

"Stick with me, darling, and you'll have plenty of chances to find that out."

"I don't want it."

"No, you hang on to it. It's lucky. If you need more than twenty pounds, pawn it. It cost a hundred and twenty dollars in the States. You should be able to get twenty pounds on it—or more if you sell it. Anyway, what are we worrying about? Wait till, that is until—"

"Till about next Tuesday week," I said.

"Till Tuesday week it is," he laughed and kissed me on the cheek, "and then if you're O.K. blue the money on a couple of dresses so you and me can step out in style when I get back from the States. That is if you'll go out with me. I do most sincerely hope you will go out with me, Lisha."

Three months later I received the telegram. It had been sent from Yarraville Post Office, and it said, "Meet me 7 o'clock tonight under clocks at Flinders Street. Andy."

That was all, and that was the first I had heard of him since the night we met. Sometimes I had looked at the watch and the money hidden in my top drawer to convince myself that it had all happened. Now the telegram made me so happy that I could not keep myself from laughing and singing as I dressed to go out. At that time I used to take the beginners' class three

79

nights a week at the Olive McSweeney School of Dancing. I rang them up and told them I had Puckapunyal throat and would not be in that night. Then I came back from the phone and told Aunt Margaret that I would be working late.

"It's a special night, tonight," I explained, and something in my voice made Aunt Margaret give me one of those searching glances, so discomforting to the guilty conscience. However she said nothing, and I explained my early departure by saying that I was eating in town with Phyl.

I arrived at the Flinders Street clocks at quarter to seven. I wore a tight pink satin frock, a full length, sky-blue Teddy-bear coat, and the famous high heels, and, in my excitement, I had slapped so much make-up on my face that I was much pestered by Americans who wanted me to go out with them, and police-men who wanted me to move on. I would move from the St Kilda clock over to the Box Hill clock every time I saw a mem-ber of the Force approaching, and at 7.10 I was just telling a youthful Yankee that I didn't care how much I resembled his kid sister way back home in Iowa, and almost weeping with annoyance and worry, when suddenly I heard a voice over my shoulder :

"What are you trying to do with my girl?"

I spun round and there he was, his hands in his pockets, his hair as unruly, his smile as insolent as ever. The Yankee melted away into the crowd, and there we were, amongst all the people. I was afraid to speak in case I cried.

"Aren't you going to kiss the man that made a woman of you?" he enquired.

I laughed then and put up my face to be kissed, and a police-man asked us both to move on, so we wandered off along Swanston Street arm in arm. He said :

"I'm sorry I'm late. It's hard to get a taxi out at that blasted Yarraville. Hell! what a place. I was chewing my fingernails all the way into town and begging the driver to speed it up. I was worried you wouldn't wait."

He said it cheerfully—as though it would have been a joke and he would not have cared much had I not met him.

"You're a hard and cagy customer," I thought, and some instinct told me that I would be foolish to act cagy, also. So I said, "I usually wait quarter of an hour, and I would have waited longer for you."

He kissed me softly on the top of the head, and said, "That's my girl. Now," he went on, "I bet you're starving. Come and I'll feed you and then we'll have a serious talk. Where do you want to eat?"

I was ashamed to tell him that I didn't really know any of the fashionable places round town, that I had never been to a night club or dined at a hotel. So I said, with what I hoped sounded like great sophistication, "Do you want to go somewhere we can have a drink?"

He laughed. "I want you to make a few decisions with your head clear," he said. "Then I'll take you and buy you all the drinks you want."

"Well I don't know," I said.

"Let's go to one of those nice greasy little Greek joints," he suggested, "where they sit you in a little cubicle and pull the curtains, and every time you're getting cosy a waiter called Spiro pulls back the curtains and asks you if you're a steak and oysters or a fried flounder."

When finally seated in the nice greasy little Greek joint, with the steak and oysters ordered, and the curtains carefully drawn, he looked at me across the table and asked, without further preamble, "Well are you O.K.?"

I was so embarrassed to realize that I was blushing that I could only nod my head.

"Good," he said. "Have you found yourself another boy friend, so?"

"I've been out with a few friends," I said. "Not like—" my voice just trailed away, and I could not go on.

"Not like you went out with me."

"That's right," I said. "Why didn't you write?"

"I didn't know what to write. I knew I would be back in time to help you if you needed help. But anyway, you're O.K. So what now? You're looking mighty pretty, kid. Did you get yourself that coat with the money?"

I took the money out of my bag and laid it on the table. Then I put the watch on top of it and pushed it across to him. "Naturally," I said, "I wouldn't use your money unless I needed it."

81

He sat staring at me. I could see that I had astonished him. I did not know how or why. Then he said, "Lisha Flynn, I think you are the first honest woman I have met in all my life. I would like you to be my girl if you will have me."

He reached out and took my hands across the table.

"What do you mean—your girl?" I asked.

He left his side of the table and came round to tell me—sitting beside me but not looking at me. He picked up a fork and kept pricking out designs on the the table cloth as he talked. "Just go with me," he said, "and no one else. I'll treat you right, Lisha. I won't go with other women when I'm away from you. I'll bring you presents from the States. If you want a flat of your own I'll keep you in it, and I won't lumber you with a kid."

"Yes," I said. "I'll go with you for as long as you want me."

The hotel at Williamstown belonged to one of Andy's friends. He was an ex-seaman known as good old Jim, and a very good friend he was; no awkward questions, no asking to see my identity card; all very maty.

"This is my wife," said Andy.

"Pleased to meet you, Mrs Kelly," said good old Jim. He swung my hand up and down as though it were a pump handle. "Got you a room ready upstairs," he told Andy. "Only got twin beds," he added quite seriously, "the best I could do at such short notice."

Andy took off his coat and threw it on one bed. He sat on the other bed and lit a cigarette and handed it to me. Then he lit another for himself and said, "Come and sit here by me."

I went and sat at the other end of the bed, leaning back against the wall with the pillows bunched comfortably behind me. He took me by the hand.

"Are you shy of me? Do you want a drink to stiffen your spine?" he asked.

"No," I shook my head, and then I burst out, "Look you've never once said that you loved me and I hate to be the one to say it first, but I just can't go on indefinitely with a love affair without mentioning it. It just doesn't seem decent."

Again he looked at me in astonishment. Then he switched off the light and came back and took me in his arms. Very gently he began to stroke my hair back from my forehead. "Lisha," he said, "I do love you, and love is something that I never believed in before in my life so you'll have to forgive me if I'm a little leary of it now; and what about you, you're such a baby, it isn't fair to go talking about love to you. Love is supposed to be for ever."

"Yes," said I, with all the confidence in the world, "love is for ever."

"Proper little fate sparrer, aren't you? Well, darling, if you're game so am I. And now, woman, get into that bed for your man's been at sea a long time."

Of course good old Jim's pub was a Jack's Ashore. Not even his best friends would have tried to deny it. The brawls, the hilarious parties, the family fights went on all night. At about 11.30 the couple in the next room set the ball rolling. Andy and I, who had arrived at the stage where we were smoking cigarettes and exchanging confidences, ceased all conversation in order to listen in. They went at it with a will while we barracked them in urgent whispers. He, it appeared, was a stoker on a tug. She, it seemed, wished to go down and see his ship. He said it was not permitted.

"The liar," said I.

"No," said Andy, "in some ships it's not allowed."

I said that men always stuck together and then I meanly shushed him before he could answer.

"I don't want to miss anything," I explained.

Small chance of anyone in the street missing anything. By now voices were raised. He was maintaining that a man felt a dill carting his wife all over the ship, introducing her to his mates, etc.

"I suppose you want a formal knock-down to the skipper," he said with fine scorn.

She said, "Nothing of the sort."

She was then foolish enough to add that it was a well-known fact that he had taken other women down into his cabin.

"That," said her spouse, "is a lie."

"It's the truth," said she.

"It's a dirty rotten stinking lousy bloody low filthy two-faced lie," he amplified.

83

"No four-letter words as yet," said Andy.

"It's the truth," from the woman next door.

"God! How did I get stuck with a nagging bitch like you?" enquired her goaded husband. "Now, will you shut up and let me get to sleep?"

Apparently she said she did not want to sleep, for his voice was raised again.

"Well I do. I'm sailing tomorrow morning" (here he paused to thank his Maker in terms more suitable for use towards an old and not very reputable friend) "and I can tell you straight that I'll be glad to be back amongst the Japanese mines to get a bit of peace. Now will you shut up for Chrissake?"

She said that she certainly would not shut up, and added that only his guilty conscience made him rave at her like this. "Because," she said, "you know that I know that you had a woman in your cabin."

"Who told you that?" he asked.

Apparently it was merely a rhetorical question for he answered it himself.

"I know. It was that lying low bastard of a Clarrie Watkins. That's his form. Doing the dirty on a man the moment his back is turned. Everyone knows about you and Clarrie Watkins."

"Good man," Andy encouraged him, "that was a smart move."

We did not hear what she said in defence of Clarrie Watkins but, whatever it was, her husband laughed it to scorn. At his first spare moment, he said, he would go aboard the dredge on which Clarrie Watkins worked and hammer him through the deck. He would also, he said, do the same by Clarrie Watkins' mate Ted Nesbitt, and for the same good reason. He would then come home and give his wife a hiding that would put her in hospital for a week. Were it not for the fact that he was an exhausted man (exhausted working for a lazy, lying bitch who made him the joke of the Australian Seamen's Union) he would start with his wife here and now. As a matter of fact, damn sleep! He *would* start here and now, etc., etc.

"You'll have to stop the brute," I told Andy.

"Don't be mean, honey," he said, "let them have their fun."

"Fun!"

"Sure. Maybe they like it. Maybe they love each other."

"It certainly doesn't sound like it."

"Ah, sweetheart, people have all different ways of making love."

Well there were no shrieks from next door, and how the quarrel was finally settled we will never know because at that moment another little diversion broke out just outside our door. Two ladies who had had some difference of opinion at a drinking party farther up the passage were now settling it during a trip to the toilet. One of the gentlemen from the party was acting as referee. Each contestant was dilating upon the moral shortcomings of the other.

"She's nothing but a bloody prostitute."

"Whose kids are on the Welfare?"

"Running around with every Yank in Melbourne."

"Kids was lousy and covered in school scabs."

"Drawing allotment money from four different chaps that's away in the Forces."

Several more of the good old traditional charges and then it was on in earnest. There was a series of the most blood-curdling yells and screams that I had ever heard in my life. They brought several more spectators running to the scene.

"She kicked me fair in the stomach," one was yelling, "the low slut kicked me right in the guts."

"For Christ's sake stop that bloody noise," yelled good old Jim from the head of the stairs.

"Get me the police," screamed she of the injured stomach, "I'm going to charge her. Get me the police or get me down to the cop shop. Alf, you come with me. You're a witness."

"Not me," said the craven Alf.

"Will you shut up or do I have to knock yez all out?" said good old Jim. "There's a patrol car right outside the door. Carry on like this and they'll be in on top of us."

The silence that followed this revelation was instant, complete and absolute.

"Well," said Andy, "that looks like the end of the fun for tonight. Now off we go to sleep."

He had hardly spoken when there was a knock at the door and somebody turned the handle and said to someone else in the passage, "It's locked."

"What do you want?" called Andy.

"I didn't know anyone was in there," called the voice from the passage, "I just want to collect some gear."

"Right you are so. Wait a minute."

Andy dragged on his trousers and his shoes (a scouse never goes barefooted to open a door. This is not personal vanity but a wise defence precaution. Indeed I have known particularly cautious souls who always took an empty bottle in one hand as well), then he switched on the light and opened the door and a tall dark man clad in nothing but trousers and half a dozen tattoos strode into the room.

"I'm sorry," he said, "Jim said he'd clear out all our gear but it doesn't look like he did."

He did not look at me but he told his mate standing in the passage. "There's a lady in here. I'll pass your gear out", which he duly did.

"Got everything now?" asked Andy, sitting on the edge of the bed and lighting a cigarette.

"Yes we're right now. Thanks again and excuse me, lady," he almost bowed towards me.

"Sorry to have to trouble you," he told Andy.

The whole affair had been conducted with such tact and so much 'excusing' and 'quite-all-righting' that I had a desire to laugh.

"Gee, he was polite," I said.

"Why shouldn't he be?"

"Well what must he think of me?"

"It doesn't matter what he thinks. He's a Liverpool boy. He knows when he'd be speaking out of turn."

"Do all the Liverpool men come to Jim's?"

"Most of them. Doesn't it sound like it?"

"It does a little."

Then he laughed : "It's funny when you think about it," he said, "we're clannish, all right. I was born in Scotland Road. I went to sea to get away from the dirt and the cold; to see the Golden Gate by moonlight and Sydney Harbour at sunrise and so on. And your father was born in Scotland Road and I've come thousands of miles to find a girl the same breed and seed as every second girl in Liverpool."

"Are you sorry?"

"Don't be foolish. If you want it that way, I'll marry you."

"Do you want to marry me?"

"I'm not a fussy man."

"You know what, I'm beginning to believe all the terrible things they say about ship's engineers."

"That's a wise girl."

And then as I was drifting into sleep someone went past in the street below whistling a song that, somewhere, I had heard before.

"What is that song?" I murmured.

"It's called '*J'attendrai*'. It's my favourite song. It's nearly a modern sea chanty. Everyone's going round the ship whistling it. All kidding themselves that some woman is saying just for them 'I will wait' and all the rest of it."

I laughed because I was frightened. "Why does someone have to whistle it under my window tonight of all nights?" I said.

"It's an omen. It's like the pictures."

"The incidental music is a bit obvious, don't you think?"

I was a little nettled at this. Much and all as I loved him, I was only sixteen and I did not see why I should not have a few trimmings if I wanted them.

"Well anyway," I said, "why be a mocker? So I will wait."

"You certainly will," he assured me warmly. "For if you don't I'll break every bone in your body."

We were jolted out of our sleep next morning by a positive barrage of knocks on the door, and then the lock gave way before an expertly applied shoulder and in burst a wild-haired young gentleman clad in the trousers and tattoos which were national costume down at good old Jim's. He brought with him a refreshing odour of whisky and hailed Andy as Clancy.

"Jesus!" he said jovially. "You look fornicating terrible. Been on the fornicating grog? Got a fornicating head myself. Fornicating terrible. On it like fornicating one thing last night. Man's a fornicating fool. What's fornicating wrong with you? What are you pulling fornicating faces for? Feeling fornicating crook? Hell! It's fornicating Kelly. Thought you were fornicating Clancy. Thought to myself 'Clancy's nose looks fornicating broken this morning!'"

"What do you want?" asked Andy.

"Just left some fornicating gear here. Going to dhobi the

fornicating stuff. What are you shushing about? Fornicating head that bad? Out on the fornicating tiles, see. No fornicating good to you."

I pushed the blankets away from my face and stretched my arms above my head, and even in the half-light and his hangover our young visitor realised that there was a female present.

"Gawd!" he gasped. "Fornicating sorry, lady. Just getting me fornicating gear."

He grabbed it and bolted, and in the passage we heard him, badly shaken, telling someone :

"Fornicating Kelly, got a woman in there. Walked in on the pair of them. Fornicating shock."

We lay there laughing helplessly. All the same Andy was a little shamefaced.

"I shouldn't have brought you here," he said, "but where else could we have gone?"

"I don't care," I said. "Just so long as I'm with you."

"Well, darling," he promised, "I'll always take you to the best from this on. Come on now," he swung himself out of bed, tied a towel round his hips and then sat down to enjoy his before-breakfast smoke, "have a bath and get some breakfast into you, and then we'll go out and spend my money."

On Monday came the terrible business of going home to face the family. I had sent them a telegram on the Saturday morning which said, "Don't worry. Spending weekend with girl friend."

On Saturday morning that had seemed quite sufficient to stave off all further trouble. Now, at 7.30 on a grey wet Monday morning, it seemed very inadequate indeed.

"Do you want me to come home with you, well?" said Andy. "I think it would be a good idea."

I shook my head trying to work things out. "No," I said, "I'll go alone. I'm frightened but I'll go home alone. I'm going to tell them that I stayed with Cathy Hughes for the weekend. She lives down at Sandringham and she's not on the phone. No good saying I was with Phyl. It's far too easy to check. About the new clothes you bought me, I'll keep them in my locker at work and bring them home next Friday. I'll tell my aunts that my mother gave me some and my father gave me the rest."

"Why can't I come with you?"

"There'll be a terrible family brawl."

"I was born and bred on family brawls."

"This one will be a beauty. Several generations will be brought into it. My mother's people hate my father's people. My father's people dislike my mother's people very intensely. The aunts I am living with are my father's sisters. My brother lives there too. He's only fourteen. Naturally my aunts don't like having us dumped on them while my mother and father are having the time of their life."

"They didn't have to take you."

"We're the same blood. I know it's very difficult to understand."

"No, I can understand that very well."

"So you see if I arrive home with you in tow both aunts will say that, it is just the sort of thing they would have expected of me—brazen, shameless, brawling, just the thing you could look for from a Ward. The Wards are my mother's people. I'm sick and tired of hearing this, so I'll go to work today and I'll go home this evening as though nothing has happened worth making a fuss about. If they want to believe the story about staying with Cathy, they can. If not, they can do the other thing. Whichever way it goes I'll live through it."

Andy still looked doubtful. He said, "All right well, I can see you're determined to carry this off like a lady. I can warn you now that it's going to be very hard to do. Try if you must; but remember, if anyone starts knocking you round, to hell with the well bred stuff and call in the fancy man. I'll come out about seven."

"Don't come to the door. You may walk right into the thick of the fight. There's a lane behind our house. Wait there."

"You don't have to go home at all if you don't want to, Lisha. Stay with me. I'll treat you right."

"If I stayed with you we could easily end in worse trouble. You know that."

"I'd risk it. Personally, I don't think there's much they'd care to do."

"That's where you don't know my family, Andy. My mother has always told me that if she ever had any trouble with me about men she would put me in reformatory for a couple of years."

"That's just a mean piece of blackmail. Anyway, little Lisha, I won't leave you alone for too long. I'll be coming out to you as soon as my work is over, and whatever you want to do, that's what I want to do. Come on now, we'll go down and dare one of Jake's breakfasts. This is not the sort of day you start on an empty stomach."

Jake was an English deck boy who was doing all the cooking at good old Jim's. The entire kitchen staff had walked out some days before and gone to a party, or into the Forces or the better paid munitions. Jake was a terrible cook but he was a great admirer of mine. I was, he said, the only good woman in the place. All the rest were a pack of gold diggers and good-time Charlies. He Mrs Kelly'd the life out of me in a tone of voice which inferred that should anyone call me anything else they would be receiving a call from Jake's seconds the very next morning. On that last morning he wrung me by the hand and said it had been an honour to meet me. He handed me into the taxi as though I were a princess.

"You've won old Jake," said Andy, as we drove away, "Mr Sentiment they call him back in Limehouse."

I said nothing. I felt physically ill with apprehension and I felt that a little English sentimentality spread around my family would not go amiss. Love! What did my family think of love? My aunts did not mention it. My father said it was a matter of sexual compulsion. My mother said it was a lot of silly nonsense, believed in by oversexed people. I had years to go before I began even thinking of marriage, and when I did marry I would find that when I had my own home and car and every debt paid, love would come. After this rigmarole she would issue her final statement on sexual morality :

"Remember, anyone can get presents if they wish to make harlots of themselves. A smart woman gets presents for no return. Always remain a virgin—you are in a three hundred per cent better bargaining position."

I was scarcely at work before the phone calls began. My father was first. He wanted to know what was the meaning of it all. Never had he been so worried.

I said, "I was at Cathy Hughes'."

He said that I should have sent word on the Friday night. A telegram on Saturday morning was not good enough. Late on Saturday morning, to make it worse. If I thought I was too old to answer to anyone I could promptly disabuse myself of the idea. (My father always became very pompous and wordy in times of moderate anger. When really enraged he became crisp to a degree.) He made a slight pause here but I said nothing so he went on :

If I thought I was too old to thrash he could assure me that I was labouring under a misapprehension. He would not be able to come out to discuss things with Aunt Margaret that evening, as arranged. Some business matters of great urgency had come up. Furthermore he would be obliged if I told my Aunt Margaret that he did not appreciate the tone she had taken when ringing him—inferring that he was remiss as a father, etc., etc.

I said, "Why don't you tell her, Daddy?"

"I shall. I can assure you I shall, at the very first opportunity."

Five minutes later my mother was on the line. She told me nothing that she had not told me many times before. That she trusted me. Of course she trusted me. As for the weekend, of course she knew I was with a girl friend.

I kindly gave her a well documented account of the Hughes' house, and how far it was from the station, and how I missed the last train and Cathy's mother had insisted that I stay the night, and then Cathy had said that it would be a good idea to make it the whole weekend. Mother gratefully accepted all this. Then, to cover herself, as it were, she added that should I decide to start running around with men she would just refuse to be bothered with me.

"It's just one thing I wouldn't stand, Eilishe. I'd put you in the Abbotsford Convent. I'd have no qualms. I'd do it without hesitation. I'd just refuse to worry about you any more."

She always delivered this hideous threat in a strange affected little voice, entirely different from her usual manner of speaking. It was as though her very vocal chords were seeking to express the measure of their disassociation. I had heard it countless times before, and it never failed to chill and irritate me—it sounded so airily mad. Had she rounded off with a couple of tra-la-las I would never have been surprised. Reverting to normal tones, she asked me to tell Aunt Margaret that she would not be out tonight. Unfortunately there was a buyers' meeting (mother was a buyer for a big city store) and she would not be able to get away.

Next call was from Phyl, who was in a dreadful state of fearful giggles, unholy glee and genuine concern.

"Gee!" she said, "what have you been up to? Your Auntie's murderous, fair dinkum, she's blazing. Come over tonight and tell me all about it."

"What did you tell them, Phyl?"

"I told them nothing, of course. What do you think I am? Look, I've got to go now. See you tonight."

Last of all was Aunt Tessie. She was Aunt Margaret's younger sister and it was typical of her that she could not wait till I got home that evening—she must ring up and fire a couple of range-finding shots, as it were, during her morning tea break.

"Well, my lady," she began, "you're going to be dealt with good and properly this time."

I let her get no further. I said, "I'm sorry, Aunt Tess, I'm not allowed to take personal phone calls." Then I hung up on her. I spent a great deal of my time being as insolent as possible to Aunt Tess, and, besides, I always became angry when I was threatened.

After that Mr Bailey, who was the boss in our department, really did forbid any more personal phone calls. "I have to get a bit of work done," he said, "I can't have the lot of you doing nothing except sit around and talk to your boy friends all day."

So after that there was nothing to do except wait till the time came to go home. And it came soon enough.

I came in through the back door, and there, at the kitchen table, was my Aunt Margaret, peeling potatoes. She looked straight at me and said, "I won't ask you where you've been. I rang both your mother and father. They'll be coming out this evening. I told them to make arrangements for you. I don't want to discuss anything with you."

I had a sixth sense, well developed in many a family brawl, and this sixth sense told me now that Aunt Margaret was enjoying casting me back at my parents. And who could blame her?

92

"This," she was telling herself, "will bring them up with a running jolt."

So I gave myself the pleasure of telling her that they would not be arriving. I delivered their messages and sat down by the kitchen table, waiting, my hands clutched together in my lap, my feet twisting round the chair legs. Then I remembered that I was a grown woman now, and I made my feet be still, and I sat back and straightened my shoulders. Aunt Margaret went red, and the tears came into her eyes.

"I won't be fobbed off and used up in this way," she said. "One or the other of them will take you tonight."

"What are you going to do? How will you get in touch with them? My father will have left work now and I don't know where he lives. Do you?"

"Very well, I'll pack up your case and take you off to your mother's. She won't get out of things so lightly this time."

"I told you, she's at a meeting."

"That's a tale."

I thought so too, but I said nothing. I made my face carefully, insolently blank, and gazed at the opposite wall.

"If by some extraordinary chance she really is at a meeting," said Aunt Margaret, "we'll wait till she gets back."

I had a sudden vision of Aunt Margaret and myself, plus suitcase, sitting grim and determined in the lounge of the very noisy, racy and convivial hotel where my mother lived. My mother was a bosom friend of the landlady and very popular with all the regular customers. She was a handsome woman in smart clothes and a smart job. She was quite queen of the establishment. A big fish in a small puddle. And now she was to be bearded on her home ground by the only adversary she dreaded. She often earned many a laugh amongst her friends by describing Aunt Margaret—her dowdy hats, her spinsterish ways and so on. What she omitted to tell her friends was that Aunt Margaret had a most awful disregard for superficialities and pose, and a most terrible ability to get to the real point of any problem in about two seconds flat, and then, worst of all, a most disconcerting habit of presenting you with the said point in the manner calculated to leave you without one tattered shred of self-respect in which to wrap the poor shivering ego.

93

I gave a sudden spurt of laughter. Poor Mum, she was in for a terrible evening.

"What's so amusing, my lady?"

"Nothing, Auntie, I'm just a bit tired and frightened. That's all."

"You're too brazen to be afraid of anything," said Aunt Margaret, making a mistake very common to virtuous women.

"Can I have a cup of tea before I pack?" I asked.

I suddenly felt exhausted. The prospect of again going upon my travels wearied me immensely. True enough, it would be something to laugh about afterwards, but it would have to be lived through first. No real harm would be done because I would slip over to Phyl's and ask her to meet Andy in the lane and tell him where to come and get me. I knew where I'd be going. Mother would let me stay with her for the night. She would give me the usual spiel which went something like this:

"God knows, darling, I'd give anything in the world to be able to have you and Michael with me. Do you think I don't want to have my own home with my children with me? Do you think I don't look at women in the tram and feel a lump come up in my throat while I think 'I suppose you've got homes and you're going back now to cook a bit of tea for the kids and then afterwards maybe you'll all sit by the fire and——'" (By this mother usually had herself deeply moved, tears would come into her lovely eyes and she would clasp her hands together as though praying for all this domestic happiness.) Sometimes she would merely falter away about here. At other times she would go on a little further, asking me didn't I see how impossible it was? There really was not enough money. The Flynns wouldn't give us a penny. (The Flynns, who were extremely generous and inclined to be revengeful, would have gladly given ten pounds a week for the fun of seeing my mother smothering in the suburbs.) And she had to put so much into her job at the store. The responsibility of running a home combined with her work, well, she just would not be able to do both properly. It would not be fair to us. So many men had gone off from work to go into the Forces. She was doing three people's work as it was. Sometimes she wondered how she could go on. She had not wanted to tell me this because it might worry me but when she had had her last medical check-up the staff nurse at the store had said to her, 'You want to watch that heart, Mrs Flynn.' "Oh nothing really wrong, darling, but I just have to be a little bit careful—"

At this point I usually said, "Yes, Mum, I do understand. It would be quite impossible. I see that."

I was fond of my mother, and I did not like to hear her rambling on, demonstrating her lack of originality, in this manner.

After I'd stayed the night with her she would take me out to her sister Molly and ask could I stay there for a few days. Then she would ring my father and ask him to try and talk Aunt Margaret into having me back. If that did not work she would have to look around till she found some hostel where I could be dumped. It was truly piteous to see my poor parents running around in circles trying to relieve themselves of this dreadful incubus, their daughter. I felt like the old woman of the sea and at this thought I laughed again. And it was while I was laughing that Aunt Tessie stormed in from work.

She did not wait to take off her hat and gloves. She stood before me, shaking with rage.

"You may well laugh, you filthy thing," she shouted. "Don't think we don't know what you've been up to, and don't you dare to hang up the phone on me."

Knowing Aunt Tessie as I did, I realised that this business of the phone had been eating into her for the rest of the day till, by now, she was quite beside herself. I was genuinely delighted to see that I had so infuriated her. I stopped laughing, leaned back in my chair, and smiled up at her. Aunt Tessie smacked me straight across the face.

I rose and began to walk away, but Aunt Tess, who had her gloves off by this time, was after me, hitting me around the shoulders and neck with her little useless hands. She was a small and very pretty woman, and not at all strong. She found it difficult to hit hard enough to hurt. I kept my back turned to her and leaned up against the wall. I made no attempt to defend myself. The saddest thing of all about my deserted and isolated position within the clan was that I longed to be accepted and admired. I never seemed to have any success and I found the ethics of the clan Flynn were almost always directly opposed to everything I felt and every instinct I had,

95

nevertheless I went on desperately trying to win approval. And I tried now. They would not be able to say, "She raised her hand to her aunt—I wonder God didn't strike it off."

Aunt Tessie tried to turn me round and attack my face. Not having the strength for this, she pulled off her shoe, swung it in both hands, and settled down to do some real damage with the wooden heel. She kept gasping, "I hate you. I hate you. I always have."

Then she ceased to waste words and energy. She just kept up a steady flogging with the shoe till my back was marked and bleeding from the shoulders to the waist.

Then Aunt Margaret, who had gone upstairs, came down and said, "That's enough, Tess. What was the use of all that?"

Aunt Tess burst into tears. After several minutes of intense enjoyment she was now horrified at herself. How was she going to square this behaviour with her favourite picture of herself— the quiet, well-bred little gentlewoman? And, basically, everything remained the same. My father still owed her money, my mother still laughed at her.

"She deserved it," wept Aunt Tess, "she'd make anyone go on like a fishwife."

I did not answer. I went upstairs to my bedroom. I knew that I was going to be very busy. I had no time to waste on Aunt Tess. "I must think. I must plan. I must be calm," I kept telling. myself, but I found that I could not think calmly at all. I stood holding open the door of my wardrobe and looking in at the clothes.

I left the door still open and wandered into the bathroom. I sat on the edge of the bath for a while and looked at the floor. Then I got up and began to wash my face. Aunt Margaret heard me in there and came begging me to go to bed. I think she was afraid I might have some sort of collapse.

"Go to bed now, dear," she said, "and don't always be starting quarrels with everyone."

I called out 'yes', and went back into my room and locked the door. I went across to the mirror and had a look at my back. It looked even worse than it felt. I began to shake so badly that I had to go and lie down on the bed.

"He'll be here soon," I told myself. "Never doubt that he'll be here soon."

I went into the bathroom again and had some Aspros for the shaking, and a drink of water because I was very thirsty. After that there was nothing to do except go back to bed and lie there fully dressed, and wait. And when the dusk was merging into night, I heard the whistle.

I stood up from my bed and walked straight out and downstairs, and through the back of the house. My aunts did not seem to be around, but it made no difference. I would have walked out had there been several battalions of Japanese in our yard. My brother was sitting in a small room off the kitchen. He had an aero modeller's kit spread out in front of him. He looked up at me and his face was very white and his eyes looked black and anguished.

"Why didn't you call me?" he asked. "I came in when it was on. Didn't you hear me? I stayed here in case you wanted me. Why didn't you flatten her?"

"Tell you after," I said, "I haven't time now. If anyone wants to know where I am, I've gone over to Phyl's for a little while."

My brother nodded and returned his attention to testing the balance of a balsa wood propeller.

Andy stood back in the shadows, a little way from our gate. It had come on to drizzle and he wore a raincoat with the collar turned up high and his hands deep in the pockets. The rain and the half-light had turned his hair a shining fox-red, and, as usual, he had the air of a patient, waiting animal. He looked once at my face, and asked, "What's happened?"

I turned so that my back was in the light that came from the lamp at the corner, then, slowly, because it hurt, I pulled my blouse down from my shoulders. I heard the catch of his breath and he pulled off his raincoat and put it around me.

"Here," he said, "you'll have to keep warm. Where can we go? You can't stand around in the rain. There must be somewhere. Down here."

He caught me by the arm and led me down to the end of the lane where the back fences formed right angles. Across one corner a straggle of wistaria had formed a roof.

"This is a fine thing," he said. "Where was your brother that he let them do this to you? Is he paralysed? Is he a cripple?"

I shook my head. "My brother loathes family blues," I said,

"they give him bilious attacks. Besides, he knows that if I'd wanted to I could have flattened the aunt who did this."

"Why didn't you, well?"

"You wouldn't understand."

"I'm getting bloody sick of being told I wouldn't understand. I understand in my vulgar, uncomprehending way that you've been beaten up badly, and you're white in the face and shaking with shock. Give me a proper look at that back."

I turned my back again, not daring to look in his face.

"Ah, Jesus," he said at length, almost in a whisper. "Ah, Jesus."

Very gently he stroked the poor lacerated skin. "Yes," he said, "I can see you're a damned refined lot, very lace curtain indeed. You're right, Lisha. It is very hard for me to understand. I've seen my old fellow haul off and knock my mother flat. If it comes to that he drove me half way through the floor more times than enough, and my brothers and my sisters too; but it takes a very high falutin type indeed to calmly and coolly take off the shoe and beat somebody to a pulp. Some of the marks you've got here, you'll carry to your grave. Well it's no good talking about it now or I'll end up going in and screwing her scrawny old neck, which won't get us very far in the long run. I can't stay long. We're sailing tomorrow. I just got a couple of hours off because I said I had to see you. You should be in bed anyway. When you go in I want you to promise that you'll get yourself a drink of something hot and then take a hot bath and go to bed and keep very warm all night. It helps with the shock and keeps the stiffness out a little bit. Now listen, darling, I'll tell you what you've got to do. It's no use your trying to look after yourself any more. I'm going to do it for you," he pulled me closer and wrapped the raincoat more firmly around my shoulders. "Now, darling, get this carefully."

When he had finished I repeated what he had said and he nodded. "That's it," he said, "now off to bed with you."

Before I went in I paused with one hand on the gate. "And what if you get sent to jail?" I asked.

"Don't worry so much. Trust your luck."

"But what if you do?"

He bent and kissed me.

"It's bugger all on a big ship," he said.

The next morning I almost fainted getting out of my night-gown. I had not had the hot bath Andy had recommended. I had suddenly felt far too tired. The pain in my body and the relief in my mind had exhausted me, and we had an old chip bath heater that would have discouraged a pyromaniac. I just did not feel up to it. I had gone to bed with my back blood-encrusted, and now my nightgown was glued to what was left of my skin. I found some kindling wood and several copies of the *Herald* in the bathroom wood box and had a very hot, if very short, shower. After that I felt a little better but I was horri-fied at the look of my face. I was white as a sheet with blue circles around my eyes. Aunt Margaret looked at me carefully at breakfast. She did not ask how I felt, nor ask to see my back. To do so would have been a breach of the famous Flynn solidarity. I could see she was worried about me so I ate a piece of toast. It made me feel sick, and I said no thank you I would not have any porridge.

Aunt Margaret said no more about taking me to my parents. Aunt Tess was still in bed. I would have liked to say goodbye to my brother, but it would have looked strange. So at quarter past eight I caught the train to the city, and I never came home again.

I remember it was a misty morning, misty and still, as though autumn were trying to prolong its time. A soft vapour lay along the top of the Yarra and I knew that later in the day the sun-light would not break through the clouds, it would just filter down in a golden web, wrapping itself around the buildings, throwing a sheen over the trees and putting beauty into the faces of the people that went up and down the streets. Mel-bourne is very beautiful in autumn and the tears came into my eyes that I must leave her on such a day, but Andy was waiting for me over by the kerb and I had never seen him so happy and elated.

"Just time enough to grab a cup of coffee," he said, "the plane leaves the airport at ten o'clock, and then look out Sydney, here we come."

Andy's ship was expected to arrive in Sydney a few days after us. She had left Melbourne the same morning as we did but the time of her arrival was open to much speculation. It all depended on how long it took her to limp up the coast.

"With a good following wind like this," said Andy, "she should do it in between three to four days."

She was very old and decrepit. Her name was the *Vale of Clydd* and she was out of Cardiff. She had been in the Home Trade for something like thirty years and she was long overdue for conversion into a coal barge. This trip out to Australia was her war effort.

"And what an effort," said Andy, who was her third engineer. "There are the poor firemen sweating away like demons, and the Old Man on the blower roaring out for double ahead, which are words that shouldn't even be spoken in her old rattletrap of an engine room, and then he abuses the Chief and the Chief abuses the Deucer, and, in due course, the Deucer abuses everybody, and especially me."

What he did not tell me until after the war was over was that when they did manage to get her up to round about five knots the effort would be too much for the poor old girl. She would be on the verge of explosion and her smoke-stack would catch alight. This would cause great consternation in the middle of the night in the middle of a blacked out convoy, as you may well imagine. The rest of the ships would immediately scatter to right and left and the poor old *Vale* would be left alone, chugging through the night, her smoke-stack a beacon to any enemy shipping that cared to come and see what it was all about.

It was not known where she would go after she left Sydney but it did not make a great deal of difference.

"We've signed on again for this next trip," said Andy, "and after that I can pay off and, with luck, get into Australian coastal. At any rate Sydney is a better town for you than Melbourne—better climate and more fun, and more chance for me to get a short run job. I might spend the rest of the war bringing coals down from Newcastle. Anyway first thing we have to do today is to go down to the Company's office and get my money paid over to you. You'll be able to collect it every pay day. It'll do you good to have a holiday for a while. You've been working too hard—in an office all day and teaching dancing half the night. It should be a few weeks before the man-power catches up with you here. So in the meantime let's enjoy ourselves."

We booked in at a hotel in the Cross. It is quite a famous hotel in its way, and it was very popular with Allied servicemen.

When we got upstairs and I saw our suite, as it was so grandly called, I was rendered almost speechless. I thought it magnificent. Never before had I seen a bedside telephone, a bedside lamp and a studded satin bedhead. And to add to my happiness the whole layout was faintly period, not any period precisely, as it were, just period.

"Isn't it wonderful?" I cried. "Just like that musical about Madame du Barry."

"It is indeed," said Andy, "it's what the experts call Louis Sixteenth and a half."

The bathroom was the ultimate glory. Those were the days when only the filthy rich had hot and cold running, and there was I with gallons of it gushing from the shiniest taps I had ever seen. I could not make up my mind whether I would bathe in the lovely green translucent bath, or stand on the rose-coloured tiles of the shower recess and press the switch that sent the water spraying out from a silver rosette in the wall. At last I decided upon the shower. I stood there a long time with my eyes shut and the water flowing, warm and beautiful, over my shoulders and running down my body. I came out, moving like a dream-walker, with a big fluffy towel wrapped around me. Without a word I lay down in the satin bed and pulled the coverings up about me.

"I'm tired," I said. "Too much excitement and too much happiness coming so suddenly."

Then I slept.

When I awoke it was too late to go to the Company's office, so we went out on to our balcony and watched the evening come down across the Harbour. We stayed there till long after dark, talking about what we were going to do when the war was over, and what we would do when we had children, and what we would do when we went on the trip round the world, and what we would do when we were eighty. After that we were hungry so we went out to dine and dance at Romano's.

The next morning we went straight out after breakfast to

arrange about my allotment. On our way we stopped at a jeweller's to buy a proper wedding ring. Wearing Andy's signet ring back to front was not really very satisfactory. It was much too big, and, at any rate, it did not look terribly convincing. "And I don't want them to think that I'm not really married," I said.

"What the hell what they think?" said Andy. "I'm not asking any Office Johnny what he thinks."

"But what if they won't give me the money, aside from anything else?"

"I'm allowed to give my money to whoever I like—besides it's been the rule since the time of Lord Nelson and probably before that 'a verbal declaration of marriage may be deemed to be sufficient', and sufficient, and more than enough, it is for those bastards, I can tell you, darling."

They were very nice to me at the office as a matter of fact, and I sat and looked at the pictures of sailing ships on the walls while Andy fixed everything. All I had to do was to give them a specimen signature and I dashed off Eilishe Kelly as though I'd been doing it for years.

Then we commenced flat hunting.

We found it late that afternoon when we'd come back to the Cross. It was really only one large room with a gas ring in a cupboard, and it cost five pounds a week, which I thought was horrifying. (By 1946 it was probably costing almost twice as much, but as it was not given me to see the future, I really did think the landlady was an old bandit.) We paid a week in advance and said we'd move in the next day.

Next morning I was sitting up in bed, with my new blue swansdown-trimmed dressing-gown around my shoulders, and drinking a cup of tea. I felt tremendously adult and domesticated because I was moving into my own flat that very morning.

"But I still think it's a terrible price," I called to Andy, who was in the bathroom. He seemed to have been splashing around for hours, and I wished he'd hurry—I soon grew very lonesome without him.

"Five quid's not so bad," he shouted.

"My aunties have a six-roomed house, eight rooms if you count the bathroom and washhouse, for twenty-seven and six.

It's very old, I know, but that's what it's pegged at, and it does seem a big difference between that and five pounds."

There was a knock at the door and I said, "I'll get it, darling."

I got out of bed, slipped on my pink feathered mules (they were also new, Andy had protested they were a bit much but I had maintained that I'd wanted a pair ever since I was twelve years old, so he bought them for me) and, with my lovely blue swansdown all billowing around me, I opened the door. Before me were two bulky looking men in civilian clothes. They were dressed almost identically, with grey felt hats which they kept firmly on their heads, even when they spoke to me.

"Are you Mrs Kelly?" asked the taller one.

I inclined my head graciously, quite the young matron. "I am," I said.

Then, for a few seconds, everything happened very quickly. They stepped into the room and closed the door. They took strange little folders from out their breast pockets and waved them under my nose. They said, "No you're not Mrs Kelly. You're Eilishe Flynn. We," they said, "are from the C.I.B."

And as though that were not enough, just to make it all the more and merrier, there was Andrew Michael Kelly stepping out from the bathroom clad in briefs and a towel around the neck, shaving lather all over the face and razor in hand. You never saw anything so conjugal in all your born days. As he came through the door he was asking, "What's going on here?"

What need to ask!

He saw the gentlemen in the grey felt hats and said, "O.K., you didn't waste much time did you? Right y'are, just give me time to get the tweeds on, well."

Down at Central Police Station there was my father, making a tremendous deal of everything, of course; rushing at Andy and having to be held back by three policemen, and all that sort of thing.

"This is getting us nowhere," said the tall detective, finally, and I gained the impression that he was a little sick and tired of my father. "So far, no charges have been laid. Now do you want to talk with your daughter or—"

"I will most certainly have him charged," shouted my father, making the fatal mistake of cutting short a police officer, "I won't be made a fool of—I hope I see him get three years for this."

"Have you seen her back?" asked Andy.

"No. Nor do I wish to see it. I refuse to discuss my sister's actions with you."

"That's convenient, then you don't have to do anything about it."

"Her Aunt felt she should discipline her."

"Discipline!" Andy laughed. "There's a difference between scratching your arse and tearing yourself to pieces."

The big detective turned aside to hide his face but I could see the smile around his mouth, and I knew, now, that his sympathies were with us. He turned to my father and said, "You know, I don't think you've got a chance of seeing this kid in jail. The way things are these days, I'd be very surprised if he got anything worse than a bond."

"I don't require legal advice," yelled my father, "I will do all in my power to see that he goes to jail."

I began to weep.

"I said I was eighteen," I said, "and he begged to marry me."

Andy came across to me and began to wipe my eyes. "Don't worry," he murmured, "just let piss-importance here keep talking, and within another five minutes our problems will be over."

"Whether you require legal advice or not," said the big detective, in a not very good imitation of my father's tone, "I'm giving you some, and," he lapsed back into his normal manner, and very menacing it sounded, I don't mind saying, "if you've got any sense you'll shut up and listen. In the first place, you've no hope of putting this boy in jail. He has done the wrong thing, we know, but by your daughter's own admission she lied about her age, and she was more than willing to go with him. Also she was unhappy and beaten up and he tried to help her. Above and beyond all that is the fact that he is anxious to marry her. There's a war on you know. It takes a good bit to put a ship's engineer in jail these days. If there is a court case, there's going to be a lot of scandal come out. You're going to be asked why you weren't home looking after your daughter. I can tell you that much right now. Why don't you let them get married all right and legal, and then forget about the whole business?"

I thought my father would take a stroke. I thought he would explode. He did everything except foam at the mouth. Gone was the careful accent, gone the Johnsonian turn of phrase. His vocabulary ranged from Liverpool to the Australian outback— a glorious blending of waterfront, road gang, industrial suburb, University and shearing shed. And the upshot of it all was that, when he had shouted himself to a standstill and recovered a certain amount of sanity, all three of us caught the plane back to Melbourne and Andy and I were married three days later in St Augustine's church at the bottom end of Bourke Street, the parish church for seamen in all the Port of Melbourne.

It was a beautiful wedding with all the trimmings—confetti and rice and gladioli tied to the ends of the seats, and an organist to play Wagner's Wedding March as I came into the church, and Mendelssohn's as I went out, and all the relatives, hastily summoned and crowding into the church in their best clothes and thinking "This is a bit sudden", but, of course, being too tactful to say so—at least while they were actually at the wedding. I was married in the only rig possible for a woman of the Flynn clan, full bridal regalia, not one trapping of virginity overlooked, a bouffant white dress, yards of Limerick lace veiling, a wreath of orange blossom round my head and thirty-six gardenias in my hand.

"Do you think," suggested Andy, "that for the benefit of sceptics you should wheel a barrow-load of lilies down the aisle?"

Lachy McLaughlin, when the *Vale of Clydd* arrived in Sydney, had been greeted by a telegram which said, "Come back to Melbourne and be my best man." This presented difficulties, for Andy had borrowed all the spare money in the ship to take me to Sydney. However, Sparks was found to have a few pounds put by which he was glad to lend in such an emergency. So there was the Pride of the Clyde, the very picture of a perplexed Wee Free doing the right thing by his benighted Irish friend. As a matter of fact the groom had, for many years, confined religious observance to barracking for Celtic football team, but what is bred in the bone comes out in the flesh and he acquitted himself very well. But Lachy! poor brave chap, there he stood like a Covenanter amidst a College of Cardinals. Had he suddenly curdled the blood of all present with a yell of 'Jesus, and no quarter' I would never have been surprised. But he stuck it out. He won through amidst hazards and embarrassments that would have caused trauma in one of a lesser breed. He didn't know when to kneel and he didn't know when to stand; so Andy had to bear him to his knees and haul him off them again at all the appropriate times. He dropped the ring, of course, and had to crawl round looking for it under the legs of all the friends and relations. But his worst moment came at the blessing of the silver and the ring. A small gilt salver was held before him. He looked at it in despair. He looked at the priest. The priest told him what he must do, at which he slapped all his pockets in an agony of embarrassment and, at last, hauled forth a sorry little collection of threepences and one sixpence, gasping as he did so, "Two and nine, it's all I have on me, will it do?"

That is what he said. I have no hope of letting you know how he sounded for I know of no phonetic system that will reproduce broad Clydeside, spoken at its broadest, by a man too far gone in nerves and confusion to remember the English tongue.

It was the priest's turn to look startled. However, he must have decided that Lachy was neither blaspheming nor suddenly gone mad, for he blessed the ring and Andy put it on my hand and kissed me—very bashfully and tenderly he kissed me, too, before all those people, and half of them must have known that he had already carried me off to Sydney out of hand.

Then it was over and we went into the sacristy to sign the book and you would have thought that would be an end of Lachy's troubles. Far from it. We came out of the sacristy, we knelt once more at the altar before turning to walk out of the church, and that last quick genuflection caught the poor heretical hero, walking behind us and expecting no such thing. He was taken off balance with one foot stepping forward, and he flew straight across my head as though I had applied a football tackle. All my younger friends and cousins were already weak with laughter. They looked at Lachy with affection. He had given them a morning of pure and heart-warming enjoyment. Lachy, safely out on the church steps, dusted his knees and looked across at Andy.

"Don't get married every week," he warned, "I couldn't live through it. It's as well my old granny didn't see me, bobbing and scraping and bowing down in the House of Rimmon, and ending up with a wee bit leapfrog to crown it all."

"Ah, you porridge-eating Presbyterian bastard," said Andy, "we couldn't think of getting married without you."

We had a reception with a four-tiered cake, and lobster and champagne and speeches and dancing, and my brother's friend Kenny McMaster strutting round the bridal table playing "Cock of the North" and the "Eriskay love-song" and "Haste to the Wedding" on his bagpipes. We had a canteen of cutlery from captain, officers and crew of the *Vale of Clydd*, a cheque for £25 from Aunts Margaret and Tess, a pigskin overnight bag from my mother, a travelling rug from my father, a cut glass decanter from Phyl, and all the usual cake stands and toast racks, and, standing amongst them, giving the complete war-time wedding touch, was a foot-high, bubble-shaped bottle of real American bath salts. It was a glorious thing with its pink ribbon and gilded stopper and label which read 'Crêpe Myrtle for all the romance and fragrance of the Old South'. It was the gift of Andy's old friend Roger Melançon, of the s.s. *Sam Tweed*, who had heard of the wedding at the last moment, and had just had time to change his clothes, seize the bath salts from his large supply of Seduction Stores, and dash to the church in a taxi.

I had a going-away frock of blue angora and paler blue accessories—this was considered very chic—and when we drove away to spend twenty-four hours' honeymoon Kenny McMaster stood on the pavement and played "Will ye no come back again", a song which makes me cry at the best of times, and which now broke me up to such an extent that I leaned from the cab window calling, "I love you all."

And so I did. My heart went out to every single one of them. My mother, my father, my grand-aunt Norah Ward with the tears streaming down her handsome, fierce old tinker face, and a terrible old hat dragged down over her frizzy tinker hair, the Pride of the Clyde, standing with his arm round Phyl, who was laughing and crying and waving all at once, my brother and three fifteen-year-old admirers of mine (Kevin O'Shea, Johnny O'Dougherty and Angus McMaster), several aunts to whom I bore a lifelong grudge, and a couple of cousins whom, at normal times, I hated with good, solid adolescent hatred.

Right there and then, I loved them all.

I put my hat down on the bed and looked round the room where we were to spend our wedding night.

"Well," I said, "I did it."

"You did what, lovely?"

"I got myself a husband before I was seventeen."

"Did you set yourself your seventeenth birthday for a deadline?"

"No, but I did want to marry very young. I wanted to show them all that I could get someone to want me. You do love me, don't you, Andy?"

"You know I love you."

"Well I can't believe it, that's all. I used to think 'nobody will ever want me'."

"And I used to say that I'd marry the first virgin I met. I thought I was safe and set for the happy bachelor's life, and then I met you and here we are, well."

"Don't joke. Please be serious."

"All right, I'll be serious. I love you. Please trust me. I'm the one that should be asking all the time 'do you love me'. I'm going away to sea, leaving you behind in a town that's full of men on the loose, and, as you say, you've married very young. Too true you've married young. How can I know if you wanted me, or just wanted someone to care for you?"

I ran across to him and threw my arms around his neck. "Oh, darling," I assured him, "of course I want you. Never, never think that I don't. That's the greatest thing about it all. I've got *you*."

"You have indeed. God help you, you poor baby."

I awoke when the first daylight was turning the night to grey and found that my husband was sitting up in bed looking down at me with such pity, love and yearning as I had never before seen on a human being's face. When he saw that I was awake he took me by the wrist and said, "Now I must go away from you."

I lay there looking at him. I could say nothing. He repeated, "Darling, I must go."

I sat up and he took me by the hands.

"What time is it?" I asked.

"Nearly six o'clock."

"Time to go."

"Yes."

"No! Oh no!"

My voice came out in a great cry. I choked it back and forced myself to speak quietly. "It can't be."

"Have a cigarette."

"It can't be. Honeymoons are not so short as this."

"It won't be long before I'm back again."

"But yesterday we were so happy."

"Please, darling."

"But look, I'm still wearing my beautiful wedding night-gown."

I looked down, plucking at the loops of ribbon and lace around my shoulders.

"For God's sake, darling, have a smoke."

I grabbed at his arms, "Don't go, don't go," I said. I was clinging to him, my eyes peering madly into his face. "Don't go. We'll run away. Deserters manage to live. We'll manage somehow. We'll go to the country and hide. Or I'll go back to work and I'll hide you and feed you. I'll get money somehow. I'll steal it from drunks. I'll steal it from soldiers asleep in the park and on the railway station."

I jumped out of bed and began to drag on my clothes. "Come on, get dressed. We'll go out and eat and then I'll hide you. You'll do it because you love me, won't you, Andy? You'll do it to prove to me that you love me. You're all I've got. I never had anyone else in the world. If you go I'll know that you don't love me. But you will stay with me, won't you? You're going to jump ship to show me that you love me. I'll hate you if you don't. I'll know that you never really cared for me. But you do, don't you, Andy? You do love me?"

There was a knock on the door and a voice said, "Here's the tea you ordered for half past six."

Andy took the tray and brought it over and put it on the

dressing-table. He poured a cup and handed it to me. "Drink it," he said.

I drank with my teeth rattling against the edge of the cup. I said, "That's a pretty design on the tea-pot."

"Yes."

"Roses and fern."

"Yes, roses and fern."

"Pretty design on your cup too, Andy."

"Darling, get the rest of your clothes on. You're shivering. You'll feel better when you're warmer."

"Yes."

"And try and eat. Have some toast."

"Yes, some toast."

"Listen, Lisha, darling. Do me a favour. Don't come into the airways office with me. Let's say goodbye here and then I'll put you in a cab and send you home to your auntie."

"No, I must be with you as long as I can."

"All right well, I'll ring a cab to take us to the city."

In the taxi I said nothing and I thought of nothing. This was because I could not speak and I could not think. I sat, clinging to his arm, and I managed to nod when he asked me, again, "Do you want a smoke?"

Before he got on the bus to go to Essendon I was able to say, "Goodbye for now, darling. See you soon. I'm all right now. I'll write every day."

He bent and kissed me quickly, and got into the bus and it went straight away.

And that was how I said 'Chin up, Cheerio, Carry on' and all the rest of it—as gutless a performance as ever was seen in any war in any time or place. But, as I stood there on the pavement with people jostling against me as they hurried along to work, I gradually became aware of my grandmother's voice speaking to me. She had been dead and buried two years, but I heard her as clearly as though she stood beside me in the flesh and she said to me what she had always said when the going got rough :

"It's a poor heart that never rejoices, Lisha darling. Live horse and you'll get grass."

And, just as always, I decided that I could go on living a bit longer. So I dried the tears off my face, and powdered my nose, and went into a little sandwich shop and had eggs on toast and three cups of tea. Then, because I had the day off from work, I set off to find a flat where my love and I could be together when he came home from sea.

It took me a week of hard searching to find that flat, and it cost much more than I had, at first, intended to pay. But we live and learn and, as Phyl said, "It's worth a fiver a week extra just to get a landlady that minds her own business."

Phyl had taken a couple of days off work to go with me and give me support when interviewing householders, home owners and other mighty ones who had any sort of shelter they wished to let.

In the matter of minding her own business Mrs Phillips was perfect. She was wont to say that she was not one to pry into other people's affairs. She had worries enough of her own.

"I was married to a seaman," she told me. "He was no good. They never are. I'm sorry for you. It won't work. It never does. You're too young for one thing. It's all very romantic now. Just wait till he starts running around with women in foreign parts. I'll tell you what I'll do. I'll take ten shillings off the rent and if you like to sub-let the spare bedroom I don't mind. Why should I? It's you that's paying for the gas and electricity."

So I paid a week's rent and was given my key.

"I'm a great believer in everyone having their own entrance," said Mrs Phillips. "Nothing is worse than having tenants, and Lord knows who else, tiptoeing past your bedroom door at dead of night. That's why the whole place is sub-divided the way it is. You come in through the front, the Rosensteins have the side door, and I use the back."

This arrangement meant that on the ground floor I had a small, carpeted hall. All the doors that led out of it had been boarded over with varnished three-ply. The Rosensteins lived on the other side. Except for this ground level entry, my flat was on the top floor, which was built on two levels as in so many old Melbourne houses. From the first landing a small flight of about six steps led towards the back of the house. At the top of these steps was a space too small to be called a hall, and from it opened the kitchen, bathroom and a spare bedroom. From the top landing opened the lounge and the main bedroom. The whole flat was newly furnished in the bulging upholstery and shining veneer of the early forties. Both Phyl and I thought it very smart. In spite of these horrible trappings the top bedroom was a lovely room. It ran across the full width of the house, and had two long windows that opened on to a balcony and gave a wide view out over the St Kilda sea front and the long stretches of Port Phillip. Down to the left I could see the shooting gallery where we had first seen Andy and Lachy.

"This is wizard," said Phyl (who was now going with a R.A.F. Squadron Leader), "I'll give you a hand to move in tomorrow night."

So the next evening I moved in, assisted by Phyl and my brother and Angus McMaster. I had not nearly enough suitcases and we arrived, already helpless with laughter, with clothes thrown over our arms and shoes stuffed into string bags, and my books (of which I suddenly seemed to have an enormous supply) in a waterproof ground sheet which Mick said he had tied with absolutely untiable knots learned in the Boy Scouts. Be that as it may, they burst apart just as we were getting in the front door and it was left to good old devoted Angus to gather books from the four corners of the hall and lug them upstairs as best he could. We were all quite beside ourselves with the relief of having half a house to range around in and no adults about to get in the way. We stayed up till all hours rearranging the furniture and packing things away, and we ended up in the kitchen at well after midnight drinking coffee and eating poppy-seed bread, and talking about life.

"I suppose we've been a bit noisy," said Phyl when I was farewelling them at the front door, "I hope everything is all right. Wouldn't do to get notice the very first evening you moved in." Just to prove that they were the most considerate of visitors they tiptoed to the front gate shushing one another and fizzing with suppressed laughter every step of the way. Once safely on the pavement, they linked arms and went off into the night singing *"Alouette"*.

I need not have worried about Mrs Phillips. Good old Mrs Phillips! I will think of her with love for as long as I live. She was the world's perfect landlady. It is true that she did give us notice at least once every time Andy came home. This was just a little exercise in keeping the hateful men in their place, and was regarded as such by both parties. I have seen the pair of them, after a particularly virulent exchange of insults, sitting at her kitchen table eating mussels from the jar and reminiscing about the fun to be had at Blackpool at the height of the season. It is proof of the affection she developed for me that when she did pass on to the astral plane (as she called dying) she left in my sole care and charge the three grand-daughters of Precious Jade, the more robust of her two Siamese cats. The other, Precious Pearl, being a delicate type, had been 'fixed up' early in life, and oh how I wished that Precious Jade had been submitted to the same gruesome-sounding process. But that is to look ahead. In the meantime, here we were in the top-floor flat, and we stayed there all the war, and for a short while after.

"It's just what we want," wrote Andy, from Sydney. "Plenty of room, and don't worry about the rent. I can make it, and more, in one game of poker, if necessary."

For the first few days I was not lonely at all. On the nights that I was not teaching dancing I always seemed to have visitors. Phyl came one evening to show me the R.A.F. type. He was handsome and charming and witty and he walked with a limp because he had been wounded in the hip.

"I think I may marry him," Phyl told me, "but no need to mention it to Lachy, just in case I don't."

"Of course not," said I.

The next evening Mick and Angus came to see me again. We had more coffee and talk about life till the early hours of the morning. Angus was in particularly fine form, as I remember. Enjoying himself to the top of his bent. It was his sixteenth birthday and he laughed a good old Mid-Victorian hollow laugh when I wished him many happy returns. He was, he told us, in love with a married woman. She was only recently married and he had not had time to recover from it. He would, of course, but—" 'Men have died and worms have eaten them, but not for love'," quoted Mick, who was a terrible chap for egging on poor Angus when he was suffering an attack of the grand Celtic soul. Angus agreed with him. That was the way it was. Nothing for it but to drag out his miserable life as best he could. He supposed that, in a way, he was lucky. He had the agony over and done with early in life. No other woman would ever be able to hurt him and so on, and so on.

"Of course you're lucky," Mick agreed, with all the cruel frankness of an old and valued friend. "Now you don't have to compete any more. What if every sheila in the world just flatly refuses to have anything to do with you, what if you're left for dead at every party and in every dance hall! Why should you care? You don't want them anyway. And what's more, you can tell them so. 'You pack of bags,' you can say, 'I love another, so you can all go and strangle yourselves, or marry Yanks or dashing R.A.A.F. pilots and rear gunners, see if I care.' "

Mick helped himself to another apple strudel and nodded, wisely. "I tell you," he said, "this unrequited love business is the greatest lurk in the world. I intend to start suffering from it just as soon as I'm shaving three times a week."

Angus attempted another hollow laugh, but it is difficult to sound really hollow when you're awash with coffee and weighed down with the wares of the nearest Kosher pastry-cook, so he brightened up a little and I allowed him to brush my hair, which always cheered him up—in a miserable sort of way.

Next night I was all alone. I started out very cheerfully, keeping myself busy and listening to the wireless that I had borrowed from Angus. I made myself a salad and grilled a couple of chops. I had promised Aunt Margaret that I would eat properly and, so far, salads and grills were all that I could manage in the cooking line. I decided that I would probably be very tired of them indeed before I was through. Considering it, I thought I could probably knock up a fairly decent stew. Heaven knows I'd seen plenty of them bubbling on the stove and filling the winter air with their good warm smell.

("Why is it called lob-scouse, Grandma?"

"I suppose, darling, because you lob whatever you can lay your hand to straight into the pot.")

I looked at the stove and suddenly felt very lonely. I decided this would not do, so I cleared away the dishes and went off to wash my hair. I had a lot of very long hair and I was very proud of it. I used to wash it with castile soap once every five days, and then I would sit down and brush it dry. And this evening while I was sitting in front of the radiator, brushing away, I began to cry. Mrs Phillips came knocking on the door about five minutes later.

"What's this," she asked, "crying for that husband of yours?" I nodded.

"Don't worry about him. He'll be all right. Men can take care of themselves. You look about twelve with your hair around your shoulders like that. He should be shot for marrying a baby like you. Cradle snatching, that's all it is."

I said that my husband was himself only just turned twenty-two. That I had not been carried off by some lecherous, dirty old man. Mrs Phillips said no need to get haughty. All men were lecherous, dirty old men, as she, who had lived almost sixty years, could tell me. But at any rate, it was no use sitting up here crying my eyes out and mooning around over something that was not worth mooning around about. I might as well come down and have a cup of tea with her. She could do with some company. She was feeling depressed herself. Her psychic powers, of which there could be no doubt, whatever some people said, led her to believe that her son-in-law was talking about her again. Also, the Rosensteins were playing that dreary, morbid, classical music again. (The Rosensteins were playing Haydn, who surely wrote the healthiest, gayest and least neurotic music in all the world. However, each to his taste, and Mrs Phillips liked "In a Persian Market" and "Pale Hands I Love".)

So I went down and drank tea and was introduced to the two precious Siamese ladies, and heard all about Mrs Phillips' girlhood in England, and how she had gone to India long before the first world war and toured all the garrison towns—singing, dancing and helping with the magician's act. She had a lot of gear from India that I thought was beautiful. A great deal of Benares brass which was not much good and some handwoven rugs that really were beautiful, and on the mantelpiece, amongst all the photos, a temple gong, shining in its teak-wood stand. Beside it was a photo of Phillips himself, dressed for polo, and looking very British-in-1910.

"Fell dead on the polo field," said his loving widow. "What a relief it was! A shock, of course. But when the shock was over, a great relief."

She walked across to the photo and looked at it a while with God knows what long dead love and anguish re-awakened in her eyes. "Ah, well," she said, "I suppose he *was* handsome."

I thought it only fair to repay all these confidences with a few of my own. I was always very fond of telling all my business to people who were almost strangers. With relatives it was different, of course. Relatives you told nothing, and if they became too insistent you told them lies. So I told Mrs Phillips about my early childhood in Port Melbourne when my grandmother had looked after me, and how my mother and father had gone to South Africa when I was so young that I could not remember what they looked like. They had intended to settle there but the awful word 'settle' must have unnerved them for, after a more than usually bitter round of fights, my father walked out and had an affair with a ballerina in a touring vaudeville show and my mother took a job with a big store in Capetown. A couple of months of this and my father lit out for New Zealand. It has never been made quite clear to me from whom he was in flight —my mother or the ballerina. I doubt if my father himself was very sure. We heard nothing of him for years. My mother always sent presents on birthdays and at Christmas and Easter, and, regularly, she wrote her letters bemoaning the fact that she was not with her babies.

I can see her now, sweeping like a film star, beautifully made-up, beautifully perfumed, beautifully groomed, into all the misery and upheaval that followed my grandmother's death. At last she had her babies. Well, the elder baby was a very skinny fifteen-year-old who had but recently achieved puberty and was doing it the hard way—pimples, tantrums and the lot. The younger baby was not quite so horrifying, being at a better age, but both of them were the very devil of a problem. So after the fight with my father she decided that Michael could stay on with the aunts and I could go and stay for a few days at her hotel. She told all her friends there that she was going to send me, as a boarder, to one of our most select convents. The mere name caused my head to spin. It was exclusive in the extreme. Only the daughters of the very wealthiest pub-keepers went there. I thought I would be sadly out of my social depth. When the day came to buy my school uniform I found I was wearing that of a much less aristocratic establishment, and that I was not going to board there, at any rate. I was going to attend as a day pupil, and I was to live round the corner in the St Celestine's Hostel for Unemployed Catholic Girls—to give it its full title. By all that's holy you should have seen the Unemployed Catholic

Girls. Most of them, as a matter of fact, were working, this being late 1940 (St Celestine's had opened in 1930), but the ones who were too old to work, the halt, the blind, the senile, the lame and the deserted, they were everywhere—breaking my heart with pity, striking ice-cold fear to my very marrow.

There was one old woman who still comes about me in my dreams. She was about seventy, with a fine handsome face and big dark eyes. She stood in the hall all day with a small suitcase beside her, and to everyone that passed she held out her hand and said, "I know your face. I've seen you somewhere before. Where have I met you before? O'Connor is my name, Eileen O'Connor. Look, my dear, I wonder if you would step to the gate and see if my taxi has arrived. I'm going away to stay with my youngest sister. My family just insist. She's sending a taxi for me. It should have been here long ago. I can't think what has happened. I can't stay in this place. I must get out of this place. I can't think how I got here in the first place."

She had got there because her brothers and sisters had put her there. Her parents had died and left her the eldest of a large family. She had never married, although, in her day, she must have been one of the best-looking women in the city of Melbourne. She had devoted herself to raising her brothers and sisters, and all the boys won C.B.C. scholarships and did well, and all the girls had married into families that were fairly bristling with lawyers, priests and S.P. bookmakers. Then poor Eileen had been worn out; completely worn away with worry and work and responsibility. Very quietly and gradually, she went out of her mind. Her memory went. She was an embarrassment to her brothers and sisters in their big homes, and before the friends they were anxious to impress. So they put her in St Celestine's, and that was her life—to stand all day, every day, in the hall, holding out her trembling old hands : "O'Connor's my name. O'Connor's my name."

One of her brothers came every week. He was grave, fleshy, very well dressed. He paid her board and asked if there were anything else she needed. He shook his head sadly. He never came in to see her. Only once while I was there did she have a visit from her sister. I think it must have been the baby sister, her pride and joy, the one who had made the best marriage of all. She was plump and grey-haired with not one atom of the distinction that marked her sister. She stepped from the big black car and positively ran through the gate; scurrying with fear lest someone see her, lest somebody passing recognise her despite the fur pulled up around her chin and the heavy veil on her hat. Somebody might say, "I saw the wealthy Mrs O'Kane (or Murname, or Kennedy, or whatever her Mick-on-the-make name was), I saw her going into a home for the deserted and poor. Who does she know that's poor?"

She stayed about five minutes. The chauffeur drove the car twice around the block and then waited a few doors down the street. Very soon she was bustling out again. She stood near the front door talking to Sister Rina. Her face was pink and crumpled up with shame and annoyance. She was thrusting some packets into Sister Rina's arms—chocolates, a pot of home-made jam, some flowers (they were white chrysanthemums) in a paper cone. "She must be made to understand," she kept on saying. "She must be *made* to understand. She must understand. She *must....*"

When she had gone Sister Rina stood a moment bowed against the door, her hand on the latch. Then she lifted her head and for one moment her face was terrible to see, haggard and hopeless. Then she sighed and went across and put the flowers at the feet of St Philomena who stood, everlastingly smiling away in the general direction of Heaven, on a small plaster pedestal in one corner. Farther down the hall another old woman was trying to make poor old O'Connor stay in her room. She stood barring the doorway with her powerless old arms, and saying, "Sit down, dear. Please sit down. Now you have a nice sit-down."

Soon after that it was tea-time, half past five. Miss O'Connor sat staring straight ahead. The obscene little pot of jam was perched there in front of her. She did not know it was there. She did not see it. She looked away across the dining-room to the windowless wall opposite, her eyes searching and searching and finding the blank wall. Her old friend beside her touched her arm, timidly.

"Eat some of your nice jam, Eileen." She picked it up and looked at the label. "Black cherry," she said, trying to put excitement and pleasure into her voice, "aren't you lucky to have black cherry jam? Let me spread you a little piece, dear."

118

Miss O'Connor shook her head. She drank a cup of tea and ate a piece of bread and butter that the other old woman put into her hand. Across the table, old Mrs Sullivan eyed the jam avidly. Mrs Sullivan was ancient and very greedy. She ate rapidly and messily, eyeing the rest of us to see that we were not getting ahead of her. If she thought we were, she would stretch out her hands, trembling with age and longing, and make a selection of what she thought best on the table. How they did it on the money we paid, God knows, but the nuns were amazingly kind to us. They tried to keep us in fruit. They baked us cakes. Mrs Sullivan was awful on cake nights, and I used to want to rise and thrust my food upon her, crying out like a sort of demented goddess of plenty, "Take it, Mrs Sullivan. Take all of it. Have my cake, have my banana, eat all the currant buns. You down at the end, there. You don't want your egg. Give it to Sully. Eat everything, Mrs Sullivan. Eat everything in sight and when you've finished I'll nick out to the fish and chip shop and get you something more, but please, Mrs Sullivan, please for God's sake, don't slobber any more stew down the front of your cardigan."

Miss O'Connor's friend would watch her, thoughtfully. She would say nothing but a fine vertical line would appear between her eyebrows. This evening she put the cover back on the jam and said, "We'll keep it then, Eileen, till you feel like having some." She gazed firmly at Mrs Sullivan. I drank a cup of tea and decided to go out and visit my brother. Miss O'Connor was plucking at the table-cloth and moving her head from side to side. "I must get out," she kept whispering, "I must get out."

Aunt Tess came back with me. She said she felt like the tram ride and a walk through the gardens. When we arrived at St Celestine's a little after ten o'clock they told us poor old O'Connor had been very bad all that evening. She was refusing to go to bed and, though she must have been completely exhausted, she was still in the hall. I had never seen her so distracted. At other times I had seen her wring her hands, or sometimes take a couple of quick turns up and down like a woman who is trying to bring herself under control. But, if she had lost her memory, she had not lost her courage, and the most heart-rending thing about her was the manner in which she would try not to make a scene, try to master her overwhelming fear and despair. Never had I seen her as she was that night. She was almost running at people, plucking them by the arm, grabbing at their hands. She was begging them, "Please help me. You have a kind face. I know you'll help me. I have to get away. I have to get away tonight. How did I get here? I should have been gone hours ago. They told me my sister was here today and she said I had to stay here. That's ridiculous, my sister would never say that. My sister would never say that."

When she saw me she became a little calmer. Perhaps she remembered that a dozen times a day I went out into the street to look for her taxi. I could not pass her by. She was the same physical type and had the same Dublin accent as my grandmother, and this put the final seal on my pity and horror. No, I could not pass her by. Now she held me by both hands. There were tears on her cheeks and her voice was worn to a whisper, but she was happy to see me. She even attempted a small joke. "You have cold hands, my dear. Cold hands, warm heart, they say. I'm sure, with such a warm heart, you won't mind stepping to the gate for me and looking for my taxi. They say my sister was here . . ."

On and on she went, looking into my eyes in an agony of pleading, while I stood there smiling politely, as though I were telling the time of day to a stranger. And inside myself I cried, "Oh God! Oh God! How can life be so cruel? How can it do this to a fine brave old girl who looks like my Gran? And, Oh God! what is to happen to me when my time comes?"

At last I managed to get free, and went off to look for the taxi. I came back and said it was coming in a minute.

"Do you want to see my bedroom?" I asked Aunt Tess.

Aunt Tess said she might as well, so we went on up the stairs and Aunt Tess sat on my bed for a while, thinking. Suddenly she looked up at me and I could see that she was being swept by one of her abrupt attacks of mercy and generosity. They were as violent and much more frequent than her sudden attacks of cruelty.

"You'll die of unhappiness if you stay here," she said. "Pack up your case and I'll take you home."

I only told the bare outline of all this to Mrs Phillips. I had a horror of being thought sorry for myself. In actual fact, of course, I had often been extremely sorry for myself, but since the day that Andy came into my life everything seemed to be shaping towards greater and greater happiness and I felt it would be ungrateful towards life to moan too much about what was over and done with, and could not be mended or changed. So I said now, "But I was very happy with my grandmother and I have been very happy since I met my husband."

"And I'm sure the both of you always will be very happy," said Mrs Phillips in so hearty a voice that I looked at her in surprise.

"I thought you didn't think much of marriage," I said.

My landlady raised her tea-cup to the photo on the mantelpiece. "Here's to you," she said to Phillips, "the greatest cad on the astral plane." Then she said to me, "If you've got that hair dry by now, run along and get some sleep, and don't worry. I shall concentrate some positive thought on that man of yours. Never, my dear, underestimate the power of positive thought."

The next day I received the last letter I would get from Andy for some time. The *Vale* had sailed. The brave old rust bucket was now limping across the Pacific and I would not hear from my husband again till he was in the States. Once I knew that he was at sea and in danger I found I could not bear to be by myself. I could not write to him without weeping and I had no hope of keeping the promise made to Aunt Margaret that I would eat properly. And not only did I moon in the manner so deplored by Mrs Phillips, but I even went out on the balcony and mooned while looking at the moonlit sea—a very foolish way to behave indeed. Finally I got into bed and cried till I was completely exhausted. I rose the next morning feeling as though I had a pickaxe driven through the top of the skull. I decided to ask Yvonne if she would like to come and stay with me.

Yvonne's full name was Yvonne Berner. She had come up to Melbourne from Gippsland at the beginning of the war. Both her parents were dead and Yvonne had been brought up by some sort of distant relative whom she called Aunt. Her mother had been a French war bride and had come from somewhere in Normandy, and that was about as much as Yvonne knew about her. Yvonne was very handsome in a big blonde fashion and most of the girls at work violently disapproved of her, but

I rather liked her. She was amusing, cheerful and tolerant, and when she did things like arriving late for work, dressed in an evening blouse and very tight skirt, and explaining to the boss, "I've just come from a party, Mr Bailey, I'm sorry I'm late", she drew the fire from me, for we worked in a prim little section and, to a lesser extent, I was disapproved of also. None of the girls had been very congratulatory about my marriage—with the exception of Yvonne. While all the rest were busy taking the 'marry in haste and repent at leisure' sort of attitude, Yvonne went out and bought me a great big orchid in a Cellophane box. She told the begrudgers that they were a mealy-mouthed pack of wowsers.

"You wouldn't marry this one and you wouldn't marry that one," she jeered at them. "Opportunity's a great thing, and that's something you all ought to remember."

Now, poor Yvonne was having great landlady trouble owing to the fact that she and a Yankee gob, by name of Frisco, had arrived at her apartment one wet and windy evening with a dozen bottles of beer in their arms. They had been met at the door by the landlady, who said there would be no liquor above stairs, and no Yankee sailors either, if it came to that. So what were Yvonne and Frisco to do? They solved their problem by retiring to the landlady's summerhouse-cum-toolshed and drinking their beer there. They had intended to do this with the utmost quiet and discretion, but by the time they had finished the dozen they were by no means so quiet as they had been before, though Frisco had become so enormously, so drunkenly, discreet that there was no holding him, and he carefully gathered up all the empties with the intention of hiding them farther down the street. This, of course, resulted in Frisco, as he tiptoed through the garden with terrific caution, tangling himself hopelessly in the wide legs of his trousers, and dropping every single one of the empty bottles with the most hideous din and uproar, right there in the middle of the landlady's nice little garden path. The landlady, who had been lurking in the ground-floor front all the evening, just awaiting such a golden opportunity to make herself unpleasant, was out like a shot. Yvonne was given instant notice. Frisco, stout fellow, waited in the hall till she had packed, and, before they left, they found one bottle that had escaped unbroken in the fall. They tied it to the door-knocker and went on their way. Since then Yvonne had been going to parties and staying the night, which, at best, is a precarious method of keeping a roof over the head. She was delighted to take my spare room.

It was a great comfort to have her. She went out almost every night and sometimes she did not come home at all but it was company just to have someone else living in the flat, and when she was in the mood she was an inspired cook. Then, of course, there were her love affairs. Reticence was a word unknown to Yvonne. She gave full details of all her men with such gusto, such frank enjoyment and amusement, that even Phyl, who did not like her much, would be obliged to laugh. "She's not refined," said Phyl, and, heaven knows, truer words were never spoken; but it was good to come home from work and find the flat not the silent well of aloneness that it used to be, but brightly lit and filled with the noise of the radio and the voice of Yvonne singing as she dressed to go out. Or even if I walked into silence and emptiness, it was reassuring and it gave me something to think about, and helped for a while to banish my own fears, to find, propped up on the kitchen table, a note which read :

Dear Kiddo,
 I've gone out with Frisco. I was supposed to meet Leroy, so if he comes looking for me stall him off with some story or another. If he hangs around like he always seems to do leave the kitchen door unlocked for a signal so that I'll know he's here and not come walking in right on top of the pest.
                                    Cheers for now,
                                         Yvonne.

My husband was at sea for my seventeenth birthday, which was in July. He arrived home about a month later, with a three-quarter length coat of silver musquash for a birthday present and still, he said, in heaps of time to have a party.

"So tomorrow," he said, "we start the celebration."

They arrived on the Friday night. There were dozens of them—half the crew of the old *Vale* with such girls as they had managed to pick up. They brought the liquor in newspaper parcels, in brown paper bags, in kitbags and seabags, and even just stuffed down the front of their shirts. There was Bourbon and Scotch, and Australian beer, and, leering away evilly in the middle of the kitchen table, several bottles of blackmarket Australian muscat which Lachy had bought in the spirit of experiment. I rushed out and rang Phyl and several friends and asked them to come round and relieve the terrible woman shortage. With glad cries of "a party", "sailors", "possibly even officers", "maybe Yanks", etc., they rushed for taxis, and, in due course, arrived. By that time the beer was flowing and a huge coffee-coloured stoker from an American ship had set up his radiogram and the strains of "Tuxedo Junction" filled the air.

The stoker's name was Calvin and when I was tired of dancing I would sit beside the radiogram and choose what records I wanted him to play. "Whatever you want, little lady," he would say. "You're the boss. It's your party."

He drank only soft drink because he belonged to the Nineteenth Congregation of the Children of the Kingdom; a sect which I confessed I had never heard of until that time, but whose members were, it seemed, very strong against hard liquor of any sort, and Alabama moonshine in particular. He was one of those lucky people so naturally euphoric and gay that he did not need alcohol anyway. The mere fact of being at a party was good enough for him. He danced, he sang, he gave imitations of every officer on his ship, he helped me with the food and he finished off the evening standing on the table singing spirituals. I can see him yet, his head thrown back dramatically, his face shining beneath the light, and the big, beautiful voice booming right up from the chest :

"Oh David was a shepherd boy
He killed Goliath and he shouted for joy.
Little David play on your harp, Hallelu' Hallelu'
Little David play on your harp . . ."

At two o'clock Phyl passed out, insisting that she was not drunk, it was just that poisonous muscat. We put her to sleep in Yvonne's bed. Yvonne had gone off with the second engineer from Calvin's ship, who said he wanted her to come and have a look at the photo of his dear old Mom, of whom she strongly reminded him.

At half past two the landlady came up and asked us to be a little quieter, and at three o'clock I went to bed and found that my pillow had a disturbing tendency to rise and revolve underneath my head. Then, to my horror, the whole foot of the bed rose, then dipped. This was followed by a similar motion at the bed head. Then slowly, sinisterly the whole mattress swung round bearing me with it. I sat up; the whole room gave a nauseating lurch and then was still. Slowly I climbed out of bed and rested both hands against the wall, whereupon the wall zigzagged in a manner that made my stomach zigzag along with it.

"This," I decided, "is extraordinary."

I climbed back into bed, where I propped myself in a sitting position with the pillows and went to sleep with my head on my knees.

"Sometimes I feel like a motherless child
A long way from home,
A long, long way from home."

The voice roused me about ten o'clock Saturday morning. I found that I had slipped from my sitting position in the night and that all the pillows and half the blankets were gone. Lifting my head very carefully I peered across Andy's body and saw that Long Jack Kelly (no relation, praise be to God) and a blonde called Claudette were sound asleep in the middle of the floor. They had the missing bedding.

I tried to rouse my husband, gave it up as a hopeless job, and went out to investigate. There on the landing, fully dressed, with one bridge coat under him and one over him, lay Specky Naughton. He was sleeping peacefully as a child, impervious to the cold of the Melbourne August. As I went past he opened one eye and requested that I shut up that bloody Pullman Sam. He added, "Tell him that I am also a motherless child and very far from home. Far, far from home and forlorn and famished and I'd like some coffee."

He closed the eye as though in pain. I went carefully downstairs, one hand on the banisters and one on my head, and there at the bathroom door stood the Alabama Abstainer. He was wielding a mop. He paused in his work long enough to bid me an old Southern 'Good morning, ma'am' and to remark, "Some poor sinner was awful sick all over the bathroom floor last night."

"Some cockeyed bastard couldn't aim straight, that's the trouble," said Andy, coming down behind me. "Was it you, Gringo?"

He leaned over the side of the bath where another inmate of the engine room slumbered with his hands folded across his chest. The Mexican was too far gone to remember any English. He muttered something in his own dialect which we took to be an indignant denial, and slumbered on. Calvin led us out to the kitchen, assuring me that all I needed was a cup of hot coffee. And I did feel better after the coffee. My backbone still felt as though it could not hold up my shoulders, and my neck felt as though it could not hold up my head, but at least I could keep both eyes open at once. Previous to the coffee I had been obliged to open one eye at a time, and as soon as I got the left one open the right one shut and vice versa. It had been very alarming and I was relieved to find them returning to more normal behaviour. Indeed, after some more coffee and rolls I felt quite cheerful and well, apart from a most terrible thirst. And the more I drank to relieve this thirst, the more full of well-being I felt.

"Strange, isn't it?" I asked Andy.

"Not at all," he said, and smiled at me across the top of a mug of coffee.

"What's amusing you?"

"Nothing, sweetheart."

Calvin carried on with his rescue work. He unrolled Lachy McLaughlin from the hall carpet, and took breakfast to Phyl and yet another blonde who had curled up and slept on the end of her bed. Phyl said she was dying but the other assured her, "You'll be all right, love. I've been like that many and many a time."

Once Calvin was satisfied that they were getting their breakfast down with a fair chance of keeping it down, he came and joined us for more coffee and we were quite a happy, if dishevelled, party when someone whose name I never knew (I'd never seen him before and I have certainly never seen him since) uncurled himself from the sofa in the lounge. He came into the kitchen, rubbing his eyes and scratching his face. He looked at Calvin and said, "A man who never drinks is always well."

I cannot describe the loathing in his voice as he delivered this tribute to the temperance movement. He then said that if he did not have a hair of the dog that bit him he would certainly die. Lachy said it was a good idea, and so did Andy, and I had a small beer to show I could kick on with the best of them.

The day wore away quickly. What with cooking breakfast in relays for the various guests as they struggled out to face their hangovers, and bracing them with small snorts to pull them together again, and pressing the clothes of those who had slept in full rig, we found it was three in the afternoon before we'd had time to turn round. Then someone said, "Let's all go to the Chow's for a meal."

So off we went—two taxi-loads of us.

There was a certain amount of excitement in the Chinese café because an American entered and asked of Calvin in a scornful drawl, "Say, where's the Jim Crow in this dive?"

Andy promptly offered to fight him.

"Man, just ignore the poor unfortunate sinner," advised Calvin, placidly.

Then who should we meet but two Scotsmen and a Taffy. The Taffy had once sailed with Andy, and the Scotsmen were his friends. They had the liquor, they said, but nowhere to drink it. That was easily settled, we decided, they must come home with us. They did indeed have the liquor—a large kitbag full of it. The Scots were called Big Jock and Wee Jock and the Welshman was just Taffy. We drove back to the sly grog where Lachy had bought the muscat and there they let us have a couple of dozen bottles of beer, provided we took three bottles of their special banana cocktail.

"Somebody may get drunk enough to try it," said Andy hopefully.

Taffy, who had been keeping nit at the corner during the bartering, returned with a scandalous-looking red-head on his arm. "Gloria is coming to the party too," he announced.

So we piled Gloria in on top of Taffy's knees and the beer in the boot and off we set. When we got home we found Yvonne awaiting us with two new Americans.

"Did Gilmer show you the photo of his dear old Mom?" I asked.

127

"Don't mention that louse to me," said Yvonne.

Feeling a little frayed around the edges, I went and ran myself a boiling hot bath with bath salts and the works. I even used up all that was left of my Crêpe Myrtle Bubble Foam. I felt I was going to need it. Andy brought me in a glass of champagne. "From my special secret bottle," he said. "I'm keeping it for my own dear Judy. How do you feel?"

"I'm fine," I said, "I just need a good long soak in a good hot bath."

"Don't be too long, well," said Andy, "Gringo may get sleepy again."

When I came out the radiogram was going full blast once again, and Phyl was dancing with one of Yvonne's Yankees.

"I'll put that bitch on her arse," Yvonne told me.

It was later in the evening, when Phyl was singing St Louis Blues (as sooner or later she always did at parties), that there was a frantic ringing on the front door bell. We rushed to open up and were confronted by a tall Australian soldier with a look of stark terror on his face.

"Hide me, hide me," he begged, "the wife's mother is chasing me."

"Say no more," we said, and locked him in the cupboard under the stairs.

We were only just in time. Two seconds later his mother-in-law appeared.

"Where's Herbie?" she asked.

We shook our heads. We didn't know.

"Well there's his hat," she said, and pointed to where a slouch hat lay on the floor making liars of us all.

She read the VX number inside the crown. "That's Herb," she said, "now where is he?"

We shook our heads again, and she departed, swearing to get the police.

"If I can't find Herb," she said, "at least I can stop the din that's been going on here for the last twenty-four hours."

Shortly after midnight the landlady arrived, with the same laudable intention. She made her entrance just when Lachy was standing on the table leading a few choruses of what he termed 'latter-day sea chanties'.

"Lower away the gallant tops'l and the good ship rides
merrily,
Lower away the gallant mizzenmast and the good ship
rides free.
Every good ship has a mizzenmast . . ."

For the benefit of those who do not know this forecastle master-
piece I must mention that, in its entirety, it is enough to stop
any landlady dead in her tracks. When our landlady got back
her breath she gave us all twenty-four hours' notice.

Herbie had stayed on to join the revels. One of the Americans was teaching him to jive. He had taken off his heavy army
boots to give his feet added flexibility. The last thing I remember he was crawling round the floor murmuring, "I know I
shed the old footwear somewhere along the line."

When I woke up next morning I found that we were now
four to a bed. I thought this a bit much, and I crawled carefully
over Yvonne and her Yankee and went into the bathroom and
was horribly sick. When Lachy had fortified me with a whisky
I felt I could face some of Calvin's coffee. I felt strangely sober
all that Sunday—sober and very cold, and inclined to shiver.
Everyone seemed to be speaking to me in a very clear voice
from a very long way away, and every now and then I thought
I saw lights floating near the corners of my eyes. When I turned
my head the lights had gone, but it was an eerie sensation.

Nobody seemed to worry about food that day and the radiogram blared on and on unceasingly. Calvin begged me to get
some more sleep but I did not want to sleep. I felt strange and
very frightened. About four in the afternoon I called my husband to me.

"Andy," I said, "don't say anything. I don't want to frighten
anyone, but do you know that the devil is on the stairs?"

"What!"

I realised that Andy was looking at me very queerly and I
made elaborate gestures to indicate that it was a solemn secret.

"Yes," I said, "he's coming to get us for being so wicked as
to sleep together before we were married. Oh look!" I jumped
out of my chair and clung to Andy's hands, "look, can't you see
his horns poking around the door?"

Andy took me in his arms and held my body close against the warmth of his. I felt great comfort.

"Oh, Andy," I wept, "I'm so cold and so frightened."

"Hush, honey, it's all right. It's all my fault, Lisha. I forgot you're a bit young for three-day parties. Come on now, we'll go out and get a cab and we'll find a chemist and get you a sedative. Then I'll wrap you up warm in bed and when you wake up you'll be O.K."

The chemist was a little terse at having his emergency bell rung on a Sunday afternoon.

"My wife's in the rats," said the boy from Liverpool. "Is not that emergency enough?"

I do not know what the chemist gave me but I fell asleep almost as soon as I was tucked in the blankets.

The party, I am told, finished at about midnight when even the banana cocktail was gone. Yvonne and Phyl did come to blows and the honours went to Yvonne. Lachy and one of Yvonne's Yankees also came to blows because the Yank called Lachy a goddam limey, and, when asked to define the word limey he said "English" and Lachy's rage was terrible to see. He came down like a charge of the clans at Culloden (I'm giving you his own description) and he carried all before him. Shouts of "not a drop of English blood in my body" rent the air, and when it was all over the Yankee and a friend who had unwisely gone to his assistance lay stretched on the lounge room floor.

Calvin and Gloria had a long talk about the Nineteenth Congregation of the Children of the Kingdom, and Gloria got salvation, which annoyed Taffy terribly.

"All that good grog wasted," he remarked.

Herb's wife came knocking on the door, and they had the big reconciliation in our hall and departed arm in arm.

I saw none of this. I slept on while Andy sat beside me and held my hand.

When Andy arrived back home from the next trip we came very near to having our first big quarrel. He had been gone only a matter of weeks, because the old *Vale* had gone a short run across to New Zealand. But I'd had plenty of time to find out for sure that I was pregnant. I met my husband with this glad news and he was not glad at all.

"This," he said, "ruins everything. I didn't want kids. I only wanted you. We should have been more careful. That's blasted parties for you."

"Didn't you ever want children?"

I was astounded.

"Not until you grew up."

I had been delighted. I had some hazy idea that a baby was like a big warm doll that you spent all your time cuddling and dressing in pretty clothes and taking for walks in a beautiful imported pram so that all the neighbours could see and admire. Yvonne, also, was delighted. Big, kind-hearted Yvonne, from somewhere in her industrious Norman ancestry she had inherited great wizardry with the knitting-needles, and now she was teaching me. Already I had finished one small singlet (it was longer at the back than at the front) and the world's smallest bootee. Andy refused to look at them. He had brought me back a lovely close-fitting dress of flame-coloured silk.

"Put it on," he ordered, "while you have some figure left and we'll go out dancing."

We went to dinner at Mario's and then on to the Embassy, and all the evening he refused to discuss Andrew junior; but that night as we lay in bed with his head against my shoulder, he suddenly burst out:

"Oh, darling, you're only a baby yourself and you're only about a hand's span round the hips. Having a baby is a hell of a business. I'm frightened."

I comforted him. "Don't be frightened. I never felt better in my life."

But after his ship had sailed I felt ill for the first time. My back ached and my legs felt strange, and I consulted Yvonne.

"Do you think it's possible I just missed a month?" I asked. "Because this month I seem to be back to normal—except that I don't feel normal. I feel terrible."

"That's nothing," Yvonne reassured me, "one of my aunts was always like that. Regular as clockwork every month, just as though she wasn't carrying. You'll have to rest up."

The doctor said the same thing. "Go to bed and keep your feet up on a couple of pillows and we may be able to save the baby. If you aren't better in a couple of days or if you feel any worse, call me straight away."

I resolved not to call him. He seemed all too anxious to put me in hospital for a curettage, and I was determined no one was going to take my baby from me. For the same reason I would not let Yvonne get in touch with my mother. Andy had paid off the old *Vale* because she was going back to England. He was now on an American tanker, earning five times the money and, though I didn't know it, running five times the risk. I wrote him a letter telling him how fine I felt. I calculated that it would reach him in Fremantle and cheer him on his way as they set out on the long weary voyage to the Cape and then up through the South Atlantic and on to Galveston. For a week I lay in bed feeling the pains in my back and my legs grow worse till I could scarcely totter between the bed and the bathroom.

"I'll lie here till the nine months are up, if necessary," I told Yvonne.

I thought in my poor child's mind that if only I could keep my baby it must live. How could I know that it would die inside my body? But that was what happened. It was late at night that Yvonne woke and found me delirious. She rang an ambulance, and they took me to hospital, dangerously ill with blood poisoning. My baby, that had been dead for days, was taken away. Mother wired Andy and, somehow, he got a plane priority and flew back from Fremantle. But I did not know him. I knew nobody. I lay in my bed and beat with my hands upon the covers, and sang lullabies and nursery rhymes and popular songs all mixed up together, and finally the new and wonderful sulphanilamide did its work, and after three days I fell asleep and woke up cool and sane again—and there was Andy sitting beside my bed. He looked very thin and he had not shaved for days. I could only look at him and smile, and fall asleep again. But when I awoke once more he was still there and I whispered to him, "Andy, will I live?"

He nodded. "Yes, darling, you'll soon be well again now," he said.

I looked down from his face to the edge of the bed where his hand gripped mine. As on that first evening, when he had put his hand under my forearm, I felt the vitality flowing out of it and into my own body.

"Oh, Andy, darling," I whispered, contentedly, "you are so strong."

Andy put his face down on my hand and began to cry.

I stayed in hospital almost a month and I was pitifully weepy and hysterical for a long time after I came out. Andy was distraught trying to comfort me but he would not let me have another baby.

"Tell you what, woman," he said, "I'll buy you a diamond watch instead."

It was a very beautiful watch; but we lost it twice at poker and the second time we never got it back.

I remember, very well, the first time we lost it.

I lay in bed listening to the men playing poker in the next room. I had no desire to sleep. I only wanted to lie there in the dark and feel happy and secure for a little while, with my husband back home for one week in which I could hold him in my arms and know that he was safe, and pretend that there were no such things as Japanese minefields and submarines.

I listened to his voice. It flowed over me in a warm reassuring wave, soft with the unmistakable softness of the Irish, but it was not quite Irish and it was not quite true Liverpool, for his mother came from Kerry and some of her accent still remained to make beauty in the voice of her eldest son, and sometimes there came the clear precise edging of a word that was Scottish (eight years amongst the engineers), sometimes the rippling singing speech that came from his Gaelic-speaking grandmother. He told me about her one night when we lay together in the warm defenceless peace that follows love-making—which was about the only time that he would ever speak of himself or the people and things that had gone to make him.

("My old granny, when she was going on for eighty she had a fall and broke her hip. She got better from it, but afterwards she just dropped about fifty years. You couldn't say she was senile. She was a young woman in her twenties just setting out for England, and not a word of English did she speak. She'd sit in the doorway nattering away in Gaelic to all that passed. She was an O'Sullivan from the Blaskets and one day she got into a right royal set-to with an O'Flaherty from Ventry Bay. Something about fishing rights, it was. None of us kids could understand a word but my mother remembered quite a bit when she had to, and it's surprising the Gaelic speakers there are who still come to Liverpool on the ships. I was always glad that the poor old lady could find some of her own to talk with in the last few days she had. She'd been a brave old girl all her life, and then on the evening she died she suddenly looked at me and she spoke in English. She said, 'Still, Sean O Duibhir a' Ghleanna, We were worsted in the game.' ")

It was easy to distinguish voice from voice in that company—Long Jack Kelly, also from Liverpool, Jock from the Western Isles, and Speckie Westcott who had grown his first crop of freckles in the old whaling port of New Bedford—brought together by the sea and the war, playing poker in a Melbourne flat. What do sailors talk about? Ships in port, women at sea.

"It's women all the time, if you ask me," I thought as I caught the drift of Long Jack's conversation. I grinned in the dark. "By rights," I thought, "I should pull the pillows over my head."

Andy was becoming increasingly conscious of his status as husband and my dignity as the little wife, and here was Long Jack, the acknowledged wit of the firemen's mess, reminiscing about the first time. According to Long Jack it was an occasion overrated both in prose and poetry and had been accompanied in his case by haste, discomfort, bad weather, expense and dire medical consequences.

"What do you expect for ten shillings on Friday night?" asked Andy the realist.

"Ten shillings was not bad at all in those days," Long Jack defended himself, "and it was a lot for a deck boy. I did expect more than the oldest and ugliest whore in Liverpool, and nowhere to go but some bit of a yard behind a greengrocer's shop and it filled with putrid bananas and rotting cabbage leaves and awash with three days' rain."

"Aye, a back yard is rough," agreed Andy.

"I wasn't expecting the pneumonia," said Long Jack, plaintively. Then, more philosophically, "As for the other, well nine times to make a sailor."

"Sure is bad luck," said the Yank sympathetically.

"It sure is bad management," said Jock.

"Be careful how you talk," said Andy. "Maybe Lisha's still awake. Lisha, woman, are you awake?" He raised his voice.

134

I made no answer.

"Be careful you don't wake her up," said Andy.

I snuggled back against the pillows and put my hands behind my head.

Never marry a gambling man, and never marry young. How many people had told me this? And I had done both.

"And yet," I thought, "I'm happy. I'm very happy—" and then the thought that I didn't want to think came pushing into my mind: "except for the parting; the parting gets worse every time."

("No weeping on the wharf now, Lisha. It's the one thing I can't stand."

"Goodbye, darling, bring back lots of presents from the States."

"That's my Judy.")

I held up my arm and watched the cool sparkle of the diamonds on my lovely little wrist-watch from Tiffany's, my best States-side present of them all so far. It was vulgar with diamonds. Even in the dim light that came from the open doorway it was a mightily flamboyant little watch.

The door swung farther open and Andy came in and went across to the wardrobe. He felt in all the pockets of the new Yankee gabardine suit and then came across to the dressing-table, where he started rummaging through drawers.

I judged that by now I could safely wake up.

"What do you want?" I yawned, as though emerging from the deepest sleep.

My husband stood looking down at me, his hands in his pockets, his head thrust slightly forward, one rumpled lock of reddish-brown hair falling into his eyes.

I knew that stance well. It meant that Andy was worrying about something—usually money.

"Are you looking for your wallet?" I asked.

Andy grinned at me. "That's my clever little wife," he said.

"It's in my bag. You gave it to me to mind when we were in town this afternoon."

"How are we holding?" he asked, standing with the wallet in his hand.

"We're holding all right—thirty pounds and two pawn tickets. We're never going to see another poor day. Now go and lose the rest of the family fortune and let your poor little wife get some sleep."

But I did not sleep straight away. I lay in the same position, arms behind my head.

"Fowl one day, feathers the next," my mother would say, "if you marry a gambling man."

"Streak of fat, streak of lean," Andy would say.

Well, apparently tonight was a lean streak, but we'd had our share of the fat, too. The fur coat and the party for my seventeenth birthday—they had represented the better part of £100 won in a two-up school. My pigskin dressing case with the silver topped cosmetic bottles (at the moment in hock)—poker in San Francisco. My snake-skin shoes with bag and gloves to match—pontoon in New Orleans. I smiled in the darkness. Streak of fat, streak of lean suited me very well. Only sometimes I thought, "It would be nice if I could try again for a baby."

"What for do you want a baby?" he would ask. "At least wait till after the war. Now any day maybe I'll get the hammer and what would you do then if you had a kid to keep?"

And he brought me home a big Spanish doll from the Argentine—a doll with six silk petticoats and a mantilla of hand-made lace.

"There you are," he said, setting the lovely useless thing on the bed amongst all the other impedimenta of the sailor's return, the flowers, the boxes of candy, the half-unwrapped parcels and the two bottles of Bourbon, "there now, isn't that better than a little wet-backsided baby?"

I smiled at him. "After the war," I said. "You promised. After the war."

After the war! Perhaps that would never be.

"Holy Mother of God, don't let me think of that. Don't let me think of that."

From the next room came the sound of bottles clinking against glasses and Long Jack began to sing softly to himself. Andy had trusted his luck far enough. Now he was bringing out the drinks. He himself drank very little when gambling, and he could rely on most of his opponents to drink a great deal.

"We'll start to win now," I thought. "Maybe there'll be a fight, but we'll start to win."

Turning on my side I fell asleep. I was awakened about an hour later by my husband shaking my shoulder.

"Lisha," he was saying, "I want that wrist-watch I gave you."

I sat bolt upright.

"I will not," I said, "it's bad enough losing everything else in the house without taking my jewellery from me."

"Who gave it to you?"

"You've got all a second engineer's wages to waste. Isn't that enough?"

"Give me that watch."

"Give you my watch and keep you for the rest of the time you're ashore. I suppose that will be it. What would you do if your wife didn't work?"

"Damn all work it is, teaching idiots how to jitterbug with Yanks. Are you giving me the watch—well?"

"You're drunk!"

Andy put one hand hard against my naked breasts and with the other he took a firm hold of the big wave of hair that fell over my right eye.

"Give me the watch," he said, "or I'll knock you right out from underneath that peroxided cockatoo's crest."

I gave him the watch and hurled a pillow after him which knocked the door and slammed it shut. Then I pulled the other pillow over my head and cried myself to sleep, and as I cried I raged to myself:

"The swine. I'll leave him first thing in the morning. Why should he ruin my life? What future is there for any girl married to a seaman—never knowing if they're alive or dead—never knowing how they're behaving. They're no good, and he's the worst of them all, with his gambling and drinking and threatening to beat me up. Him with his bad temper and his brawls—look at his nose! Smashed in two places and he's not yet twenty-five. Fine sight he'll look when it's broken in a couple more spots. He won't think he looks so wonderful then, with his muscles and his red hair. If I had a little boy I'd like him to have hair that colour. I'll leave the brute in the morning. I won't stay with him to waste the rest of my life. Maybe if the boy did have red hair it would fall down in one big lock across the forehead. Like father like son. Hair like that looks good under an engineer's cap. There's his cap hanging on the top of the mirror. Funny how the big full-length looking-glass reflects nearly all the room. If I were staying I'd move it over to opposite the windows and then it would reflect some of the sky on a clear day. Lovely to wake on a bright morning with the windows filled with light on one side of you, and the mirror filled with sunshine on the other. I love that mirror. I love the way it swings and tilts in its old rosewood stand, and the way the frame is finished off with the true lovers' knot carved on top. And the cap has been hanging there caught on the true lovers' knot since the first time he came home here to this flat. It was pouring rain that day, I remember, and he was in a hurry so he wore his uniform. It's the only time I've seen him in his uniform. He never wore it again, no matter how much I begged. He always said, 'Darling I'd never live it down. I can just hear the boys—"Get a load of the third going ashore in his uniform, our fitters and turners take themselves a bit serious these days".'

"And now he's a second. Deucer on a big Yankee tanker. I'm leaving him. I wouldn't care if he were bloody Lord Nelson. It's a year now since he came home in all that pouring rain. He was a day or two earlier than I'd expected him, but even when I heard the taxi door slam I knew who it was. Straight away, I knew who it was. And I went running down the stairs, and there he was, just getting in the door with all the parcels and packets in his arms. And we were clinging together and kissing and laughing, and I was crying, and the parcels were everywhere and it seemed like ages before we got them all upstairs. And when we got up to the top landing the bedroom looked so warm and sheltered with the long white curtains filtering out the greyness of the sky, and the radiator glowing and pulling all the sweetness out of the early hyacinths that I had in bowls everywhere. He stood a moment in the doorway, and he looked at it all. Then he took off his cap and he threw it, and it went skimming straight across the room and landed on top of the mirror.

" 'Leave it there,' he said, "if anyone wants to know who owns it, you say "That belongs to my husband, there's no fancy man round here".'

"('Fancy man, gee that's a funny old-fashioned expression, Andy.'

" 'It is that, darling. The old people say it a lot, and it always made me laugh, for I never saw one of these romantic characters that looked so very fancy.')

"I've left it there ever since. Many's the time when he was away that I've taken it down and dusted it and stood holding it against my cheek, and kissed it before I put it back. 'That belongs to my husband. I'm the wife of the red-haired man.' If I did have a little red-haired boy, how I'd love him. We'd dress him all in Yankee gear and get him a gold chain wristlet with his name on it like the one Andy has in hock this moment at Dinny O'Brien's in Newcastle. Everything's in hock. I'm leaving in the morning. I haven't seen Newcastle. Maybe next time we're in Sydney we'll go and have a look at it. I'm leaving in the morning. We could get up there and back in a day from Sydney—I'm leaving—"

And then it was morning and I was still lying alone amidst the tumbled bedclothes, and the air was heavy with stale cigarette smoke and there was an empty bottle on the dressing-table, and Andy was coming in from the kitchen bringing me a breakfast tray. He was red-eyed and he smelt of whisky. He needed a shave and it was obvious that he had not been to bed all night, but he was smiling at me, and he put the tray on the dressing-table and handed me a cup of tea without a word; and there on the saucer was the diamond-studded watch.

"Andy!" I bounced up in bed, ignoring the tea and clutching the watch in my hands. "Andy, you got it back for me!"

He put the tea on the dressing-table and took me in his arms. "It looks like it, doesn't it?" he said.

"Oh Andy, darling!" I smothered his face in kisses. "I do love you."

"And I love you too. You're my own dear Judy."

"Did you get back any of your own money?"

"No, darling. I had to get your watch first."

"What does it matter, love? We're holding O.K. It should bring forty pounds in hock. We'll go straight out after breakfast and put it in."

"After breakfast, darling," Andy ran a hand across the stubble on his chin, "I think I'll have a shower and shave and turn in for a little while."

"Didn't you even get a wink of sleep? Not even with your head on the table?"

"Nary a wink. It was seven-thirty before I got your watch back. Then I made you pancakes. Here, eat them. They're no good to you cold."

"Oh darling! Up all night just to get my watch back. You could have got your money back instead."

"I couldn't have rested if I hadn't got your watch."

"Andy darling, you're the best husband in the world."

I threw my arms around him again.

"And you're the best little wife. You'll never leave me, sugar?"

"Never, Andy! Never!"

And we ate pancakes and honey together in great peace and harmony while Long Jack Kelly slept curled up like a cobra on the lounge-room floor, Andy's jersey under his head, Speckie's raincoat over him, a bottle half full of whisky ready to hand, and in his shirt pocket, for Long Jack did not believe in any nonsense about debts of honour and gentlemen's agreements, the IOU Andy had given him for the price of the watch.

That grand old marital landmark, the first black eye, was passed some time shortly after the following Christmas. There was I one hot summer evening mooning around the flat and feeling discontented and sorry for myself. Everyone in Melbourne seemed to have somewhere to go. I was the only one staying home and wasting the lovely summer weather. I wandered in to Yvonne's room and idly moved her collection of graduation rings around on her dressing-table. Slowly I spaced them out till they made the outline of the Gulf of Mexico. I spaced them down from New Orleans to Galveston.

"What are you going to do with all these?" I asked.

"Go into the scrap metal business," said Yvonne. She held up her hand and waved it backwards and forwards, waiting for her nail polish to dry. "Why don't you come out with me," she said, "if you haven't got a dancing class?"

She had just come from the shower and she was sitting in her brassières and briefs, and I reflected that she was putting on a lot of weight and also that she was not working very regularly, which, of course, was her business not mine. She had her glorious hair piled up on top of her head and it gleamed with steam from the shower. She shook it down and began to comb it out into a long page-boy style.

"Come on, kid," she urged, "what they don't know doesn't hurt them."

Discontent had made me bad-tempered so I answered that I considered it a lousy thing to do to any man, going out on him the moment his back was turned.

"Don't you trust yourself?" asked Yvonne.

That settled it. I said I would go. After all I was not going out with a man. I was just going dancing with a girl friend.

"I always keep cheerful," said Yvonne, "the brave boys at the Front expect it of me."

"Yvonne, you're awful."

"Come on. You won't come to any harm with old Aunt Yvonne for chaperone."

Much hope anyone had of going to a dance and remaining alone in those days. At half past eleven Yvonne found me and she had a Yank on each arm. Sorrell, she said, was going home with her for a while, and couldn't his friend walk along with me for company?

Sorrell's friend had the slightly indecent name of Amos, but he was a nice lad and he listened to my chatter about my husband with interest and courtesy. There is nothing so courteous in all the world as a courteous Yank.

When we got home I discovered that Sorrell was indeed to come home for a little while. I had decided that we would not ask them in, but Yvonne turned at the door and said with great savoir faire that she and Sorrell were just going upstairs, and there was I left standing in the porch with Amos who was as embarrassed as I was. We made feverish conversation. Amos told me he was two-thirds Indian (Cherokee) and came from Oklahoma. One thing is certain—if the Indians of Oklahoma are all like Amos, then the Cherokees are a handsome, sensitive and very witty race. At last my rage overcame my sense of what was the right thing to do. I said, "Why should we stand here freezing all night, waiting for those two? Come in, there's a crayfish in the fridge and I'll make you a cup of coffee."

In the fridge we found a bottle of beer which we decided would be better with the crayfish than coffee.

Now in those days, for obvious reasons, they published no shipping news, and as far as I could judge Andy was in Sydney on his way home from the States; so picture my horror when the door burst open and there he was—Second Engineer Kelly home from the seas. The whole scene suddenly crystallised like a still from a movie. There was the Yank tilting back on his chair, a glass of beer in his hand. There was I, sitting on the table, cracking crayfish claws and swinging my legs. There was my husband with murder in his eye. With that wonderful facility for saying the wrong thing in a terrible moment, I said, "Andy I can explain everything."

For about the tenth of a second the scene held—and then there was action. Andy said not one word. He swung into the room and lifted the American out of his chair by the lapels of his jacket. At the same time he lowered his head and brought it forward, crash, between the American's eyes. I screamed. The deadly Liverpool butt! I had heard of it but this was the first time I had seen it. Amos was half conscious and his nose was pouring blood but, somehow, he got to his feet and covered up. I ran forward crying, "Don't kill him, Andy. Don't kill him."

"Get out of it, you whore," yelled my husband, and I caught the full force of his open hand across my face, "get out of it or I'll kill you too."

I tried to run in between them again and this time I ran straight on to his arm as it swung out to push me away. I went spinning back against the table in a way that knocked the breath out of my body and for the next few minutes I could only watch through swirling mists of pain and listen to the thud of shoes against flesh. My own body quivered at the sound. As I hung on to the table I saw Amos sink slowly to the floor.

"You've killed him, you've killed him," I sobbed, "and he was only waiting for his mate who's up with Yvonre."

Andy took no notice. He grabbed Amos, hauled him to his feet and shook him till he opened his eyes. Then he dragged him off to the front gate.

Poor Sorrell was wakened from a sound sleep and sent off after his friend. He went without argument and was altogether very biddable and docile indeed—such is the psychological effect of being caught without your trousers. Then Andy turned his attention to Yvonne, who was ordered to pack and go, forthwith, and never to come back again, turning the Kelly ménage into a brothel, etc., etc. She packed but, of course, did not go.

Then he looked for me and I was found, huddled in the

kitchen with a black eye, shivering with fright and crying with the pain in my side.

"I'm cold," I kept saying, "cold, and I can't stop shaking."

When they got me to the hospital I was found to have two broken ribs and to be suffering with shock. They gave me a sedative, strapped up the ribs and kept me there over night. They appeared to be very incredulous regarding my story that I had fallen downstairs. When Andy came to collect me next morning the doctor in Casualty remarked:

"One of our gallant lads in the turtle-necked sweaters. Well! Well! Well!"

And the fire-eating Andy took it without a word, his eyes swollen with tears.

I think it was on my husband's next trip home that there occurred the frightful seduction scandal. Not that I was seduced, not that I wished to be seduced, not that I knew that Howard Harrod was trying to seduce me; but then, as my husband remarked, I was so young and silly that I would not have known if the proverbial night cart had crashed into me.

It all began when we quarrelled about the low-cut black velvet dress. We were staying in a hotel for a few days because our landlady had finally roped in her son-in-law to paint out the flat. Several of Andy's shipmates were staying at the same hotel and we had arranged to meet and have drinks and then go to the Silver Grill for dinner.

"Do you think," enquired my husband, "that I'm going to have that pack of wolves panting round you while you parade around in that?" He waved one hand dramatically at the neckline of the black velvet. "For one thing," he went on, "I think you look bloody ridiculous slinking around in black velvet with three-quarters of your bust bared to the public. You look as though you're trying to look like the Madam of a whorehouse."

"Decent people don't know what the Madam of a whorehouse looks like."

"We're talking about my friends. And at any rate I still say you look bloody ridiculous."

"I'm sure your friends won't think so," I said, because I thought this would be the remark most likely to infuriate.

I was right.

143

"Will you take it off," he shouted, "or do I have to tear it off your back?"

"I won't take it off."

"Well it's coming off even if I have to knock you down and undress you."

"Knock me down then. Do you plan to put me in hospital every time you come home?"

He looked at me as though he were seeing me for the first time and didn't like what he saw.

"You bitch," he said at last, "you wicked-tongued little bitch. Surely to God you know I'll never lay a hand on you again as long as I live."

I was sorry then, and that made me meaner.

"I'm relieved to hear it," I said. "For a moment you gave me the impression that you thought you were back in Scotland Road."

"That's a very corny old jibe. Surely you can do better than that. Look, Lisha, don't let's fight. I'm not a patient man."

That 'I'm not a patient man' was a mistake. I replied that I was not a patient woman and that no strong-arm artist was going to dictate to me, and that I would wear what I pleased.

I looked down at the black velvet. Its wide skirt spread over a taffeta underskirt that rustled as I walked and the controversial neckline was not only low cut—it was wide cut in a deep square that went almost out to the armpits.

"Half an inch lower and you'd be run in for indecent exposure," declared Andy.

I picked up a heavy gilt choker necklace and clipped it around the base of my throat. Now I was bent on tormenting him to the point of madness. So I laughed the gay little laugh that makes husbands strangle their wives.

"That half an inch makes a world of difference," I said.

"It does if you don't bend over."

"Oh, I suppose I'll only bend over if I'm leaning across to let somebody light my cigarette. Like this, see."

I sat on the edge of the bed and demonstrated. My husband, half in and half out of his shirt, stopped in his dressing and gave me so long and hard a look that I straightened up and giggled with fright.

"At any rate," I said, "how lucky I am to have a good firm bustline to show."

"Such a pretty little navel too."

"Don't be disgusting."

"You're the one that's being disgusting. Just remember I'm your husband. Who are you to say how much neckline you'll have cut out of your dress? Every inch of you belongs to me."

Now in my secret heart I found this speech both flattering and reassuring, but of course I had to pretend that I had my pride. I sprang up and began hunting for my bag and gloves.

"I belong to myself," I announced, "and I say what I'm going to wear, and tonight I'm wearing this dress to go to dinner."

Andy took off his shirt. "Then you go alone," he said.

"We're late now," I said, "Howard and Roddy and Jack are waiting for us in the lounge. I'll go with them."

"You won't go out that bloody door."

I turned at the door and invited him once again to knock me down.

"All right, you harlot, go."

"I'm going."

We were both shouting by this time.

"Go then. Get right out of my sight."

"Expect me when you see me."

Both Andy and I suffered with *esprit d'escalier* in our quarrels. He put his head round the door several times to fire various parting shots. I made at least three trips back from the head of the stairs because I had thought of things that I felt were too good to be left unsaid. Finally I stamped down to the lounge with tears of rage in my eyes.

"Andy won't be coming," I told Howard, Roddy and Jack.

"What's wrong?" asked Roddy.

"He objects to my wearing this dress. Do you think there's anything wrong with it?"

"Not at all," they assured me.

"It's charming," said Howard. He came from South Africa and he had a lovely, special planter-in-Kenya sort of accent. "Anyway," he went on, "don't let's be miserable. Let's all have a beer."

"Yes," I agreed, "let's have a beer and forget about him."

"I'll go up and talk to him," said Roddy.

"If you do," I threatened, "I'll walk straight out that door. After the way he's gone on I wouldn't spend the evening with him."

"Surely it's not that bad," said Roddy, pacifically.

"He called me a harlot."

"Shhh," Howard smiled at me as he put down his glass, "you're just upset now. Don't tell us anything that you'll wish afterwards you'd kept a secret."

What an operator that boy was. In that one short speech he contrived to let me know that he understood, he sympathised, he found my temper impetuous and charming; but at the same time he considered me to be a completely loyal wife.

"Give him another chance," urged Jack, who worked side by side with Andy.

"Well really I don't see why we should," said Howard, "after all, if he cares to behave like a spoilt little boy—well!" He shrugged his shoulders.

"That's right," I agreed, "he's behaving just like a kid."

"Well what will we do?" asked Roddy.

"We're going to the Silver Grill, aren't we?" asked Howard.

"Do you think we should go now?"

"I for one don't propose to rearrange my evening to suit Kelly."

"Well I for one," said Roddy, "don't fancy having to rearrange my face after Kelly has finished with me."

He rose and put down his glass.

"Frightened, Roddy?" asked Howard.

He looked like Douglas Fairbanks Jnr., even to the quizzical little moustache (and believe me, in 1944 that was really something) and now, as he tilted back in his chair and smiled up at Roddy, he looked dashing to a degree. Roddy looked as though he would like to backhand him where he sat.

"Well it's not the right thing," said Jack, uncomfortably.

"Are you suggesting," asked Howard, "that Lisha is not the best judge of what is the right thing?"

He looked as though he were going to suggest pistols at dawn.

Roddy said, "I don't know. We'd like you to come of course, Lisha, but," he paused, miserably, "it's just that Andy's our friend."

"I have no friends," said Howard, "nobody loves me."

He gave me another smile. This time he raised one eyebrow. Andy maintained afterwards that he spent hours before the glass practising with that eyebrow.

"I don't think I should go out without Andy," I said, "even though I am furious with him."

"Just what I thought you would say," said Howard. "Why don't you two run along and play where it's safe," he turned to Roddy and Jack, "I'll just have dinner here with Lisha—if I may."

"Of course you may," I said warmly, "I hate eating by myself."

"What if your husband comes down?" asked Roddy.

"Heavens above!" Howard sounded bored. "You weary me, Roderic, my boy. Honestly, you weary me. When all is said and done this is the twentieth century, and I do happen to be staying in this pub. I have a perfect right to eat here. Any complaints?"

Roddy contented himself with saying that it would be more to the point to ask if Andy had any complaints, and Howard begged them both not to worry about him.

"We'll run along then," said Roddy. "Good night, Lisha, take care of yourself, and listen, will you promise me you'll go up and make up with Andy as soon as you've cooled down a little?"

"Well I'll think about it," I said.

He still seemed unwilling to go, and he repeated, "Take care of yourself."

"She's not a child," said Howard.

So Roddy and Jack went and Howard and I had another beer.

"I think old Roddy had just a little bit of a cheek," said Howard, "trying to exact promises from you."

"Everyone tries to run my life," I said, darkly.

"I suppose you know why that is?"

"No I don't."

"It's because you're so feminine, my dear, and, let's face it, so very pretty."

I laughed, trying to cover my embarrassment. "What's that got to do with it?" I asked.

"Men always try to dominate a beautiful woman. I suppose we're all cavemen at heart."

"Are you?"

"I have my moments, Lisha, but at least we can try to be civilised about these things."

I felt a sudden rush of affection for, followed by a sudden spurt of anger against, the red-headed wretch sulking in his room and refusing to be civilised about anything.

"It's a shame my husband can't try and be civilised," I said. "If you weren't here I'd have to try and get a place all by myself amongst this beer-swilling herd."

I made a gesture of what I hoped looked like sophisticated distaste towards the noisy, overcrowded dining-room.

"Well, of course, poor old Kelly is not quite himself at the moment," said Howard. "We shouldn't talk about this little blot on his copy-book."

Having thus established himself as a man of strict impartiality and tolerance, he then managed, in the course of the meal, to slip in several well timed remarks concerning my unfortunate man, so that by the time I had finished my soup I was quite certain that I had married a clod, and by the time we got to sweets we were roasting him with relish and without camouflage. Howard, while appearing to excuse him, had attributed his possessiveness to inferiority complex. And what had caused this inferiority complex? Well, any man married to a woman as lovely as Howard said I was might well feel a bit inferior. And add to that the fact that the man in question came from the toughest part of Liverpool, still had a very fair remnant of a scouse accent, did not have a particularly fortunate social background ("We'll put it that way," said Howard with his charming smile, leaving me with a mental picture of the whole Kelly family sitting in the Lime Street gutter), well it just added up to the fact that I was class and Andy was not—and knew it.

"Enough to make any man a little difficult, don't you think?" asked Howard. "But anyway I shouldn't be talking to you like this. After all, the man is your husband and anyone but a fool can see that you're the sort that would stick to a man come hell or high water."

We had had a dry sherry before dinner ("Wouldn't you know that he'd go for the old dry sherry routine?" was Andy's comment when he was told the tale later) and several beers while we ate, and now I saw myself through a faintly alcoholic mist as a woman of breeding, poise and beauty who had married a boor and was nobly making the best of it.

"Love is for keeps with you, isn't it, Lisha?"

Howard's voice sounded deep and tender. I nodded and smiled a brave self-sacrificing smile.

"I guess I'm foolish," I said, "but that's the way it is."

Howard covered my hand with his for a fleeting second. "You're a woman my dear," he said, "a real true woman. We'll just let it go at that and have another drink. Would you like a Bénédictine with your coffee?"

I had never tasted a Bénédictine in my life and when it came I thought it foul. And at any rate, what the hell did one do with a Bénédictine? 'A Bénédictine with your coffee.' How did you manage that? Did you pour it into your coffee? Or perhaps have it sip for sip with your coffee? What *did* you do with the cursed thing? Finally I threw it down at one gulp. It almost suffocated me, I do assure you.

Howard stirred his coffee thoughtfully. He said :

"I just want you to know, Lisha, that I realise that you love the man and nothing will ever change that, and if you know it you'll understand that I'm not making a pass at you. That's what Roddy and Jack quite evidently felt."

"Did they?" I was genuinely shocked.

"Of course ! Lisha, Lisha, I'm afraid you could never understand the dirty little mind of the average sailor-man. Well they're simple souls with only one ambition with regard to women. Why discuss them?"

"But you're different."

"After all, Lisha, I'm a man too," he again made with the eyebrow, "and don't think I don't find you very attractive. I do. Any man would. But when it comes to thinking of anything like that in connection with you—well there are just some women who are loyal and some who aren't, and you're definitely in the former category. Besides (the eyebrow was working overtime by now) I know this sounds a corny old line but I've a kid sister back in Jo'burg and you're very like her, Lisha. That's how I feel towards you. Just a big brother talking to a kid sister who maybe needs some advice about her marriage."

"We can all do with some advice at times."

"Look, Lisha, I'll tell you what we'll do. Let's get away from this crowd. You're not in the mood for them. Neither am I. I've got a few bottles up in my room. Let's thrash this thing out properly over a few drinks."

I hesitated. Silly as a wet hen I undoubtedly was, but at this I hesitated. Howard smiled at me.

"Come on, Lisha. You're not going to turn suburban on me after all I've said?"

"Well I don't know."

"O.K., forget it," he sounded hurt but tolerant, "I just feel a bit of a fool, that's all."

"Why, Howard?"

"Oh, it doesn't matter."

"But it does matter."

"Well, I mean to say, here I've been talking to you the way I've never talked to anyone else in my life. I thought we understood each other, Lisha."

"But we do, Howard," I protested, wishing the Bénédictine had not given me such a howling headache.

He smiled a bitter sort of smile and shook his head. "You don't understand me, Lisha, if you think I'm like all the rest of the firemen's mess."

I felt a heel. "Look, Howard," I said, "I'm sorry. I'll come up and have a drink. Where's the harm?"

"Remember," he assured me as we went upstairs, "I know a loyal wife when I meet one."

I was told later that he had a favourite theory to the effect that old lines worked best. He would frequently have the whole mess holding their sides as he entertained them with stories of women who should have known better, who had fallen for the old fair damsel treatment as though it were the newest thing under the sun. He must have been promising himself the laugh of his life after this night's work.

Once in his room he installed me in an arm-chair and poured me out a stiff whisky. He sat on the bed with his drink and we chatted decorously of this and that for ten minutes or so. It was at the second whisky that he said, "That chair's not very comfortable. Why don't you sit over here?"

I hesitated again. He was right about the chair. It was the typical hotel-in-wartime article with springs that had given up the struggle somewhere about '40, but no matter how bent I was on appearing sophisticated and not suburban, yet the fact remained that I did come from the suburbs, Port Melbourne to be exact, and in the language of the unsophisticated Port Melbourne suburbanite a bed was still something primarily intended for love-making—all the eyebrow-raising and moustache-twerking in Jo'burg couldn't alter that.

Howard laughed at me. He said :

"Lisha, Lisha, what a careful little thing you are. Casanova himself would have no hope with you. O.K. I'll sit on the chair. You come over here and be comfortable."

So we changed places and it was just unfortunate that, as I sat on the bed, my balance forsook me and I swayed back against the pillows.

"Lord," I thought, "after all this woman-of-the-world act I can't let him know that I can't hold my grog."

So I remained lying back against the pillows as though that had been my intention all along, and announced, "That's better. I have a bit of a headache."

"A headache," said Howard, "we'll soon fix that."

He poured us both another drink and came and sat on the edge of the bed.

"Now," he said, "just relax."

He put one hand behind my head and started to massage the back of my neck. I began to think, belatedly I'll admit, that perhaps I had started something that I might not want to finish.

"You have beautiful hair," he said. "I don't know, sometimes it makes a man furious."

"What does, Howard?"

He jumped up and paced up and down with his hands in his pockets. Then he said, in the voice of one who has suddenly decided to blurt out some home truths, "Well, Lisha, if I don't tell you probably somebody else will. I'm not the only one to think this way. All the chaps on the ship are wondering. I'm wondering too."

"Wondering what?"

"Wondering why you tied yourself up to Kelly. Kelly is all very well in his way. But you ! Lord, girl, you're class. I suppose it's none of my business, but when I think of the way he treated you tonight, well it just makes my blood boil."

He came and sat beside me on the bed and said more gently,

taking both my hands in his, "Don't you honestly think, Lisha, that he deserves that we teach him a little lesson?"

"What sort of lesson?" I asked suspiciously, and it was then that my husband was heard at the door.

Howard sprang up with a most regrettable exclamation—it sounded more than usually obscene coming from under such a well bred little moustache.

"This ruins everything," he said.

On the other side of the door Andy could be heard stating that he had been down to the Silver Grill and had found only Roddy and Jack. He was now going to take the hotel apart, brick by brick and board by board, till he found Howard and me. When he found us he would kill us both, etc., etc., etc.

"Open up there, Harrod," he yelled, "I know you're in there. I can smell you, you bastard."

"Don't let him in," I ordered, in a high-pitched, drunken little voice. "How dare he make a show of me like this!"

And at that my husband kicked the door down and the fight was on. It is fortunate that the hotel manager had all types of bottle parties on the premises. The revellers were booked in as guests, and therefore he did not dare call the police lest they calculate from his register that he was either trading after hours or else had people sleeping ten to a bed. This was the only thing that saved us all from ending up in the Black Maria. As it was the room was a shambles, even the wardrobe was lying on its side, and we laid Howard on the bed tenderly nursing a broken jaw. He opened one eye and said, "I haven't touched her, Kelly."

"I should think not," I said with dignity.

I had lost both shoes in the mêlée and the lovely black dress was splattered with gore.

"As for you, Andrew Michael Kelly," I went on as I retrieved the shoes, "don't ever speak to me again."

"Ah, get up to bed," said my husband, "and give no cheek or I'll screw your neck."

I turned to walk away. "You peasant," I said scornfully, "all a civilised person can do is just ignore you."

Then it was that Andy kicked me straight up the stern. It was not a hard kick, but it was unexpected and, unfortunately for my attempts at dignity, I fell flat on my face up the stairs.

He picked me up and I said, "Hands off me, you drunken brute."

Whereupon he kicked me again with exactly the same effect except that this time I lost the shoes once more; so he picked me up in one arm and tucked the shoes under the other, and took me up and dumped me on the bed.

"You're drunk," I declared. "Stand aside, you hooligan, you lout."

It infuriated me further to see that he was not impressed by this dowager duchess style of vituperation; that he was, in fact, laughing at me.

"Surely," I said, "two civilised people can have a drink together without all this. Do you think I can't look after myself?"

"Yes," said Andy.

"You think everyone is like yourself."

"Look how well you looked after yourself with me."

"You rotter."

"Oh you boundah, you cad."

"Well say just for the sake of argument that he was trying to, to—"

"To lay you," Andy helped me out.

"Yes, to use an expression you will understand."

"I can think of others if you like."

"Don't be any more revolting than you can help. Well, say he was trying. Andy, he would never, never have succeeded."

Andy said, "Hmmm."

He went on to say that one more drink, and I would have been unaware of anybody's whereabouts unless they had coughed.

"That," I shouted, "is the finish. I'm going."

"You're going nowhere," said Andy.

He pushed me back on the bed and I sat down with such a jolt that the padding over which I'd piled my Pompadour hair style flew right off the top of my head.

"As Howard would doubtless say," said Andy, " 'yours, I think'." He handed it back to me with tremendous politeness.

I grabbed it wrathfully and sat it flat on the top of my hair, where I clutched it with one hand, still fighting to maintain poise, still trying to appear dignified, outraged, sober. Andy laughed again.

"Lisha," he said, "you're full as a newt. You're blinking away like an owl with a Bath bun on its head. Why don't you give up?"

And at that I did give up, and we sat laughing on the bed, hugging each other and glad to be friends again. Then Andy helped me to undress and put me gently to bed. When I woke in the morning I found the Pompadour padding still hanging drunkenly over one ear.

Yvonne had left us soon after the affair of Amos and Sorrell. She said there were no hard feelings, as a matter of fact she thought Andy absolutely right, but she was not going to be a fool and work her guts out all her life, so rather than embarrass us she would move on. We parted the best of friends but she seldom came to see me after she left. In fact, we had begun to bore each other a little. After my initial efforts as an adult drinker I had decided that getting drunk was a boring business, and Yvonne had very little to talk about except parties, and how she'd passed out at this one and 'was I drunk at that one' and how uproarious Colorado had been when he'd had the run in with the cop, and how so-and-so had fallen into the big lake in the Botanical Gardens and all the rest of it. I responded as desired. I laughed uproariously and yelled "Priceless" or "Wizard" or "Solid Jackson" as the speech mores of the day demanded—but privately I thought it deadly dull. I had already decided that, when drinking yourself silly and half aware, you could have been, if sober, buying clothes, dancing, reading poetry, listening to Rosenstein's radiogram, or making love. Look what a farce drink made of love-making! No. It was not worth it.

Therefore I went to fewer parties and Yvonne went to more and I had not seen her for almost twelve months when she rang me up one evening towards the end of the war, all excitement and supplication.

"Listen, kiddo, just do this one thing for me and I'll never ask you anything again. It's life and death. Honest, it is the most important thing in my life, sweetie."

"O.K., Yvonne, get off the bended knees. I'll do it. What is it?"

The gist of it was that Yvonne wanted to come and stay a few weeks.

"Just say I've been there all the time, kiddo. I've got to have a job and a respectable address and someone to give me the big wrap-up—I'M MARRYING A YANK."

"Wacko! Lucky you. Pack the grips and bring them round."

With what glee we all entered into the deception of the Yanks. The Yanks who had the damn cheek to send officers around to check on our girls who were engaged to their men. One and all, young and old, rich and poor, Labour and Liberal, we all came forth with the slogan: *Any* Australian girl is too good for any other nationality you care to mention. We are not a humble race.

And there was Yvonne, a picture of virtue, on the night the investigating officer called, sitting on the sofa, dressed in a blue jersey shirtmaker, knitting and chatting away about her job in munitions. And she really had got herself a job. We did this thing seriously.

"I wish I'd been able to do more," said Yvonne. "I really have not been in munitions so very long."

"How true, how very true," communed I unto myself, praying to God that the Yank would not ask just how long.

My prayers were answered.

"I was months at home nursing Aunt Edith," said Yvonne.

Mrs Phillips, as the delicate Aunt Edith who had suffered every complication known to man after an attack of pneumonia, was superb. She quite took the honours from Yvonne and me. With her top lip drawn into a thin line which always, with Mrs Phillips, indicated a desire to laugh, and with every muscle of her face pregnant with scorn of male stupidity, she spoke glowingly of Yvonne's devotion as a nurse and her perfection as a lodger—no drinking, no men, no being behind with the rent.

When I went to the kitchen to make coffee the poor bedazzled Yank followed me and told me how lucky I was to have such a good responsible friend.

"I know what it is for you young married kids with your husbands away," he assured me, "it isn't always easy. Yvonne must help a lot."

"Oh she does, she does," I assured him.

So Yvonne is in America today. Her name is Mrs Van Storen.

She calls her husband Specky. She lives in Connecticut in a two-storey wooden home of which she has sent me innumerable snapshots. She has put on weight, seems always to wear a jersey shirtmaker, and has three sons called Brent, Warren and Brooke (which I suppose is an improvement, however slight, on Hank, Butch and Chuck). She wears the glory of her hair in a smart roll around her head. It looks tidy but not Yvonne. Her letters over the years have become stranger and stranger—full of prattle about the American Way and Pilgrim's Pride (whatever that may be) and last November, inflamed I presume by the Thanksgiving ceremonies, she sent me a recipe for cranberry sauce. She also enquired on a note of tender reminiscence, "Do you remember what a funny wild kid you were?"

My old friend Phyl Foley could have married a dozen Yanks, but when it came to the point she always said, "I couldn't leave Mum. I'd die of loneliness if I had to go that far away from all my people."

But she wanted to marry all the same and as the months and years went by she took to stamping and weeping with rage when the engagements of much less beautiful friends were announced in the papers.

She took to doubting everyone's virtue and told hair-raising tales of the numerous cads who had put the hard word on her and with what scorn she had repulsed them :

"Otherwise I'd be married today like half the rest of you."

As she knew my full story I thought she was tactless to talk this way to me, but I was sorry for poor Phyl and she had been a good friend for a long time, so I bore with her. But my brother and Angus McMaster said she was becoming just plain tiresome, and in view of her many testimonials to her own continence they called her Rocky Ned,* which I thought very crude of them. She persisted in believing that Lachy McLaughlin was dying for love of her and would always warn me if she came to see me, escorted by another admirer, "Don't tell Lachy."

* "Kye yi yippee yippee yi
  Hi there hold his head
  Many have tried but few can ride
  The outlaw Rocky Ned."

Old Australian folk song about a famous killer horse that was star of Skuthorpe's Rough Riding Show, many years ago.

This harmless vanity wrung my heart, for Lachy, with his soft rolling voice and golden hair and sleepy eyes the colour of cairngorms, was the greatest flirt unhanged. He appeared at all hours of the day and night with all types of females, and he treated each one as though she were the only woman in existence, and each believed that she *was* the only woman that did exist as far as Lachy was concerned.

One evening towards the end of the war Phyl and I were discussing the marriage question. Andy was home and was reading a book over by the window.

"The trouble is you've got to have money," said Phyl, "and all the ones that have money are old or ugly or both—or else just plain straight-out idiots. I like rank but anyone above captain is sure to be an old man of forty at the least."

"That's it. Money and looks never seem to go together."

"Well I want money and looks *and* rank." Phyl was at her most petulant. "You've got a second engineer so why shouldn't I?"

Andy looked up from his book. "I'll come back Chief next time just to spite you."

It was always easy to laugh Phyl out of a bad mood and she laughed now, but she kept to her point.

"If you marry for love," she said, "you find yourself in some dump and you have kids swarming all over you and you're finished. Remember the Port when we were kids? God! what a place. I don't think I could ever go back there."

I agreed, and even while I agreed it seemed to me that some of the happiest days I had ever lived had been spent in the Port, but then I remembered Lila Clancy humped over the table in agony, and Jimmy Clancy dead on his parents' bed and the damp wall behind him, and Paddy Barton dead from overwork and worry, and my grandmother counting coppers at the kitchen table, her face haggard and terrible with worry. I knew that these were things it was criminal to forget and so I said, "Yes, I know what you mean."

Andy threw away his book and stood up with his back to the window so that his face was in shadow. "Well," he said, "I think you're a bloody mean pair. Mean and small-hearted. To begin with, no matter what you say, neither of you have seen a real slum. You should see good old Scotland Road or, better

157

still, Errol Street, Lachy's old home. I've actually seen the dark stinking single-ender where Lachy first saw the light of day—if you can call it light of day. His old Granny still lives there, that is if the Germans have not blasted it off the face of the earth, and it'll be a blessing, in the long run, if they have. I can tell you two that's so anxious to make ladies of yourselves that it would give you a new respect for the working class if you could see the smelly, bug-ridden box in the wall where he was conceived and born—something as beautiful as Lachy to come out of that."

By this time we were opening and shutting our mouths and trying to get out a word or two of self-justification. But the champion of the masses swept on :

"Instead of crawling after those that are just waiting to kick you right back where you come from it would do you both good to identify yourselves with your own. You say you had a lousy time in the thirties? Didn't we all? At least you had fresh air and sunshine out here and if you did have such a tough time all I can say is that it's taught you nothing. All you can think of, the pair of you, is running away to the more comfortable suburbs, never mind the poor bastards you leave behind. Doesn't it ever occur to either of you that instead of trying to claw your way out of it you'd be better employed trying to make sure that the Port was never again the place it was in 1932?"

"I've heard talk like that before," said Phyl, "it does no good. What can people do?"

"Only a hundred years ago children of five worked down mines. So did women like you two. Sick, well or pregnant they crawled along dragging trucks of coal behind them. Children worked in spinning mills for hours that would have killed a grown man, and it did kill them too, in their thousands. What stopped all this? Unionism and unionism alone, and standing solid with your own people."

"My people were not like that," Phyl was furious, "old mill hands and that, and Lisha's grandfather was a ship's captain."

"Couple of toffs, aren't you? Well, my father was a Liverpool Irish stoker, so was my grandfather, and the fact that I'm a second engineer and Lisha's grandfather was a captain and yours is in the public service is beside the point. We all come from the same people and instead of ratting on them you should be proud of them."

"Well what are we supposed to do about it?"

"You could both of you stop whingeing because you can't live like film stars, and get into a Union and stop in it."

He turned from the window and suddenly he was embarrassed. He said, "Ah! Why do I bare my guts to you. You can't see what I'm talking about."

I went up and put my arms around his neck. "I know," I said, "I know all too well. I'll make you a cup of tea."

I hurried out into the kitchen. Had I stayed, I felt, I would have embarrassed us all very much by bursting into tears or kneeling down and kissing his hands.

Phyl and Andy joined me as the kettle began to boil. They were linked arm in arm and shoulder to shoulder and, with Andy conducting, they were singing :

"Solidaritee for ever,
Solidaritee for ever."

And while we drank our tea Andy gave us his famous Hyde Park speech on the equality of man :

"I've got them, comrades. You've got them. The Duke of Gloucester's got them. Three hundred yards of them! And to what do I refer, comrades? ENTRAILS!!!"

While speaking of the workers I feel that now is the time to mention that veteran of the I.W.W., Uncle Shaun. He was in England when the war began and he promptly put his age down ten years and sailed as peggy on a cargo boat on the North Atlantic run. He had the time of his life. To hear him recount the story there was never a man enjoyed a war more. Twice his ship was blown out of the sea from under him, and on the first occasion he was afloat in an open boat for ten days.

"The young chaps collapsing like flies," said Uncle Shaun. "It takes us iron men from the wooden ships every time."

I only saw him once during the whole six years of the war. He arrived on an evening when Andy had the flat full of Yanks whom he intended to pluck at poker. I thought it a poor way to spend a lovely late summer evening, so I wandered down to see the Rosensteins. Rosensteins were playing the Beethoven

Pastoral Symphony, which I felt accorded well with the beauty of the evening and the stillness of the sea, so I went and sat on the verandah and listened to the music and watched the darkness come down. And then, suddenly, there he was, coming up out of the dusk like a figure in a dream. I ran and threw myself upon him.

"Don't go in, don't go in, Uncle Shaun," I babbled. "The flat's full of people. I want you all to myself."

And I had him all to myself, for we crept into the kitchen by the back way and there we talked and drank coffee. How we talked! And every now and then Uncle Shaun would smile at me and say as though it were a matter for wonder, "Well, you're a grown-up old married woman now."

About ten o'clock we realised that the noise in the lounge room was growing in intensity. It did not sound like fighting. We could not be sure what it was. We went to find out. As we approached the door we heard a voice that sounded as if it came from San Francisco saying, loudly and proudly, "I had a full bottle of whisky inside me before I went in to have this done and when I came out again I was stone-cold sober."

He had removed his shirt and was displaying a huge American eagle that stretched in red and blue across his chest. They were showing their tattoos. One was stripped to his underpants but hastily donned his trousers when I appeared. T-shirts had been cast aside in all directions. Andy's markings I knew—five aces on one arm with Good Management written underneath and on the other a monstrous shamrock, inscribed Erin Go Bragh. I had never seen such a collection of hula girls, and Crosses and Sailors' Graves and Mothers and flags and ships and sea serpents. They were magnificent tattoos from all the ports in the world. But I still remember the silence that came down, the silence that was almost reverent, as they clustered round to look at the Hold Fast on the back of my uncle's gnarled and ancient hands.

The end of the war came the next August, the fifteenth. I heard the people shouting in the street and then Saul Rosenstein came tearing upstairs shouting, "It's peace, it's peace."

Then Phyl was on the phone with the same cry. "Town's going wild," she said, "come in and see it."

So Saul and I dashed into a taxi and got into the city through streets that were suddenly jammed with taxis and people. We collected Phyl outside the shop where she worked and the rest of the day remains in my mind as a confusion of sun and laughter and singing, and dancing the hokey-pokey in the middle of the roadway

(You put your right foot in
 You put your right foot out
 You put your right foot in,
 And you turn it all about)

and running, laughing and pleasantly hysterical, under the belly of a mounted trooper's grey horse, and dodging soldiers I was too shy to kiss, and watching the fireworks, and joining the Chinese in a Dragon Dance in the middle of Little Bourke Street in the evening—and at last getting home after midnight, and suddenly finding myself with my head on the kitchen table and sobbing wildly, "He's safe, he's safe, he's safe. He can't be blown out of the sea now. He's safe. Oh God, he's not in danger any more."

It was a relief to speak the word danger, for ever since I had married I had not allowed myself to think of it at all.

Mrs Phillips came in and found me and astounded me by putting her head down beside me and weeping almost as frantically.

"You'll pardon me, I know," she said, "but I drove an ambulance for the Red Cross all last war, and Phillips was in the front line almost all the time. I know all too well what war is. The last was a sort of dreadful pudding of mud and blood, and as for agonising over the men, I know all too well what that is, too. Phillips was one of that sort who could always make a woman go to any lengths to be near him—even to the extent of driving an ambulance in Flanders."

I looked up at her and wiped away my tears. "You loved him," I said. "You loved him very much all the time."

"Yes, I did, the bounder, but it takes an Armistice to make me admit it." She looked at me with the same old smile that was both warm and ridiculous. "What a pair we are," she said, "crying on such a night, and about men, of all things. Come, we must celebrate."

She produced the port (to Mrs Phillips and her buddies an almost sacrosanct tipple which was indulged in only on the greatest occasions) and we had a small glass each.

"Now," she said, "a good warm bath and off to bed. You're overwrought."

As I drifted off into sleep I could still hear the sound of music and laughter down on the Esplanade.

The war being over I lost no time in demanding of Andrew Michael that he let me try to have another baby. He refused. He said that never again could he live through the terror of that time in Fremantle when he had received the telegram, "Eilishe dying in Women's Hospital", and he had gone to his cabin like a man in a nightmare, and put his money in his pocket and walked off the ship without a word to anyone, still wearing his boiler suit. He could not remember getting to Perth, nor what he had said to the booking clerk at the Airways office, but he had managed to get a priority and the next day was in Melbourne, where he sat and watched me dying, as he thought, for two days.

"Don't ask me to go through it again," he begged, "don't ask me."

I pleaded religion (no effect), maternal instinct (slight effect), and finally fell back on the old Physical Blackmail. It is amazing how long he held out but in the end he capitulated.

"The Ladies," he said, "the grand old Union that's never lost a strike."

My son was born in September 1946 and we called him Owen Michael after Andy's father and mine.

"Looking back on it now," said Andy, "I realise I was fond of me Da—hard-hearted old bastard that he was."

My brother was godfather and we had a grand christening party, and the baby lay amongst the ribbons in his bassinet and slept while people came and gave him gifts and said how beautiful he was.

There is no triumph in all the world, no happiness, to compare with the birth of a first child. He was born at ten at night. It was in the small hours of the morning that I became aware of what was happening, for it had been a breech birth and instruments had been used and I had been under anaesthetic quite a long while. But when I knew that I had borne a boy I demanded to see him and they brought him to me looking like a tadpole in a pink bunny rug. His outstanding beauty struck me immediately and I spent the rest of the night lying and smiling at the shadows the nightlight made on the ceiling, rubbing my hands over my body that was soft and light once more, and whispering over and over till I fell asleep in the early light of morning, "I have a son. A son. I have a man child."

Andy, who had paid off in the August and waited round for a month in a state of panic and funk embarrassing for a loving wife to see (begging me to get a taxi to the hospital every five minutes and declaring that he had pains in *his* back so I *must* have them in mine), now told his friends that it was bloody painless and we intended to have six. He got on the Tasmanian run and had a good deal of time at home, all of which he spent hanging over the bassinet maundering on at his son.

"Ah luke at him, he's smilin' at his Da."

"Ah luke! He's shaking his fist at his old Da."

This went on all day.

He believed that a sip of stout was good even for the extremely young and he thought that babies should be nursed every waking moment.

("Ah luke at the faces he's pullin' at his Da. Ah luke, now he's been sick all over his Da's new suit. Yes you have, Lar. You're a bad babby but your Da loves you.")

Apart from the stout, about which I was obliged to be very firm, and the fact that he had never heard of schedule feeding and thought it very cruel, he was the perfect father.

Those months were the happiest time of my life.

The Christmas of 1946 was the biggest festivity since the peace celebrations. Christmas 1945 had possessed a sort of serenity that perhaps we will never see again—the first Christmas of the peace and all the killing over. But still it was an austerity Christmas. Goods were in short supply and there was a certain amount of rationing and all the boys were not yet home. But by '46 everyone was back, back to their children, back to the wives they'd married on final leave (some of them were even already divorced), and the shops were filled with beautiful things to buy. There were things we had not seen in

163

years—crystallised fruit and luxury chocolates, and the first of the glorious post-war dress materials, and caviare and champagne, and tiny tinsel Christmas trees to stand in the windows. And everybody had plenty of money, so we bought. There were still just enough shortages to make shopping exciting. I was very triumphant when I procured for myself a cut glass bottle of 4711 and a pair of midnight-blue silk stockings, and for my son a lovely little girl's frock of the new and wonderful nylon. I loved pink and decided I would indulge myself while he was still too young to care about the sexual connotations of the shade—a happy state which little boys soon outgrow.

It was while I was hurrying home, with the frock under one arm and some very precious French plums and Dundee shortbread under the other, that I saw the man who still remains in my mind as the very picture of that wonderful post-war time. He was a stout man in early middle age, and obviously he went at life with great gusto. He had been shopping with a vengeance. Amidst several unidentifiable parcels he held a magnificent doll in a Cellophane-covered box, a four-pound box of chocolates, a big Cellophane packet of assorted nuts, almonds and raisins, the most glorious ham that I had ever seen and a small Christmas tree. And then the ham, which was clutched under his elbow, began to slip, and once a ham begins to slip in circumstances such as these there is nothing that can be done. The doll followed suit and then the Christmas tree. I darted forward but, alas, too late, and our poor friend, in the horror of his plight, cast both armfuls to the street, clenched both hands above his head and, to the delight of everyone on the south-west corner of Collins and Elizabeth, shouted to the heavens:

"Oh BUGGER!!!"

It put us all in a wonderful mood. We retrieved the goodies for him and wished one another Merry Christmas from the very bottom of our hearts. We were all very happy that Christmas.

Andy was home, also Lachy. Mother was to have Christmas dinner with us. Mrs Phillips was having it, as usual, with an old friend of Indian days, called Hilda, but she said they would both call in the afternoon, so we got in a bottle of port. My brother was away in the Occupation Forces in Japan, and we sent him an enormous food parcel. We sent another to Andy's sisters in Liverpool. Andy had managed to get me, heaven knows where, a record that I had sighed for during almost all the war years. It was a big mystery but I knew that it lay there on top of the wardrobe—the Huddersfield Children's Choir singing "Nymphs and Shepherds", and accompanying them a most wonderful chap on a golden-toned recorder. With what innocence and strength and joy that recorder went soaring up in the roulades of Purcell's music—music such as must have sounded when Creation was fresh and new and the hills were appearing with verdure clad.

Four days before Christmas I said I would put up the Christmas decorations. Most people already had theirs up, and the stores and streets of town had been bright with them for weeks. But I liked to have them fresh for the day so I hung mine late. Andy, who was no good with decorations at all, said he had promised to meet Lachy and do some last minute shopping, and they'd have a few drinks and see if they could get a dozen of beer anywhere. I encouraged him to go because I wanted to play my record again, and he went off at about eleven o'clock when he had finished bringing up his son's wind after the ten o'clock feed. ("Up with it, Lar. Don't be embarrassed, your Da's no toff.")

As he went I called down from the balcony to ask him to try and get me a music box that played a Christmas carol.

"What carol do you want?" he called.

"Anything except 'White Christmas' and 'Silent Night'."

He began to sing in his pretty voice :

"I saw three ships come sailing in—

How about that, Macush? It's me favourite carol."

"Anything you like. I love you."

"I love you too, old woman."

He went off down Balaclava Square with the sunlight on his hair, and his whistle came up to me in a glitter of sound :

"And all the bells on earth shall ring
  On earth shall ring—"

Lachy came to me about two hours later when I was in the kitchen having an omelette for lunch. He was white-faced and shaking, and he put his hand on my arm and said, "Lish, you must come to the hospital straight away. Andy's hurt."

"Hurt badly?" The floor was heaving beneath me.

165

"Pretty bad."

"For the love of God, what happened?"

"We got into a fight with some Dutch sailors about the Indonesian business and Andy's been hurt. Come, Lisha, I've got a taxi. You've got to come now."

I took the sleeping child in my arms. Mrs Phillips offered to take him but I shook my head. I was beyond speech but I knew that Andy needed all his life around him now. We went in silence, except that once in the taxi Lachy said a strange thing:

"How old are you, Lisha?"

"Twenty-one."

Then Lachy said, "Oh God!" and buried his face in his hands.

We tore up the hospital steps and into Casualty and there a nurse was waiting for us.

"Are you Mrs Kelly?"

"Yes."

She held a little silver and gilt music box in her hand. . . .

"I'm sorry, Mrs Kelly, you're too late. Your husband died ten minutes ago."

PART III

AND THEN JOE

It was at one of Dotty Steele's parties that, feeling lonely and looking round, I suddenly saw Charlie Barton sitting over against the wall. I had not seen Charlie since my school-days, and I saw that he had fulfilled his early promise of being good-looking. He had the same well shaped face and regular features as his father and the snowy blond hair had darkened to golden, but the eyes! The eyes were changed and they made me afraid. Almost all the time they were the same wide-set eyes of green flecked with hazel, but every now and then they became blank and unseeing, deliberately unseeing. It was as though a shutter was drawn down behind the pupils, as though he had looked on horror and could look no more, as though he could not bear the sight of outward things, particularly people, and then all his gaze would be turned inward to some terrible secret world of his own.

I was happy to see him sitting there amongst all those people who were not my people, and I went across and put my hand on his shoulder and said, "Charlie!"

He looked up and I saw the happiness and recognition in his face, but, before he even greeted me, he said, "I'm Carl now."

"Carl! Whatever for?"

"Sounds prettier."

"Carl, where do you live now?"

"Johnson Street."

"Good old Johnson Street—on to the bus and straight down to the Port."

"That's right. You ever go to the Port now?"

"Haven't been for years. It would break my heart to go back. I'm a widow. Did you know?"

"I heard it."

"Who told you?"

"The Swede."

"How did he know?"

"The Swede's got ways of finding out things."

"Where did you meet the Swede?"

"Round about. What are you doing with yourself?"

"I teach dancing. What have you been doing?"

"I'm a wharfie."

"W.W.F.?"

"You don't think I'd be a Permanent and Temporary, do you?"

"Never, never—not a boy from the Port."

While we spoke we were laughing and wringing each other by the hand. We were both very lost and lonely.

"What brought you here amongst this shower?"

"I came with another dancing teacher."

"I came because I was told: 'You'll have a wonderful time and meet some exceptional people'."

"Who brought you?"

Charlie (now Carl) nodded towards a slim young gentleman who was sitting on the bed with Dotty. They were both very drunk by now and were chanting obscenities and then roaring laughing at their daring in the manner of very small, very naughty children from very sheltered homes—this, in fact, is exactly what they were. Every few seconds they would become so delighted with their boldness that they would fling themselves backwards, arching their bodies in semi-frenzy. The young man in the blue jumper was obviously homosexual and I wondered if Charlie knew. He knew it well enough, as I was later to discover. Now he was saying, "I've been on ships and I've been on the wharves, and I've been inside, but I've never heard filth like this before—let's blow." I also wanted to go away. Dotty must have been one of the most basically humourless people in the world, and I did not see why I should sit and drink bad muscat and be bored, bored and depressed, all night, while she showed off. She was famous for her mad parties and the things she said. Her coterie described both as fabulous. Well, each to his taste but, like the good old Dean, I have always felt that true genuine dullness, when it offers to be witty, is no longer pitiable, nor should we waste our charity upon it.

I had not wanted to come in the first place, but Marty, who

was the niece of and successor to the Misses McSweeney, was always rushing round trying to cheer me.

"Nearly two years without a man, it's just not natural, honey," she would say, and she meant so well, and was so genuinely kind, that, to humour her, I came.

And what a fiasco it had been till I met Charlie. Dotty had greeted us, not at the door, but at her window, which was in a basement—to make it all the darker and damper and more depressing. She had just moved in (this was a flat-warming) and already there was some little difficulty about the rent. Dotty had, in fact, very wealthy parents, but she was always carrying on with this tiresome rigmarole about not paying the rent. I suppose it was fabulous or mad or something. I don't know. Personally I have always found it more convenient to pay. What's the big deal about dodging bluey servers all round the town? I'd had enough of it by the time I was ten. At any rate this night all guests were met by Dotty gesticulating at the window, and we had to climb over the area railing and slither and clamber over the sill. We all roared laughing, not wishing to seem deficient in appreciation of such a brilliantly unconventional situation. I laddered a very expensive stocking. More than ever, I began to feel that the free life was not for me. Once inside we were given a tumblerful of muscat, and we sat in damp and semi-darkness while someone with a beard played blues records on the radiogram. I like blues but I like them better when I don't feel that I am about to go down with a rip-roaring attack of rheumatic fever. I took a sip of the muscat to keep out the damp (I LOATHE muscat) moved away from the wet wall and decided that much more of it and I'd be gouty as an old colonel. So I was vastly relieved when Charlie reached down and took my arm, and said again, "Let's get out of here."

And I looked down at the hand that gripped me below the elbow and I remembered that evening so long ago when Andy had held me by the arm and said, "Lean on me."

"It is all being re-created," I thought. "Two years' loneliness and misery, and now! Now I can be happy again."

But I felt nothing—nothing at all.

"Oh God!" I cried within myself, "it must happen again. It will. It must. I will make it."

Getting away was not so easy, for the slim young man who was sitting on the bed with Dotty put on a scene. He said that he had come with Charlie and he expected to leave with Charlie. Charlie leaned back against the wall and watched him. Again the eyes were shuttered off. Obviously the slim young man was suffering and Charlie did not care. Nor did I. I had been unhappy too long, and now anyone who tried to take my happiness could burn for all I cared. I did not worry what happened to them. I did not worry what happened to myself.

"What is the strength of him?" I asked.

"He's a bloody queen," said Charlie.

"How did you get to know him?"

"I never saw him before today in my life. I didn't know what he was. I was drinking in the lower bar at the Australia and I got talking to him and a couple of his mates, and they asked me would I like to come to a party and meet some exceptional people—they're exceptional all right."

"They're not really. There are thousands of them all over the place."

Charlie looked at them with most active dislike. "*I've* never met anything like them before. Come on, let's go."

The slim young man said he would stay and his friends said they would drive us home. His friends were big and rugged-faced. They looked as if they could work and fight but, some-how, they seemed even less heterosexual than their slender friend. At the very last moment the poor slim one came out and I could see that he pleaded urgently with Charlie about some-thing. Seated in the back of the car I looked out, puzzled. Charlie was obviously annoyed and yet he kept strangely patient. Why he should waste so much time with someone who was being so irritating and embarrassing was more than I could understand. I had yet to learn that men can be very patient indeed in cases of mutual blackmail.

At last Charlie joined us and we set off. When I arrived home at the flat I was sharing with Marty it transpired that the two craggy-faced friends expected to take Charlie to their house at Frankston for the evening. I paid off Owen's baby-sitter and I felt uncomfortable and even afraid with the two hairy fairies sitting there. Then they got up and walked, sneering, round Marty's little lounge room. They laughed at her collection of liqueur bottles, the blue ceiling, the water-melon pink walls, the red and gold travel poster above the fireplace.

"There is nothing so pretentious as half a dozen different colours used in a small space," said the taller of the rugged ones (they were both over six feet). "This whole little room would be better done all over in cream or flat white. It would look bigger."

"That's obvious," I said rudely, "but it's not my flat."

I wished they would go, but they sat on and on. They wanted to play Marty's records but I said the people upstairs would complain of the noise. They asked was there anything to drink and I said no there was not. And all the while Charlie sat sprawled out in the one arm-chair, and he pulled me down towards him till I was sitting on the arm with my body leaning against him. He put one arm around me and drew me closer and his breath came quicker and he kept running his hand up and down my arm and turning his face to kiss my hair. I looked across at the rugged ones and saw them watching. Their faces were filled with hatred, pain and loneliness. One of them said:

"Well, if you've nothing to drink at least you could offer us coffee. We *did* drive you home."

I shrugged and stood up. "It's late," I said, but I went out to the kitchenette and put the percolator on the stove. While I was out there fixing cups on a tray the three of them went past to the lavatory, which was downstairs in an ablution block. We shared it, and a bathroom, with the flat below.

No sooner had Charlie and his friends gone down than I shot into Marty's room, which overlooked the courtyard and had a fine command of everything that went on in every lavatory, bathroom and wash-house in the building. Marty was always complaining of the excellent acoustics. Now in the bedroom the window was open and I stood to the side amidst the curtains and spied on the men below. It struck me, even then, that I must be going mad. What did I want to learn? What strange compulsion would send me to eavesdrop in this manner. Sure enough, the voices came up to me:

"You must be bloody well mad," the taller rugged one was saying. "What's gone wrong with you?"

"Nothing that I know of," came Charlie's voice.

"But you promised."

"Did I? I'm a bastard, well."

The rugged one spoke more softly: "You don't know what you're saying, you're drunk."

The answer came with the maximum brutality: "What difference does that make? I've been drunk for a frigging week if it comes to that."

Soon after that the rugged ones left. Hope had gone out of them. They drank their coffee and went away, and Charlie and I sat before the gas fire and made love.

Marty came in very late and very gay and good-tempered. She had been brought home by a final year medical student.

"His father is a big specialist in Collins Street," she exulted. "Useful, very, very useful."

Charlie said he would sleep on the divan in the lounge and there we left him, but after a while, when Marty was asleep in her bedroom with the golden walls and rose-pink cushions, he came in to where I lay in the darkness and he whispered, "Do I come in to you or do you come out to me?"

My little boy had slept beside me in that bed many a time when he was teething and restless. Now I looked across to his cot, which was a shadow of white, heaped around with mosquito netting, in the far corner of the room.

"I'll come out to you," I said.

"If you think there's something wrong, don't go out at all. If you don't want to love him in your bed, then don't love him on a divan," said that horrible little voice that represents one's cerebral equipment, and is such a bore and embarrassment—particularly in love affairs.

I protested frantically at myself: "It's not that. It's not that at all. It's—I don't know what it is. I mustn't think."

So I went in to the divan and, in the shadows, his face became soft and handsome; the face of the Charlie Barton with whom I had gone to school in the days when he had truly been one of my own kind. And I told myself that the thickness of his shoulders and the solidity of his muscles comforted me because they were like Andy's—but I felt nothing. I was completely frozen, and when I got up in the morning I made coffee and fruit juice and toast and was very gay. I told myself how happy I was and I was very affectionate to Charlie. But something had happened to Charlie. He could scarcely bear to speak to me (or to Marty either, if it came to that). He did not want his breakfast and he said he felt lousy and he blamed the hangover and the fact that he had had no sleep for days, and he said what was the use of anything anyway and, finally, he said he'd be getting home and he'd be seeing me. Then he must have felt sorry for me because he asked would I like to go into town for lunch, and I said yes. I was sorry as soon as I said it because I was not accustomed to men who became sunk in gloom after sleeping with me and, unbidden from some place within me where I still had a little pride and sense, there came a swift desire to tell him to go to hell. But I choked it back.

"Stay with him," I told myself. "Don't be alone again. You can't be alone again."

So I just said, "I'd have to take Owen."

"Bring him," said Charlie, "I love kids."

We trailed off and went into the city, and we scarcely spoke to each other. It was Sunday and there was the usual trouble to find any place that was open. Charlie said, "God! What a dump", and told me I should see Times Square.

At last we found the usual small Greek place and had half-cold eggs on toast. Charlie picked at his food and pushed it away almost untouched. He cheered up a little when the waitress paused to talk to us for a while. He told us all about his travels to the States when he was in the Merchant Marine and, even as he talked, I knew he was lying. It was nothing that he said. He had been too much amongst wharfies and seamen to make any obvious mistake, but I had listened to sailors' tales all my life, and I knew he was lying.

"Well," I thought, "you can't blame him for wanting to seem romantic."

After lunch he said, "Look, I'm bad company today. I'm going home to see Mum. See you soon."

He went down to Flinders Street and I caught the bus down to the Port.

It was a long time since I'd been in the Port. Not since a few months before Owen was born, and now he was just over two years old. As well as the visit when I was pregnant, I had gone down once after I was married. Gone in a taxi and dressed up to the eyebrows in my silver fox and carrying the crocodile-skin bag. All my friends had been very generous. They had been delighted to see my riches and splendour. They fingered my fur coat and were amazed at the fineness of my American stockings, and congratulated me upon getting a ship's officer for a husband.

"And you're so young, too," they had said.

It had been a very triumphant visit.

Now as I got off the bus at the foot of the ramp that leads up to Station Pier I saw that the Port was still the same—and yet how changed! The houses, that had remained untended and unpainted all the depression and the war years, now burgeoned forth with new fronts painted in colours that we would never have seen before the war. White houses with pink doors, blue houses with yellow window sills, little old panes of glass knocked out and replaced by wide landscape windows that let in a decent amount of the good clean light and air of the bay. And in and out of the bright gay houses little children ran, shouting in all the languages of Europe, and I sat and watched them and knew that my people, as a race, were gone. The old Australian speech, with here and there overtones of Ireland, that had been the patois of the poorer suburbs was a dead language. With all its beauty and roughness, and strange taciturn expressiveness, it was gone. None of these little Sicilians, Yugoslavs, Poles and Germans who played up and down the street would think in it or speak in it, as I would till the day I died. And I thought of the wonderful autonomy that had been ours. Of the songs and the stories that had gone to make us. How our brothers had marched on St Patrick's Day and our fathers on Labour Day, and how the Scottish would turn out on Burns' night and go to the big concert in the Town Hall, and how they would rise at the end and sing :

> "Let kings and courtiers rise and fall,
> This world has many turns."

How the little black-haired Taffies always had such beautiful programmes on the wireless on St David's Day, and how there was always a couple of them dashing in and out of the fray in all strikes and Union business, and making speeches fit to fire any working man's blood. And I thought of how these same people, from mountains soft with mist and fields so green that they could not even describe them to the Australian born, had gone into the desert and the loneliness, amongst the sheep and flies and cattle and dust, so that all our vast empty country was blessed with their courage. I looked at the culture bearers from Europe—and I wondered if they would have as much to give. Then I looked at my son as he played down on the sand, and my heart rose. He was a proper little scouse, as his father would have said. He was small, dark and barrel-chested, and one of these days when I lay in the earth with a Celtic Cross above me his seed would go on to enrich the Australian race.

"Come on," I said, "I'll show you where Mummy lived when she was a little girl."

We went and bought an ice-cream at the shop where Johnny and I had bought potato crisps and then we went on over the ramp, past Prince's Pier and down Stawell Street—and where I had lived was a heap of rubble with, here and there, a chimney piece or part of a wall still standing. Every house for half a block lay in that rubble and a sign-post said that here the State Housing Commission was to build a block of flats. But I found the fig tree! I found it standing there amidst the ruin, brave and bare in the pale spring sunshine. And by some miracle the back wall of our kitchen still stood and the branches of the tree etched themselves, sparse and dark, across the whitewashed bricks. I remembered the day that I had painted that wall. I had been reading about the Mexicans and their houses of white- and pink-washed adobe and I had decided to touch up our outside walls and give a Spanish-American flavour to our Port Melbourne back yard.

"You wait and see, Gran," I had said, "it will positively drag in the sunlight."

Gran had said that if it could do so it would be doing well, and she had helped me mix the whitewash.

I worked away all one autumn day. Not only did I do the wall. I touched up the lavatory and back gate as well, and Gran said that if the landlord saw such astounding improvements he would surely raise the rent.

Standing now amongst the fallen bricks, I remembered how, in summer, the green of the fig leaves would gleam against the white and I would sit in the tree saying to myself "Under the glassy, cool, translucent wave". And I saw, rising up before my eyes, the face of my grandmother a few days before she died. She had come out to sit a little while in the sun, and the sun was white and the wall was white and she sat there in the stillness of the winter day—not a strand of her hair loosened, the air around her motionless, time motionless, her image imprisoned there for ever. Her profile was ageless and beautiful in the timeless light and the shadow of the tree, sparse and wintry, falling on the wall behind her.

Then I saw another figure coming out of the time that was gone. This time a true figure of living flesh. It was Lily Dale swinging down the street, leaning into the sea wind as she had always done so that it tossed her black curls around her head and swirled her skirts against her slender legs. I had heard that she was now a grandmother, but she brought with her the same old aura of sex and vitality. She stopped before me and held up a strand of my hair.

"But it can't be," she cried. "Lisha Flynn was so dark. You bad girl, touching up like that," and she threw her arms around me and then stood back beaming into my face. I indicated Owen.

"Meet my son," I said.

She knelt down and held out her arms and Owen ran to her.

"Come on," she said, "you're both coming home to tea."

She stood up, swinging Owen up and holding him against her shoulder.

I enjoyed sitting and eating cold meat and two kinds of salad and jelly and scones with jam and cream. Owen ate a dozen small scones and nothing else. Lily said what wouldn't fatten would fill. And while we ate we were told all the news. Lily told gossip with no spite or sniggers of disapproval, but as one who had a tremendous love and tolerance for the human scene. Gracie was present with her husband, who was a Pole, and her little boy, who was called Wayne, and I heard all about the wedding, and how Eugene was to marry next month, and how Johnny had done electrical engineering for his Rehabilitation after coming out of the army, and was now installing telephones for the P.M.G. Clarrie Harrop had spent most of his army career stealing guns and selling them, for which he did a stretch in Bendigo. He was now dishonourably discharged and ambitious of becoming a big shot in the underworld, but Bluey Gleeson said, and he should know, that Clarrie would never be anything except a small-time shit kicker if he lived to be a hundred. Bluey had made a fortune during the war and was now said to be suffering with heart trouble and tending towards religion. He had closed the Little Compton Street houses and given a whacking great donation to St Antony's Orphanage. Young Bonnie Gleeson had likewise made a fortune and earned herself the local nickname of poxpants. This name was, of course, mere hyperbole, Bonnie being far too smart and professional to come by anything so inconvenient. She had gone off to America on one of the first war-bride boats—married to a Major and wearing one fur coat and carrying another over her arm, and surrounded by pigskin suitcases that had been procured from heaven knows where on the black market.

When I had heard all the news I found myself saying that I had something to tell them—that I would shortly be remarrying. They were delighted. Lily said it was not natural for a woman to live alone, especially one who was so young.

"Who's the lucky man?" Gracie wanted to know.

"Charlie Barton."

Then their delight suddenly cooled. The smiles grew fixed on their faces and for a moment there was silence. Then Jack Baker said :

"Charlie Barton, he was always a nice boy when he was a little kid. I haven't seen him for years."

"Didn't I hear that—" said Gracie, and then she saw her father's eye upon her and finished off, lamely enough, "Oh no, I remember now, it was someone else."

I decided to carry it off, as Marty would say.

"He has been in jail," I said, "if that's what you heard, but only for fighting in the street and assaulting the police and that sort of thing."

This lightened the atmosphere. We all understood about assaulting the cops. It was the sort of thing that could happen to any decent chap. So I went on to tell them how we had met again, and I found myself supplying details as to the approximate marriage date, and how I was going to wear an oyster satin ballerina, and Charlie was buying me a fur for a wedding present.

"He's working on the wharves and making terrific dough," I told them.

"The wharf's wonderful now," said Lily. "There's money in

177

the Port now and at Yarraville and Altona. Everyone's doing up their houses and buying things for their kids and buying cars. You've got no idea. Young Clancy made forty pounds last week, 'course he was working twilight. Both boys are on the wharf and they're wonderful to Lila. They bought her a washing machine and everything new. The house was supposed to be condemned, but the landlord said nothing about it and they've got it lovely now. Everything's new and all electric. They bought her a radiogram and an electric dishwasher and all. Ted hasn't been too good since he was in Changi but he's got his pension and the boys are wonderful to him too."

"Better if they put money on a block of land and build house," said Gracie's husband, who had scarcely spoken all the evening. "First most important thing is get the own home."

"Who wants to live way out beyond the black stump?" said Lil. "Anyrate the housing can't get any worse, it must improve, and they'll be able to get something decent closer in. Where are you and Charlie planning to try and get a place, Lisha?"

I said I didn't know, just wherever we could, I supposed. Housing being what it was.

It amazed me to discover how happy I felt, sitting there the centre of attention—the heroine of this glowing fairy story. The fact that it was not true seemed to make no difference at all. Going home in a taxi, with Owen asleep in my arms, I still felt exhilarated and excited. I found myself chatting to the taxi driver about my approaching nuptials. I was beginning to learn the immense power of a compensation complex.

Back home, I put Owen to bed and pressed an evening frock because I was dancing in a competition the next night. Then I made myself a cup of tea and sat in front of the fire.

"What have you done with yourself since your husband died?" Charlie had asked.

What had I done?

At first I had done nothing. I had sat numbed with shock and unremembering. I would begin to write to him because he must be away at sea—letters that were never finished, for when my mother saw that I had forgotten them and was gazing blankly before me, she would take the paper out of my hands and go away, weeping, and burn it. During all that terrible time the only clear recollection I have is of my mother nursing me with the strength and tenderness of a Peter Damian.

"Baby, try and eat something."

"Lisha, darling, your meal is getting cold."

"Lisha, dear, I'll go down the street with you."

For I could not be allowed anywhere on my own. I could not remember my name, nor where I was, nor what I was supposed to be doing. I knew only that I had a baby and I must feed him, and, from some atavistic source of strength, I *did* manage to feed him. He was the only hold I had left on life. I would sit nursing him for hours, and Mother would take him away to bath him and dress him and take him out in the sun. She did everything for him and for me as well.

"Lisha, get into your bath now. I've run you a lovely hot bath with jasmine bath salts. Come on, darling, Mother will help you undress."

She fed me, watched me, guarded me, and when sleep released me and I woke weeping and with terrible cries of grief, she put me off again with brandy and hot water and sugar (we knew of no drugs) and I would lie in oblivion for just a little while.

I do not know how long this went on. Perhaps it was three months, perhaps a little more. But, strangely enough, it was the fact that Owen began to look very much like his father that brought me to realisation of what had happened. One day I was sitting looking at him, and suddenly he lowered his head and looked at me from under his brows while a lock of hair fell down across his forehead, and in that instant I knew that Andy was dead and all that was left of him was here, held in my arms. The pain of loss was terrible, but at least I knew I was in pain.

They told me that people had been very kind to me. That Phyl had come almost every day and sat and tried to talk to me; that Mrs Phillips had refused to take any rent and people had brought me money. The crew of Andy's ship sent a cheque, and Lachy and Uncle Shaun had sent every penny they could scrape together or borrow. From my father I received nothing. Some time before Christmas he had gone off to New Zealand with a very beautiful half-Maori whose father, according to my father, had treated her vilely. He had left her, as a child, to run the streets of Auckland and, as a direct result, said Father, she had contracted T.B. while over here dancing, and she had a very beautiful soul ("Soul indeed," snorted my mother) and Father was going to look after her. We have seen and heard nothing of Father, or of her of the beautiful soul, from that day to this. My guess is that some day he will reappear with the news that the soul did not turn out quite so beautiful as expected.

It was soon after I began to recover that there was a ring at the front door and when I went down to answer it I was surprised to find the eldest Miss McSweeney there : Miss Olive, looking as severe and distinguished as ever with her tall spare figure and her upswept hair and her long, thin, beautiful face. She did not greet me. She simply followed me up the stairs saying, "Lisha, this will not do."

How often had I heard that 'this will not do'.

"My dear Rose Murphy, 'this will not do', that is the worst third position I have seen in many a long day."

"My dear Lisha Flynn, you are ruining the entire reel. You have been told a dozen times that the top of the body must not move. You look like a tinker dancing at a cross-road. 'This will not do.' "

I gave a shaky giggle and asked Miss Olive if she would like a cup of tea.

"No, thank you, Lisha. I have not come to sit over the tea-cups and tell you what an unfortunate young widow you are. You have had quite enough of that sort of sympathy, I should have thought, from well-meaning but impractical friends. I have come to suggest what may be done. Ordinarily I would consider it an impertinence, but in this case it is somewhat different. I have known you since you were a little girl and," she leaned forward and placed one hand on mine, "you see, my dear, we are both dancers, and so I know certain things about you that perhaps even your own grandmother, God rest her, would not have known. I am an old woman, and I'm sure I always appeared old to you, and I suppose it would seem impossible that I could ever have loved and lost my love, but I assure you it did happen, a long time ago, the time of the Boer War. And remember I was less fortunate than you. You married and you have a child. I did not marry. I was just starting the school then. I used to teach children deportment and adults used to come to learn the waltz and the Lancers and newfangled dances like the Boston. Mother and Father were drowned, you know, going down to Geelong in the old paddle steamer *Zerelda*. She went down just off Gellibrand. We girls were all alone and Martha was still at the Convent and Sally was only a baby. So I had to think of them and I felt I had not the right to marry for a few years, and when the telegram came to tell me he had been killed at Mafeking I felt I had nothing left. I cursed God and I hated my little sisters. But I was wrong, you see, for I did have something left. God always leaves us with something, and I found that when Martha played the piano for classes I could still dance. And you will find the same, and your body will live on though your soul wishes to lie down and die, and in time, for time is very kind, all of you will become alive again. You will even be happy again, though you do not believe me now. Well, I think I will have that cup of tea. Talking about one-self is thirsty work and I don't usually indulge in it, but I wanted you to know that I know of what I am speaking. Now, to business. As no one knows better than you, we girls retired before the war and the city studio has always been run by young women. My niece, another Martha, is manageress now, and we would be glad of you on the staff. Jitterbug, I am happy to say, is in eclipse. They perform a milder version of it called jive, but the great thing now is something called the samba. Now Latin American was always your speciality. You could be a great help. Of course with the baby you will only be able to work part time. I realise that. Nevertheless this is not charity that makes me offer you the job. I want my Latin-American classes taught well. Another thing is that you cannot go sitting here any longer in a much too expensive flat which must be filled with memories which you should not dwell on at the moment. My niece Martha has a flat much too big for her in South Yarra. She would be glad of the company and the assistance with the rent. She is a girl from a big family and she loves babies and children. At the moment she is trying, desperately, to be smart and woman-of-the-worldly. Hence she has moved out into this large and strangely furnished flat, but she is lonely and she would be happier if you were there. I would be happier too. Now for the tea and a look at this young man of yours."

And that was how I came to go back to work and to be living

at Marty's. The happiest part of the arrangement was that Marty adored Owen, and spent a great deal of time dressing him up and taking him into town to meet her smart friends. She missed her own big noisy family very much.

"But they're hopeless," she would say. "I think the world of them, of course, but I had to leave. I'm not going to stick in Brunswick all my life."

I had taken nothing away from my home in Port Melbourne except the photo of my grandfather, Hughie Ward, and the big oleograph that used to hang above the kitchen door—"This nation laments its murdered patriots Allen, Larkin and O'Brien", and there were the 'noble-hearted three' standing proudly upon the drop. It was a hideous old picture, but I took it with me in honour of dignity in the face of a terrible death, and in memory of my first lessons in history and politics.

In like manner I took nothing from the flat except clothes for Owen and myself, the photo of Andy in his boiler suit, and the cap which still hung on the cheval glass. At Marty's I left the Manchester Martyrs in the bottom of my trunk, for I felt that they did not go with Marty's décor, and the photo of Andy and the cap I took out but I had not the courage to look at them. I put them on the top shelf of the wardrobe. My grandfather I put on the mantelpiece, and the thin tough face with the big tender eyes looked out at me as though to say, "Keep your courage up, girl, there's a lot of life before you yet."

I found Marty a very good friend and very easy to share with, and I found that Miss Olive had been right. Numbed as I was with misery, I could still respond to the beat which to a dancer is the very core of the music. The rhythms of tangos and rhumbas went through me in a warm revitalising wave that relaxed my body and comforted my mind. While I was dancing I was happy and when I was not teaching I was too tired to think very much about anything, and gradually I healed. The time came when I could think of the happiness and richness of my marriage without weeping and I could remember Andy with gratitude and joy. Thinking of him now, and the strength and courage and honesty that had made his twenty-seven years of life a victory over the rules of social cowardice, I suddenly found myself weeping that I, who had lived with such splendour, should now be reduced to living in lies.

After so unpromising a beginning it is amazing the amount
of fun I managed to get out of my affair with Charlie. Sensually
I continued to feel nothing for him and I was to discover that
he was an unpredictable lover. He was skilled enough while the
love-making was in progress; it was afterwards! One never knew
how Charlie would be afterwards. Sometimes he would be the
simple worker :

"I'm tired, woman. Go to sleep."

Sometimes his cruelty was dominant and he would get out
of bed and stand gazing out the window, silent, or else volun-
teering such remarks as :

"I don't know, I must be oversexed."

Once I made some trivial remark about his father, and he
laughed and said :

"God! It's a nice time to talk about him now."

His mother, I realised, was of course too sacred even to discuss
with me. And yet there were other times when he would lie with
his head in the hollow of my shoulder and tell me how he loved
me and make foolish and pitiful dreamlike plans for our future.
One of his favourites was that by some miracle he would get
his matriculation and go to University and, in time, become a
great surgeon. "We'd have money and we'd have a big home,"
he would say. "We'd dress for dinner every night and dine by
candlelight, and we'd have a grand piano and lots of kids. I
can just see you, all soft with a lot of little kids around you.
Remember how you were before life mucked you round?"

I suppressed a grin, for the top of his curls brushed my mouth,
and suddenly I was very sorry for him and kissed the curls
gently, for life had mucked him round to some purpose.

Until his father died he was the luckiest and most looked-
up-to little boy in the street, and suddenly he found himself
enmeshed in utter horror, caught in a terrible trap from which
there was no escape. He and Brian and Terry went into St
Antony's Orphanage, and their mother went to work at a
country hotel where she could keep the baby girl with her. And
it was not only that his father and his home were gone, and
his mother far away—his careful clothes, his knitted sweaters,
were soon replaced by the orphanage uniform, and he wore it
like a hair shirt. Instead of having his mother there to acclaim
him for wanting to be a priest, he had a swarm of companions

who said he was a crawler and only talking of a vocation to curry favour with the Brothers. And he was not any good when tried out for the St Antony's brass band, which was one of the best in Melbourne, and he was small and not clever, and he had never been much good at sport which involved teamwork. He did not like being in a team. He liked being out alone. He had been the first born, the best loved—the white-haired boy.

As his curls turned from lint to honey and his body filled out with puberty he discovered that he could fight. At St Antony's they were proud of their gym. They had trained many a fighter. Countless careers, famous in Australian boxing, had commenced at St Antony's. They tied the gloves on Charlie Jarman Barton and told him that he might be a world welterweight one day. One day! In the meantime he was one out again, on his own and going to win and the other boys admiring him.

Then, when he was good enough, the Brothers took him and another boy to the stadium and they fought an exhibition bout, and when it was finished the crowd cheered and threw money into the ring. This also was an old St Antony's tradition, but Charlie sat in his corner with murder in his heart while the money danced on the canvas before his eyes.

"I think it was then I began to hate people," he told me, "all up there kidding themselves they were so good, tossing a few pennies to the poor little orphan boys. Not that they tossed pennies, they were very generous and that only made it worse. Some big glad-handers amongst the bookies in the crowd even threw fivers. I hated them and I hated the Brothers for making us look like beggars."

About that time his mother remarried and he hated his step-father.

"For a while," he said, "I even hated Mum."

"You still do," I thought, "Charlie, you still do."

His mother worked like a slave and so did the stepfather to get a house partly paid off so that the boys could come home. Brian and Terry were glad to be home, but it was too late for Charlie. He stayed away from home as much as he could. He had fourteen professional fights and went around with the stadium crowd. And because he was not a world-rank boxer after all, he was soon pushed out to the fringe where hovered the gamblers, the confidence men, the criminals.

His chief advantage as a lover was that his way of life provided plenty of excitement. I very soon discovered that the term in jail had not been for fighting but for stealing cars. There was a great boom in stolen cars in those years after the war—those glorious old years when we were still short of consumer goods. In fact, Charlie was not a very clever thief. I have seen him and an accomplice go to work on an early model Holden, one jumping on the back bumper bar, the other on the front. This is an amateur's method at the best of times. Charlie's skill lay in driving—getting the stolen vehicle away to the N.S.W. border where, in those days, one needed only a licence to drive, whereas in Victoria you had to have ownership papers as well. Perhaps this is still the case. I do not know. I have long since lost interest in the used-car business; but at that time I became avidly concerned with it and with all affairs of the underworld, where they were enjoying the post-war boom the same as everyone else. It was the hey-day of the famous Normie Morrison, and his lieutenant, Freddie Earnshaw, who stalked beside him, waiting for him to die. Directly beneath them came Johnny Lockwood, who was considered to be the stupid one of the three but who outlived them all. The ostensible reason for Charlie's living in Johnson Street was because it was easy to get to the Port from there. The real reason was because it was close to the headquarters of Maurie Flower, a solid middle-class criminal who was aiming at the aristocracy and who was Charlie's chief. Maurie had not quite reached the flat in Toorak. He lived above his office, as it were, in 86 Glastonbury Street. Maurie and Charlie had boxed together when they were preliminary-round boys. They had never got past being preliminary boys when they were in the fight game, but it was thought in the underworld that if they each stuck to their own speciality (standover for Maurie and cars for Charlie) they would go much further— particularly Maurie, who drank much less than Charlie. Charlie drank a great deal, but he was afraid of drugs. Except for benzedrine once in a while when he felt particularly depressed, I never saw him take anything. Maurie, on the other hand, always hopped up before a big job. And when he was drugged he would do anything. He was a gentle fellow when normal, and the only criminal I ever knew who was gentle and kind to the unfortunate. I have seen him give five-pound notes to the bedraggled mothers of Fitzroy, but Maurie, drugged, did some of the most brutal standover jobs in Melbourne, and worked some of the most ruthless protection rackets, and when he was broke (and it is extraordinary how these people will suddenly find themselves without five shillings) he lived off his woman.

Bonnie Gleeson had been Maurie's girl when he was a boxer, and he had known then that she was a prostitute. He had not liked it, and he had beaten her up on several occasions. It was after one row when he had half murdered her that she met the Major, who had been left behind in Australia after the war to wind up some U.S. Army business. Maurie was in jail for the wedding so he made no trouble there, and poor little Bonnie packed her pigskin trunks and told herself that she was making a new life for herself, and that she was very happy. And about a month after I met Charlie she came back. She brought with her a new fur coat (sapphire mink), piles of lovely clothes and some very good jewellery, for the Major was wealthy and Bonnie was a very smart girl. She moved in with Maurie in the big front room on the top storey of No 86 and it was as though she had never been away, except that she retired from business. She was a strange girl, Bonnie. She was completely honest, and she loved to read, and when she had read a book she loved to discuss it. All this is very unusual in a prostitute, and don't let the intellectual-sentimentalist novelist tell you otherwise. We talked together a great deal, for she would come to the flat and talk with me when Maurie was out on a job, or perhaps merely casing the various baccarat schools that he protected. On one occasion she was telling me of the glories of the Major's home somewhere in Vermont.

"Why did you come back to Maurie?" I asked.

"I loved him, and besides," here she paused and thought a while, "I couldn't live without the excitement," she finished.

If it was excitement she wanted she got plenty of it at No 86, which was run by her grandmother. At last I had discovered who was Bonnie's grandmother. It was not Pat Gleeson at all. Pat had merely been the Madam for whom Bonnie's mother worked. Bonnie's grandmother was an old Cockney woman, and she was complete mistress of many trades. She was a fence, a Madam, the proprietress of a sly grog, and, of course, she plied a little blackmail as a sideline. Naturally such varied activities made life at No 86 fairly lively. It had, long ago, been declared a disorderly house, and the police, without warrant, or let or hindrance, or thank you, or kiss my foot, could come traipsing through at all hours of the day or night—which they did; the Vice Squad, the Licensing Squad, the Gaming Squad, the Larceny Squad, and, on a couple of very uncomfortable occasions, the Homicide boys. And they are no fun. They're much too serious.

Old Dora had No 86 arranged in business areas. The family (herself, Bonnie and Maurie) lived on the top storey in considerable splendour, if not taste. Down underneath, the three front rooms were divided in half by plywood. This made six cubicles that small-time pros hired by the day, hour or night. In the big room at the back was the slyg. (beer 7s. 6d. a bottle) and in the shed in the back yard, and in the back yard itself, were the stolen goods, in all sorts of unlikely places—diamonds up the walnut tree, etc., etc.

The boys cached their guns somewhere, but where I do not know. Charlie always had the decency to tell me very little of what he did. I remember once when I had not seen him for three days. I was not worried and I had long since ceased to be hurt for it always happened like that. He would come in at all hours of the night. He would get up in the morning, have a bottle of ice-cold beer for breakfast, and say, "See you", and then he'd be gone.

He might be back the same evening. He might be back in three days or a week's time. He might be back drunk or sober, good-tempered and witty, or taciturn and moody.

"I'll always come back to you some time," he would tell me, lying with his cheek against my shoulder on the rare occasions when he was not feeling disgusted with himself after love-making. "Always be sure that some time, some place, I'll come back to you."

Well, this time he had been gone three days and, suddenly, as I was walking along Elizabeth Street, going to Couties to get a supply of practice shoes, I saw him. He was wearing a hat, which was something he never did at ordinary times, and he sat at the wheel of a black Humber Hawk. I went across and said, "Hullo, Charlie."

He looked at me and said, "I don't know you."

"But, Charlie—"

"For Christ's sake get going. Get across the road."

He turned on me a look of such urgency and rage that I swung round, walked to the back of the car, crossed over to the Post Office, mixed in the crowd there and went down the Bourke Street steps. There I caught a taxi and got myself out of the city as quickly as I could. That evening the *Herald* came out with headlines "Big Warehouse Payroll Snatched—Unknown Gunmen escape in Getaway Car". There was the usual rigmarole about how the police were combing the city and they expected to make an early arrest. So far as I know they have not made it yet. Charlie came in a week later. All he said was, "I was working it a bit hot and I panicked a bit."

"Charlie, I saw you in Elizabeth Street the day the payroll went off."

"Not me."

"Charlie, I could swear it was you."

I realised that this was an unfortunate choice of words. Charlie was looking at me with his terrible shuttered eyes.

"Not me," he repeated. "You didn't see me."

"Then you must have a double."

"Must have."

I tried again in the early hours of the morning when he was lying beside me having a cigarette and saying that it was good to be home.

"But, Charlie, you were in a black Humber."

The arm that was round my shoulders did not even stiffen. The glow of the cigarette went backwards and forwards in the dark. The most experienced police officer would have sensed neither tension nor strain—only withholding, complete withholding. He said, "Sure it was a Humber? Could have been a Mercedes. Could have been one of Angie Randazzo's boys."

I said no more. Even I knew the difference between a Mercedes and a Humber, and also I knew the face of the man who slept beside me. However, it was obvious that I was to be told nothing, so I shut up. But Charlie was in a marvellous mood for a week or so. He drank comparatively little. He was gay and loving. We went to the races and dinner at the Australia and then on to the Tivoli. We drove down to Portsea where Normie Morrison had bought himself a summer house. Normie, also, seemed in excellent spirits. Never had I seen such geniality in the underworld. Then Charlie said he would buy me a fur.

"Freddie Earnshaw's got his woman dripping with furs so you'll have one too."

"I am now the complete gunman's moll," I told Marty.

It was about a week later that I, wearing the platinum fox, stopped the traffic outside the Tankerville Arms Hotel. I had taken all the morning classes and the afternoon was mine, so I collected Owen from the kindergarten and dressed him in his new summer suit. Then I arrayed myself in my new outfit— the skin-tight dress of pale pink satin that had been Charlie's first gift, my sheerest stockings, my highest-heeled shoes, and the silvery, lovely fur around my shoulders.

"My God! You look like a gangster's girl, right enough," said Marty, and she loaned me her new antelope handbag to round off the ensemble. Then I set off to No 86 to do a little showing off to Bonnie and old Dora. I suppose they were not very impressed with the platinum fox; especially Dora, who had managed to work off within twelve months the fifteen minks that Johnny had removed from the store rooms of Silberstein and Samuels.

I did not stay long. Both Dora and Bonnie professed ignorance of where Charlie had been after the payroll job, and they both pretended to believe that Angie Randazzo's boys had done it. This irritated me, and Dora, watching me with her eyes of a shrewd, sinful old lizard, said, "Look, kid, you're still a cleanskin, and if you've got any sense you'll stay that way. The less you know about anything the better."

This excellent advice, naturally enough, irritated me further, and then one of the girls came in with a customer, and this depressed me. So I finished up my tea, said I still had some messages to do in town, and went out again, glad to be back in the streets and the sunshine. I told Owen that I'd take him across to the Fitzroy Gardens and show him the fairy tree. He seemed pleased with this arrangement and we wandered along to the corner, looking for a cab. By the standards of Collins Street, I would have been about the most execrably clad woman in Melbourne; but by the criteria of Johnson Street I was superb. I think that the first blast of a taxi siren came from my old friend Angus McMaster, who, as luck would have it, was having his petrol tank refilled at the garage opposite the Tankerville Arms. His appreciative performance on the siren caused all the other waiting customers to join in the fun. They blasted away on their car horns, they whistled and wolf-called. All the bowser attendants whistled as well, and the men waiting outside the Tankerville Arms, getting a bit of sun between drinks, raised one ear-splitting shout. Never did a new fur, allied with a new brassière, have a greater triumph.

And then the taxi came swinging into the kerb, and the passenger who sat in the front seat with the driver was leaning out and calling to me. Glancing sideways I could see a small golden brown face, high cheek-bones and white teeth, and suddenly I remembered Uncle Shaun talking to me of his wife who had died when she was so young :

"She had a little smooth face and skin like golden satin."

It was this that made me turn. On a sudden wave of longing for Uncle Shaun and all the honest, healthy people amongst whom I had once lived, I turned towards the taxi and the lad with the golden face.

"Hullo," he said.

"Hullo."

"May I drive you anywhere?"

"No, thank you."

He spoke almost without accent, just enough to let me know he was an Australian, and now I was looking at him closely I could see he was a white man. Despite the high cheek-bones and the almost black eyes, there was nothing of the East in his face.

"Is that your little boy?" he asked.

"Yes."

"Then you're married?"

"I'm a widow."

"No boy friend?"

"No boy friend."

I must be going mad! Didn't I love Charlie with all my heart?

"Then what harm if I drive you where you want to go?"

Owen smiled at him. Owen liked adult males. Sometimes he seemed a little bored with the feminine company supplied by myself, Marty and Phyl. Now he said, "Mummy, why can't the man come and see the fairy tree?"

"There you are, see. Your little boy likes me."

This made it easy for me to give in gracefully and we all went off to see the fairy tree and Captain Cook's cottage and to have tea in the kiosk. We ate out on the verandah in the leaf-dappled sunshine and fed crumbs to the sparrows. Our new friend's name was Joe Ferelle and he spoke very little, just smiled such a smile as I had never seen matched for gaiety and brilliance since my grandmother died, and looked after Owen and allowed me to be silent and drink the sunlight and the clear air and the quiet into the very marrow of my bones.

I lingered over my third cup of tea. I felt deeply contented sitting there with the little brown birds hopping round my feet and the old-fashioned metal tea-pot before me. Leaning back in my chair I looked at Joe across the top of my cup.

"Where do you come from?" I asked.

"I'm Australian."

"Yes, of course, but where do you come from in Australia? You're much too brown for someone from Melbourne."

Joe looked down at his hands. "I was dark to begin with," he said, "and I'm a seaman and I've just finished a season's mutton-birding, and that puts a fine healthy tan on anyone."

"Where were you mutton-birding?"

"Down on the Furneaux Islands."

"Do you come from there?"

"No, I come from the Bellereve Group. It's four small islands a little to the nor'west of the Furneaux. My old grandfather discovered them and named them. He said they were the islands of his dreams. He came from Jersey in the Channel Islands and he sailed his own eighty-tonner out to Tasmania. He was on a fishing trip when he discovered the Bellereve. He came into harbour driven by a terrific southerly, and he used to tell us how the moonlight came through the clouds and shone on the masts of the *Emilie* and the surf was breaking on the bar and he thought 'It's now or never' and he said to his brothers like General Beauregard is supposed to have said, 'Come on, you bastards, do you want to live for ever?' and he put the wheel round hard to starboard and followed the track of the moon across the bar and the little *Emilie* went in with the southerly at her stern as sweetly as a sea-gull, and suddenly the clouds lifted for a moment and there they were in a perfect little bay, with the moon all silver on the water. It was like a dream of heaven, he said, he has never seen the bay so beautiful since. And it was there that we settled."

I was silent. When romance at its most perfect enters the life of man, for perhaps only once in that lifetime, I always feel that comment becomes blasphemy. Joe finished his tea and turned to help Owen, who was sitting on the floor trying to coax a sparrow with a piece of cream cake.

"You just keep the cake in your hand," he said, "and stretch it out and sit there as still and quiet as can be. That's it, gently, gently, *doucement, doucement.*"

He drawled out the French word with a sort of lingering lilt like one who is repeating some incantation in a language old and magical and more than half forgotten.

"Have you ever been on the big ships?" I asked.

"During the war I went to England on a Pommy and from there I went in a convoy all the way up to Archangel. But I like the little boats and the little rocky islands. I love Bass Strait. I've been sailing around it since I was eight years old."

"Did you come up to Melbourne for a holiday?"

"Not really, I'm not very fond of Melbourne. I usually holiday in Sydney. I came up on the *Emilie* with a cargo of mutton-birds."

"Not the same *Emilie*?"

Joe laughed. "Lord no, this is *Emilie Ferelle the Third*. They were all called after my grandmother. The old *Emmy* wouldn't have known this one. She's a hundred and fifty feet with an auxiliary engine and freezing capacity for ten thousand pounds of fish. Grandfather and my eldest brother have shares in her and I'm mate."

Emilie Ferelle the Third! What a name for a schooner—white sails and raking masts, and coming home with the surf booming and the lights flickering on in the grey stone houses ashore. Men who carried guns and took cocaine seemed a long way away.

I rose regretfully. "I'll have to go now," I said, "thanks for a very good afternoon."

Joe rose and helped Owen to his feet. To my intense relief

he had not once said that he loved kids, but he handled Owen in an off-hand reassuring sort of way. "I've got a tribe of little brothers and sisters myself," he had said.

Now, as he handed me my fur, he said, "May I see you again?"

"I'm sorry, Joe, it's impossible. Don't ask me why, but it is. If we walk over to the Parade now could you catch me a cab?"

"Well, may I take you home?"

"No. Please don't press, Joe. It's not possible."

He smiled and his smile was so charming that I almost weakened, and then I thought of Charlie's heavy shoulders and those fourteen professional fights. Instinctively I knew that Charlie did not care enough about me to be jealous. The question was, did Charlie know it? Joe was too young, too slender, built in too Gallic a mode. I could not allow him to take the risk of finding out Charlie's reaction, but I was unwilling to see the last of him, so I said: "Could we drop you anywhere first?"

"The *Emilie*'s berthed just below the King Street Bridge. I would be glad if you could drop me back there."

The *Emilie Ferelle* was as beautiful as I had imagined she would be. Joe slipped 10s. into my hand for cab fare and went off, waving to Owen, who had been so charmed with him that he blew him a kiss. Joe kissed the back of his hand in our general direction. Then he waved and was gone. Down on the South Melbourne side of the Bridge I got the taxi driver to stop. I ran back and looked down over the parapet and there was Joe, standing on the deck. He was talking to someone who was obviously a relative, though not so dark and a little taller. He had pulled off his white shirt and now it fluttered in his hand as he gesticulated to add point to his words. His body was the same golden tan right down to his waist.

A couple of days later Charlie came in and was very silent, though good-tempered in an off-hand sort of way, all through dinner. Afterwards, when we were drinking our coffee in the lounge, he said, "I hear you had an escort away from Number 86 the other day."

I decided to answer interrogation in the manner which he always used. I said, "Did I?"

Charlie reached out and caught my arm and dragged me towards him. His eyes that usually shuttered in anger were now wide open and receptive of me. I have seen the same look in the eyes of a boxer as he sized up his opponent just one second before he administered the Sunday Punch. I could have laughed out loud. Carl Barton, the great big fast car expert, the clever operator who could lose any police car in Melbourne, was now looking at me with some sort of respect. I was a threat to his vanity. He would have to study me at last.

I smiled and said, "It wasn't important."

"Why didn't you tell me?"

"This is the first time I've seen you since. Besides it wasn't important."

"Like you said, it's not important—why did you go?"

"Everyone on the corner was whistling and going on. I just wanted to get away. Half the people in the Tankerville know you look after me. I didn't want to look a fool."

"Weren't there any other taxis? Ah, Jesus! What does it matter? You please yourself what you do and I'll do the same."

I knew he would be in a terrible tantrum of wounded pride if he had to ask me another question so I said, "It's not as though he knows my address, or is going to see me again, or anything."

"I don't give a frig when you see him."

After all this you may imagine my very mixed feelings when, on going to take a private class a few days later, I find that the private pupil turns out to be none other but the earliest of all my admirers, the first of the few, as my brother called him—Swede Ryan!! And he'd paid for an hour and there was no getting rid of him. I had heard them talk of Swede at No 86 and I had been told that he was doing very well. He was spoken of with respect. Swede Ryan, the best tank man in Melbourne. I confess to a certain amount of regard for the tank man, myself. Where the others use their gun or their muscles, the tank man uses his skill and brains. He is usually a quiet chap without the flamboyance and paranoia of the average criminal. He does not feel the need to assert himself. He knows he has talent. Well, there Swede sat. His face was as puffy and his eyes as heavy as ever —and his hands were just as beautiful. They were white, and better tended than mine, the nails filed down even, and the fingertips rubbed soft with emery paper. He looked up as I came in and he said, "I want to learn to samba."

194

I think this was meant to be a joke. Actually, it sounded most extraordinarily menacing, and I found myself laughing nervously and saying, "Swede, fancy seeing you."

Just fancy! Just bloody well fancy!

Thank God he did not want to dance. He had come to declare himself and, without any more preamble, he did so. He said that he always remembered that when I was a little girl at school I had promised to be his girl. I did not remember any such thing but his eyes were so wild and his face twitched so terribly that I decided he must be coming out of a prolonged bout of cocaine. At such times the boys are always very short-tempered and touchy and do not brook contradiction—so I didn't contradict. Swede went on to say that he had lived on that promise.

"Honest, kid, it meant a terrible lot to me. When I was in Royal Park and I heard you were going with Dawson I nearly went mad. When I came out, I was getting into the big time then, you realise that, Lisha, and I could have had acid on his face in five minutes if I'd liked, but you weren't with him any more and I thought, 'What's he to me? Let him live.' "

I dared not show disgust. I had to sit and listen.

"And then when you were married so young I kept away. I've got great respect for marriage. Honest I have, kid."

I fully expected Swede to come in here with the information that, though personally not a very good Catholic, he still had the deepest regard for the Church, the State, the Establishment, etc., etc., etc. They're a dead respectable lot, are the criminals. However, he must have considered that he had already come out strong enough as a moralist for he went on to say that I was wasted on Charlie.

"He'll never make the big time," said Swede, with scorn. "You know what he'll be in less than ten years' time? He'll be an old drunken ex-pug rolling other drunks for a couple of bob."

I thought this very likely, myself.

"There's a lot of things I could tell you," went on Swede, and I knew that he was afraid of Charlie's fists, and maybe even of the Smith and Wesson that he carried under his full drape coat.

"Look, Swede," I said, "it's no good talking like this. Will you have a drink?"

Swede said he drank milk. He had milk and I had a brandy

because I felt I needed it. By this time Swede's hour was almost up and he insisted on paying me. He would not, he said, impose upon the time of Charlie Barton's girl, and he did not need money. He had, he told me, three thousand stashed away and he owned three houses and his own car; he didn't have to go stealing cars.

"Think about it, honey," he advised me.

I thought about it. I thought about it all day, and when Charlie came in that evening I told him about it.

"Couldn't you keep him away?" I begged. "Just give him the word to keep off?"

But Charlie knew that Swede was no sexual menace to any man alive so he roared laughing.

"You can take care of yourself," he said, "you're the little charmer that can find men in taxis to protect you outside the Tankerville Arms. You'll be all right."

"Charlie, I'm sure he dopes."

"Of course he dopes."

I burst into tears. "God Almighty, Charlie, I'll have to go away. I can't live this sort of life. It's O.K. for Bonnie Gleeson. She's used to it and she likes it. But I'll have to go away."

Charlie was sitting on the divan and he was stone-cold sober. He pulled me down beside him till he was looking into my face. Then he wiped the tears from my cheeks. He was very gentle.

"To go away," he said, "yes, that would be best. To go away; that's what we all want, isn't it, darling? Anyway I'll keep the Swede off. Don't worry about him any more."

I was so relieved that I continued to cry in an exhausted sort of way, my face buried in the cushions of the divan. Charlie stroked my hair till I was calmer, then he lifted me up and wiped the tears from my cheeks.

"You're a nice girl," he kept on saying, "you haven't changed so very much. You're still a very nice, good girl."

When I was quiet again he said, "Tell you what, you're tired and fed up. How about we go down to Normie's beach house for Christmas? We've been invited."

But I cried out against this with such vehemence that Charlie was startled. I had not realised that Christmas was so near. I had become inclined to shut my mind against Christmas, but it was only two weeks away. Nothing would stop its coming.

And all the bells on earth shall ring
On earth shall ring . . .

No! I knew that if it were to save my life I could not spend Christmas Day with Charlie or any of his friends.

"Charlie," I said, "I think Christmas Day should be spent with the family. Owen and I are going out to have dinner with Mother and we'll probably stay the night."

Charlie nodded. "You're right," he said, "it's one day you should spend with your mother. I'll get them a few presents and have Christmas at home myself. Mum'll like that."

Filled with good intentions he disappeared on the morning of Christmas Eve and did not appear again till about a week after New Year. He looked swollen and yellow and sick, and he was almost weeping as he described the fiasco he had made of his mother's festive season.

"I was just about one pony shandy off the D.T.s for about a week," he kept saying. "I sat bloody stupid all through Christmas dinner. I couldn't speak. That's how bloody rotten I was. I couldn't even speak. The priest was there and all. God! A man ought to be shot, doing that to his mother at Christmas."

He talked about it for the rest of the week, castigating himself, living it over, rolling it round his memory. He had shamed his mother on Christmas Day, before the priest, before all the relatives. Revenge is very sweet.

It took about a week of quiet living and unlimited raw eggs with Worcestershire sauce and cups of Bonox before he was back in his full strength and then we all went down to Portsea to spend the weekend at Normie Morrison's. Normie's beach house was beautiful. It was set in a fold in a hillside and the windows looked out on to a wide sweep of ocean. Its position and its plan were both so good that not even the colour and furnishing expert called in by Normie had managed to spoil it. Normie, in this set-up, played the gentleman of culture, money and leisure. Arrayed in faultlessly tailored slacks, or tuxedo, depending upon the hour, he met guests at the door. They were then handed over to George. George was an old retainer, an ex-pug ex-safecracker who was now on the square and had taken up religion. Reformed though he was, he missed the company of criminals, so he worked as a sort of butler-cum-houseboy for

Normie (whom he admired tremendously), and very well he played his part. For many months I thought he was English. It came as a surprise to learn that he had been born in the Fitz-roy Narrows. George led the visitors to their bedrooms where the carpets were beautifully deep and the mattresses were made of foam rubber, and there was hot and cold running water, and the built-in wardrobes had room for dozens of dresses and suits. He always addressed guests as Sir or Madam, and criminals, who at other times had a fair sense of humour, would take it all with so solemn a face and so pompous a bearing that the whole affair became one great pathetic charade. And do not think for one moment that one only encountered the criminal element amongst all this luxury. I have met almost the only members of high society that I ever knew down at Normie's. Big business men who played baccarat, all glad to be known as friends of the big boy. Little girls who had just left finishing school and were ambitious of sleeping with a big-time smash-and-grab boy. Usually they achieved this dream—and the smash-and-grab boy ended up borrowing several hundred pounds from them and not repaying it; or they developed a taste for the life and finished by supporting the smash-and-grab expert and weeping into their gin and telling all who would listen about how they had been nice kids once, a long time ago. They were the greatest bore of the lot. But such confessions were considered non-U and were not encouraged in the upper-crust atmosphere that prevailed down at Normie's. There we swam and sat in the sun on the patio and discussed our trips to Surfers' or the States, and talked of cars (big expensive ones) and of buying houses. We women admired one another's clothes, jewels and accessories, and Owen was kissed by a great many beautifully groomed ladies who all loved children. (One thing I can say with confidence is that my son should be well and truly inoculated against harlots.)

In accordance with the general tone, Charlie was always Carl down at Normie's and he got around smelling of Prince Gourielli after-shave lotion and saying, "As they say in the old country" and "As Socrates said" till I longed to thump him under the ear. At some stage of his career he had taken a few piano lessons and had learned a couple of pieces by rote. So down he would sit at Normie's Bechstein Grand and, after a few preliminary ripples, he would be well away with the *Dream of Olwen* or the Theme from *Laura*. I can tell you there was gracious living laid on down at Portsea.

True to form, after being so good all the weekend at Normie's Charlie decided to be in a vile mood by the time we got home. He wandered about the flat in moody silence, and had I asked him what was the trouble he would have shrugged and said, "Nothing."

But I did not ask him. By this time I played a little game with myself. It consisted of ignoring Charlie's megrims and then watching the manner in which he behaved when being ignored. It was pathetic to see him watch your face for reaction. If there was none he would try something else. Now, on this Monday evening, he stopped mooching round and came and sat in the kitchen doorway—his back supported against one door-post and his feet placed about the level of his head on the other. When in his present frame of mind he always ignored the more conservative posture and seating accommodation. A Czar of vice was above them, as it were. Now he looked at me hopefully. On one occasion when I had been dashing round dressing for a competition I had said, being irritable with nerves, "For God's sake, Charlie, can't you find somewhere else to sit? I'm tired of stepping over you."

He had moved his foot about one thousandth of an inch. "Name's Carl," he said.

But tonight I had nowhere to go and nothing particular to do. I felt calm and relaxed. I went on chopping up greens for the salad. Then the kitten, Napoleon, came up and patted him with one paw, and Charlie stroked him gently under the chin. Napoleon loved this. He stalked around Charlie, arching his back, and Charlie stroked him from the tip of his nose right down to the end of his tail. The kitchen was filled with Napoleon's purring and then he climbed bodily into Charlie's lap. Charlie took him up and cradled him against his chest. The little cat closed his eyes in ecstasy and Charlie's face was very tender; softly, softly he rubbed his chin down against the kitten's ears. Then, suddenly, he put the poor little animal on the floor and spun it away from him with such force that the unfortunate Napoleon was rolled over and over till he was brought up short by the side of the fridge. This went on for about three minutes, with Napoleon being alternately cuddled and tormented till he did not know where he was.

Finishing the salad preparations, I said, "That's a strange way to play with a kitten."

I did not say it in anger. Charlie had been angling for anger all the evening. I spoke as though I were discussing some abstract problem.

Charlie looked up at me. "They like it," he said.

"Do you think so?"

"Everything and everybody likes it—women, cats, anyone, there's no difference. First you throw them away from you and then you take them back. That's how you make them stick to you."

"Not me, mate," I said, "never, never me."

"Don't be too sure." Charlie grinned at me. He had gained some sort of response at last.

Suddenly I could not be bothered what Charlie thought. If he wished to think I was speaking because I was hurt, well then, let him think so. In a swift moment of truth I knew that I did not love him and I never had. I did not even like him particularly.

I said, "Charlie, you've known me all my life and yet it is very obvious to me that you don't know me at all—so I'm going to enlighten you. If you imagine I relish that silly love-and-rejection routine you're much mistaken, and I'd never stand for it for five minutes."

"What are you getting so hot under the collar for?" Charlie was genuinely delighted now. "I'd never leave you. I might go away but—"

"But I'd always come back to you," I finished off rudely. "I'm getting sick of hearing that, Charlie. In the first place it sounds like the script of a B-class film, in the second it's so damn condescending, and in the third place it's a bore."

Charlie put down Napoleon and looked at me.

"You're very independent all of a sudden," he said. "A man ought to shoot through for six months just to show you who's boss."

"You shoot through any time you like."

"Thanks for the permission, baby."

"And while we're talking about what bores me, Charlie, I might as well open up the little soulcase and let you know something else : irritating as I find such silly remarks as the one that began this row, I find the women who fall for that kind of line even more tiresome. I'm getting sick of women with sixty quids' worth of suit on their back and a fiver's worth of hair style from Jacques of Collins Street and the whole ensemble set off by a whacking great black eye, getting round telling anyone who's silly enough to listen, 'Gawd, I love that man. He treats me like a dog but I love him.'"

"Maybe they do love him, at that."

"Well I'll never love anyone in that way. I wouldn't be such a crawler."

I was surprised that he did not leave that same night but, having walked out for no reason at all on numerous occasions, he now decided to stay and be placating. But now it was my turn to be silent. I pitied him, and I made no plans to leave him because I could not contemplate being on my own, but I could not be bothered talking to him except in the most impersonal manner. Not only was I impersonal, I was cheerful and impersonal—a combination which Charlie never could stand. After three days of it (and three nights as well, if it comes to that) he disappeared and I did not see him for over a week. When next I encountered him he was standing outside the Green Gate sweet shop. He was dressed as though he had just come from the wharf and he was talking to a very fat red-head. While talking he was leaning up against the window of the Green Gate and, with both hands on her hips, he was trying to draw her towards him. The red-head was acting coy. I said "Hullo, Charlie", and the look on Charlie's face was such a blend of surprise, guilt and rueful amusement that I almost laughed aloud. Perhaps my sense of humour would not have been in such tremendous form if the red-head had been anything to worry about, but she was neither pretty nor smart, nor even very clean. I went home, bathed, had a swift facial and made myself up with great care. Then I waited for Charlie. Sure enough he arrived at about eight o'clock—all ready for the big explanation. He began by saying that both he and the red-head had had a few drinks and that she meant nothing to him. I laughed in his face. I said that I had taken it for granted that he was not madly in love with someone who was five stone heavier than he was. As far as I was concerned she became Rosabelle McGee ("Her name is Rosabelle McGee, and she tips the scales at 303") and that was all there was to it. She became a family joke. This griped Charlie somewhat, for he did not relish any of his possessions being ridiculed. On the other hand he could not protest, for he knew that if he did I would make a greater joke of it than ever. It may be gathered from all this that for sheer immaturity we were about evenly matched, but that I had a stronger strain than usual of the good old feminine bitchiness, which gave me the advantage.

Early in April I asked Charlie to take me to Sydney or Cairns for the winter. The mere thought of another Melbourne winter terrified me. I had already had one very bad cold and it was on an evening when I knew that I was coming down with my first dose of flu for the season that I asked—and he refused. Not that he refused straight out. He hummed and ha'd and said he could not let down his mates in his gang on the wharf.

"Charlie," I said, "I've never asked a favour of you before. God Almighty knows I can't stand this bloody bastard of a place in winter." I was desperate. "It's cold enough to kill you now. What will it be like in July?"

Charlie moved himself into a more comfortable position on the end of the bed. "I dunno," he said, "the air's lovely and fresh here. When I was going down to the wharf this morning it was all lovely and misty and clean. I thought it was beautiful."

In that moment I loathed Charlie. He had a stocky well-fleshed body already beginning to put on a nice insulating layer of beer-fat. I had long skinny limbs that burned with fever as soon as I began to sneeze. It made no difference to Charlie where he worked. There were wharves in Sydney and Cairns, but his boss, Maurie Flower, had finally grown tired of explaining to the police why he had not a regular job and had adopted the usual course in these circumstances. He had joined the Painters and Dockers. This reflected a good deal of glory on Charlie. He did not want to go away to some wharf where he was nobody. Hence all this poppycock about not wanting to let down his mates.

He was very good to me for the next few days. He paid the

doctor and went down to the nearest Chinese café every night and brought me back meals to tempt my appetite. When I was comparatively well again he paid for me to have a hair set and face pack, and bought me a big hand-knitted Italian jumper to keep me wrapped against the winter wind; but he would not take me away. I had become a point with him.

"No woman's going to arrange my life for me," he said.

But the ironical thing was that, just when April was passing into May, Angie Randazzo's boys made a few arrangements for him with which he was obliged to comply whether he would or no, and it happened in this manner :

The baccarat schools of Melbourne were divided almost equally between Angie and Normie Morrison. When Maurie Flower decided to open his own school, Normie, who could not be bothered with one small school more or less, and who was rather friendly with Maurie, refrained from demanding any protection money on the condition that Maurie did not branch out any farther. For some weeks the school flourished. Clarrie Harrop and a nephew of Bluey Gleeson provided protection and Charlie drove such customers as did not wish to come in their own car. Maurie was delighted and talked of having a small cabaret as a blind in the front room. Then Angie Randazzo decided to move in. Angie had been bred in a sterner school than Normie Morrison—Sicily to wit—and his thrifty continental mind was troubled at the thought of even one small establishment functioning without paying anything to him. After giving it due consideration he called his boys together and set them to the terrorising of Maurie Flower. They went about their task with great *élan*. They sent a shower of tommy gun bullets through the front windows of No 86. As we know Maurie and Bonnie slept upstairs so nobody was hurt, though several of the girls who had hired the downstairs cubicles for the night were obliged, with their clients, to rush into the back lane in considerable disarray—which was interesting for the neighbours but off-putting for the clients.

After this initial failure the Randazzo push really got down to business. Driving one of the big Randazzo Mercedes they attempted to run down Bonnie when she was driving a Holden. She was about eight months pregnant but her nerves were in their usual superb condition so they did not do her a great deal of harm. They were, however, tougher on the Holden, which they rammed up against an iron lamp-post.

Maurie said he would not be stood over and doubled his guard and carried on business as usual. The Randazzo strong-arm squad decided to call in person, which they did late one night about a week later. Their intelligence service must have slipped up (an extremely unusual thing in the Randazzo combine) for they came on the very evening when Maurie was being paid a social call by Normie Morrison, Freddie Earnshaw, Johnny Lockwood and several of their boys. It was old Australians versus new, as you might say, and who knows what the outcome might have been had it not been for the fact that the Gaming Squad also decided to drop in.

Maurie was tipped off about three minutes before the raid commenced. He managed to get all the players off the premises, and there was a most exciting throwing away of guns and racing for cars. Maurie's car went off with Charlie in the driver's seat and Clarrie Harrop beside him nursing his trusty Owen gun which he himself had turned up on a lathe in his beautifully equipped back-yard workshop. In the back of the car sat the Big Three—Normie Morrison, Freddie Earnshaw and Johnny Lockwood. Now the Randazzo clique, not having been told of the tip-off (why should they? they didn't pay for it, as Maurie so reasonably said) were under the mistaken impression that the Australian faction was in flight before them. Several of them jumped into a Mercedes and gave chase. The school was in a converted warehouse in South Melbourne and Charlie headed into his home ground of the Port, where he soon lost the Randazzo car amongst the alleys and back streets that he had known all his life. As he said later, the Randazzo driver was a new boy who had leaped to the wheel all dash and Latin impetuosity, but he did not know Melbourne and only twelve months before he had never driven anything except a donkey cart. He was no match for the Victorian champion. However, our boys exulted a little too early for, as they drove towards Glastonbury Street where they intended to wait for Maurie, they saw that a police car, alerted by radio, was following them, and gaining on them into the bargain. At that time they were coming along Punt Road. Normie leaned forward and said to Charlie, "Get into Richmond as fast as you can, turn under the railway bridge, then straight to your right and first turn to your left." This brought them into a small side street which had two streets running out of it. The right hand street led into Swan Street, the other was a cul-de-sac. Normie calculated that the police, knowing that one street led into a main thoroughfare, would expect him to take the other—therefore he took the one that led into the main thoroughfare, and as the police swore and raged and reversed in the cul-de-sac Charlie turned the corner into Swan Street. And as soon as they were round the corner Normie barked "Slow down", and in the instant that the big car came almost to a halt he and Freddie Earnshaw threw out Johnny Lockwood. They threw their guns on top of him and Clarrie Harrop thoughtfully jettisoned his Owen gun at the same time. It is to Charlie's eternal credit that his Smith and Wesson stayed where it was. So it was that the police, tearing into Swan Street, were forced to brake lest they run over Johnny's prostrate form. It is possible that Normie and Freddie would have preferred to throw Clarrie Harrop to the pursuing cops. They were quite fond of poor old Johnny; but Harrop was nursing a gun and the unfortunate Johnny was unarmed—always a foolish way to be when amongst friends, as Normie said when telling the story afterwards. Johnny, famous for the hardness of his head, came to as the police picked him up off the road from the small private arsenal wherein he lay. While under observation in St Vincent's Hospital he disclaimed all knowledge of the whole preceding evening. He said that a bump on the head had resulted in amnesia. He continued to cop it sweet and did his two years for illegal possession of a lethal weapon without a word. Freddie and Normie looked after his wife and son while he was inside. They sent him lavish supplies of tobacco and other forms of prison currency and when he came out he stepped straight back into his place in the Morrison machine. When Normie, now that nothing could be done about it, was inclined to laugh at the picture of Johnny sitting on a pile of revolvers in the middle of a Richmond road, Johnny said nothing except that he who laughs last laughs longest—and today only Johnny walks the earth. Normie and Freddie lie under extremely expensive headstones in Fawkner Cemetery, one in the Presbyterian section, one in the Catholic. Freddie Earnshaw died in a car crash; but who blew Normie's brains out one wet August evening outside his biggest two-up school? Nobody saw who did it. A man stepped from behind a truck and there were half a dozen of Melbourne's leading gunmen around Normie, but nobody saw the face of the man who fired the shot. Nobody saw him at all.

But all this was in the future on that wet autumn night when Johnny found himself on the roadway with the police car pulled up beside him. For the next week there were the usual raids by the police, threats and counter threats by the rival gangs and smuggling away of vital witnesses. Charlie disappeared completely, and I heard that he was in Sydney and heading north. I did not see him again till the next summer.

It was about the middle of that winter when I received a letter from Lachy McLaughlin. This was unusual. Lachy never wrote. He just arrived. He had, he wrote, met the most wonderful woman in the world. This, also, was unusual and not at all Lachy's form as I knew it. She was not, the letter continued, a girl. She was a little older than Lachy and had had a bit of trouble. Indeed she had, I thought, as I read on further. She had been married to a Jamaican trumpet player who had gone on tour and never returned. As he was now living with a strip-tease artist it looked as though he would not be returning. Therefore Lachy was looking after the most wonderful woman in the world, who had three children and loved Lachy to desperation. All this came from an address in Tiger Bay.

I was very unwilling to tell this news to Phyl. I knew how she liked to keep her admirers. "Not that I want them but it's nice to have them around," she would say, and she had been particularly fond of Lachy. No, I did not want to tell her at all. However, she was coming over to tea that night and I decided to get it over and done with. I gave her the letter to read while I was washing up, then I turned my back and busied myself at the sink so that I would not see her face as she read. I had been prepared for a certain amount of chagrin. I had not been prepared for a frantic outburst of weeping and Phyl crouched down before the fire with her hands over her face. I could think of nothing to say and when I did speak I was so powerless to comfort that it would have been better had I remained silent. I said :

"Phyl, I didn't know you were so fond of him."

"Fond!" Phyl turned on me angrily. "I loved him. I loved him all the time."

"I didn't know."

"You must have known. Everyone must have known. He must have seen."

All this from the beautiful Phyl Foley who was supposed to have a heart of stone.

"Oh Phyl," I thought, "my best loved and oldest friend, why couldn't you have been a little more forthcoming? The day is gone when if you smiled graciously at a man he was ready to be your true and faithful knight for evermore. Or rather, the day is gone when you smiled graciously at a young man and perhaps invited him home to tea and social convention did the rest. When it was just taken for granted that the young gentleman would in due course go down on bended knee and into the old 'Fair damsel wilt thou be mine' routine." They were face-saving old conventions but they were at least fifty years out of date, and we had been reared in them.

"Never let a man know you love him."

"Let him make the first move."

"Never let him take you for granted."

"Men don't want women that run after them."

How often had I heard these maxims, particularly the last, from women who labelled anything beyond the barest civility as 'running after'? But I had not believed and Phyl had.

I let her cry on while I went to get her a brandy. It was the only thing I could suggest—a stiff brandy swallowed at one gulp. It steadied her a little and after a while she managed to stop weeping, and went into my bedroom and repaired her make-up. When she came back she sat for a while looking very lost and white-faced before the fire. Then she said :

"Do you remember what a good dancer he was? He was better even than Andy, and Andy used to laugh about it and say they had the best dance halls in the world in Glasgow. 'Every facility,' he used to say, 'a man can be shaved while he dances,' and Lachy would say, 'You're way out of date, you ignorant scouse.'

"Remember the time they won two hundred pounds at Stokes' two-up school and they came home with it and we had a party straight away, and Lachy and Andy had the argument about the football or soccer or whatever it is they play over there, something about some decision or something that Andy said should have been given to his team, and they went out on the Esplanade to demonstrate how it had happened, they had a roll of toilet paper for the ball, remember, and an A.I.F. chap that they'd met at Stokes' went with them to show how it was done according to Australian Rules, and the lot of them got arrested for obstructing the traffic and we had to go down to the station and bail them out, and no sooner were they out than the row was on again and Lachy came home singing to the tune of the Red Flag

'The Celtic goalie never saw
Whaur Alan Morton pit the ba''

and I said 'What on earth language is Lachy singing in?' and Andy was trying to sing him down with

'The workers' flag is scarlet red
It's wrapped around our glorious dead'

and the Aussie was finishing it all off, same tune different words,

'The working class can kiss my arse
I've got a foreman's job at last'

and out came the coppers and arrested them all again, drunk and disorderly, do you remember?"

I nodded. I remembered all too well and the little worm of pain twisted in the bottom of my heart. They had been such good days and now we were alone. But I had had so much and Phyl had not been so lucky.

She came over to see me a week later and announced that she was going up to N.S.W. to visit her Aunt Alice who had married 70,000 acres of the best sheep country in Australia.

"Aunt Allie's always asking me to come," said Phyl, "she's been saying for years that she'd get me a husband amongst the money. Well now's her chance."

So Phyl, having come to grief on the old Irish method of making the women unapproachable, was now falling back on the other fine old Irish institution of the matchmaker. Well, good luck to her.

I was very lonely after she had gone, for Marty, who had flung herself into the jungle that was post-war café society, with determination, even if without much enjoyment, had managed to procure for herself a very rich business man indeed. He was quite a prize and Marty had won him from two models, one call-girl and three society beauties. She was very proud of him. He made more raincoats than anyone else in Melbourne. He was a good twenty years older than Marty, being nearer fifty than forty, and, being of the older school, he liked his comfort and his privacy. Consequently Marty spent most of her time over at his flat in Toorak. I took almost all the evening classes now and I actually opened a bank account. Owen would come to classes with me and sleep on the couch in the dressing-room. I was beginning to depend on Owen a great deal. I spent my free evenings telling him stories, teaching him nursery rhymes and talking to him about matters he was twenty years too young to understand. Not that I need have been so much alone for it is axiomatic in the underworld that as soon as a man goes inside or into smoke his woman is given every opportunity to transfer her affections. Once I was taken to Claridge's by the great Freddie Earnshaw. Freddie usually looked much higher than dancing teachers, but he had just parted with Peggy, the lovely Canadian model with whom he had been living for the last twelve months, and I suppose he was at a loose end. He was in a particularly expansive mood the night he took me out and was pleased to say, before quite a party of people, that I had the sweetest legs in Melbourne.

"You can quote me on that," he said.

That's condescension for you. I swear I was quite overcome.

Shortly afterwards I was invited to one of the really big Earnshaw parties. A sort of criminal Queen Charlotte Ball. Anyone invited had really arrived. It was when the night was warming up that one of the small-timers present had words with his woman, and, perhaps to impress the big boys, perhaps to keep her interested, he tipped the fluid from his cigarette lighter down the side of her neck and, before she had time to step back, he held the lighter against her bare shoulder and flicked the wheel. She screamed and all one side of her neck went up in flames.

"Next time, doll baby," he told her, "it'll be your face."

No one seemed to take a great deal of notice of this. The party went on with unabated verve. Indeed it seemed almost the better for a little excitement, but I went home and did not avail myself of any more opportunities for social climbing. The Earnshaw parties, I decided, were too strong for my stomach. For the rest of the winter when I was not working I sat at home and read and in the early summer Charlie came back.

He looked tired and sick and shabby and was very reticent about what he had been doing. This making a mystery of his activities was one of Charlie's most irritating habits. It irked me particularly now when he seemed to know everything that I had done since he left.

"Hear you went to Claridge's with Earnshaw. Hear you went to Flemington with Normie and Beryl and some big boy from the States."

It was quite a little war of nerves. I countered with :

"And what have you been doing, if I may ask?"

"You may not."

"That's what I thought you'd say."

"Then what are you griping about?"

"I'm not griping. I'm not sufficiently interested."

"Good! That makes two of us and nobody's hurt."

This was not a very promising exchange at the resumption of a love affair. Charlie came across to me and took my hand.

"Don't be sarcastic and hard to get on with," he pleaded. "I've missed you, honest I have, and I nearly went mad when I heard you were running round with Earnshaw."

But I was determined not to give in so easily. Had he left me to risk bubonic plague I would have been more ready to forgive, but he had gone off and left me to the Melbourne flu and that was something I could not overlook.

"Running round with Earnshaw," I scoffed, "since when would Freddie be ready to take your leavings? I went to Claridge's one evening and I was silly enough to go to a party at his place. That's the running round with Earnshaw that you're talking about. Most of the winter I've been indoors sneezing my head off while you've been lying round in the sun."

"Do I look as if I've been lying round in the sun?"

"As a matter of fact you don't."

"Well, that's it. Look, I'd tell you what I've been doing if I could. I got into a bit of trouble up there and I can't tell you about it. Come on, Lisha, let me stay. I thought about you all the time. Let me stay."

So he stayed, because I had been lonely and when he was at home he was someone to talk to; but I felt a little critical of myself. Here I was living with a man whom I did not even like particularly because I was too immature to face the greatest of all trials to the human spirit, being alone. That was really what it amounted to and there was no more to be said.

I was soon to discover the secret of his activities in Sydney and points farther north. It was one pleasant afternoon when Marty and Owen had gone driving with the raincoat king that I decided to go and see a film and, as Charlie had been missing for twenty-four hours, I went by myself. I cannot remember now what film I saw but I shall always remember the look of horror on Charlie's face when he saw me coming down the steps of the Regent Theatre. It was obvious that he wished me a thousand miles away, so, perversely, I stayed where I was, chatting on about this and that and the next thing while the unfortunate Charlie fidgeted and squirmed and threw fearful glances up the steps and in the direction of the Regent's Ladies' Lounge (as they so delicately call it, if I remember aright). At last the poor harassed chap threw discretion to the winds and said, "Look, I can't be seen with you here. I'm with the fat piece. She was keeping me, like, when I was in strife up in Sydney."

So that was it! I thought it over all the way home and I was horrified at myself to find that I just did not care. It just was not decent to live with someone to whom I was so indifferent. Of course I did have a certain amount of misgiving regarding the hygiene of the affair, and I broached this aspect of it when Charlie arrived that evening, as I knew he would, all apologies and explanations. Leaving tact to take care of itself, I plunged straight into the heart of the matter. I said :

"Look, Charlie, if you get the clap from that dreary-looking drab and bring it home to me I'll cut your throat while you sleep. That's not a threat nor a promise, Charlie. Nor is it drama for the sake of drama. It's a plain simple statement of fact."

Charlie, who sprinkled four-letter words through his speech

as though they were some sort of conversational garnishing, could, upon occasion, be most terribly mealy-mouthed. He chose now to be shocked and horrified at my bluntness. He said that he had not touched her since he left Sydney, and she knew how to keep herself clean, and Good God! what did I think he was, and it was no way to talk anyway.

I said I'd talk as I liked.

"Not to me you won't," said Charlie, who could never be made to realise that my first pitiful longing to make him the hero of a love affair was now long over and I had become very objective about him indeed. "No woman's going to speak the way she likes to me. As Socrates said—"

"Ease it up, Charlie. Don't give me that 'Raffles the gentleman crook' routine. It gives me the stomach ache. We've all had plenty of opportunity to observe that you know that there once lived a chap called Socrates. Now I'm going to tell you what Horace really did say. 'The vulgar are the primmest people on earth.' That's what he said, Carl the Socratic authority, and I think of it every time I hear you solemnly talking about the sacredness of motherhood, and the dignity of marriage, and at times such as this when you're editing my language for me. I do indeed hope, sir, that Rosabelle McGee is sufficiently refined in her speech—especially when handing over her earnings."

"I don't bloody take her earnings. It's just I was going bad for dough in Sydney and she gave me a quid now and then. I never stood over her for it. She's wrapped in me, see."

"Poor bitch."

"I'm no bludger and you needn't take me for one."

"I take you, Charlie, for a small time crim on the skids."

"Am I? We'll see if I am. I've got a couple of big jobs coming up this week. I'll show you if I'm finished or not."

But he had no jobs coming up, no jobs at all. Even that loyal old friend Maurie Flower had been obliged to give up trying to help him.

"I've give him a few jobs for old time's sake," said Maurie, "but it's no good, Lisha. You've got to have a steady hand on the wheel, and last time he arrived plastered to the eyeballs, full as a State school. We had to get young Bertie Stone to do the job, and he's that young he doesn't hardly know how to let in a clutch. I'm sorry, Lisha, but Charlie's had it."

I thought so too and I was very sorry for him and regretted that I had been so cruel at our last meeting. No one should be told that they are on the skids—particularly when they are.

He rang the studio about a week later and said he was dying of misery, and he had broken with Rosabelle and he was working regularly and if he did not see me soon he would very probably cut his throat. I did not believe this last, naturally enough. I have never seen myself in the role of female destroyer, and I could never visualise Charlie as being destroyed by anything except alcohol. However I told him he could come out to the flat that evening.

When I got back to the flat about five o'clock that evening I heard an unknown voice coming from the kitchen. This unknown voice was announcing that someone called Tricia was doing wonderfully well in a solicitor's office, where she was already a private secretary, though only sixteen. Marty came into the lounge. Her face was a study. She jerked a thumb backwards towards the kitchen.

"Bloody Auntie Connie," she whispered angrily.

I began to laugh. There was no need to say anything more. The situation was all too crystal clear. Auntie Connie would be staying the night; perhaps several nights.

"She's come down from Ballarat," continued Marty, "to do her Christmas shopping in the big wicked city. God knows how long she's staying. She arrived just after lunch and she's done nothing except talk about her blasted daughters, Tricia and Pamela, since she arrived. I'm nearly up the wall. No need to laugh, Lisha Kelly. Wait till we've had a couple of days of it. I was going to Ciro's with Evan tonight. I've had to put him off." Evan was the raincoat king.

"Wait till you've heard my bit of news," I told her. "Charlie is dashing out all ardour and enthusiasm this evening. The big reconciliation is on."

At this Marty began to laugh.

"Well it will just have to be off again," she said, "Auntie Con has the divan. When is he arriving?"

"Any time, you know Charlie."

"That's choice," said Marty.

Fortunately, when Charlie did arrive Auntie Connie was in

213

Marty's room looking at Marty's clothes and telling her about the beautiful dresses that Pamela designed and sewed for herself.

"What gives with that old bat in there?" asked Charlie.

"That's Auntie Connie."

"Who's Auntie Connie?"

"Marty's Auntie Connie from the provinces, as Socrates might have described Ballarat."

"That fornicates everything," said Charlie.

He went across to the window and stared out. "Lucky Jim they call me," he said. He followed me into the bedroom while I put Owen into his cot. "What are we going to do?" he asked.

"What can we do?"

"But I'm busting."

"I feel for you, Charlie."

"Where's she sleeping?"

"On the divan."

"Well can I sneak in here after she's gone to sleep?"

"Oh Charlie, is it worth it? Besides, maybe she doesn't go to sleep. Maybe she sits up all night and talks about Tricia and Pammie."

"I'd never be surprised," said Charlie gloomily. Then he had an idea. "We could go to a pub or something."

"I'm not terribly keen. It seems a lot of trouble."

"I want you."

I felt sorry for him again. "How much money have you got?" I asked.

"I haven't got any. I thought you might pay."

This naïve assumption was too much for me. I roared with laughter.

"God! Charlie," I said, "you must think you're the five-alarm charmer. Rosabelle has spoilt you, that's what it is. I'm a virtuous woman. I've never given a man money in my life."

"Is that what makes a virtuous woman?"

"As far as I can see."

Charlie was silent for a moment. Then he made the remark which finished our affair for ever :

"I know how I can get it easy enough. I'll go into Thel's Coffee Lounge and get it off one of the cats."

For a moment I could not speak. Then I walked back into the lounge.

"Damn and blast it, what's got into you now?" asked Charlie, following me out. "I don't know what's wrong with you lately. A man never knows where he is with you."

So I told him exactly where he was.

"Charlie," I said, "you will never touch me again as long as you live."

Charlie looked at me and his eyes narrowed. He said, "What are you getting at? Come on, spit out your mouthful. You think I'm trade, is that what it is?"

"Don't try bullying me, Charlie. It doesn't make any difference to me if you are or not. The big thing is that you disgust me."

"Do you want a belting?"

"Try it Charlie, and—"

"And what?"

"It doesn't matter. If you wanted to beat me there's nothing much I could do, but you'll never sleep with me again, never ever. And now you may as well go."

"What's wrong with you? They're only bloody poufters when all's said and done, and I told you I'm not trade. I gave one a hell of a beating only the other night for getting too cheeky."

"Please go. Go before you make me vomit."

He came across to where I sat on the divan and, standing over me, he slowly raised his right hand. I looked at it, fascinated. I had never seen a hand so charged with the power to smash and kill.

"In one second," I thought, "he will have knocked me out and it will have served me right for ever having had anything to do with him."

He looked into my face for a long agonising moment during which fear turned me to stone. Then slowly, terribly slowly, he dropped his hand.

"Ah, you bloody thing," he said, "I wouldn't be bothered touching you."

He picked up his coat from the divan and I heard the door shut behind him; but I did not look after him nor call goodbye, and so it ended.

We sat together at the table nearest the door marked "Gents". In night-clubs this table is always reserved for the dancers, singers and musicians. Don't ask me why. I think it is compulsory under the old Rogues and Vagabonds Act.

"Oh!" said the Latvian dancer, looking straight ahead and being terribly, terribly tragic, "Oh, it was dreadful. She shuddered. "I cannot tell you how terreeble it was. The Rassians they come and they rape all the Latvian women and now there is no pure Latvian race, just Rassians, Rassians, little half-Rassians."

"Ah yes," the Polish prostitute sipped her coffee and also stared ahead dramatically, "it was terrible. Rape! How many times have I been raped?"

"Surely not you, a Frenchwoman," said I, which was mischievous of me, for poor old Marisa indulged in the harmless and popular Polish fantasy that she was French and it was difficult enough as it was to keep it up without my slipping in my sixpennorth and making it just that little bit more impossible.

Marisa sipped her coffee and gave herself time to think. "I was in Germany then," she said.

("I'll bet you were, Marisa. I'll bet on that.")

"I was taken to Germany for my work in the Underground."

"Oh, I see."

"Oh the Rassians, they were *terreeble,*" the Latvian was away again, "I cannot tell you. Oh I cannot tell you how dreadful they were."

It was eight-thirty on a Friday night, and we who handled the entertainment at the Femina Cabaret sat drinking coffee and waiting for the patrons to arrive. Not, of course, that Marisa was officially on the staff, but she was a fixture as it were. She usually arrived about eight, wandered into the kitchen and got herself some coffee. She drank coffee till about nine o'clock and from then on such vodka as was passed to her under the table. She departed about one in the morning, supported by the customer for the night, so blind drunk she could scarcely walk.

The Latvian and I were the floor show. She did an Egyptian belly-dance and something vaguely Indian. I did flamenco. It was not very good flamenco by any manner of means, owing to the fact that I had never seen a flamenco dancer in my life; it was, as it were, a sort of Andalusia via Cuba. However, what the odds? I had decided I wanted to buy a house and to make a little extra money I had gone into show business. What matter if I were a phoney? We were almost all phoneys at the Femina Cabaret, most particularly the patrons, a large proportion of whom were, as far as I could see, disappointed Nazis who now had to pretend that they loved the democracies, and very irksome too did they find this dissembling. As the evening wore on and the vodka went down and their morale went up their scorn for Australia and things Australian became so monstrous, so overwhelming, that it is miraculous they did not die of it.

At that time Melbourne night life was just struggling to its birth. Aside from the two big rivals, Ciro's and Claridge's, there were only a few hotels where they staged small floor shows in the weekends and a string of tatty little coffee-lounges-cum-cabarets, mostly run by Middle Europeans. I had a feeling that this was where I would be starting, and sure instinct had told me that no Australian would be getting work there. They had completely sold themselves on the idea that all talent, all charm, all ability to entertain came out of Europe. However I soon overcame this little difficulty. I became Marie Babanine, whose father had come to Singapore from Russia via Shanghai, and in Singapore had met a French governess. They married and I was the result.

Did I speak Russian?

Well, no. My father had died when I was so young that I did not even remember him. We had a photo of him wearing the uniform of a cadet in a crack Cossack regiment. That was all. He had fled from Russia, not in October 1917, but, being a Kerensky supporter, a little later.

It is dead easy to put this sort of tale across the average New Australian. "Where would an Old Australian have heard of Kerensky?" they argue. "Silly barbarians, they know nothing except football and how to drink beer. Obviously she is half Russian. She knows the name Kerensky. She even knows the difference between a Bolshevik and a Menshevik."

They believed me implicitly.

My father had been heir to large estates near Poltava. ("There you are, you see. She knows where is Poltava.") Babanin was really a Tartar name. Anyone who wishes to acquaint themselves with the rest of my background I recommend to read *The Journal of Marie Bashkirtseff*. They'll find most of it there.

Our estates, of course, were gone, all gone, taken by those uncouth Communists. (Oh, we were a pack of bloody toffs, we Babaniñs, as Andy Mick would have said.)

Papa had gone first to Harbin, then down to Shanghai, and on to Singapore. Once at Singapore I was on firmer ground. Anyone with any seafaring relatives knows a certain amount about Singapore. I had been born there and educated at the Patterson Street Convent. Mother and I had fled before the fall. I had been back since but, alas, it was not what it was—those Communists again—so Maman and I had decided to make our home in Australia.

How did I like Australia?

To answer this, one raises the shoulders, lowers the corners of the mouth and gives a superior smile.

It always worked. Yes, the interrogator never failed to understand perfectly. He felt the same way himself. He would say that life was very different here. I would agree. Yes, indeed it was.

("My bloody oath it's different you big, fat, cold-eyed, no-back-on-your-head Nazi bastard, and are you kicking yourself that you backed the wrong horse!")

Did I speak French?

Just a little; of course, as a child, I had spoken Malay with the servants.

"Maman m'a dit, 'Vous parlez français comme une vache espagnole'." This sounds terribly fluent to those who don't know French and is good for a laugh from those who do. But not many did. German is the language of the D.P. camps.

I commenced my career as the big overseas artist in a very small way. It was during the pitiless winter of 1951 that I was engaged, with one of our few men students, to do an exhibition tango at the United Licensed Victuallers ball. The Licensed Victuallers pay very well (why shouldn't they?) and we had a vaguely Spanish-type evening dress which I had worn in the 1950 Latin-American contests. So off we went—Marie and Maurice, straight from Singapore's famous Coconut Grove!!

Maurice's name was Paddy Talbot. He was a long lean Spanish-Irish-looking type. He came from North Melbourne and had learned a little Italian (or Sicilian) fighting with the little boys in Peel Street, so, getting on to this foreign kick, he blossomed out as a French-Italian mixture.

Did he speak French?

Well, no. His father had died when he was so young that he did not remember him.

Did he speak Italian?

A little; of course he had always spoken Malay with the servants. Mamma would say to him, "You will forget your mother's language, (wagging the forefinger) *cattivo*! You are *cattivo*!" We removed the enemy-alien stigma (which seems to cling so long to the Italians who did not want to fight us anyway, and not at all to the Germans who were simply bursting to be at us) by shifting all Mamma's family out to Singapore in about 1923. They had been leading Roman anti-Fascists.

Why Singapore?

Well Mamma's father had been a railway engineer who had supervised a great deal of construction out in the East. He had always loved Singapore.

That about took care of everything. It may be seen that I trained my corporals well.

And now I was to star for a month at the Femina—Friday, Saturday and Sunday nights. For this I received six guineas each weekend. Mr Pearl, proprietor of the Femina, drove a hard bargain. On that first Friday evening I was met on arrival by a morose-looking teenager who, besides the twin trials of a shabby suit and a very Semitic nose, had a bad whang of adolescent spots to further test his spirit. He sat at the top of the stairs and, in a very bad light, he was reading *Buddenbrooks* and eating a pie.

"You're early," he said, gloomily. "Doesn't matter. I've been told off to meet you. They tell me my big brother Bruno hired you."

"That's right."

Bruno was a photographer who did a good deal of work amongst Marty's gold medallists and competition winners.

"Typical of Bruno," the gloomy student of Thomas Mann finished his pie and stood up, "all charm. Hire them, then leave it to brother Hymie. Let him show the victim round. O.K.! this is it."

He gestured towards the empty chairs, the cigarette-marked tables, the forlorn murals of various capital cities of Europe. (I recognised the Eiffel Tower and that big Ferris wheel which has been representing Vienna ever since they made *The Third Man*.) Seen thus the Femina Cabaret was nothing but a large ill-lit room with a small dance floor and a slightly raised platform for the band. It was depressing, also very chilly on this wet September evening.

"Uninviting, isn't it?" said Hymie.

"It will look different when it fills up with people." I was being diplomatic.

"People," Hymie was reflective. "Yes, I suppose you could call them that."

Suddenly he turned on me and asked, "Do you know how Kramer, the Beast of Belsen, began his defence? He said, 'I was a white-collar worker. I was a clerk. For three years I was unemployed. The Nazis came to power. What could I do?'"

Hymie paused and gazed at me. The words with all their dreadful import hung between us in the silent chill of the room.

Hymie's big intelligent eyes looked me up and down. "I don't know," he said, "what your affiliations are, but those words could be said by almost everyone, or at least every second one who comes into this place; pathetic people, pathetic and frightening. They tell me you were not reared in Europe. So much the better for you. Now back to business. There is no profit in politics as my old grandmomma so wisely says. I must break it to you that there is no dressing-room."

"But where do I change?"

"In the ladies' toilet, which is down those back stairs in the basement."

"That'll be O.K."

Poor Hymie was so ashamed and ill at ease it seemed only kind to help him as much as possible.

"Seeing as you've taken that so well," he continued, "I may as well tell you the rest. On Sunday night you do an extra job. Did you know that?"

"No."

"I didn't think you would. They leave it to me to tell you. My God! What a pack of momsers! Well, Poppa has another little sly vodka shop round in Barkly Street. It is smaller and sleazier and more spirit-crushing than here. It is called the Casbah."

At this I laughed. The Algiers I could have taken, but the Casbah was a little too much.

"It has," said Hymie, "red pumpkin-shaped lamps and three imitation windows of tin painted to look like iron grilles, and the waiter wears a fez. It only has a floor show on Sunday night. You are the floor show at no extra fee. I drive you round there in the car."

I really thought the unfortunate Hymie would fall down dead of embarrassment, so I said I did not mind about the Casbah job. Privately I did mind, but what could you say to poor suffering Hymie?

He looked at me with gratitude. "You're very good," he said. "You should have heard how Vera performed. Not so much about the Casbah, she's been in a few Casbahs in her time, but the toilet dressing-room really sent her off. Never had she been obliged, etc., an artiste of her standing, etc., etc. You haven't met Vera yet. You will. She's our other dancer, finishing her season next Saturday. Poor thing, the Germans spoilt her when they were in Latvia. In Vera's memory every Private Hans Pfiffler has become an officer with a monocle screwed in his eye. Do you want some coffee?"

I said I would like some and he wandered off to the kitchen and came back with a cup each. He put them down on the bandstand and we sat down with our legs stretched out before us. It was uncomfortable but somehow more cheerful than sitting at one of the tables. The bandstand may be cramped and draughty, it usually is, but it is the place of the music makers. A slight feeling of happiness and creativity lingers there even in the saddest of cabarets.

"You don't eat here," Hymie told me. "Actually it is a matter for congratulation. The food is as bad as the coffee, but of course it is not philanthropy on Poppa's part that makes him refrain from feeding the artists. He does not feed anyone whom he does not have to feed. You may have all the coffee you wish. However one does get hungry. That is the trouble. I am always hungry; growing boy, and also I am studying. I am a first year University student. I am doing Arts. My family think it is a most terrible waste of time. Poor Poppa did not know what to do. He didn't want to waste my earning power here and now, but then he would ask himself 'What of the future?' Also he did not want to waste my brains. I won a Commonwealth Scholarship, you see. It almost killed him making up his mind. At last he hit upon this brilliant compromise. I go to the Shop and I do all these little jobs such as tonight. You'll be thinking my Poppa is a momser. He is not, but he is tough, very tough, otherwise he would be dead, and we who depended on him would be dead likewise. You wait till you see him. He is five feet four, perhaps he weighs nine stone, and it is all endurance and guts. Ah, here comes the music now. I must introduce you. This is Walter."

Walter set his piano accordion case down and took out his instrument. He made me a little bow. "The rest of the boys will be here soon," he said, "would you like me to run over your music with you so that you may rehearse a little?"

This was kind of him. I was to discover that Walter was invariably kind and considerate to work with. He was Viennese. As well as piano accordion he played the piano. There were two pianos in the band, two baby grands pushed back to back. I thought this rather Continental and strange.

"Poppa took one in exchange for a bad debt," explained Hymie.

That first evening passed off quite well. I was very enthusiastically applauded for, generally speaking, New Australians make an easy audience. There was only one untoward episode. When the last ex-stormtrooper had gone home, when the last Pole had departed—drunk and abusing the ex-stormtrooper—when Marisa had fallen downstairs, taking with her in her tumble the customer of the evening, a large fat Rumanian, when most of the lights were out and Hymie had begun to stack the chairs on the tables, then Mr Pearl, who had asked Vera and me to stay behind, called us all into the kitchen. He appeared doomed, tragic, bowed down with worry. I expected him to tell us that bankruptcy was imminent and he must dismiss us all. He stood before us. There was a moment of agonising silence, then! the black head went up, the black eyes flashed, the eighteen-inch shoulders were thrown back. One arm was flung out in a superb gesture :

"WHO?" demanded Mr Pearl, "HAS BEEN EATING THE MARASCHINO CHERRIES?"

I laughed. The drummer, who was a Slovak from Nitra, also laughed. But the pianist who played the second piano! Never will I forget his reaction. He was a Pole, a brilliant graduate of Warsaw Conservatoire. We called him Young Frederic. It excruciated him to play at the Femina at the best of times and now, on top of the musical humiliation, came this preposterous interrogation. His rage was magnificent. The following exchange with Mr Pearl was entirely in Polish. Hymie, sitting beside me on an empty box marked 'china', translated for my benefit:

"Young Chopin here tells my father that he is the offspring of a toad and a camel—the toad leprous and the camel with syphilis."

"My father replies that he is not in Poland, the Goys' earthly paradise now, and only Poppa's charity prevents him from starving."

"Young Frederic now says that Poppa should be dragged backwards through every ghetto in the world."

"Poppa says that, in a manner of speaking, he has, and it leaves him only the more determined that Frederic will not get off with his maraschino cherries."

"Frederic says that if everyone were in the job that suits him best Poppa would be washing the small towels in a brothel."

Here the Slovak drummer laughed and Mr Pearl turned upon him. Hymie again translated:

"Poppa now switches to German and tells Ladislav that, if everyone had the job that suited him, Ladislav would be beating the drum outside the tent of the gypsy strong man at the country fair."

Hymie stood up. "We may as well go. That will be the end of it. Ladja and Poppa roar at one another but they do not really quarrel for Ladja is three-quarters gypsy and the fellow feeling is there. Come on, I'll drive you home."

When we were safely outside and getting into the car I asked, "Hymie, do you know who *did* eat those cherries?"

"I did," said Hymie.

It was during my third Sunday at the Femina that I looked across the room and saw, through the blue haze of cigarette smoke, Swede Ryan sitting watching me. Swede, when he was out of jail, had become the most unutterable nuisance. Fortunately he had spent most of 1950 inside, and when he was out Charlie had kept him away. Charlie, when I had at last managed to convince him that the big love affair was over, had remained a very good friend.

"You see," he had said, "I talked like a fool but I did love you a lot, so let me hang around sometimes and do anything I can for you."

So I had given him the little chore of keeping the Swede away. But now, unfortunately, Charlie had been arrested at the N.S.W. border driving a stolen truck piled high with stolen refrigerators. He was doing six months. Meanwhile here was the Swede, larger and healthier than life. It was one of the Swede's most irritating idiosyncrasies that when he was hopped up, and he usually was, he saw fit to be very sinister—soft-voiced, downward-looking eyes, monosyllabic. He now blew smoke down through his nostrils and motioned me to come over. I sent a message by the waiter :

"If that gentleman wants to speak to me he can come over to my table."

Swede's answering message was that he had something very important to tell me. He then turned sideways, leaned his elbow on the table and spent half an hour looking at me out of the corner of his eyes. While I danced he remained in the same position, still blowing smoke through his nose.

At last he could bear it no longer and came across to me.

"Someone's been looking for you," he said.

"Who?"

"Just someone. Some bloke that met you outside the Tankerville one day."

"I don't remember anyone."

"Sure you don't?"

"Come off it, Swede. You've been sitting there making a big silly ass of yourself all night, and now this third degree. Stop hamming your plaits off. I've said I don't remember."

It was Joe. It must be Joe and my heart turned over with fear at the thought of what Swede might do to him.

"Sure you don't remember?"

"Look, Swede, I'm getting sick of this very old-fashioned performance. If I remembered I'd tell you. Why shouldn't I? You don't pay my rent, a fact which you seem to be forgetting. I haven't been in Fitzroy for twelve months, so that's all there is to it. At any rate, who told you?"

"Bon Gleeson."

So that was it. I had considered Bonnie a friend. I should have known that when her hunger for excitement and violence was aroused her first loyalty would be to her own world.

"Seems there was this chap in a taxi one day about twelve months ago, or more. Remember now?"

"Yes, I remember, what about him?"

"He's not getting you. I am—if I have to do murder to get you."

"Here we go again. Why don't you get off the snow, Swede? It makes you a great big bloody bore. Now what about this man who's been looking for me?"

Swede raised his eyelids and looked at me; then he took a small blue bottle from his pocket, uncorked it and held it upside down. Drip by drip he poured the contents to the floor. There was a strange acrid smell and I saw the small hole eaten in the boards beside my feet. I did not know if Swede carried a gun. Usually he did not. My rage was so blinding I would not have cared if he had. My hand shot out and I smacked him across the face with all my force.

"You filthy thing," I gasped, "you filthy, rotten thing. Never come near me again, and remember, Swede, that I've put up with a lot from you, but this is just one threat I don't take from anybody. You ever again mention acid-throwing to me and I'll see you inside for as long as any evidence of mine can make it."

Swede sat grinning at me. The marks of my fingers made purple weals on the white doughiness of his face.

"Remember," he said, "I've told Bon to tell him where to find you and it's up to you to tell him. Bye bye now, doll baby."

He made his exit in great triumph, every musician in the band, and half the people in the room, watching him.

Joe arrived the next Saturday night. I had just finished dancing and was having a cup of coffee before I went home. I was feeling depressed and alone and when I saw him I felt such a swift gladdening of the heart that I knew I had been waiting for him ever since Swede's warning the week before. He came towards me, his smile as brilliant as ever. There was something about Joe which could only be described by the old-fashioned word 'dashing'. Amongst the dreary and defeated who crowded the Femina he was radiant with vitality. His black hair shone, his dark eyes sparkled and he carried his slender body with a kind of gay arrogance that said: Look at me. I am not a big man, but I am alive—all alive.

He had, under one arm, a bunch of early spring roses. There must have been three dozen of them, white, red and golden. Their fragrance drove back the smell of cigarettes and Tabu which was the distinctive odour of the Femina. He put them on the table before me.

"These are for you," he said. "I thought you might be having a nice quiet evening at home and I brought these round to cheer you up. Your little boy's baby-sitter sent me on here and I find you living it up."

"I'm working," I said, a little stiffly.

"Of course. The baby-sitter explained all about it. Little did I know that day that the famous Miss Marie Babanine was riding in a cab with me. Miss Babanine, may I have your autograph? You have long been my favourite star."

He gave me a wink of musical comedy proportions and I laughed but could think of nothing to say to him. The thought of what Swede might have said made me feel awkward and constrained. Then I saw Marisa undulating towards us between the tables.

Marisa was only slightly in liquor and was wearing her famous white rabbit stole over her equally famous slinky black satin. She sat down with a great jingle of costume jewellery and the air became charged with brandy, Jean Didier violet perfume and sexual acquisitiveness. She eyed Joe, not with her usual professional eye, but with a much deeper interest. She had decided she would have him. I decided she would not.

"This," I said, "is my friend, Joe Ferelle. He speaks French too."

"I don't really," said Joe, being truthful to a fault as they say. "Mostly I only remember old nursery rhymes and songs that Grandmother taught me, like

En passant pour la Lorraine
Avec mes sabots,

that sort of thing. You know."

Marisa said, with great dignity, that since coming to Australia she had only spoken English. She did not choose to speak French. She thought it bad manners. After all, when one was in a country one should speak that country's language, and so on. Marisa had a long spiel which she always brought forth on these awkward occasions. It sounded far from convincing and she knew it. She discovered someone right across the room whom she must see. She rose and begged to be excused.

"Goodbye, darlings," she said.

"That gets rid of her," said Joe. "Now can we go or do you have to dance again?"

I stroked the heavy velvet of the rose petals. "No," I said, "I don't have to dance again. Let's get these home before they're poisoned with nicotine."

Once at home I put the roses in water and then made tea for Joe. On an impulse which I could not explain I set up a tray with the best china and the only linen tray-cloth I possessed. For some reason this fisherman from a wild and remote island engendered in me a desire to create an atmosphere of intense civilisation.

"It's gracious living tonight," I said as I put the tray down before him, "not everybody gets the white supper-cloth, let me tell you."

"Why do I have the honour?"

"I don't know. Perhaps because I want you to tell me about your island. I love stories about islands."

"No, tell me about yourself. That should be much more interesting. Why wouldn't you meet me again, or even tell me your name? For almost two years that has puzzled me, really intrigued me, and when I think about it I always come to the conclusion, 'Joe, *mon gars,* she just didn't want you.' Simple enough, eh?"

"Well where did you actually find out my name and address?"

"I went into that pub on the corner where we met and there was this little blonde in the lounge and she said she heard that I'd been asking around, and I said 'That's right', and she said

227

she had a message for me. All the time she was talking to me and giving me your name and the addresses of the dancing school and your flat, there was this big white-faced hopped-up-looking bastard making like Sydney Greenstreet over in the other corner. Who the hell does he think he is? I'm going to have to fight him, I can see that."

"Surely you don't think he is the reason that I couldn't see you again last time?"

"Never. I'd never think that. I know you're a woman of taste, and, all else aside, he wouldn't be much use to any woman. He's stoned to the eyeballs to begin with, and even unstoned I don't think he'd be capable of much."

"How practical you are, Joe. I never thought of that but I believe you're right."

"I'm right. You can believe me."

"Well, now you've met those people, surely you have some idea of why I was frightened to have anything to do with you?"

"I know old Sydney Greenstreet thinks he's a big boy, if that's what you mean, and I know the crowd round Johnson Street were scared to tell me anything about you, and the little blonde warned me to be very careful because there were some big dangerous boys after you. She likes trouble and murder and mayhem, that little blonde does, and she nearly got it. I was right on the point of going across and flattening hophead there and then but I didn't want to end in jail or get my face messed round till I'd seen you."

"When did Bonnie tell you all this?"

"Only yesterday evening, and I went back on board and bathed and shaved and dressed up and I came back into town and then I went to the pictures, all sad and lonely and by myself, because suddenly I lost courage. I'd wanted to see you for so long and then—well then I just couldn't front."

"After eighteen months searching? I must say I'm flattered, at any rate."

"I wanted to begin looking for you eighteen months ago but I didn't. For the first twelve months I told myself, 'If she wanted to see you again she would have told you where to find her. She doesn't want you', and then about six months ago I thought, 'Well, what the hell! She can only rubbish you. What's that to

228

you, Joe Ferelle? You've been rubbished by experts.' So I began the big search."

"Who rubbished you, Joe Ferelle?"

"It's a long story and I'll tell it to you some other time."

"Then tell me about your island now."

"My island! My island is so lovely that it's hard to talk about it. I'd like to take you there in the summer, not in the winter; if you don't like the winter here you'd hate it on Bellereve. And yet it's beautiful then too—all grey rock and tossing green and grey water with the big molly hawks gliding above it with the wind that comes howling up from the ice-packs in the south, and the surf crashing on the beaches and the gulls screaming on the cliff tops and the seals coming up to sit on the rocks. And in summer! In summer you get the feeling the sea is rocking the whole island in its arms, gently, very gently. Right in the middle of the island with the little green hills around you, and the smell of grass and peppermint gum and Bellereve daisies, you can still feel the sea, rocking you like in a cradle. You'd love it then. My grandmother has an almond tree beside her kitchen door and when the first green comes on the almond we go out and we whitewash the whole house, and when the blossom is on the tree it glows against the white walls, and down on the beach below the house we get out the small boats and go over them and repaint them and repitch the seams. All the beach smells of wood shavings and tar and fresh seaweed, and over all the boat houses there are nets spread out to dry in the sun. You would find it beautiful then with the sun shining and the wattle beginning to show on the hill-sides and the mutton-birds flying down all the way from the Arctic Circle. One day I'll take you there and I'll take you out to the smaller islands where there are nothing but mutton-bird burrows and small shrubs and the wind blowing over the grass, but now," he stood up abruptly, "I must go. It's after two o'clock and we sail at six."

"Joe! Sailing so soon and we've only just met again. Can't you ask your brother to wait a few days?"

"I'm not on the *Emilie* now. When I decided to look for you I went back into coastal. I thought I'd have a better chance of finding you. I'm on the *Denman*."

"Where are you going?"

"Yampi Sound, north about."

"How long will you be gone?"

"Seventeen days there, two days at Yampi and seventeen days back. You see, I have it all worked out. It is a pity I must go so soon, but the sooner I go the sooner I am back and we must be philosophical, as my grandfather would say. Tomorrow is Sunday. Sunday sailing means I get an extra day's pay and overtime. There is good overtime in this ship and when I come back I shall have some money and then we must have a serious talk, eh? Come now, show me your door."

At the door he took me by the hand and asked, "May I kiss you?"

I, being a little too bright, as one invariably is at such times, gave what sounded in my own ears as a very affected little laugh and said, "What a quaint, olde worlde question."

"It's a dead serious question," said Joe. "I'm damn sure I'm never going to kiss anyone who doesn't want to be kissed."

"I am quite serious too. Do you want to kiss me?"

"Very much."

"Then go ahead."

He kissed me hard on the mouth and then turned and went off into the darkness with the sweet springing stride of a man who has spent most of his life in sail.

That night I was strangely troubled by the thought of Andy as I had never been troubled in the time of Charlie Barton. It was as though my subconscious had known all along that Charlie meant nothing, whereas Joe, that strange mixture of romance, practicality and gaiety, I found very charming, and perhaps I would love him. I felt it very possible that I would love him, and I was haunted by feelings of disloyalty. And yet—and yet there are all types of love in the world and no one can live alone for ever and Andy, who had always had a strange foreknowledge of his own early death, had so many times said, "I'll never make old bones, and after I've croaked make sure you get a good man to look after you, for one thing's certain, you'll never be able to look after yourself."

And Andy was dead. Dead and gone. My first dear love, my first.

I spoke aloud to him in the night: "Oh Andy Mick, there

will never be another like you. If I loved a thousand there would never be another like you."

"Which is about all that can be said about first love."

In my mind I could hear his voice saying it. His voice with the laughter behind it.

I was comforted and I fell asleep.

Before Joe came back again I had found my house. I had intensified my search about six months previously when Marty had parted with the raincoat king, and become engaged to a young garage mechanic from Brunswick. He did not own the garage where he worked but he did home repairs on his friends' racing bikes and planned to open his own business in about twelve months' time. He had his eye on a likely little workshop in North Coburg. When he had enough money to get it he and Marty would marry and live in the three rooms behind it.

"Mum says I'm mad," said Marty, "but, as I tell her, you can't expect everything at the start and it's something to work for together."

(Some of Marty's friends said it was hilarious, some said it was tragic. I said nothing, not even 'Remember when you said', and time has proved me right for Marty and her mechanic and her three kids—and another expected—are all very happy.)

These plans of Marty's meant that some time in the not too distant future I must give up the flat. I could not afford to keep it on when Marty left and twelve months was not much time in which to find a house in the housing shortage of the early fifties.

I saved every penny I could, and slowly the house I wanted took shape in my mind. Firstly it must be painted white. I could not conceive of my home being of any other colour. It would have a wood stove in the kitchen as well as a modern gas range, and Swedish earthenware on a shelf. My son's room would have a bright striped quilt on the bed and a hooked rug on the floor, and shelves for books as he grew older, and red curtains at the window. The lounge room would have sea-grass matting and white walls and furniture covered in golden saddle-bagging, but in the bedroom I could let my dash of Pompadour run riot with a bed of gilded iron and mirrors in curly frames, and silk-covered cushions everywhere, and to hell with good taste.

"I must be getting old," I told Marty, "all this wanting to settle down in the little nest and so on."

Marty looked up from the sweater she was knitting for the mechanic. "Every woman worthy of the name wants to make a home," said Marty.

About a week after Joe left I went down to the Port to visit Lily Dale. I was missing Joe and Lily was good to visit when you were feeling low. However, she was out and I called in on Lila Clancy to get all the news. Lila still lived in the house where we had laid out her dead baby so many years ago, and though they had spent a fortune putting Stockholm pitch on the walls and trying to repair the roofs, it was still almost as damp as ever, and not quite so smart as it had been a couple of years before. The Seven Dwarfs in the garden needed a coat of paint, Snow White had some plaster off her nose and the bright pink front door was beginning to peel; but inside there was a monstrous fridge which took up half the kitchen. Lila showed it to me with pride. She said, and I agreed with her, that it looked as though they would never be able to get out of the place and they might as well have a few comforts.

"We've applied for a Commission house," she said, "but there's about thirty thousand on the list ahead of us. What can you do? The boys had the sink put in. It's marvellous after having to traipse out to the gully trap for every drop of water for years."

Mary Teresa was married and Ted was in Heidelberg Repatriation Hospital. He went in and out, but the boys were still with her and still wonderful boys to her. They were paying for her false teeth that week.

"And about time too," I thought, which was ungracious of me, for Lila was not of the school that considers dentures necessary. Not until you've had a new perm, bought a rabbit coat and a full set of crystal ornaments for the front room—all of which she had. It was quite true that her boys were wonderful sons to her. She was completely gone to seed, her face lined, her figure swollen, her arches fallen; and she was still a relatively young woman, not much over forty. But she had never been a fighter and life had knocked her around, and now, as she sat in the kitchen and drank tea, her big bust resting comfortably on the table top, she seemed to have forgotten the hell she had been through. She chattered on about the sales in town and Mary Teresa's lovely wedding clothes, and films. Pictures! she seemed to have been to thousands of them, every film that had ever been shown in town. But then she said that things were not so good on the wharf as they had been. They were still good, mind you, but the five boom years of after the war had gone. Terry, who was mad on politics, said it was the system, that was how it worked, war, boom, bust, war. He said if we didn't get the Labour Party back in it would only be a matter of time before the wharf would be the same as it was in the thirties, but she said it could never be that terrible again. It just would not be possible. Did I think so? The poor dazed eyes looked at me.

"I think I'd shoot myself, Lisha, rather than live through that again."

So she had not forgotten. She had not forgotten at all. I felt sick with pity for her.

"It couldn't be like that again," I assured her. "People have too much sense to let it get like that again."

I sincerely hoped that I was right in this, and it comforted Lila.

"You always had a brain in your head," she said.

She asked me to stay for tea but I wanted to be away in the sunlight by myself. The little room that still smelled of gas and damp held memories that threatened to close in and choke me. I said I had to be home early, and I went out and walked along the sea front with the spring wind lifting my hair, and suddenly, when I was a couple of hundred yards past Bay Street, I saw the house.

I had seen it many times before for it belonged to old Mrs O'Grady and she was a great friend of my grandmother. I had visited there. But now it had been renovated and remodelled and the result made me stand still in the street and say to myself: "This is my house."

Originally it had been a small brick cottage built to a very early Australian pattern. There had been two rooms downstairs and a skillion-roofed kitchen at the back. The two main rooms had each a roof consisting of a long high gable which ran the full length of the room. The house faced east and west, and the north and south ends of the gables were of brick and each gable made a long attic room with small windows in each bricked end.

There had been a verandah out front. Now someone had removed the verandah and built a wooden porch over the front door—not a square boxlike porch but a delicate pergola on which climbed Mrs O'Grady's famous Cloth of Gold rose. Whoever had removed the verandah had preserved it so that the main stem, twisted with the strength and growth of twenty years, climbed up beside the porch, and the new wood, already studded with the first golden buds of the season, frothed out against the whiteness of the walls and over the blackness of the old Cumberland slate that was still well weathered and waterproof on the roof. Just where the roses ceased to reach, the roof had been cut back on two sides and a small French window built in on the third side so that it was as though half of a box had been cut diagonally out of the roof to make room for the window, and the space thus left before it had been turned into a small widow's walk about four feet long and two deep, with a railing of black wrought iron.

And nailed to the front fence were the words which had really brought my heart into my mouth and caused me to stand stock still on the footpath; the magic sign which told me I could hope —a big red FOR AUCTION sign.

The auction was dated for the first week in December. I decided to find out more about it and I went up and knocked at the door. I expected it to be opened by an Italian woman who would tell me that she did not speak the English. I was surprised beyond words when old Mrs O'Grady stood before me. She must have been well in her seventies and her eyes were still clear and aware, but I could see at a glance that she was sadly bent and crippled with arthritis.

"Lisha Flynn," she cried, "you're doubly welcome, for your own sake and your dear grandmother's; but I mustn't call you Lisha Flynn, now. Kelly was the name of the chap you married, wasn't it? Ah well, we outlive the men, don't we? And how are you, Lisha?"

"I'm well thank you, Mrs O'Grady. How are you?"

"As well as can be expected, dear. I still struggle around. As you see the arthritis has made a crock of me, but I still manage to look after myself and the place."

She led me out to the kitchen and I saw the two front rooms had been knocked into one. It was a vast improvement. The

234

two rooms made one of good clean restful proportions and the enlarged window let in so much light that the afternoon sun on the sea set ripples dancing on the ceiling.

"Leo did that last time he was home on leave," said Mrs O'Grady. "I used to complain that all my life I'd been pigging around in little rooms where you couldn't swing a cat. I was a bustling sort of woman," she sighed, "and I liked a lot of room, and Leo used to say that the first time he had a bit of money he'd have that wall down, but he never had any money till he was in the army. He was a sergeant you know." She nodded towards the mantelpiece where stood the photo of him in uniform. Sergeant Leo O'Grady's bones mouldered somewhere in the mud of the Kokoda Trail.

"Well, dear," she sat back and folded her hands and looked at me, "what can I do for you? I have a feeling you've come about the house."

"I have," I admitted. "I didn't even know you lived here any more, but it looked so beautiful and I saw the auction sign and I thought I'd make enquiries. After all these years I'm surprised that you want to move away."

"Believe me, I don't; but you can see for yourself that I'm little better than a cripple. I still manage to get around and that's about all. The doctor says I won't get better and I must have rest or I'll get a lot worse, so I'm going up to Templestowe to my married daughter, Gladdie. It's like this, Lisha. The price we hope to get is two thousand five hundred. It seems a terrible lot for a little three-roomed cottage but some Italian or Greek would pay it all the same. I want the money for Gladdie, and a bit for myself to come and go on. I'll have my pension but I don't want to come to them with empty hands. Could you pay me two thousand five hundred?"

I laughed.

"Well then, we'll have to think of terms. God knows I'd like you to have it. Your grandmother was my best friend. She saw my children born. Gladdie and her husband need five hundred to pay off their house. Could you give me five hundred pounds down and five pounds a week?"

I knew exactly how much I had in the bank—three hundred pounds. I also had in hand fifteen pounds, which represented three nights' dancing at the Hotel Crescent. "Surely," I thought, "with the people I know I can raise two hundred."

"I'll do better," I said, "I'll give you five hundred and fifteen pounds down and some weeks I'll be able to give you more than the fiver."

Mrs O'Grady looked towards the photo of her dead son. "Remember," she said, "how he used to talk, and how every Sunday morning I would go to Mass, and every Sunday evening he would go off to the Rationalist Society, and I could never convert him to my way and he could never convince me; but one thing he used to say stays in my mind now, and I know that, in that at least, he was right. He would say, 'To each according to his need, from each according to his ability'. Well, you need a home and I'm able to help you get it, so it's a bargain."

She leaned across and took my hand, but her eyes were on the photo of her dead son.

Then began the dreadful business of raising the wind. Mother, who with a friend was running a very expensive hat shop in the Block, gave me £50 which she said I need not repay. The bank lent me £100 and my strange friend Mr Pearl gave me the other £50. Mr Pearl was extraordinarily generous to those he considered friends and, once he discovered that I was not descended from a long line of propertied Russian Jew-haters, he roared laughing, and said I was a clever woman, and I had my little boy to keep and it was a pleasure to help me. After that he always paid me for my work at the Casbah and saw to it that Hymie had the car to drive me home. Now he handed the money across to me, his dark eyes searching my face, as though trying to read there in my features if I had enough stamina to go through with the task I had undertaken. He must have been satisfied with what he saw for he nodded and said, "Yes, you are one of the ones who can build a home and look after their own. We who are like this must help each other." I felt flattered beyond measure—to be numbered amongst the ones who can endure.

Joe arrived back just in time to take me to Phyl Foley's wedding. About eighteen months previously Phyl had started her engagement to a young pastoralist to whom she had been introduced by her aunt, who was as good as her word. "I'm fond of him, even if not madly in love," Phyl had written. The wedding was to be a big affair with Owen as page boy in dress Stuart tartan kilt and buckled shoes. Suddenly Phyl decided it was love or nothing, marriage on any other basis was dishonest—and there was her mother tearing her hair and with the invitations all ready to send out. And then the young man whom she could not love had broken his spine in a car accident, and Phyl tore off back to N.S.W. to watch by his bedside in hospital and to help his mother nurse him when he came out. By the time Laurie (that was the young man's name, Laurie Delaney) had lain in plaster for twelve months Phyl was blazing with love for him, and would have laughed in your face had you mentioned Lachy in the same breath.

Laurie was still not very strong so it was a quiet wedding after all, on a golden morning of early summer. Phyl was indescribably beautiful beneath the folds of her Limerick lace veil, and she still had Owen in kilts to hold her train and I was matron of honour. After a small reception in the afternoon they went off to Hadley's Hotel in Hobart for two weeks' honeymoon. When they came back they visited me. I was still in Marty's flat but moving out the next day and they could not stay long because they were driving through to N.S.W. that same evening; but amidst all the bustle and confusion Phyl followed me into the bedroom with the air of someone who has something important to impart.

"You know all the sex business," said she, pink-faced, "which I said would never interest me and you used to say 'wait and see'? Well, you were right. I didn't know what I was talking about."

So my old friend Phyl Foley was one of the lucky ones. She got love and money and a satisfactory sex life. What more could you ask? And it could not have happened to a girl who deserved it more.

Joe gave me £50 towards paying off the house. To take it brought back the same uneasy feeling of disloyalty towards Andy, but Joe said Mrs O'Grady must be a great old girl who deserved paying off as soon as possible. "She isn't well and she may need it to come and go on," he said, and when he put it like that it was hard to refuse.

Six weeks from the day I had first called on Mrs O'Grady the 'For Auction' sign came down, the house was mine and I moved in the same night. Mrs O'Grady had moved three weeks before and Marty and I had already been working like galley slaves in the empty rooms. All the furniture I owned was Owen's bed and I had no money to buy more. Also I had not the wherewithal to get floor coverings or curtains. So we stained floors and polished them and I went to the job shop at the top end of Bourke Street and bought yards of dotted muslin (a job lot, slightly shop-soiled) for 1s. 6d. the yard. With this I made curtains for every window in the house. On the night we moved in I slept on a new inner-spring on the floor and Marty loaned me the blankets. Had it not been for Patterson's Proprietary Limited Easy Credit System I would have been sleeping on the bare boards. Mrs O'Grady had left behind her old gas stove and I decided to make do with it for a while. Time enough to go into debt with the Gas Company when I had paid off P.P.L. Marty's mechanic made me a larger-than-double-bed-size divan out of spare crates that were lying around the garage. I think Jawa motorbikes had arrived in them but I'm not sure. We had great fun during the making of that divan. It had to be put together in my bedroom because it was too big to get up the stairs in one piece. Marty said the size was prophetic and one day I would have half a dozen children bedded down in it. Miss Olive McSweeney donated a handsome cedar chest of drawers and Mrs Phillips presented me with a round table with a brass top on which Owen and I exotically ate our breakfast porridge.

I had taken the front room upstairs for my bedroom and Joe painted it white with just a hint of blue in the ceiling to heighten it and help it reflect the morning light from the sea. Like all sailors, he was clever with the paintbrush, but it was in the garden that he excelled himself. There was not much in the front. Just a small lawn and the rose and a little ti-tree sighing, always sighing, in the south wind; but the back was a wilderness of grass-grown brick paths and moss-covered fruit trees, and dog roses all along the back fence. When the morning sun was on it, gleaming against the worn red of the paths and the silver of the tree trunks, it was one of the loveliest and warmest places in the world. Here Joe trimmed back grass from the paths and cut the dead wood from the apple tree and the two ancient

238

lemons that stood covered in tiny, stunted golden globes. He worked fast and with assurance, and I was filled with admiration to see the skill with which he gently weeded the grass from around the roots of the grape hyacinths and the freesias, the last of the season, where they stood in a patch of fragrance behind the wash-house, a wooden building mouldering away contentedly amongst the hollyhocks.

"It's easy to see you've done plenty of gardening," I said, as I knelt and picked myself some freesias, for these heady-smelling bulbs are my favourite flower. I love them better than anything else that grows because of the beauty of their perfume at once so delicate and magnificent, so wild and yet so highly sophisticated.

"My grandmother had a garden like this," said Joe, "many the time I've pruned the roses and tied them up for her. You want to keep that apple wood. It smells sweet when you burn it."

He stretched out on the grass and turned his face to smell the freesias. He took a deep breath. "How good they are," he said, "I like flowers that smell good."

I was glad to hear him say this and felt a swift spurt of fondness for him. We freesia lovers are a stout band and hay fever sufferers hate us. Had he said, as so many do, "They give me a headache" or "They make me sneeze", I would have been disappointed beyond what one who is not a freesia fancier could consider possible. I changed the subject for I did not want to feel this empathy with him. I said :

"You always talk about your grandparents. You never mention your parents."

Joe rolled over on his back and looked up at me with his long black eyes. "Are you dying of curiosity?" he asked.

"Frankly, Joe, I am."

He gave his sudden flash of a smile. "Well," he said, "I will tell you. *Toujours la politesse*, as my grandfather says, and I have always considered it terribly discourteous to be all silent and mysterious about oneself. Not to waste any more words, my mother doesn't like me. I can't remember when she ever has. She rubbished me when I was eight years old. I am like my father, you see, and she has often mentioned to me, in passing, that she hated him. She was a MacKinnon. The MacKinnons

239

come from the Isle of Skye and they are the only other family on the island. My father married her when she was eighteen because she was expecting my eldest sister. There was no other reason at all for their marriage. I have three sisters older than I am and an elder brother and two younger sisters and a brother. We were all born by the time my mother was thirty. Reason enough, I suppose, for hating any husband. Then, when I was about seven, he was drowned just off the Reef. They never even got his body, and, within twelve months, mother married one of the Adamsons from Hobart. The Adamsons live on an island down in the mouth of the Derwent. They have a couple of boats and a few sheep. They've been there since the convict days and they're inbred and strange. Stan Adamson had known my father and they had once had a fight about some lobster pots or scollop trawls or something, I was too young to remember, and they carved each other up with their deck knives. It was a fair fight but Dad did a little more carving than Stan, and Stan hated him ever afterwards. When the happy couple got back from Hobart he took one look at me and said, 'That one is the image of Jules. He must go.'

"I went then and there—down the hill to my grandmother's. There was a howling wind that night and pouring rain, quite the classic stage effects, and I arrived on my grandmother's doorstep, sodden wet, with my clothes under my arm. I was only a little boy and I cried bitterly for my brothers and sisters. Grandmother and Grandfather were very good to me. I was happier with them than I had been at home, but I used to feel strange when I would play with my brothers and sisters on the beach and they would go home one way and I would go another. It made it hard for me to forget that my mother had not wanted me. Sometimes I would go home to chop the wood or help her mind the young ones when she was busy, for she would always say, 'He's like Jules in that way too; he's wonderful with children', but at night I would go away again. So now you know why I do not speak of my parents, and you also know why I did not decide to look for you for such a long time. 'Who would want you, Joe?' I would ask myself. 'Who has ever wanted you?' Well it makes nothing now. Two things I have learned. Stan Adamson taught me all that a stepfather should not be and my Gran taught me many pretty songs—like this one."

He whistled *"Auprès de ma blonde"* and buried his face again in the freesias. He looked like a lithe, black-headed cat stretching his body there on the grass, and I knew that I wanted him and I longed to say so; but all I said was, "Joe, it's four o'clock. Let's clean up and have a meal and go to the pictures. We've done enough work for one day."

The film we saw was a beauty. Owen was in the seventh heaven of delight and I must admit it was the kind of film I enjoy myself. It was set in Alaska at the time when it still belonged to the Russians, but there was this brave Yankee sea-captain up there all the same. He had a lovely little ship called the *Pilgrim of Salem* and he married a beautiful Russian Princess who, being a Russian, did not feel the cold at all and cavorted round the Alaskan seaboard in full evening dress, and very *décolleté* evening dress at that.

"Lucky fellow," said Joe, as we came out, "what a lovely boat he had and what weather luck! Going north he had a fair wind and then when he turned her about due south he still had a fair wind. I've never seen the likes of it. And what a man amongst men he was. How was he with those barmaids? That's the way to treat your women."

Without warning, he picked me up and slung me over his shoulder.

"Excuse me," he said to the startled crowd in the foyer, "I sail with the Boston Man."

Owen followed behind, helpless with laughter and saying, "Oh Uncle Joe you *are* funny. Carry me too, Uncle Joe. Carry me too." And so we went half way up to the corner.

I was speechless with laughing and embarrassment when he put me down. Joe was not even out of breath. He could only have weighed a couple of stone heavier than my eight and a quarter, but he was wiry—small and wiry and cock of the walk as all the most attractive men of only 5 ft. 9 in. must look, if they are to hold their own at all.

Then while we were still laughing we saw Swede Ryan standing on the corner looking at us. He turned and walked away and further down Swanston Street he got into a taxi.

"Why won't you let me flatten that big bastard?" asked Joe, as we caught a cab down by Flinders Street.

"Because he's a dangerous man, Joe. He might do you some terrible injury."

Joe laughed. "What could he do?" he asked. "He only needs fronting. Front him and he'd go to water. Creeping round town after us. Who does he think he is? The next time I see him it's on."

We were to see him sooner than expected for when we arrived home he had arrived before us. He stood beside the gate with one hand in his pocket.

"Take the child inside," said Joe, "and stay there."

I got the front door open and got Owen upstairs at the run. My legs could scarcely carry me, I was in such terror, and even as I reached the top of the stairs I heard a blow and someone moaning, and a noise that was like weeping. I pushed Owen into his room and told him not to move, then I ran downstairs, catching up, on my way, a block of wood left behind by Marty's mechanic. I had some idea that if Swede had thrown acid at Joe I would kill him. But it was Swede who was weeping; without even waiting to pay the cab fare, Joe had walked straight up and hit him, once on the jaw and once in the short ribs. It was enough. Swede was collapsed beneath the ti-tree, his hands across his face. In the light from the street lamp I could see the tears running between his fingers.

We paid off the cab driver and hauled Swede into the kitchen, where we made him coffee. He sat on a kerosene box, blubbering and shaking.

"Poor man," said Owen, "don't cry. Cheer up, there's a good boy. Drink your nice coffee."

But Swede could not be calm. He wailed on, stripping his soul bare before us, and the childish unformed language which was all he knew made the whole confession even more horrifying and pitiful.

"Why do I never get the women? I'm quiet and I don't drink. I don't even use bad language. I've got money and I know how to behave myself, and I've never had a woman in my life. I never carried a gun in my life or knocked anyone around and the only time I got up enough guts to show her a bottle of acid she (he waved towards me) turned on me like a wildcat.

She was never cruel to me before. She was so kind, even when we were little kids at school. I used to do her sums. The other little girls were nasty to me. They would say, 'Go away, Swede, you're ugly', and my father would say what did I throw? A suet pudding that the water got into? But she never said anything like that. She was always nice to me and I thought about her a lot. When I grew up and made dough I used to make up stories that we were married and had a real nice house, but I couldn't get her, and, in the end, all I knew was that I could frighten her. I've felt real big following you round town these last couple of days. You never knew I was there. It gave me a real big feeling; but then I follow you home and this cheeky little bastard is with you. It's hopeless, it's hopeless."

I felt a great desire to comfort him, and I said, "Swede, Joe doesn't stop here. I'm like yourself. I'm all alone."

Swede drank his coffee and stood up. "I have to be alone," he said. "You needn't worry, I won't pester you again, not after dropping my guts in front of you like I did. Goodbye, Lisha. Thanks for letting me do your sums."

When he was gone Joe said, "You should have let him think I stopped here. It's not safe for you to be by yourself. I ought to stay here even just for tonight. Could you take Owen into your bed and I could turn in in his room?"

I felt that the strict propriety of this suggestion was almost insulting, but I nodded, for the truth was that I was still a little afraid of Swede.

(I need not have been. I never saw him again and six months later he died of an overdose of cocaine and lay in his room for three days before anyone found him.)

I had very little rest that night. Owen was soon asleep, curled up against my body with his head on my arm, but I lay awake and listened to the sea and thought of Joe on that first day standing on the deck of the *Emilie Ferelle,* laughing, with his shirt in his hand and his body golden.

He was up early in the morning and I heard him making porridge and frying eggs, and as we came downstairs the smell of coffee came up to meet us.

"See how good in the house I am," he greeted me. "Doesn't it make you wish to have that serious talk about marriage with me?"

"What an early one you are, Joe. The act of getting up almost spoils the whole of every day for me."

"Then I shall cook breakfast every morning, for I get up with daylight. I have always done this. Every morning of my life I have been afraid I might miss something if I lay in bed."

"Mummy," said Owen, "I've finished my egg. May I take my toast out into the back yard and play?"

"Very well, darling."

He ran out and disappeared into the wash-house, which Joe was helping him turn into a cubby house.

"Now," said Joe, "please talk with me, Lisha, and put me off no longer. I lay awake all last night in torment, and how much longer I can go on playing this friend-of-the-family role I do not know. I am not very patient, Lisha, and I love you very much."

He came around from his side of the table and cupped both hands under my chin. He kissed me so hard that I gasped and then I clung to him and kissed him back. Suddenly I found that I was weeping. He knelt before me, wiping my eyes.

"Don't cry, darling, don't cry," he begged, "but just tell me. Will you marry me?"

Marry! But I was married. I was married to Andrew Michael Kelly who had died with my music box in his pocket.

"Oh Joe," I cried, "I can never marry."

Joe poured a cup of coffee and handed it to me. "Drink this," he ordered, "and I'll go down the street and get some Aspros for you."

"The shops won't be open yet. There are some in my bag upstairs if you would go up for them, please."

He was gone only half a minute but in that time I had managed to steel myself. "Now," I thought, "comes the time when I must throw him out."

So I said, with deceptive calm, "I'm O.K. now Joe. I was not really upset, but never mention marriage again to me. It is quite out of the question."

"How long has your husband been dead?"

"Almost exactly five years."

"And you have lived a *vierge* all this time?"

"No. For twelve months or more I lived with a gunman who used to be in Swede's crowd. That is why Swede and Bonnie and the rest made such a big mystery about me, but you see I am being quite truthful with you."

"This gunman, did you love him?"

"No, I didn't even like him very much."

"So you thought your husband wouldn't mind?"

"I suppose that is what I thought."

"You're a very strange woman. No, on second thoughts, I suppose it isn't strange at all. At any rate you need someone. You don't love me! O.K. It makes nothing. Love is a luxury. One can live without it. But you do need a man to look after you. You have taken on more than you can manage in this house here, and with crooks wandering around it in the night you are not safe. Let me stay here with you. Let me be the man who looks after you. I merely mentioned marriage because so many women seem to like it. You are the only one I ever knew who was shocked at the bare idea. For myself, I don't care one way or the other, but if you would have me I could take care of you well. I could sell my share in the boat. My brother would be glad to buy it and then we could pay off a little more on this place and furnish it. I don't like to see my loved one sitting on a kerosene box. We could have an arrangement, as Grandmother would call it. I could send you money every week while I was away and I could get on a short run. What do you say, Lisha?"

What did I say? All the while he had been speaking the anger had been rising within me. The cool French practicalness of what he had said had chilled me to the bone. I had wanted him to beg for marriage, to persuade me against my will, as it were, and he had shrugged it off, almost as though relieved.

"It makes nothing."

"We could have an arrangement."

Childishly I fanned my anger with these words as though it were his fault that he did not know the more evasive phraseology of the English, he who had been reared by the French. "An arrangement." That's what he thought was good enough for me. He thought I would sell myself to get a house paid off. And the furniture! He offered to put me amongst the furniture. The romantic French, nobody like them. Well if it suited him it suited me. Certainly it would be a help.

And down at the back of the bottom of my mind was another thought I was not honest enough to admit: "And if I had a baby I'd have to marry then. It would be out of my hands. Andy would understand that."

I sat silent and he took my hands and asked again, "Lisha, what do you say?"

"An arrangement," I said, "yes, that would be all right."

He gave a little laugh and took me in his arms, but this time I did not cling to him. I sat unresponsive, raging against him in my heart.

He stood up and stepped back from me.

"All right," he said, "you think I'm trying to make a tramp of you. Because you told me about that silly unimportant gangster you think that I think less of you. You think that, in some way, I will do you harm. I'll tell you who did you harm, Lisha. That same gunman. I don't know why you lived with him if you did not want him, but I think that many women, when they lose their husband, don't know what they're doing for years—sometimes for the rest of their life. It doesn't matter to me if you slept with him a thousand times. What does matter to me is that he brought down your pride. You say to yourself, 'All men are the same and what does it matter?' you could live with one, you could live with another. This is good enough for many women but not good enough for my dear one. So I am going. I will not leave you without help. I could not bear to think of it. I'll send you money. You'll need it and Owen will need it. If you want me and if you get enough guts to say to yourself that your dead husband, wherever he is now, would not expect you to be bound to the grave for the rest of your life, then write to me. I'll still be on the same ship."

He paused in the doorway, and said, "I'll be saving all my overtime for you, Lisha." Then he was gone. I went upstairs and cried till my face was a swollen mess.

Well, of course, I still had my pride, and a damn silly thing to have under the circumstances, and very miserable it managed to make me during the next month. I told Marty, who received the information with obvious scepticism, that I had my house and my work and my son and I had never been happier in my life. To prove it I gave a very gay Christmas party for Owen and all Marty's little brothers and sisters, and Mrs Phillips and Saul Rosenstein. Saul loved that sort of thing. Indeed, in red flannel and whiskers, he was the hit of the afternoon as he handed the gifts from the tree.

"Am I not the perfect Goy?" he exulted as the children, toys under the arm and sated with cocktail sausages, ice-cream cake, bread and butter, and hundreds and thousands, fruit jelly and other dishes which protocol rigidly demands must be served on these occasions, departed to the back yard to play Indians beneath the lemon trees. Saul plucked off his whiskers and wiped the sweat from his brow. "I think," he said, "that Santa deserves a nice cool lager."

He collapsed in the chair of honour, the only chair, the chromium kitchen chair which Marty and her mechanic had placed beneath the tree for me, but he was only half way through his lager when he sprang up with a yell and, still in Father Christmas outfit, dashed out to his car.

"Gifts for you," he cried, "gifts for the lady of the house. Santa nearly forgot them. This is from Momma and Poppa (indicating the beautiful Indian rug over one arm) and this is from old Santa himself."

And there under the other arm, with a pile of records perched precariously on top of it, was his battered old portable radiogram. It was his greatest treasure. It was a ghost, an old and friendly ghost, from the days of my marriage. Someone was playing the Bach Christmas Cantata on it the first time that Andy came home from sea as a married man. On it I had first heard played Eli Eli and Kol Nidri. I took it on to my lap with the tears starting in my eyes.

"Come now," said Saul, "old Santa is going away to drive a tractor on a kibbutz early next year, and so he is getting rid of all his old junk. He must travel light or his reindeers will complain. There are a few of your favourite records there. Some Haydn, Maggie Teyte singing *"Plaisir d'amour"* and so on, and a few for dancing. Now what lucky lady wants to be first to dance with Santa?"

Mrs Phillips, who had had two ports, said she would teach him the Turkey Trot, which in no time at all they were performing with great spirit.

"I value spirit above mere technique," announced Saul.

For a highly successful Christmas party, always throw in a little dash of Jewish euphoria. I can truly recommend it.

Early in the New Year Uncle Shaun arrived back in Australia. Uncle Shaun was a very old man now and he found it difficult to get ships, even though the age he signed on his articles did not approximate to his real age by more than ten years. He had been in the Home Trade for almost four years, trying all the time to get a ship to Australia, and now at last he was here and I wept for joy on his shoulder. For all my pride I seemed to be in a very weepy condition in those days and Uncle Shaun's appearance brought the first feeling of real joy that I had experienced for weeks. For the first time in my life I saw him with some luggage. Uncle Shaun always sailed schooner rig and paid off in the same style.

"What point is there in lugging possessions all round the face of the earth?" he would ask.

But this time he had a sea bag with him and a big brown paper parcel under one arm which turned out to be a leather pouffe bought in Suez.

"I said to myself," he explained, "my dear niece is bound to be short of furniture in this new mansion of hers, so when Ali Baba and the several thousand thieves came out in their boats I bought you this, and, as I thought, it's very much needed."

He put it down at one corner of the Indian rug and sat on it.

"Very comfortable it is, too," he said, "now dry your eyes and make your old uncle a cup of tea." He took Owen on his lap. "This one is Hughie Ward over again—skinny and dark. The tinker blood takes a long time to die out and thank God for that, for it's a tough and strengthening strain."

He stayed almost a fortnight. It goes without saying that Owen loved him and trailed around after him all day. They spent most of their time out walking together on the beach or else in the back yard, where Uncle Shaun was cutting up the wood from the wash-house and turning it into a corner wardrobe for my room, and a set of bookshelves for the lounge. And through the sound of carpentry would come Owen's voice:

"Tell me a story, Uncle Shaun. Tell me another story."

And Uncle Shaun answering him:

"Did I ever tell you about when I was in Frisco at the time of the big earthquake?"

"Did you ever hear of the sea-serpents off Dondra Head?"

"I'll tell you about the time I was captured by Chinese pirates?"

Good stories, all of them. I remembered most of them myself. And then one night, when Owen was in bed and we sat in the kitchen drinking coffee and talking of the times that were gone, he looked at me across the table and said, "Well, Lisha, the wardrobe and bookcases are all lacquered a splendid shiny white and the windows are all clean. I think I've done all my little jobs and I must be on my way. I'll be leaving you to-morrow."

"Oh, Uncle Shaun," I cried, "don't go. Please don't go. Stay with us. We've been so happy to have you here and if you're worrying about the money you could get the pension. We'd manage very well."

"It wouldn't be fair, Lisha. In a couple of years I may be a bed-ridden old man and it wouldn't be fair to you at all. Besides I don't deserve it. I'm a great believer in the old saying that as a man lives so shall he die, and what have I ever done except wander wherever I wanted to go? I've left you alone in many a struggle and your grandmother before you. Not because I didn't care, I do want you to believe that, but because my eternal rambling had landed me in some place where I couldn't help no matter how much I wanted to be with you. I have no excuse except that I was always what these clever chaps now call a compulsive traveller, what the old seamen called a wandering foot. But it wouldn't be fair, now that you're getting a little home together, to come and put myself upon you and spend my last years in the comforts of home and the company of my family. I must look after myself. I never worried much about looking after anyone else."

"Uncle Shaun, you were always the best uncle in the world."

Uncle Shaun smiled at me. He said, "You're still young enough and generous enough to think that a good singer of songs and teller of stories makes a good uncle. God help you, you're not much more grown up than your own son. See your grandfather Hugh Ward, there. Well he couldn't dance much and he couldn't sing in tune. It was the greatest grief of his life for he was a musical chap, and he said that sometimes his head was fair roaring and ringing with glorious symphonies that would never be reproduced. He was a worker. He was the eldest of six boys and his father died of T.B. when Hughie was eleven. When his father knew he had not much longer to go, he got a forged birth certificate for Hugh and apprenticed him to the Blackwall Line, which didn't take boys under twelve. Hughie used that certificate for the rest of his life. He was a mate by the time he was eighteen and he managed to put all his young brothers through their apprenticeship. He married before he was twenty-two and no two people have ever loved as he and your grandmother loved. He looked after her as though she were a princess, and he worked for her and his children till a week before he lay down and coughed up his lungs. He was a man and he could neither dance nor sing."

"Uncle Shaun, you always sent us money. All those bad years you always sent money when you had it."

"There's more things than money, if you'll pardon my being obvious. I should have been here keeping an eye on you. Little Owen, he talks to me. He says, 'Uncle Charlie used to stop with us and then he went away, and then Uncle Joe came and he didn't stop very long. I liked him and I wish he'd come back.' Now, dear, I'm not accusing you, and I know there are things that cannot be discussed between people with the space of two generations between them. But I do know this—no woman of our clan has ever before been forced to depend on an Uncle Charlie or an Uncle Joe, and I felt that had I been here it might not have happened to you. It hurt me in my heart and in my pride, and I want you to forgive me, darling, if you can."

"For God's sake, Uncle Shaun, let there never be any talk of forgiving between you and me. Joe was only a friend, and Charlie! Charlie was just one of those things that happen when you're mad with loneliness, if you can understand."

"I understand all too well," said Uncle Shaun. He patted me on the head as he did with Owen. "Please, darling, don't feel that you have to say any more; but I have to go away. I'm not going back to sea. I'm too old to get work. I'm too old to sail, even as a peggy, which is the job I've been doing ever since the war ended. So I'm going up to this friend of mine who has a shack and a fishing boat up near Broken Bay. He wants me to go in with him and if we can work up any sort of a little fishing business there'll be my share to come to you when I'm dead."

"It sounds like terribly hard work."

"Lazing round in a small boat? Never!"

"Joe," I said, "is a small-boat man. He's spent most of his life on the Bass Strait schooners."

"Good seamen, those Bass Strait men. They have need to be. Is he Australian?"

"Australian born. He's half Channel Islander and half Hebridean Scottish."

Uncle Shaun laughed. "A good seaman, indeed," he said. "Is he a good man?"

"He's generous and kind and he's got guts."

"Do you love him?"

"Yes I do."

"I'm asking a lot of questions tonight, Lisha, but answer me just one more. Why did he go away?"

"I sent him away. He wanted to marry me and I thought of Andy, and then we quarrelled."

Uncle Shaun said flatly, "Andy is dead."

"I can't believe it."

"You must believe it."

"Living or dead, it makes no difference."

"It makes the hell of a lot of difference, as Kelly would be the first to point out. Ruining the rest of your life is no way of keeping his memory. That is such an old piece of wisdom that even an uncle my age can scarcely be pardoned for pointing it out to you. Remember how he used to worry that, if anything happened to him, you wouldn't be able to look after yourself? Do me a favour, Lisha. Write that letter."

I was silent.

"I never asked a favour of you before."

After a moment I spoke: "I want to write it, and I promise I will, but just give me time. It will take a couple of weeks to bring myself to it."

"To get rid of your dirty Irish pride, you mean?"

"That's it."

Uncle Shaun smiled at me. "How alike we are," he said. "What a stiff-necked old crowd! Surely it helps you to understand why I can't stay here?"

"Please, Uncle Shaun."

"Don't beg me, Lisha. I'm doing the best thing. The weather is good up that way, the fish plentiful, the scenery beautiful,

and my old friend Nobby is a very easy man to work with. I
expect to enjoy myself. It's a much better arrangement than
sitting around in a sailors' home waiting to die, and that is the
only alternative. So, Lisha, let me be a working man a little
while longer."

"Sing to me, Uncle Shaun."

"What do you want me to sing?"

" 'Venezuela' and 'Lowlands'."

A month after he had gone I had still not written the letter.
Or rather I had written it twice, and on neither occasion had I
posted it.

And then, at the end of a still, hot day in February, there
came a wild southerly buster that brought a violent electrical
storm and pelted the rain in from the sea. Owen was sleeping
in his own room and I drew back my window curtains and
lay on my bed watching the purple and gold of the lightning
flood the room. At times I was lying in pools of coloured fire.
It was a wonderful night.

And then the knock came to the door.

I ran downstairs, thinking it must be Marty, and as I opened
the door, the force of the wind tore it from my hands and flung
it back against the wall—and there, with the wind howling
around him and the thunder rocking the blazing sky behind
him, stood Uncle Shaun. He wore a deck coat, turned up
around his ears, but his head was bare and shone silver against
the night. On his face was a look of such love and longing as
I had never before seen on human countenance and he tried
to speak to me. And then he was going away from me—down
the garden path and away. At the gate he turned and I saw
only the face transfigured with love, and then he was gone.

I cried out to him and ran into the street calling his name;
but in the street there was no one—nothing but the wind and
the rain and the roaring of the sea.

Slowly I went back up to my room. I took my grandmother's
rosary from where it hung beside the mirror of the chest of
drawers, and I knelt and prayed for my uncle who was dead.

Next day I posted the letter to Joe.

I was not surprised when, about a week later, I received the
letter from the old friend Nobby. I had expected it. Uncle

Shaun had died on the night and at the time that he had come to me.

"He took pneumonia," the letter said, "and he was too old for these new drugs to do him any good. He soon went unconscious and died without pain, but while he could still talk he said he had a bit put by for his funeral and the rest was to go to you. Bury the old hulk cheap, Nob my boy, he said, and send the rest to my niece to buy herself a real slap-up guitar, she aways wanted to learn the guitar. So I enclose £50 hoping you are well as this leaves me at present,

"Your Uncle's old friend,
"Royston Clarke.

"P.S. They always expect you to say something in these letters but we both knew him a long time so we don't need to say anything."

Acceding to my uncle's last wish I bought a £20 guitar (on which I can now play four chords. Two more chords and a pair of sandals and I can seriously think of joining Melbourne's coterie of brilliant folk-singers). I tried to give the other £30 to Mr Pearl in part payment for what I owed. He handed it back to me.

"You can dance it out for me some time," he said.

On the day that I received the telegram from Joe, Marty came to me. Owen was still at kindergarten and I was sitting up in my room looking out at the ships coming in. I was in a species of happy coma. Marty sat down on the bed, lit a cigarette and said she had important plans to discuss with me. I said to go ahead, and continued to stare out at the bay.

"Well, are you listening?" asked Marty, a trifle sharply, understandably enough.

"I'm listening, Marty. I promise you. I concentrate better this way, honestly I do."

"It's like this," said Marty, "I'll be marrying soon and I won't be able to teach for ever because I'm going to have two children as quickly as I can. You know the rent has gone up sky high on the city studio. As a matter of fact city rentals are becoming impossible and business just isn't as good as it was for those first few years after the war. We've just got to face it—the boom's over, but I don't want to give up the business altogether. It just wouldn't seem right if the McSweeneys weren't teaching dancing somewhere, and we're still a name to juggle with, or whatever that saying is, in the Port. Women who went to Aunt Olive, and their daughters too, if it comes to that, now have kids old enough to learn national and tap. So what I've been thinking is this : you've got a great big room downstairs which it looks like you're never going to be able to furnish. I'd help you with the rent. I'd pay you three quid of the fiver and give you a wage, depending on how many classes you took, if you let me turn it into a studio. Hal can fix in the big studio mirror and a barre and, if you could take national and ballroom, I'd look after ballet, tap and acrobatic. Don't think I've got a cheek, but it would help me and it would help you to pay off the place. And you know something? There's a new ballroom craze coming in that I don't think I'm going to have enough time to learn. The old Charleston's back. The samba's finished. Play a samba and you empty the floor. You can Charleston, can't you? The only thing is, I suppose it's a relief to get into town to work. Could you put up with it, being stuck in the Port all day every day?"

All day every day!

Just around the corner from here had stood the house where I had lived all the days of my childhood. My first memory of my father was of his teaching me to Charleston in the kitchen of that same house. I could not have been more than three years old and he was back on his only trip home from New Zealand. I was very small and he had put me on the table, the better to watch my feet, and up there I had learned to shuffle and double shuffle and cross my hands across my knees while I sang in my baby voice :

"Chicago, Chicago . . .
Oh you'll have the time, the time of your life . . ."

My father was very young and golden-haired and laughing. "She'll be a champion," he was saying, "she'll leave the Powells for dead."

On the wharves, which I could see just by leaning out the window, I had seen, in the same year, the police put in the scabs in the '28 wharfies' strike. I had seen them marched down four abreast, with an armed policeman marching with every third line. I had heard the shuddering roar that shook the street as a scab's house was bombed and I had stood at the window in my nightgown as he and his wife and children came staggering out into the night, their eyes so filled with plaster that they thought they had been blinded—and the hungry thin-mouthed women of the Port took in his children and his wife and comforted them, but they turned their faces from him and left him to stagger in circles in the road, dazed and in deadly fear and crying, "The kids, Oh God, what has happened to the kids?"

In this street that I watched now I had seen the unemployed marching. I had heard their friends call 'Good luck' to them. I had seen their banners—"We demand work, our right as Human Beings". And perhaps on this day they were marching to somewhere they were not permitted to go, for the police vans were drawn up at the Bay Street corner, and there was Uncle Shaun doing great execution and knocking out three policemen before they got him into a van, and, the Flynn adrenals being so superb, he came to in the van and before they could turn around he was out again, and had accounted for a couple more before he collected the rabbit killer that finally put him out of action.

Down this street I had dawdled on my way to school and here, in the bad years, I had seen a woman flog a child half unconscious because she had fallen with a bottle of milk and broken it, and there was no money to buy another pint.

"And we have a baby in the house," the poor woman had screamed. "Oh God! Oh God, what shall we do?"

I had seen this street bloom with the money that came with war, and now, if we were to have the poverty that came with peace, I would face the fight here where I was already a veteran in poverty and struggle.

Here I had walked with Johnny Dawson, and I had walked alone in the rain with the hood of my raincoat up and my rubber boots squelching through the puddles, and singing to myself,

"None but the lonely heart could know my sadness
    Alone and far apart, etc., etc."

That was at about fourteen when only Tchaikovsky understood.

255

On this very seawall, at about the same age, I had harangued the sea-gulls :

"They are not long, the weeping and the laughter,
Love and desire and hate,
I think they have no portion in us after
We pass the gate."

On Station Pier I had sat with my grandmother on the last day of her life and watched the ships come in past the Gellibrand—("When I first met your grandfather, he was on a little boat not much bigger than that—").

And tomorrow, or at the latest the next day, Joe's ship would be coming in and I would see it far out there as it went to anchorage at Williamstown. And when they passed the Gellibrand they would be within harbour limits, and they would begin to top the gear, and up forrard the bosun would be walking out the anchor. Joe would already have his going-ashore clothes laid out on his bunk, and when they were tied up at Williamstown he would be amongst the first ashore and catching a taxi to come home. And I would know to the hour when he would arrive because I would ring Dockhead, and I would wait up here at my window till he got out of the taxi and stood a moment in the street, the sunlight shining on his thick black hair—

"Dreamy," Marty's voice was exasperated, "I said 'Can you Charleston?' "

I laughed and turned away from the window.

"Yes, Marty," I said. "If there's one thing I can do, I can certainly Charleston."

Australian Selection

OTHER BOOKS IN THE SERIES

OUT OF THE SMOKE

Ray Parkin

1942, and Japan has struck with all its force at Java, in one of the most bitter sea battles of the second world war.

The Australian cruiser *Perth*, one of the two surviving combat ships heading south for allied shores, runs into an immense Japanese fleet in the Sunda Strait. *Out of the Smoke* tells not only of the *Perth's* last magnificent fight against such overwhelming odds, but also of a small party of the shipwrecked crew who try to sail a derelict lifeboat to safety — only to land at a port in enemy hands.

This outstanding story of courage and endurance is vividly recounted and illustrated by one of the survivors. Ray Parkin's moving and exact honesty makes this a classic tale of war at sea.

'Unique . . . It has a dimension rarely found in stories of action . . . which gives spiritual meaning to physical experience.'

Melbourne *Age*

'Here the ferocity of war at sea is experienced at its most intense and bitter.'

London *Observer*

JIMMY BROCKETT

Dal Stivens

Fiction – or fact? Jimmy Brockett is that archetypal character – charismatic, ruthless, playing for high stakes in politics, sport, business and the underworld. In the great tradition of Australian con men, he exploits the greed and weakness in others to build his own power.

He toughs his way from the Sydney slums to wealth, fame and influence. Brockett elevates the corruption and brutality in his personal and public life to a level which is bizarre but all too believable.

'. . . a work of importance, a thoroughly Australian work, written with an Australian idiom and tang . . .'
Jack Lindsay

TIRRA LIRRA BY THE RIVER

Jessica Anderson

Life has become a series of escapes for Nora
Porteous. The tightness of a small-town family life,
a sanctimonious and mean-hearted husband, the
torpor of suburbia—these she endures and finally
escapes. On her flight from cruel realities she is
sustained by desperate courage, discerning
intelligence and ebullient humour. Spanning seventy
odd years, the action moves from Brisbane to Sydney
to London and back again. This is a beautifully
realized novel, enriched by the bitter-sweet tang of
the past.

In 1978 *Tirra Lirra by the River* won the Miles Franklin
Award.